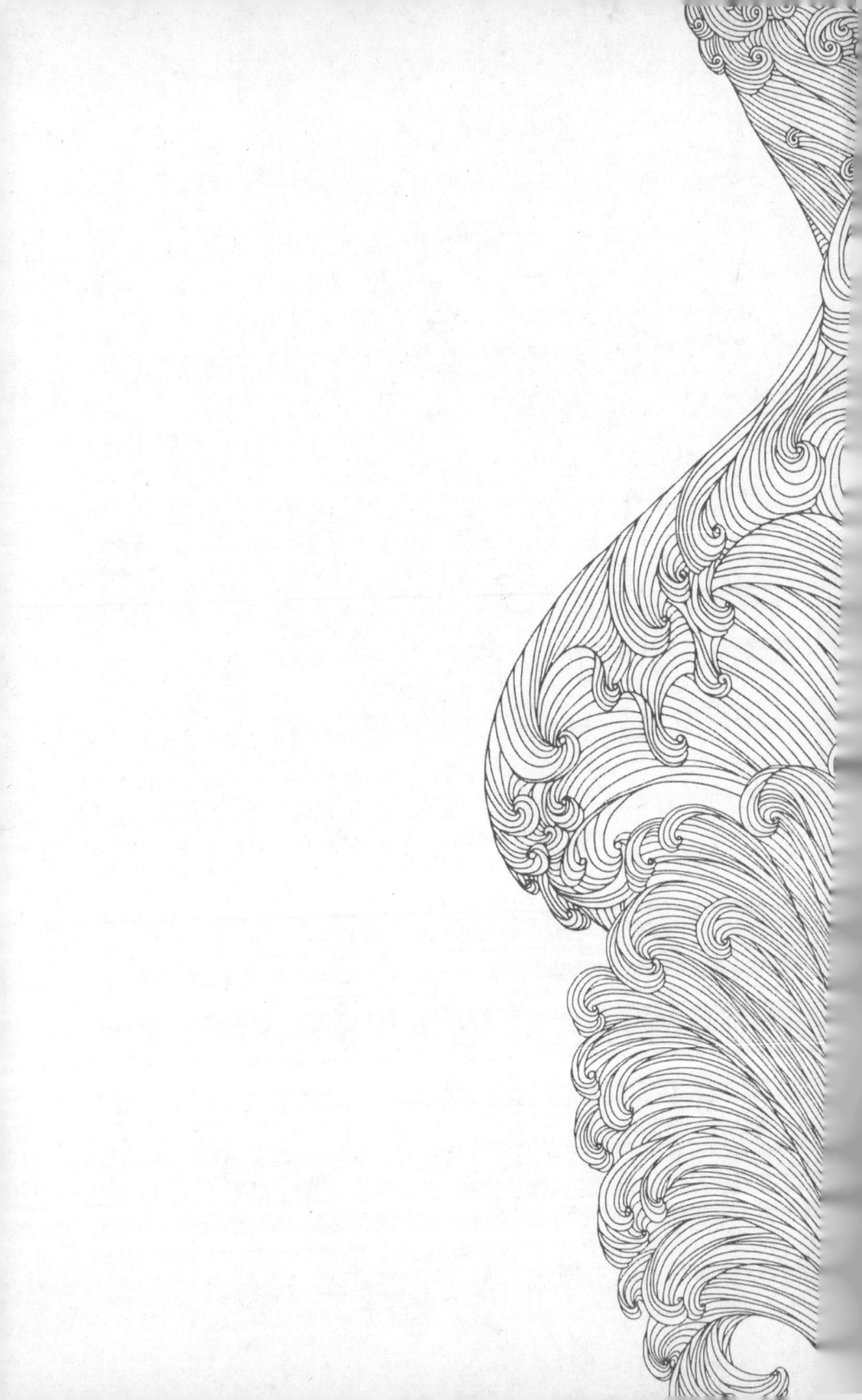

THE PLANS I HAVE FOR YOU

A Novel

LAI SANDERS

SIMON & SCHUSTER
New York   Amsterdam/Antwerp   London
Toronto   Sydney/Melbourne   New Delhi

Simon & Schuster
1230 Avenue of the Americas
New York, NY 10020

For more than 100 years, Simon & Schuster has championed authors and the stories they create. By respecting the copyright of an author's intellectual property, you enable Simon & Schuster and the author to continue publishing exceptional books for years to come. We thank you for supporting the author's copyright by purchasing an authorized edition of this book.

No amount of this book may be reproduced or stored in any format, nor may it be uploaded to any website, database, language-learning model, or other repository, retrieval, or artificial intelligence system without express permission. All rights reserved. Inquiries may be directed to Simon & Schuster, 1230 Avenue of the Americas, New York, NY 10020 or permissions@simonandschuster.com.

This book is a work of fiction. Any references to historical events, real people, or real places are used fictitiously. Other names, characters, places, and events are products of the author's imagination, and any resemblance to actual events or places or persons, living or dead, is entirely coincidental.

The views expressed herein are those of the author(s) and do not necessarily reflect the views of the United Nations.

Copyright © 2026 by Lai Sanders

All rights reserved, including the right to reproduce this book or portions thereof in any form whatsoever. For information, address Simon & Schuster Subsidiary Rights Department, 1230 Avenue of the Americas, New York, NY 10020.

First Simon & Schuster hardcover edition March 2026

SIMON & SCHUSTER and colophon are registered trademarks of Simon & Schuster, LLC

For information about special discounts for bulk purchases, please contact Simon & Schuster Special Sales at 1-866-506-1949 or business@simonandschuster.com.

Simon & Schuster strongly believes in freedom of expression and stands against censorship in all its forms. For more information, visit BooksBelong.com.

The Simon & Schuster Speakers Bureau can bring authors to your live event. For more information or to book an event, contact the Simon & Schuster Speakers Bureau at 1-866-248-3049 or visit our website at www.simonspeakers.com.

Interior design by Wendy Blum

Manufactured in the United States of America

10 9 8 7 6 5 4 3 2 1

Library of Congress Control Number: 2025936656

ISBN 978-1-6680-8792-3
ISBN 978-1-6680-8794-7 (ebook)

A NOTE FROM THE AUTHOR

Dear Reader,

On a cloudy day in November 2023, I stood in a museum, crying. Yet another rejection had rolled into my inbox that morning, and the truth was becoming clear: The latest book I had written, a story that I had poured my heart into, had also failed to find a literary agent.

That week, I happened to be in New York, staying at a hotel in the Garment District. In my hotel room one evening, I felt drained, defeated, mired in decades' worth of painful memories. Getting rejected by nearly all the colleges I'd applied to. The embarrassment of wearing donated clothes and eating free lunch at school. Being the only person at work who never got promoted. Not being believed after an assault. By this point, I was no stranger to disappointment and failure—so why did it hurt so much, still?

An idea came to me that same night.

In my head, I saw two women sitting in the lobby of a hotel at midnight, engaged in a raw, strange, almost dreamlike conversation. One was in her thirties, hiding a tortured past behind the thin façade of a perfect wife and perfect mother. The other was younger, desperate and hopeless, her once promising life having just gone up in flames. What might these two women say to each other? United by a shared trauma, pushed over the edge by the pressures of family and society, just how far would they go to unleash their pent-up rage?

- A NOTE FROM THE AUTHOR -

At its heart, *The Plans I Have for You* is a book about rejection. It asks painful questions like: What does it mean to be rejected as a child? A friend? A lover? A daughter in a culture that favors sons? A young person trying to get past the gates of an elitist, nepotistic institution? And what the hell are you supposed to do when you are rejected by a whole career?

I am still pinching myself that this book found its advocate in my agent and its home in my editor. And now, incredibly, it has found its way to you. This story is angry. It's uncomfortable. Many times while writing, I'd cringe, thinking, *What will my family think of me when they read this? What about my coworkers?* That was when I knew I was doing something meaningful. I hope you will find within these pages recognition, catharsis, and perhaps even a bit of healing.

Thank you so much for reading,
Lai

THE PLANS I HAVE FOR YOU

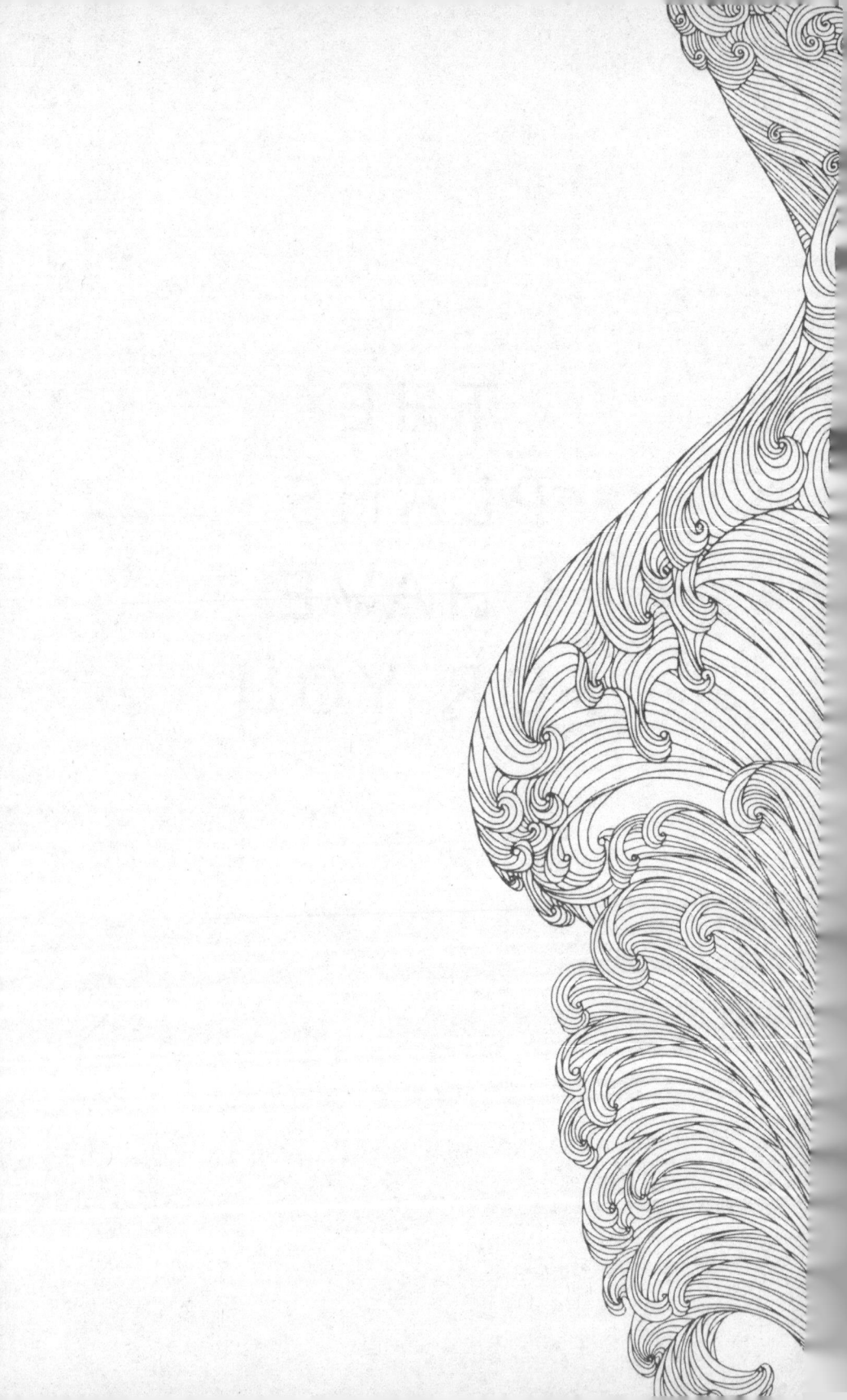

Part One

NIGHT SHIFT

SHELLEY

December 2016

"I don't want to lie to you," she said. "I know who you are."

We sat across from each other at one of the small tables in the lobby. The whole place looked like a sunken pirate ship, and that was on purpose. The walls were aquamarine. The chairs were round, plastic, and clumsily painted in strokes of colors that gave the rough suggestion of wine barrels. And the pièce de résistance: The front desk where I worked, with its wooden wheel and glow-in-the-dark fish tank, was the stern of the ship. Glittering gold doubloons hung in strings. I was in a bright salmon shirt and a balding plastic lei, the same ones I always put on when I showed up for the night shift. I had drawn the line at wearing an eye patch.

It was two in the morning and the lobby was empty. Her eyes were moist, almost glistening. I didn't know what to say to her. I took a sip of my coffee instead.

She had checked into the motel two nights before, arriving just minutes after I took over reception at ten thirty. Her husband was circling the parking lot in what I imagined was a minivan, looking for a spot. She'd led her kid inside by the hand and come up to me and said in one breath, "I'm so sorry to trouble you, but would it be all right if he uses your bathroom before we check in? We've been in the car for hours."

It was one of those questions that instantly flipped my brain to autopilot. I jabbed a thumb behind me. "It's right through this door."

Before she shepherded the kid around the corner, she'd looked into my eyes and said, "I appreciate you so much."

I could tell right away they were Korean. She had a small, pale, oval-shaped face and frizzy black hair pulled back into a loose bun. She was wrapped in a light-colored coat that made her look not rich but comfortable, like an ad for Everlane. When they finally checked in, she picked up a pen and I saw an audience of rings, cheap, dainty little things, across all five fingers. Stars and moons and obviously fake gemstones.

As for the dad: There was less to say about him. He was lanky. He wore a baggy gray sweatshirt that said CORNELL. And he had that energy a lot of men had, where if he came into the same room as you and stood there quietly, you wouldn't even hear him breathe.

Not long after I moved back to Florida, my mom became convinced that we were being punished by a jinn.

It's angry at us for some reason, she'd say, pacing the length of the kitchen table. *I can feel it. It's in the air.*

I didn't ask her any questions. In those first days back, I had pretty much stopped talking. In the mornings, after we ate breakfast and my mom left for her shift at the motel, I'd pile the dirty dishes in the sink, slip back under the covers, and let the daylight hours waste away like sand. In the afternoons, when I finally talked myself into getting up to pee, I'd catch a glimpse of my reflection in the mirror on the armoire, gray and hunched over the edge of the bed, the collar on my T-shirt greasy with sweat. *Another day.*

Also: The jinn stuff was old news to me. It had been there all along.

I was six years old when my grandmother first told me about the jinn, not long after my dad died and she and my grandfather had moved in with me and my mom. It usually visited her at the tail end of her long afternoon naps, emerging from the shadows in the walls and crouching over her body: a dark, silent, faceless figure that took its rest directly on her beating heart. I couldn't see the jinn, but I could see the force of its weight. I'd see the tiny tremors in her fingers and toes, the way her chest quivered with shallow breaths. I'd see my grandmother's eyes, glassy with terror, her tears carving a glistening trail down her papery face.

Over time, we'd learned the best way to deal with it. I'd lay my head over her chest, my ear to her heart, and count out loud for her. *One. Two. Three. Four.* By thirty, her heartbeat would start to slow. By sixty, she could move her fingers, wriggle her toes. By two hundred, sometimes three hundred, she could find her voice again. *I'm okay*, she would say, straining to raise her arm so that she could stroke my hair, her palm damp with sweat. *It's gone. It's gone.*

Count yourself lucky that you can't see it, she would say once she was back on her feet. *These things make themselves best known to those who have experienced the greatest despair.*

My grandmother was right, it turned out.

Because here I was eighteen years later, back in the ratty little apartment I'd grown up in, no job, no Columbia Law, no friends, no reputation, no future. Nothing left in my life but my mom and the vast, bitter disappointment that she hid behind a flimsy veil.

The day after I returned to Kissimmee, lying in the bed where my grandmother had once slept, I saw the jinn peel away from the shadows and slither onto my bed. This time, it had come for me.

And this time, there was no one who could make it leave.

A month after she picked me up from the Orlando airport, my mom burst into my room with a red plastic pail. "Look what I got for you," she said.

It was filled with water and about a dozen small dark-green turtles; some were paddling wildly across the surface, while others were motionless at the bottom, either resting or dead. "Manuel from maintenance got these from his brother-in-law at the pet store for a discount," my mom said. "Twelve turtles for less than two hundred dollars."

"I don't want twelve pet turtles, Ma."

"They're not pets," my mom said. Her face was shining with an animation I hadn't seen since the day I told her that I'd landed a coveted internship at one of the biggest law firms in New York City. "Get up and get dressed. We're going to do a life release ceremony."

At Lake Toho, we found a quiet dock overlooking a marshy mass of lily pads and bulrushes and yellow-tinged water. In the distance was a gray bark-like thing that was either driftwood or a snoozing alligator. I looked down at the pail in my hands, where the turtles were stirring uneasily, and back at my mom. "So what am I supposed to do?"

There was a pause, and that was when I realized she hadn't thought this far ahead. "I don't know," my mom said. "Just pour them into the water gently, I guess."

"Should we even be doing this? We don't even know if they can survive in this habitat. They could get eaten by a gator."

"They're not going to die," she said. "We're giving them a new life. That's why it's called a life release."

She stepped forward to stand next to me. "Put them in the water, and I'll say something. A prayer."

As I tipped the bucket, my mom clasped her hands together. "Dear Buddha," she began, her voice tentative. "Dear Guanyin bodhisattva, my daughter has saved these turtles from a pet store, and she is now giving them back to nature. So please . . . please bless my daughter. Please give her good fortune and protect her from evil things. Thank you."

The last turtle fell into the lake with a *plomp*. My mom and I looked at each other. "You lied, Ma," I said.

"What?"

"You lied to the bodhisattva. You told her I was the one who got the turtles when really, it was Manuel. So now the karma's going to him instead."

For a moment, I saw my mom's brows come together, a deep ridge forming in her forehead; then she relaxed. "Oh, what does it matter who got them?" she said. "You were the one who let them go. The karma belongs to you."

In the car, as we put on our seat belts, my mom became pensive again. I watched her absentmindedly rub the car keys between her fingers, and after a while she said, "If this doesn't get rid of the jinn, maybe next week we should go to a mosque and ask for the imam's guidance."

I couldn't help it, then. I let my head fall back against the headrest and exhaled. "Jesus, Ma, are you for real?"

"Don't say that. And I'm serious. There's a big masjid in Orlando that has a Chinese person on staff, a Hui like us. I saw a flyer on the bulletin board in the Chinese supermarket."

"When was the last time you even stepped foot in a mosque?"

"Three years ago," she said. "I went to one with your little aunt when I was visiting her in Henan. You know she's become very devout in the last few years. She's even applied to the Chinese government for permission to go to Mecca. And she prays five times a day, like clockwork."

"Yeah, only because she found out she has cancer."

My mom winced. "Don't say that."

"It's true, though," I said. "Didn't you guys stop being Muslim during the Cultural Revolution because you were afraid of getting beat up by the Red Guards or something? That's what Laolao and Laoye told me. And then Dad died, so you were born-again Christian for, like, five minutes because you thought that would help him get into heaven, and now you're tossing turtles in a lake and praying to Buddha because you think that's going to get me out of the shit I'm in. But it doesn't work like that. Religion isn't a buffet. You can't diversify your portfolio by investing in multiple gods. You can't be . . ."

There was no other word for it. "You can't be so fucking Chinese about it, Ma."

The car was silent. My mom was no longer looking at me; she was staring into the bushes at the end of the parking lot.

When she finally spoke, she said, "You know what's going to get you out of the shit you're in? A job."

In the lobby, the Asian mom smiled at me. "I was hoping to get your advice on something."

It was the first time I'd seen her since they checked in. She was wearing this formfitting lavender jacket, the sporty kind you go jogging in. "I'm thinking about going out for a walk."

The clock on my desk said *02:27.* I said, "Out by yourself?"

"I can't sleep. My son and husband, they sleep like logs. But lucky me—I'm a lifelong insomniac."

Then she said, "It looked like a busy block when we were driving around in the daytime. There's that pizza place nearby. Lots of hotels and souvenir shops. But I just wanted to ask—do you find it safe, personally? You know, for people like us?"

There was a pause.

I said, "I would probably stay on the premises if I were you."

"Yeah?"

"Yeah. I mean, I don't think you'd necessarily get mugged if you went out. This is a pretty safe area. It's just—"

She finished the sentence for me. "It's late."

"It's late."

The mom nodded slowly. "I guess I'll stay put, then. Thanks for the advice."

She half turned, glancing at the brochure stand by the front desk, and that was when she noticed the pot of coffee sitting out. "Oh, look at that! Just what I was looking for."

As she reached for a paper cup, I said, "That's not decaf. Just a heads-up."

"Oh, that's sweet of you. But I'm way past that. Caffeine, decaf, melatonin, even prescription stuff—none of it makes a difference. I haven't had a good night's sleep for decades."

She turned to face me. "I'm Korean. Well, Korean American, but also Korean Korean. My parents and I moved from Seoul to Massachusetts when I was eleven. We had this family joke that I never got over the jet lag. I nap during the day. At night, that's when I'm wide awake. All of my best work, I've done at night."

When she brought the cup to her lips and took a sip, I saw that her fingers were long, thin, and bare. No rings.

She said, "I know this might be strange, but would it be all right if I gave you a hug?"

"Um," I said.

She didn't wait for permission. She picked her way around the desk, stepping gingerly over a box of opened brochures, and wrapped her arms around me. My limbs froze; my brain went wheels up. I considered wriggling out of her grip. Clearing my throat and saying, *Okay, thanks for that.*

But I didn't. She kept hugging me, the soft fleece of her lavender jacket pressed against my skin. Time seemed to move differently. Everything slowed down. She smelled faintly of pine trees and snow; the gurgling sound in the fish tank behind us was like a lullaby. When she finally let go of me and we looked into each other's faces, something about her was different.

She was crying.

"Oh," I said. My mind was still reeling. "Oh, um . . . are you okay?"

"Yes. Yes, I'm wonderful, actually. I'm just really happy right now."

I passed her a tissue and watched as she blew her nose quietly and folded the used tissue neatly, into a square.

She said, "The reason I'm so happy is because I finally got to meet you. It wasn't easy to track you down after you had deleted all of your social media accounts. I had to call a lot of hotels in Kissimmee before I found you at this one."

It took a few seconds for the words to sink in.

"You were looking for me?"

"I was."

"Are you a journalist?"

She shook her head.

"I'm not a journalist. I'm an artist. But more importantly, I'm a friend. To you. Because I have . . . I have been exactly where you've been, you know."

I blinked at her.

"It's why I came all the way to Florida, in fact. I came here to tell you that everything you've gone through, I have gone through. Every emotion you have experienced, every fear, every moment of despair—I've felt it. Because what happened to you? It also happened to me."

She smiled at me, and I felt the hairs on my back stand up.

She knew. Fuck, she knew.

Everything about her was suddenly too close. Her hair, her breath, the warmth of her body through her lavender jacket. I got up from my chair and shoved it against the pigeonhole behind me; a stack of letters fell out with a clatter. She was still, quiet, watching me.

I said, "You also had a mental breakdown on the 6 Train, exposed yourself, and had the whole thing filmed by a reporter from the *New York Gazette*?"

Her voice got a little quiet. "No, I didn't."

"Then excuse my language, but how the fuck would you know?"

She nodded at my phone. "Look up the name Soyoung Kim—or, actually, don't, there's so many people with that name, the results are all muddied now. Search for 'Cornell Hobo.' Or 'Homeless Heather.' Read the first news article that comes up, and when you're done, come have a coffee with me."

I watched as she refilled her cup. She went to a chair in the lobby and sat. Her pale face was turned towards me, calm, waiting.

Against my better judgment, I followed her. I typed the words *Cornell Hobo* into my phone, and in that silence punctuated only by the occasional hiss and gurgle from the fish tank, I began to read.

SHELLEY

"I think I've heard of this story before," I said.

"Oh, I don't doubt it," the mom said. "It's turned into a bit of an urban legend in Asian circles. *Did you hear about that crazy Korean girl who pretended to go to Cornell? She snuck into the dorms and pretended to go to class. It took the campus police five months to find her and kick her out.*"

"So you're the person from the article? You're Soyoung Kim?"

"I was Soyoung Kim. Now I'm Sophia Moon."

She said, "I changed my legal name soon after that, when I became a US citizen. Naturalization is one of the easiest ways to have your name changed, you know. Marriage is the other one. Without that, a lot of states make you jump through hoops. You have to take out an ad in the newspaper to announce that you're changing your name. Which kind of defeats the purpose, doesn't it?"

I said nothing. Sophia Moon leaned back in her chair.

"Do you want to hear about what happened to me after that story came out?"

After a pause, I said, "Yeah, I guess I do."

She smiled at me. "Before that, why don't we get a pizza first? I saw that the place next door is open twenty-four seven."

Sophia made the call, one large, half mushroom, half pepperoni. She gave her credit card info over the phone. Then she put down her phone, crossed her legs, and looked at me. "You have a question."

"I have several."

"Go ahead—ask me anything. We have all night."

There was a garland dangling from the mantel behind Sophia's head, and it was dotted with plastic fish-shaped ornaments and tiny twinkling lights. Half of the lights were already dead. But in that moment, I had this feeling that I wasn't sitting in the lobby of a horrifically decorated motel anymore. I was in Sophia's home, in her confidence. I really could ask her anything and get a straight response.

The first question that came to mind was "How did you know to find me here?"

"I googled your name. It had been all over Twitter for hours at that point: your full name, where you worked, where you went to school, but it was no use emailing your work or school addresses. I had a hunch you were drowning in hundreds, if not thousands, of disgusting messages. There's not a chance you would've seen anything in your inbox. And I was right, because a week later, you were fired from your internship at the law firm. And possibly expelled from Columbia, if I read it right."

"They didn't expel me," I said. "They just . . . suggested that my best option was to drop out. There was no point in going anymore."

Evenly, Sophia said, "You couldn't become a lawyer after this."

"I was supposed to go into IP law. When you're an attorney, you're an officer of the court. And your reputation has to be . . ."

She finished the thought for me. "Immaculate."

Then she said, "I'm really sorry you won't get to practice law. Having your lifelong dream ripped from you? It's positively heartbreaking. There's no other way to put it."

It was obvious, what she'd said. It was bordering on saccharine.

But it wasn't wrong.

A lot of people would have been devastated to trade their life in New York City for a hopeless existence in muggy Florida. Not even in Orlando proper, but a little no-nothing town on the outskirts of the Happiest Place on Earth, a miserable sprawl of gimmicky motels and faded billboards and dying palm trees. Orlando was the destination.

Kissimmee was the place you passed through to get there. Disney tourists paused here just long enough to fill up the tank, take a dump, maybe lay their head for the night. Whatever we could wring from the wallet in their cargo shorts, we were grateful.

Of course I was one of those people. I was devastated. Yet strangely, I wasn't disappointed. In a way, I'd even anticipated it, that worst-case scenario. Of course I couldn't hack it in New York. Of course I'd ended up crawling back to the same place I'd worked at in high school, a pirate ship–themed motel with an enormous animatronic mermaid perched over the entrance, her tail wagging slowly and creakily, the color of her hair just a shade away from triggering a copyright-infringement claim from Disney. Every time my mom came home from one of her shifts, still coughing from the cleaning chemicals, wedging a hot-water bottle between her lower back and the couch cushion, she'd remind me that I had to fight for what I wanted. Fight to make the debate team. Fight for first chair in marching band. Fight for every college scholarship I could get my hands on. So I did: I went into every fight with my chest puffed up, my fists ready. I came out on top every time.

Except my legs never stopped shaking. They never found solid ground.

I said, "You still haven't said how you found me."

"Ah, right. Google. I found something on page ten of the results. There was no picture, so I couldn't be sure it was you, but I had a feeling. It was a website blurb from your old high school from a few years ago, back when you won a writing competition in the tenth grade. Do you remember that?"

I shook my head. Sophia said, "It was a competition for all the high schools in Osceola County. You'd written an essay about what it was like working at the same motel as your mom, you being at the front desk while she was cleaning rooms in the back. The judges loved it. They said it was"—she used air quotes—"'a thoughtful reflection on the immigrant experience through the lenses of language and privilege.'"

The competition had taken place at another high school on a Saturday morning. My mom had driven our only car to work, so I'd asked Mrs. Alvarez, our elderly neighbor, to give me a ride. In a classroom with concrete walls, we wrote our essays in thin blue booklets, heads down the entire time, the only sound in the air that of pens scratching on paper. When they announced the following day that I'd won first place, the sole prize was a paper certificate signed by some county official, but Mrs. Alvarez still insisted on taking me to Zaxby's for celebratory fries and Sprites. The side of my right hand was still smudged with ink residue, and I had looked at the black marks over and over again in the booth, grinning to myself.

I said nothing, and Sophia said, "From that, I gleaned three things. One: You were originally from Kissimmee, Florida. Two: When you lived here, you used to work at the same motel as your mom. And three: You thought you were too good for a place like this."

She picked up her coffee and took a sip. "Which is why I guessed that this was where you'd end up."

My face burned.

I was on the verge of telling her to get fucked.

Except that's when the pizza arrived.

Sophia gave the guy a cash tip. She set the box down on the table and opened it, and I had to admit it smelled fantastic. The grease was practically crawling all over the cardboard. Sophia passed me half of the stack of napkins. "Come on. Dig in. I always get hungriest this time of night."

I had bitten off half a slice when she said, "I knew that you'd need a moment to crawl into a hole, lick your wounds after what happened on the subway. But I also knew that after that, you'd get back up and go back to work. Asian women like us? We don't know how to sit at home and do nothing. I figured the easiest point of reentry for you was the motel in Kissimmee—but which one? Lucky for me, it only took about twenty calls. I just had to use the right voice. Call up the front desk and say, *Hey, is Shelley working today? She was supposed to give me a ride to school.* It was too easy. People were so quick to trust a voice on the phone, something they couldn't see. That's how I found out you were working the night shift at the Mermaid Inn."

She nodded at the slice of melting cheese in her hand. "This is pretty good. Not as good as NYC pizza, obviously, but decent enough. Do you ever miss the pizza?"

"I have bigger things to worry about."

"Your mom," she said, "does she still work here, too?"

I got up, taking my cup with me, and walked around the corner to the bathroom, where I dumped the cold coffee in the sink. Then I went back to the coffee maker and poured myself a fresh cup. Sophia had stopped eating and was watching me, her face a little tense. I sat back down across from her.

I said, "I think you're forgetting something. We're not here to talk about me. We're here for you to answer my questions about you."

She looked at me for a moment, unblinking. Then her face relaxed a little, and she smiled. "Of course. Anything."

"Why'd you pretend to go to Cornell?"

The question surprised me. But I genuinely wanted to know. "With me, at least it was spur-of-the-moment. But your shit was premeditated. You knew you were on thin ice the whole time. People could find you out at any moment. And you still stuck it out for, like, four months. Why?"

Sophia nodded. She didn't seem offended.

"I suppose it just snowballed," she said. "A small lie turned into a bigger lie turned into a bigger lie. At first, I just wanted to get my parents off my back. I didn't want to go to college, at least not right away. I wanted to take a year off. See the world. Become an artist. But with my parents, that was never an option. It was the Ivy League or Stanford or nothing. I was my parents' only child. I had the hopes and dreams of my entire family riding on my shoulders.

"I applied to all the Ivies, like they asked. Then it was decision season, and every day I got home from school, there was a flat little envelope in the mail waiting for me. Rejection, rejection, rejection. I hid them in my backpack, but I knew time was running out. So I downloaded a pirated copy of Photoshop and faked an acceptance letter. It was so beautiful, with the right emblems and fonts and colors and everything. Then I thought, *Hang on—that was so ridiculously easy, I should just make another one.* And I couldn't stop. It was like this bad joke, or maybe even a performance. I showed them one letter after another, and they were so happy. They had nothing critical to say about me for the first time in my life. There was no *Oh, you did a good job on this one thing, but you're still bad at this other thing.* I'd reached a pinnacle. A state of completion.

"I had to operate within the parameters of reason, of course. I wasn't delusional enough to fake an acceptance from Harvard or Yale—but everything else was fair game. I don't know why I chose Cornell, in the end. I think there must have been something at the subconscious level drawing me to it. Fate, even."

I remembered the beat-up gray CORNELL sweatshirt, the guy quietly rolling three suitcases into the lobby. "Didn't your husband go to Cornell?"

Sophia smiled. "He did. We met there the first week of orientation."

There was something about the way she phrased things that irked me. *Choosing the school. Going to Cornell. First week of orientation.* Sitting here in front of me, all these years later, she still talked about that hot-air existence she had pantomimed like it was real. As if she'd actually gotten accepted. I said, "Does your husband know that you, uh . . ."

"Oh, he knows."

Sophia answered without hesitation. Picking up another slice, she said, "My husband and our parents are the only people in the world who know that Sophia Moon used to be Soyoung Kim."

"And the judge who granted your name change."

"Well, that's true. And now you do, too."

"And he was cool with what you did? I mean, I assume he was a legit student there. Was it weird for him to find out?"

Sophia didn't answer immediately. She was chewing on her pizza, looking thoughtful.

"He was kind about it," she said. "But then again, Paul has always been a much better person than I."

There was something in her expression I couldn't figure out. But it made me believe her a little more.

I said, "How did you get into the dorms? The article said you didn't have a student ID, as far as they could tell."

Sophia made a face. "Oh, that. Social engineering at its simplest."

"What do you mean?"

"Getting into dorms and libraries was easy. In a place like that, all you need is to be young, Asian, and dress the part. I had a backpack dangling from one shoulder, hoodie, flip-flops, the whole getup, and I'd hang out by the entrance, pretending to be on the phone. Whenever someone swiped their card, I would dawdle over with my phone to my ear and enter after them, like I was barely paying attention. *Oh, thanks for getting the door.* In four months, no one ever refused to hold the door open for me. All I had to do was act like I belonged."

I didn't want to show it, but I was impressed. The woman had . . . not balls, but what was it, exactly? Gumption. A certain swaggering resourcefulness. I tried to imagine myself sauntering into Columbia Law without having been admitted, slipping into seminars with a laptop, inserting myself into small group discussions. It would've taken a quality I didn't possess.

She was fucking insane.

I said, "So what happened after you got caught by the police? After they kicked you out?"

Sophia looked down at her hands. Then she looked up at me.

"My parents drove all night from Brookline to Ithaca to pick me up. No one said a single word. When we got home, my dad carried my things into the house, and my mom closed the door and drew the curtains. I'll let you use your imagination as to what happened next."

All I could think of was "Fuck."

"Yes," she said, calm. "But it was a long time ago."

"They locked me in my bedroom for weeks, bringing meals to my door until I had convinced them that I wasn't crazy in a dangerous way—just a sad way. Then one day, they let me out and put me on a plane. My mom and I traveled to Korea, except we didn't stay in Seoul. We drove to a little town in the mountains, and there she took me to see a manshin. A Korean shaman woman. They're said to have healing powers. They serve as bridges between the human world and the world of gods."

"Did the manshin heal you?"

"What?"

Sophia raised her eyebrows, evidently surprised by the question. Then she laughed, soft and derisive.

"Of course she didn't heal me! She was a fraud. They all were."

She leaned forward in her seat, her hands clasped on the table. Her eyes were glistening again, boring into mine.

"No one healed me, not my parents, not the manshin. *I* healed me, Shelley. Have you ever heard of the Japanese art of kintsugi? When a ceramic jar shatters, they put it back together and trace over the fault lines with gold powder, emphasizing the imperfections. After I shattered, I doused myself in coats of paint and glaze until no one could see that there were cracks to begin with. I changed my name. I reinvented myself. I carved out a new life for myself, a career as an artist, a beautiful family, a home in New York. Don't you see? I put myself back together. *I* did that. I made myself whole."

She waited.

"No, that's great," I said. "You look very . . . very whole."

"You don't believe me?"

"It's not that."

She cocked her head, a little quizzical, and I said, "I do believe that you are who you say you are. It's not about that. It's more—so what? So you fucked up twelve years ago and ruined your reputation. And now you're living in Hoboken and you have a family and a career. What are you trying to say to me, exactly? That I shouldn't give up and it's all going to be okay in the end? Because you didn't need to drive all the way down from Jersey to deliver that message. You could have just called. Saved yourself a lot of gas."

"Oh, no," Sophia said, "that's not my message at all."

Her face had grown serious. A little ridge had formed between her brows, and in the dim lighting, there was something deep and eerie about her eyes. They were utterly focused on me. I couldn't look away.

She said, "I drove all the way down from Jersey to tell you three things. The first one being: You're not crazy. You were never crazy."

"Okay."

"The second thing is that the universe owes you a debt. What happened to you—what *is* happening to you—doesn't make sense. There's something very, very wrong here that needs to be fixed."

My mouth was dry.

"As for the third thing," Sophia said, "it's good news, actually. Because I'm here. And I'm going to help you get what you deserve."

The biggest lie the *New York Gazette* published about the worst day of my life, among many others, was that I was arrested by MTA police as a result of The Incident and led from the 6 Train in handcuffs. I was not arrested. On July 7, 1992, responding to a group of activists who challenged New York State's penal laws as discriminatory and unconstitutional, the New York Court of Appeals ruled that women were—incredibly—now permitted to exist while shirtless in public. In this, I was afforded a basic human right long enjoyed by my grandfather, who, when he was alive, liked to scrunch up his sweat-stained cotton tank tops all the way past his nipples whenever our AC conked out on a sweltering Florida day. I was born exactly one month after the court of appeals' ruling was issued. I don't think that's a coincidence.

Another lie the *Gazette* peddled (and again, there were many) was that I was fired from my internship for what I'd done. I was not fired.

The morning after The Incident, after Twitter had identified me as Shelley Hu, 2L student at Columbia Law and summer associate with the Midtown firm Ingram, Russo & McAllister—after I had silenced my phone and set all of my social media accounts to private—I had sat down at my kitchen table and started writing an email to my boss, Gene Struzik, to ask if I could work remotely for the next few days. But Katharine from HR had beaten me to it.

For one week, I was placed on something called administrative leave while IRM investigated my behavior during The Incident. During this time, the video sprouted legs and ran a marathon around the country. It was just too goddamn good. Too emblematic of the national zeitgeist in the months leading up to the election. A middle-aged, well-dressed white woman on the NYC subway, going head-to-head with a younger, slightly less well-dressed Asian woman, the two of them embroiled in a virulent yet shapeless argument no one could make heads or tails of.

They tried, of course. It earned write-ups in *The New York Times* and *Slate*. *The Atlantic* published a five-thousand-word think piece on the intersection of race, gender, and polarization in modern-day America, as reflected through the microcosm of one powder keg moment on a packed Manhattan subway car. That was the classier coverage I got. Fourteen-year-olds on YouTube dubbed me the New York Subway Naked Lady. The video launched a thousand reaction videos, and the things we said were parodied and auto-tuned. In the comments section of online news articles, people diagnosed me with a spectrum of mental illnesses ranging from schizophrenia to bipolar disorder. And worst of all: Though the original, uncensored video was removed from Twitter, it soon made the rounds on sketchy porn websites, the kind that didn't have any English and was hosted on servers in faraway countries. The kind that was impervious to takedown notices.

Eight days after The Incident, I tendered my resignation to IRM. By this time, no one from the firm or Columbia was talking to me, not even to send texts laced with false concern (*hey girl! just wanted to see how you're holding up*), and I spent my days lying on the couch of my studio apartment, crying, hyperventilating, drinking cheap sour wine, eating tortilla chips, and watching old episodes of *Parks and Rec*. A week later, I dropped out of Columbia Law.

Six years earlier, as the salutatorian of my high school class, I'd been accepted to five colleges. I ended up going to UF because it was the only place my mom could afford to send me. It was 2010, the height of the financial crisis, and we spent our lives fortifying ourselves against the outside forces that could break us. Staying in-state was real. Studying prelaw was real. Getting a job in UF's fundraising office, cold-calling alumni for donations, that was real. It was bricks on a house, laying down a steady foundation.

New York wasn't real.

New York was mirrored skyscrapers and cold faces and steam rising out of manhole covers on the street, swallowing up the pedestrians like stage fog.

The hard yellow-and-orange benches in the subway car. The floor warm and filthy and sticky under my bare skin. Legs and feet, sneakers and sandals and beautiful ballerina flats, all shrinking out of the way as my limbs flailed. My nude-colored bra lying next to a metal pole, facing upright as if someone had posed it all delicate. The scream. *The scream.* People had their hands covering their ears. People were saying, *Stop it, hey, stop it, lady, that's enough.*

It wasn't until I tasted blood in my throat that I realized the scream had been coming from me.

Once I had made a new pot of coffee, I brought it over to the table and poured it for both of us. Sophia took hers with a lot of cream and sugar. The off-white powder crumbled in her cup like chalk, and she stirred it with one of those little red plastic straws. I had the feeling that this was pond water compared with the coffee she usually drank. It had started to drizzle outside; behind us, I could hear the rain drumming on the window.

I said, "You said you could help me get what I deserve."

"I did."

"What does that mean? What I deserve?"

"It means that there is a karmic imbalance," she said, "and I want to help you claim the things you are owed."

I opened my mouth, but she held up a finger, preempting me. "Let me be up front with you, though. I can't help you get your old life back. Unless you find a way to turn back time, erase the memories of everyone who saw that video—that life you had in New York five months ago is gone. It's never coming back."

There was a stinging sensation at the back of my nose. My vision was foggy. To steady myself, I took a big gulp of coffee and cleared my throat. Then I said, "So if I can't get my life back, then what . . . what can I get?"

She smiled at me.

"The right to come back as a new person. To start again."

"So, what, I should change my name?"

Sophia waved a hand, dismissive. "Changing your name is nothing. A simple legal procedure. What I can do for you—what you are capable of—is so much more than that."

She was quiet for a moment, tracing the bottom of her cup with a finger. I waited.

Then I heard her say, "I'm going to tell you something I haven't told anyone, not for a very, very long time. The thing is—I'm Chinese, too."

My brain short-circuited. Instinctively, my eyes ran back over her face, her eyes, reappraising the way her features fit together. I said, "Didn't you just say you were Korean, like, five minutes ago?"

She inclined her head. "I *am* Korean. And I'm Chinese. Is it really so difficult to imagine that someone could straddle multiple identities at once? I would think you of all people would understand."

That was when it finally clicked. I put down my coffee.

"Hang on," I said, "so you're—"

"Chosonjuk. Korean Chinese. My ancestors were forced to move from Korea to northeastern China in the nineteen thirties, when the

Japanese invaded. I spent most of my childhood in a small village a few miles outside Yanji with my grandparents."

"I thought you said you were from Seoul."

"I said that I *moved* from Seoul," Sophia said. "An important semantic distinction."

She was quiet again, gazing into her coffee. A moment passed before she said, "Do you know what it was like to grow up Korean in China? For me, it all comes back in bits and pieces now. Not a complete story; just fragments. I remember working with my halmeoni in her little brick house, helping her brine cabbage leaves in jars to make kimchi in our cellar. I remember going to school one day and an older student tying a red scarf around my neck, and the teachers saying, *Now you're all brand-new members of the Communist Youth League.* There used to be a strange woman in my village who never left her house and spoke to no one. People said that she had escaped from North Korea by swimming across the Yalu River, and that a man from our village had bought her as his bride because she had nowhere else to go. One day she was gone, and we joked that she'd been arrested and sent back to North Korea. Why did we say things like that? We were just children. And already we had an astonishing capacity for cruelty in our bones."

She smiled at me, and I was struck by how sad her expression was: an ageless sadness I had only seen in the faces of my mom, my grandmother.

"I didn't have a father, either. He was a drunk, I heard. He'd disappeared by the time I was born. My mother left me with her parents and moved to Korea to find work, the way many Chosonjuk did. The way many still do. South Koreans look down on people like us, as you can imagine. They think we're Chinese country trash. That our accents are strange. That we deserve only the dirtiest and most thankless jobs. My mother cleaned nursing homes. She nannied other people's children. She found a job caring for the sick wife of a South Korean businessman, and a month after his wife died, she married him. She was always a highly pragmatic person, my umma. She must have sunk her claws into him well before his wife died—a young, beautiful, healthy body, always eager to cook for him, clean for him, warm his bed in the way his dying wife no longer could. How could he have looked away? A few years after that, she was able to send for me to come live with them in that glittering city. I became a Seoulite. I became a *real* Korean, you could even say."

We were both quiet.

"Sounds like your mom made a lot of sacrifices for you," I said.

"She did, didn't she? And so did yours."

Sophia leaned towards me.

"The thing about your mom and my mom—the thing about you and me, Shelley—is that we will never have a stroke of luck in our lives. Just by being born as Asian women, we've drawn the short end of the stick. You and I, we have to fight for our places in a world where we will never have anyone to lift us up, never have anything to fall back on. If we succeed, we're expected to bring up a host of others with us. But if we fail—we get nothing. No forgiveness. No second chances. No unconditional love. We fall back into the abyss, and we don't get to come back."

My mouth was dry as I watched her. There was a faint ringing in my ears.

Then I heard her say, "But what if I told you I could bring you back?"

The air in the lobby had become still.

"I can build you back, piece by piece, brick by brick, until you become the person you were always meant to become, just like I did. I can save you from this life and help you create a new one. A life where you can step out of the night and walk freely under the sun, without shame, without humiliation, without the fear of being judged for something you had done in a past life. Can you imagine that? A new beginning. All it takes is a *yes*."

Sophia reached across the table then, and she touched my face. She held her left hand against my cheek and cupped it.

"Tell me," she said. "What really happened in that subway car?"

Her voice was so gentle. But it broke me. I opened my mouth, and in the next moment I was bawling, churning, gasping for air. I could feel her arms close in around me; her pine cone smell was everywhere. She ran her fingers through my hair. "Tell me, darling," she said. "Tell me how it feels."

Between the hiccups, I managed to get some words out. They came out as gasps and sputters.

"It was so unfair. It was s-so unfair."

"I know. I know it was."

"I know—I know I was being a bitch that day. I was wrong. But she was—she was so mean. I had already had a b-b-bad day and I . . ."

"You were a bitch," Sophia said, "and you were wrong."

Her voice was no longer soothing. It was cold, and I looked up at her, startled, dazed. "What?"

"You were those things, yes. I watched the video many times. This is what happened, as best as I could tell: It was a quarter to eleven on a Thursday morning. You were sitting on the 6 Train, in the seat closest to the door. You had a large purse and a duffel bag taking up the seat next to you; beyond that, there was another empty seat, and there was a man in the seat next to that.

"A white woman got on at some point, before the video started. She asked you to move your things from the seat next to you. You told her she could sit in the free seat between your things and the man. She refused and again asked for the seat next to you. She said, *Did you buy two tickets for the subway? Why do you think you're entitled to take up two seats?* and you said, *Leave me alone, oh my God, just shut the fuck up and leave me alone.* Neither of you would acquiesce to the other. It escalated into a screaming match, which was when a reporter from the *New York Gazette* named Auggie Flores decided to film the encounter and post it to Twitter. Do I have the facts right?"

The woman had worn burgundy pants.

They were deep and dark, the color of wine, and they fanned out at the bottom, fell elegantly over her open-toed leather heels. As she shouted at me, I had looked down at her pearly pink toenails and imagined bringing my foot down on them. The way her bones would crunch under my heel. The ring of green-and-purple bruising that would form. She'd have to hobble around for weeks.

I said, "She didn't want to sit next to the homeless guy."

"The homeless guy?"

"The guy next to the open seat. He was quiet, not bothering anybody. But he reeked. And she didn't want to sit next to him—that's why she asked me to move my stuff."

"Why didn't you?"

It was the way she had asked. No preamble, no *Sorry, do you mind?* I had heard her step onto the train, *clack clack clack*, then her heels coming to a stop. Scanning the seats between me and the homeless guy. The loud, clear, commanding voice. Someone who was used to getting what she wanted. *Can you move your stuff?*

And she had seen the tears on my face when I looked up, the snot snaking from my nostrils. Had I even said anything to her in response? I remembered shaking my head dumbly, I'm not here, I'm not listening, don't talk to me.

And then she had raised her voice and asked again.

Can you move your stuff?

"I wanted to make her sit next to the homeless guy," I said.

"Of course you did," Sophia said.

Her arms were still around my shoulders. She reached up and nudged back the hair that had gotten wet and clumped across my face. Her touch was like a feather.

She said, "Do you know who that woman was?"

I shook my head.

"Her name is Amy Cloverfield," she said, "and she's a vice president at an advertising agency in Chelsea called Meek LeClerc."

Amy Cloverfield.

I had thought of her every day for the last four months. Sometimes I saw her in passing delusions, those burgundy pants swishing for a millisecond before vanishing into the air. I heard her voice, at first in my head, then in the room all around me, even in the dead of night.

Can you move your stuff?

Hello? Hello? Excuse me. I'm talking to you.

Did you buy two subway tickets? What makes you think you're entitled to take up two seats?

No, I don't want that seat. I want this seat.

Do not yell at me. No, excuse me. Excuse me. Do not raise your voice at me. Do not tell me to shut up.

We can stand here all day. Oh, we can absolutely go at this all day. I'm more than happy to oblige.

Jesus, what is your problem? Do you not speak English? What part of "you can't take up two seats on the subway" do you not understand?

I'm racist? I'm racist? Oh, that is laughable. That's absurd. I literally traveled around the world to China to adopt my daughter. I've been a registered Democrat for thirty-five years. I sit on the board of a charity that helps underfunded inner-city schools. But please, go ahead and call me racist.

Where do you work? I want to know where you work. I want to know your name, I want to know the name of your employer. I think they'd be very interested in hearing about this.

I said, "How did you find out who she was?"

Again, Sophia waved her hand. "It was easy."

She started typing on her phone. "In the video, she was carrying a branded tote bag. I took a screenshot of the logo and upped the contrast. It was from a professional association called New York Women in PR. I looked at their website, and voilà—she was a former chapter president from 2013 to 2014. Her picture was on the About page."

She showed me the screen, and I saw the same woman smiling at me from a group photo, her reddish-brown hair cut into a shapely bob. She wore a green piece of jade around her neck, and when she smiled, as she did in the photo, she was vaguely attractive: Her jaw was a little square, her front teeth a little big, but her eyes were pretty. They burned bright. Steady.

Just seeing her face set something off inside me. I felt sick. I turned my head and brushed the phone away. "Okay."

"How does it feel, seeing her?"

After a pause, I said, "Not good."

Sophia nodded. She ran her hand over my hair again.

She said, "It's not fair, is it?"

I looked up at her.

"You're right about what you said earlier. You were a bitch. You lost your temper at her. You were wrong to take up two seats on the train. But you paid for what you did. You lost your career, your reputation, your future. You were wrong, and you paid the price a hundred times over. But what about her? She saw that you were crying. Distraught. She should have deduced that you were having a bad day. And yet she barked at you, she got in your face, she pushed and pushed and pushed until you snapped. Why did she get to do that?"

Sophia's eyes had become pools.

"You were humiliated in front of the entire world, Shelley. But have you ever asked yourself why she walked away from this encounter with no consequences, no disastrous Google search results, no shameful memories keeping her up at night? Why did Amy Cloverfield get to simply walk away?"

The last remaining lights on the garland were beginning to dim. I watched one of them struggle to keep the spark going, sputtering a few times, before it finally gave out.

In a small voice, I said, "Yeah, but she didn't make me take off my shirt."

"No," Sophia said, "but your boss did, didn't he?"

It was a visceral reaction. I jumped in my chair, jerked the whole thing back, and it almost knocked her to the floor. But she held on, and she collected herself. She took the other chair and dragged it over to my side and took a seat, still holding on to my arm.

I couldn't look at her. I said, "How did you . . . how did you . . ."

"New York can be a village sometimes."

Then she said, "Paul has a colleague who used to work at Ingram. You were interning for Gene Struzik, weren't you? He has a reputation."

I couldn't feel my fingertips. Sophia took one of my hands in both of hers, and she rubbed it, breathing life back into it.

"He has . . ." I tried to say, and my voice was a rasp. "He has a reputation?"

Sophia nodded, and I closed my eyes. My vision had become blurred by tears.

"Fuck," I said. "I didn't . . . I didn't know. No one at the firm said anything. No one warned me."

"Why would they? Most people don't care. If anything, they were happy to see it happen. There's something about a bright young woman, someone who's untarnished by the ugliness of the world. People want to see her tarnished. They want to see her taken down a peg, the uppity bitch."

"We'd just come back from DC that morning," I began, and I could hear the tremor in my voice. "It was a—a work trip."

"Go on," she said, gentle. "What happened in DC?"

And finally—finally—I told her about Gene.

Gene Struzik. My old boss at Ingram, Russo & McAllister. The IP law juggernaut. The star senior counsel who was slated to make partner in just two more years.

By the second week of my internship in Gene's practice, I had started feeling uneasy. Like something was off, but I couldn't put my finger on what. Because Gene and I had gotten along famously. We'd had our getting-to-know-you lunch at an upscale hotel restaurant, and he'd goaded me into ordering a fancy bottle of wine, flashing his company card and saying, *Daddy Loic's buying.* (Loic was one of the partners.) I'd gotten comfortable teasing him about his cycling gear, the bright orange helmet and lime-green vest that he wore biking into work each day. We'd hang in his office and shoot the shit over beers, decompressing after a long client meeting. More than once, he made me listen to him strum on his guitar.

But then things started to change.

Gene started bringing up conversation topics that ranged from the debatably innocuous to the decidedly intrusive. Whether I had a boyfriend—or a girlfriend, he wasn't one to judge—at school. Whether I might find fellow Asians less sexually attractive because they presumably reminded me of my relatives. Whether I thought women truly derived any pleasure from giving blow jobs (asked drunkenly and earnestly just before he'd put me in a taxi home after a work happy hour).

Of course I'd talked to HR. I went and sat in Katharine Browne's office, head down, hands in my lap, shaking, the qualifications pouring out of me nervously. *I could be wrong, of course. I could be reading too much into it. I don't want him to be fired or punished or anything, obviously.* Katharine had promised me they'd look into it. *I want you to know we are taking what you've shared very seriously,* she'd said that day, handing me a tissue across her desk. *And I will be sure to keep you updated on next steps.*

Three weeks later, walking back to our hotel rooms after a long day of meetings in Arlington, Virginia, Gene had come up behind me and pinned me against my door. It was just like how Sophia had described it: The memories existed only in fragments. I remembered the wetness of his breath, the sour taste of booze, the slippery feeling of his tongue in my mouth. I remembered standing frozen, my back against the door, the peephole digging into the back of my head. I remembered the ugly geometric pattern of the carpet that stretched all the way down the corridor, navy-blue abstract circles on flat beige. When I closed my eyes, they were burned into the back of my skull.

I remembered laughing. *Okay,* I remembered saying. *Okay. Okay.*

And Gene saying, *Come on, you're not going to invite me in?*

And I had laughed and laughed and laughed like he'd said the funniest thing in the world. *Sorry,* I had said. *Sorry, I actually have a headache. I'm feeling a little bit sick today. I'm so sorry.* And I'd kept on apologizing even after the door had closed behind me, even after I'd clicked the lock into place. *See you tomorrow, Gene. Have a good night.*

On the flight back to New York, Gene had rested his hand on my knee. *You know,* he'd said, *I'm not usually drawn to women with short* hair. It's just not very feminine, in my opinion. But you're just—look, my wife is Asian, too. I have a weakness, I'll admit that. And if I did anything that was untoward or made you feel a certain way, you have my apology.

And he'd said, *If word of this gets back to the office, it's going to make things difficult for you in a way that you don't want it to be. I want you to take some time and really think about that.*

I had thought about it, sitting next to Gene on that eighty-six-minute flight.

And three hours after that, I'd boarded the 6 Train.

"I wish I had murdered him back at that hotel," I said.

"Do you?"

I sighed. "No. No, of course not. It's just . . ."

I trailed off, and Sophia squeezed my hand. "No need to explain," she said. "I get it."

She took a deep breath, and suddenly, she had become small, fragile. She reminded me of myself.

"I'm so sorry, Shelley," she said. "That never should have happened. Not to you. Not to anyone. I wish . . . I wish I could turn back time for you. I wish I could take it all away."

We were both quiet, listening to the hiss of the fish tank.

"The thing is," Sophia said, "I know it's strange that I'm here."

"It's okay."

"No, I mean it. I know how it looks. You must think I'm crazy, driving all the way down here from New Jersey just to talk to you. You must think I'm some kind of lunatic stalker."

"It's okay," I said again, and I meant it. "You know what it's like."

She nodded, and a thought occurred to me then, surprising me in how certain, how complete, it was. "You've . . . you've done this before, haven't you? You've helped someone else. Someone like me."

I thought I saw something in her eyes, a fog, a passing haze. She nodded again.

"It was years ago," she said. "A friend from art school. Her name was Casey—or it had been in the before. She'd moved to San Antonio to be with her partner after graduation; we'd lost touch. And one night, out of the blue, I got a call from her, whispering on the other end. She was sobbing, hysterical, hiding in the bathroom. Could I come and get her? I was on a plane three hours later.

"I set up a private space for her to sleep in our apartment—we lived in the East Village back then. I helped her file a restraining order, change her name, land a job at the same ad agency where I was working as a designer. By the end of the following month, she'd moved into her own place. She was back on her feet, happy, living a new life."

"How's she doing now?"

"Good, I think. I haven't seen her for a long time, not since I had a baby and left the agency to go freelance. When you become a mother, friendships erode. People drift away. But I know she's in a much better place now."

I nodded. I felt her hand tighten around mine again; her lips were open, eager, hesitant. I waited for her to speak.

She said, "Can I tell you the truth? The whole truth, and you won't judge me for it?"

"Yeah."

Sophia picked up the coffeepot and refilled my cup. She handed it to me, and I took a sip, but I was barely paying attention. I was hanging on to her every word.

"The truth is," she said, "I couldn't stop thinking about you after I saw you in that video. Most people watched that video and saw a crazy woman who was having a mental breakdown. But I saw *you*. I saw the pain that was inside you, and I could feel it. It was the same thing I felt twelve years ago, when I was just as alone and helpless as you are now. It was the same thing I heard in Casey's voice the night she called me.

"You've taken the long and steady road your entire life, haven't you? You were a first-generation college student, not legacy admissions. You got every job, internship, and interview through applying cold, not knowing anyone on the inside. You never cheated, never called in favors, never screwed someone else over so that you could get ahead.

You had one bad day. One. And you lost everything over it. How could that happen? How is that fair?"

My hands were shaking. I pushed the cup away, my eyes still trained on her.

"And you know what's the worst part? The three people who'd made your life hell—Gene Struzik, Amy Cloverfield, Auggie Flores—will never get what's coming to them. Haven't the events of the last month taught you anything, Shelley? There's no accountability for men. There's no accountability for people in places of power. There is no justice for people like us."

Sophia squeezed my hand. When she looked at me, she was clear-eyed, compassionate; she held me in her gaze. I felt a surge of warmth.

"Which is why," she said, "you and I, we're going to make our own kind of justice."

SHELLEY

These were Sophia Moon's conditions for helping me.

One: I had to legally change my name. "You'll need to do it while you're still in Florida," she said. "In New Jersey, they make you take out an ad in the newspaper. Here, the process is more discreet. I'd be happy to cover the fee on your behalf."

Two: I had to move in with her, Paul, and their kid, Ory, in Hoboken. The three of them lived in a small white house at the end of a sleepy, tree-lined street. There was a guest room on the first floor that I could stay in. Sophia showed me pictures on her phone. "We painted the front door cobalt blue after vacationing in Greece last summer. Now it feels like coming home to the Mediterranean."

Three: She was the one who would come up with the plan. I just had to trust her.

I told her no that night. Of course I did.

She wasn't even fazed. She just nodded and reached into her pocket. "I want you to have this, then, for when you change your mind."

It was a business card. Snow white and crisp, with a name and an email address printed on the front. SOPHIA EUNJIN MOON. The back side was blank. I said, "You gave yourself a new Korean name?"

Sophia shrugged. "It's a tool. People expect you to be American, to get rid of your accent and fully assimilate, but they also want a little bit of an ethnic edge in there. It's one of the ways I make myself more palatable."

Then she put her hand on my back and rubbed it, briefly. "My door is always open, all right? It doesn't matter if it's a day from now or a year from now. Whenever you get to the point where you feel you need me, I'll be there."

She was almost at the elevator when I spun around. "Sophia."

We looked at each other. I took a deep breath.

"What you're proposing to me, the things you want to do, it's . . . it's insane. I might have had a bad moment once, but I'm a normal person. I'm not crazy. I need you to know that."

Then I said, "I mean, really, what makes you think I would in any way, shape, or form reach out to you?"

Slowly, Sophia began to smile. In her eyes, I saw the moon. They were crescents, slivers of light deep in the darkness.

"I never claim to know things for certain," she said. "But this one, I'm pretty sure about."

The elevator doors opened, and Sophia walked in. She was still holding my gaze.

"Remember my words, Shelley," she said. "All it takes is one yes."

The doors closed. I was alone again.

Sitting there at the table, I was visited by a sudden, startling realization.

During the time Sophia Moon and I had spoken, no one had checked in. No one had checked out. There hadn't even been a single other guest walking through the lobby, coming down the stairs. It was almost five in the morning, but we were days from Christmas. High Disney season. The motel was fully booked.

It was as though for a little while, as we sat together at that table, time itself had slowed to a stop.

Suddenly, there was a bright light in the lobby, washing away everything in my field of vision. I raised my arm to shield my eyes, and the light passed: It was a huge SUV pulling into the parking lot, high beams on. I could hear the sound of doors opening, kids whining, luggage being unloaded from the back. Wheels rolling towards the entrance, passing through shallow puddles on the pavement. At some point, the rain had stopped.

I rearranged the chairs and threw away the pizza box. Then I reinstated myself behind the front desk and got back to work.

That weekend, my mom invited a Chinese exorcist to our apartment.

I'd thought she was joking when she brought up the woman at dinner the evening before. "I found her ad on the bulletin board inside the Chinese supermarket. Her name is Dali, but she goes by Dolly in America. The cashier said she was the real deal."

I said nothing, and my mom said, "She's going to get rid of the jinn."

At this, I looked up. It had been days since the jinn last visited me; the shadows in the walls and ceilings of the apartment were empty. Perhaps the jinn had gotten wind of this exorcist and vacated itself. My mother deposited a chicken leg in my bowl of rice.

"It's become too much," she said. "First it was your father leaving so early. He should have had more time with us. Decades. Then your grandparents, gone. The way your grandfather lost his mind and forgot his family at the end. And now you! Doing that horrible, shameless thing for no reason, like you were possessed by a demon. It's not right. Something is not right."

It was the first time I had heard my mom explicitly reference The Incident since I had come home. She put down her chopsticks and rubbed her temples.

"I didn't want to believe in it before. When your grandmother told me about a jinn in the apartment years ago, sitting on her heart, I just laughed it off. Her and her silly old-world superstitions. But in the pit of my stomach, I always thought, maybe, just maybe..."

But then her face shuttered, and she said, "Anyway, she's coming at eight tomorrow. Make sure to tidy your room."

She got up to refill her bowl, and I said, "Wait, how much are you paying this person to get rid of the jinn?"

My mom wouldn't look at me. "It's worth it."

"I'm serious, Ma. How much?"

But she wouldn't say.

That night, after my mom had gone to bed, I sat in the kitchen with a cup of instant coffee, staring out at the empty wall.

Outside, the night was still. For a passing second, I thought I saw Sophia Moon in the doorway. She was wearing that cream-colored coat, and when she smiled at me, the rings on her hand glittered. Her business card was sitting in the top drawer of the desk by my bed.

Maybe the jinn really was gone after all.

"Oh yes, I see a big problem immediately," Dolly said. "The feng shui in the apartment is unacceptable."

She had arrived twenty-six minutes ahead of schedule, after calling my mom to inform her that her previous exorcism had wrapped up earlier than expected. Immediately after changing into house slippers at the door, Dolly had dropped her bulging purse on the floor and walked straight into the kitchen. She took in the room without removing her enormous sunglasses. "It's your feng shui," she said in Mandarin. "It's all screwed up."

I could sense the tension in my mom's shoulders. "Is it easy to address?"

Dolly rejoined us in the entryway. She took off her sunglasses, and she was younger than I'd expected. Early forties. She had thin, overplucked eyebrows and coral-orange lips.

"Your front door. It opens right into the heart of the apartment, no wall, no barrier, nothing to deflect the bad energy that enters and bounce it back outside. You'll need to put up a screen at the entryway. Even a tall bookshelf could work."

My mom was taking notes on the back of an expired calendar.

I watched as Dolly spun on the spot, taking in the rest of the apartment. Her eyes flew over the awards and certificates framed on the wall, the accolades I'd brought home over the years. Then they settled on me, and she drew a sharp breath, the sound reproachful, like I had stepped on her foot.

"This is her," my mom said, and she gave me a sharp jab in the back, nudging me towards Dolly. "My daughter, the one I was telling you about. She's been having some troubles."

Dolly gave me a long, appraising look. Instinctively, I crossed my arms.

"Yes," she said slowly. "Yes, I see it now. It's in her glabella."

"It's in my what?"

She pointed at her own face. "Your glabella. The place where your eyebrows meet, just above your nose."

Then she said, "I can see a darkness lurking there."

My mom clapped a hand to her mouth.

Dolly put her bony hand on my shoulder, and I had to fight the urge to shrug it off. She said, "There's a spirit bothering you, isn't there? I can tell that it has become tethered to you. It refuses to leave."

"I don't know what you mean."

But it was too late. My mom was already hooked. She took Dolly's hand into both of hers and shook it back and forth, like she was trying to shake loose sprinklings of good fortune.

"Please," she said, "you have to get rid of it. My daughter, she was perfect before this. Top of her class, a prestigious internship, a bright future ahead of her. I never had to worry a day about her. Then out of nowhere she lost her mind, and now her entire life is ruined. Please, you have to make the . . . the thing go away. You have to make it leave my daughter so she can get her life back."

Dolly nodded. I could see her eyes working, that sideways little twitch, running the calculations in the background. She reciprocated the gesture, taking my mom's hands into her own.

"It's going to be difficult," she said.

"Difficult?"

"Oh, yes. I can see the darkness twisted around her body. It has taken some very deep roots. It must have settled inside her long before this. Years."

My mom let out a little gasp. "Can you help her? Please tell me you can help her."

Dolly let the suspense build for a few more seconds before she smacked her coral lips together. She put a hand on my mom's shoulder.

"It's an extremely complicated situation," she said, "but I have seen this kind of case before. A boy in Chengdu. It took a lot of work—I had to put in a lot of overtime—but in the end, I was able to help him and his family return to a normal life."

That was it. I could no longer stop myself. I said, "So is there a surcharge for extra-difficult exorcisms? Or can we do an annual subscription and get some kind of loyalty discount?"

They both looked at me.

My bag was already hanging from the coatrack by the door. As I reached for it and slipped into my shoes, my mom tried to stop me. "Shelley, don't go. Dolly came here to help you."

I ignored her. To Dolly, I said, "You know what? You're a fucking crook, and you should be ashamed of yourself."

She didn't even flinch. She met my gaze straight on, calm, in a way that was almost amused.

"Shelley," my mom was still saying. Her hand was on my arm. "Dolly is going to help you get your life back. Don't you want that?"

I shook her off, and I saw the hurt in her face. But my heart was pounding, and I had two things to say.

"Ma, first of all, there is no jinn. You can make up all the stories you want, blame all the fucked-up shit in our family on things that don't exist, but a spirit didn't make me do those things on the subway that day. I did that. It was all me. And second—"

The words that followed, I had to force them out.

"The life I had in New York is gone. I'll never be able to get it back. And you're just going to have to live with that, like I have."

We were both quiet, me waiting for her to say something. Anything. My mom closed her eyes, and when she opened them again, she had become calm, too.

Looking straight at me, she said, "So this is it, then? You're accepting that this is the life you will have?"

I didn't slam the door like they do in movies. I left it open as I walked to the car and got in, started the engine. They didn't come after me.

I drove around for miles. From the wheel, I saw the city as it always had been, this petri dish of cheap, synthetic consumerism. The winter sun was flat and colorless, and the shadows of the cars before and after me stretched out faintly across the asphalt. They came from all over. Georgia. Florida. Illinois. South Carolina. In my mind, I saw Sophia Moon in the back of her family car, her husband driving up front, her kid in a booster seat next to her, pointing out the license plates to each other as a game. I hadn't seen them leave. They had checked out in the morning, after my shift had ended.

In the passenger seat, my phone was buzzing. My mom, calling again.

It was half past ten when I pulled into the parking lot of a strip mall. Ahead of me, there was a dental clinic. Next to it was a Dairy Queen, a Dominican restaurant, a coin laundry, another motel. I turned off the engine and picked up my phone and opened the Mail app. I didn't need the business card; I had already committed the email address to memory.

In the subject of the email, I wrote, *Is the door still open?* And I hit send.

The answer came only four minutes later.

Yes, she wrote.

Under that was a phone number.

SHELLEY

January 2017

The only other person changing their name that rainy afternoon was a guy with an Iranian name, one that was so long I won't even try to reproduce it here. In his petition to the court, the guy had chosen the new name of Mark Taylor. When we heard the names read out loud one after the other, Sophia and I glanced at each other, and we had the same thought: *Makes sense.*

Sophia had flown down to Florida on the day of my court hearing for moral support, after having first sent me the $400 administrative fee via wire transfer. As we sat together in that small, musty courtroom in the row behind the guy soon to be known as Mark Taylor, waiting for the judge to appear, it occurred to me that this was both my first time—and possibly last time—appearing in court. In the two months that I worked for Gene Struzik at Ingram, Russo & McAllister, I had split my time between doc review and other legal assistant busywork, like prepping conference rooms and rescheduling Gene's many appointments, including, once, lunch with his wife. She'd been understanding, at least.

When the judge came in, we all stood, and he heard Mark Taylor's petition first. The background check had already been cleared and the fingerprints taken weeks ago, so this was just a formality. In a disinterested voice, the judge read out Mark Taylor's old name, stumbling over the syllables, and then the new name with far greater ease. He confirmed with Mark Taylor that the spelling on the petition was correct. And then it was over. "You're all set, Mr. Taylor," the judge said. "You can see with the clerk on your way out about getting copies of the signed order."

It was my turn next. Sophia squeezed my hand and mouthed, *You've got this.*

The judge took a little longer to read my petition. At one point, he looked up at me, adjusting his glasses as he did so, and I wondered if he had recognized me from The Incident. But then he looked down again, and he sounded bored as he said, "And the name you are requesting to change to is Erin Callaghan?"

I had to swallow before my voice would come out. "Yes, Your Honor."

"Everything seems to be in order here," the judge said.

Then he pressed his pen to paper and signed the order. "Your name-change petition is approved. Congratulations, Miss Callaghan."

Sophia and I were both silent as we filed out of the courtroom. The door closed after us, and we looked at each other in the hallway, the green fluorescent lighting washing over us. We didn't even say anything. We just moved in towards each other and hugged.

I said, "I can't believe I just did that."

"It's a big change," she said. "The shock will wear off in a few days."

"Still," I said. "Erin Callaghan. I mean—how the fuck am I going to explain this to my mom?"

"Maybe you tell her it's what you had to do. Or maybe you just don't say anything. It's up to you."

I nodded. I felt dizzy, like I had just been spat out from a moving roller coaster, trying to regain my balance on the ground. I said, "Let's not say anything to her for now."

We walked slowly down the hallway, Sophia's arm still around me. She said, "You did tell her you were leaving, didn't you?"

"I did. She took it well, actually. I think it made her hopeful again."

"Good. She should be. Because you're not just doing this for yourself. You're doing it for her, too."

On the way to the clerk's office, we ran into Mark Taylor again, clutching the certified copies of his name-change order. We made eye contact, and he said, "Hey, uh, good luck with everything."

He had a Texan accent, which—and I would've felt like an asshole for admitting this—threw me a little at first. After a pause, I said, "Yeah, you too."

"I'm guessing you did it for the same reasons," Mark Taylor said.

I knew what he was referring to. "Yeah," I said. "Crazy times we're living in."

He nodded at me, once, before he walked away.

Sophia helped me pack up while my mom was at work. We didn't touch most of my stuff. I had a closet full of clothes that I'd bought for internships throughout the years, polyester button-down shirts and black pants and patent leather shoes from TJ Maxx, a couple of niceish blazers from Zara and Banana Republic. But Sophia told me to leave it all behind. "You won't need them anymore," she said. "Not as Erin Callaghan."

I'd tried my best to clean things up before Sophia arrived, but the apartment remained an intense, controlled explosion. My mom was the type that held on to everything: old calendars, expired biscuits, school portraits of me leaning against a tree with my arms folded awkwardly. Even my dad's clothes were still hanging in the back of my parents' armoire. When I was younger, I used to go in there and wrap an armful of his shirts around my face and smell them. Eventually they lost their smell. Or maybe I'd just forgotten what he smelled like.

In my bedroom, as I put a rolled-up shirt in my open suitcase, I said, "I know why we had to do it, but it still feels so jarring that I have a white name now. Am I allowed to even call myself Chinese anymore?"

Sophia was sitting on my bed; she looked at me now with amusement. "You think just because you have a white name, you can't be Chinese?"

In 1998, a week after my dad died, my mom had printed a black-and-white photo of him at Walmart and stuck it in a thick black frame.

She set it on the top shelf of our bookcase, right next to the TV, and every few days, she'd change out the fruit offering in front of the photo. Usually it was a small clementine. Sometimes it was an apple. Once she ran out of fruit and had to use a Snickers bar. Then she became a born-again Christian, and one day I came home to find the top of the bookcase empty, my dad's photo and the offerings gone. She ended up drifting away from the church, eventually. But the altar never made a comeback.

In the bottom drawer of my dresser, I found the framed photo and held it up to show Sophia. "Look."

She turned the frame over in her hand. "Is this your dad?"

"Yeah."

"You look like him," she said. "You have his eyes. His bone structure."

"I know. That's what my mom says, too."

Then I said, "We used to have this in the living room when I was a kid. And my mom would put up these little fruits, like—"

"Things for him to eat in the underworld," Sophia said. "I know." She looked at me. "Did you know that in Chinese mythology, the underworld is made of water? A long, flowing river. It's called the river of forgetting. The ancients believed that after you die, your spirit floats along the river, and once you've reached the end, you'll have forgotten everything from this past life. You'll be ready to start anew."

"See," I said, "I didn't know any of that. My Chinese is ass."

"How old were you when your dad passed away?"

"I was six. It was in 1998."

"Do you still remember him?"

I frowned at her, and Sophia looked abashed. "I'm sorry," she said. "I shouldn't have . . . It's just that Paul also lost his father when he was young, so I've always been curious."

"It's not that," I said. "I made that face because I genuinely don't know. Sometimes I do think I remember what he looked like, but then I don't know if that's just from seeing him in photos."

"So you were okay, then. You weren't . . . broken by what happened."

"Maybe I was okay. I don't know. It's hard to say."

I said, "I remember that after he died, there was this... this emptiness. Even the times when I was happy, it was like there was always this hole at the bottom, and the happiness would eventually leak out. I felt that all through my childhood. I still feel it sometimes. In a way, I guess that was me missing him. Maybe it's why I'm still so fucked up as an adult."

Wordlessly, Sophia passed me the photo, and I looked at my dad's smiling face. "That's the one good thing about him not being here," I said. "At least he doesn't have to see me throw away his name."

We had dinner at home one last time, me, my mom, Sophia. My packed suitcase was in the hallway, zipped and standing upright, and there was something oddly shameful about its presence; my gaze kept flitting back to it as I ate.

To my mom, Sophia said, "Auntie, this fish is absolutely incredible. I wish I could live here and eat your cooking every day."

She was great. She had my mom in a chatty mood. Now my mom used the communal pair of chopsticks to break off two more pieces of fish and transfer them to her bowl. "You must eat more, then. Eat more. Eat more."

Then she said, "Sophia, what do you do for job?"

"I work at a marketing company. And my husband, he works for the city government of New York. He's in finance."

This got my mom's attention. "Oh, you have a husband."

"Yes, and we have a little boy, too. His name is Orion, and he just turned five in October."

Sophia showed my mom a few pictures on her phone, swiping through them slowly, and my mom drew in her breath. She pulled down her glasses to take a closer look, because she was at the age now where her vision was starting to go. "Very cute," she said. "Very, very adorable."

I said, "Sophia and I met at a networking happy hour for Asian American professionals earlier this year, I want to say... When was it, April?"

"I feel like it was earlier than that," Sophia said. "Maybe February, even."

It was surprisingly easy to come up with these details on the fly, to ping-pong falsehoods between us without even thinking. She said, "It was back when you were still in law school, I remember that."

My mom stiffened. She looked up at Sophia. In a subdued voice, she said, "You know about the . . ."

She couldn't bring herself to finish the question. Sophia reached for my mom's hand and squeezed it, the same way she always did with me.

"I know," she said, "and it is so, so unfair what happened to Shelley. She's the brightest, sweetest, most incredible young woman I know. It never should have happened."

My mom's bottom lip was trembling. She nodded, then turned her head away and dabbed at her eye with the sleeve of her sweater. It killed me to see her like that.

I said, loudly, "Ma, Sophia found a job for me at her company. I'm starting there on Monday. I'm going to start over, I'm going to work hard, and—and I'm going to find my way back. You'll see."

My mom nodded. She took both of Sophia's hands in her own. "Thank you," she said. "Thank you for helping my daughter."

I slept in her bed that night while Sophia stayed in my room. My mom was on the outside, just like how it was when I was a kid, and after we had both changed into our pajamas, I ran through her chin-length hair with a wooden comb. When I was younger, we used to play this game where I went through her thick black hair and plucked out the rare white ones. Now she had a head full of gray.

My mom said, "Sophia is such a good person."

"I know. She's been amazing."

She turned to look at me. "Don't waste it," she said, "this precious opportunity she has given you. You have to take it and run with it. Run as far as you can. And one day, after you've succeeded, you're going to pay her back for everything she has done."

"I will, Ma. Don't worry."

We had lain in the dark for barely ten minutes before I felt I had to tell her. "Ma? There's something else."

I could hear her even breathing. "What?"

"I changed my name. This afternoon, Sophia and I went to the courthouse, and I got my name legally changed by a judge. My new name is—" I hesitated, and I had never felt more stupid than I did in that moment. "My new name is Erin Callaghan."

There was a pause. My mom said, "Your new name is what?"

"Erin Callaghan. I changed—I changed my whole name."

She was silent. I held my breath, waiting for her judgment.

Then I heard her say, "Okay."

"Okay? What does that mean, okay?"

"I think it's a good idea," she said. "Now no one will know you are Shelley Hu anymore."

My head was spinning.

"And when you apply for jobs in the future, they see that name on your résumé, they'll think you are a white person. So that's even better for your chances."

I sat up. My mom had blackout curtains in her room, so I couldn't even see her outline. I just felt her there.

I said, "So you're not mad at me? You don't think I'm . . . I'm betraying my heritage or something?"

In the darkness, I heard my mom laugh, almost as if to herself.

She said, "You know that in Zhengzhou, back in the old village, your dad's family still has a shrine?"

"A shrine, like for the ancestors?"

"Yeah. They had to burn it down during the Cultural Revolution, when everyone had to denounce ancestor worship and other old traditions. Then they pooled some money and rebuilt it in the eighties. They reconstructed the Hu family tree, too. It goes back to the early Qing dynasty."

Then she said, "You're not on it."

"Wait, seriously?"

"They don't record daughters on the tree. Your dad got into an argument with your great-uncle over this when you were born, but they said it was tradition. Daughters are like a bowl of water, the saying goes. When they marry, they're poured out the door, and they'll never be yours again."

In the dark, my mom reached out and patted my hand. It was as if she had night vision.

She said, "Your heritage isn't your name. It's what you want it to be. Me, your dad, your laolao and laoye—all we've ever wanted is for you to have a good life. So don't worry about things that aren't important. Just hold on to what really matters."

I found Sophia in the kitchen after midnight, sitting at the table with her phone and a glass of water. She smiled at me. "How are you feeling?"

"Can't sleep," I said. "I think I'm still on night shift mode."

For a moment, I saw something fragile in her face. She said, "Can I ask you for a favor?"

"Sure. Anything."

"I'm serious." Her eyes were pools again. "It's the only thing I'll ever ask of you."

I nodded, and Sophia said, "I need you to promise me that you will never, ever tell my family what you and I are doing."

"Oh, that's easy," I said. "Done. I won't tell them."

She looked down at her hands.

"Ory's too young to understand, so I'm not worried about him. But Paul—he can't know. He just can't. What we're planning, everything we've said to each other, it has to stay between us forever. Paul isn't a part of it, and he never will be. Can you promise me that, Erin?"

The sound of the name on her tongue—the newness of it, the two syllables landing one after the other like a pair of raindrops. That was the moment it really settled. I wasn't Shelley anymore; I was Erin. And she was the only person in the world who knew why.

"I promise, Sophia," I said. "I won't tell Paul anything, I swear. He's not in the game."

That made Sophia smile, just a little. "He's not in the game."

She changed the subject. "Do you have any snacks? I always get so hungry at this hour."

"We have half a bag of tortilla chips. No dip, though. I know, it's a jailable offense."

She laughed. "I think I'll manage."

As I turned to open the pantry, I caught sight of something black and shapeless in the hallway, and I froze for a moment. But it wasn't the jinn. It was my suitcase, standing right where I had left it.

Sophia was looking at it, too. Now she turned back to me. "It's gone," she said, calm.

My voice caught in my throat. "What?"

"You don't have to worry anymore. It's left the house."

That was when I felt it, too.

The jinn was gone.

My legs were shaking. I stumbled to the table and sank into the chair next to her, and for a long time, I just stared at the wall, at what it no longer was.

The jinn was gone, and for the first time in my life, so was my fear of the things I did not know.

Part Two

THE HOUSE WITH THE BLUE DOOR

ERIN

January 2017

The taxi dropped us off just after five in the afternoon, in front of a quaint little house that looked just like the one in Sophia's pictures: white walls, two stories, a deep blue front door. There was a tangle of trees peering out from the back, dark shapes with naked branches. Sophia noticed me looking and gestured with her hand. "Our cherry trees. They don't do so well with fruit bearing, but the flowers are gorgeous."

As we brought our suitcases to the door, I could see Paul, the husband, appear in the living room window. Their kid was slung over his shoulder, asleep; he'd caught some sort of bug from school, she'd said. On the other side of the glass, Paul made a questioning gesture, and Sophia nodded and gave him a thumbs-up.

Then Paul's eyes flicked to me.

His vibe wasn't friendly. It wasn't hostile, either, but there was something cold in his face, something that could have been read as a sort of wary disapproval. We made eye contact for a prolonged moment, and then he moved and disappeared from view. A second later, the blue front door opened, and Paul was there with the kid, who was now stirring sleepily in his arms. "Look who's back, Ory," I could hear him saying. "It's Mommy. Mommy's home."

It was the first time I had heard Paul speak. In Kissimmee, it had been Sophia who'd checked them in. Sophia who had come down to the lobby in the dead of night and changed the trajectory of my life over a pot of coffee.

Next to me, Sophia beamed. She touched me on the arm lightly, as if to say, *Be right back*, and then she was hurrying to Paul, taking Ory from his arms. All of her attention was focused on the kid. "Hi, my baby. Mommy's here. Mommy's here. How are you feeling? Does your head still hurt? Oh, Paul, can you bring Erin's bags to her room, please, and show her the house? I'll be down to help with dinner as soon as I can."

As Paul reached for my suitcase, my hand tensed around the handle. "Thanks, but I don't want to trouble you. I can take it myself."

"It's no trouble," Paul said. There was no warmth in his voice.

I followed Paul through the front door; immediately, there was a staircase, and Paul went around it, going past an open kitchen and a small laundry alcove. The guest room was at the end, and when he pushed the door open, I was pleasantly surprised to see that it had two large windows. The cherry trees in the back were all in view, as was a small, manicured Japanese garden: ferns, stone pagodas, an earthy pond lined with mossy rocks, plus a slim wooden bench. "Must be nice in the springtime."

Paul set my suitcase down by the desk. "It's not bad," he said.

Then he gestured at the room. It had been tastefully furnished: There was a full bed made up in blue-and-white-striped linens, a small teal armchair, a simple floral pattern running across the wallpaper. The only thing that surprised me was that there was no art on the walls. Just the wallpaper. "My mom stays here when she visits, so we try to have the basics stocked year-round. Extra linens, pillows, towels are in that closet. There's an en suite bath. If you need something else, just let Sophia or myself know."

"No, that's perfect. Thank you. I doubt I'll need anything."

We were both quiet for a second. Paul said, "Let me show you the rest."

The house was beautiful. They had bought it in 2013; before that, they had lived in a comfortable one-bedroom apartment in the East Village, which quickly became unbearably cramped when Ory arrived. The renovations had taken eight months, but Sophia had had a vision, and it all came together, despite how eclectic everything was. The doorways were round arches, and the kitchen and bathroom floors were covered in Portuguese tiles. There were rugs and cushions from Morocco. Wicker baskets from Indonesia. Lanterns and tatami mats from Japan. And Sophia's art was all over the place. Clean, whimsical ink-wash paintings framed in white squares. Sculptures of enigmatic faces and bodies. There was a gallery wall of black-and-white photos of Ory from birth to present day, often accompanied by Paul, taken with a professional camera by Sophia. The kid was effortlessly photogenic. He flashed a big, toothy grin and crinkled his eyes like moons in all of the pictures, and Paul smiled in most of them, too. I was surprised to see that he'd once had voluminously curly hair, much like Ory's; it was now tame and cropped.

Paul was not smiling now as he led me down the hallway, around the staircase to the living room, and back to the kitchen. "Laundry is over there. There's a magnet on the fridge with the Wi-Fi password."

Then he opened one of the cabinets and took out an empty glass. "Can I get you something to drink?"

It was clear that Paul was not going to show me the upstairs of the house, where he, Sophia, and Ory lived. But I knew I'd see it at some point. Sophia would invite me up. She and I, we were the ones who shared a secret between us.

"Tap water's fine," I said. "Thanks."

I wasn't thirsty, but I drank a few sips just to be polite. I could feel Paul watching me. He said, "It's Erin, right?"

"Yeah." I smiled my customer-service smile. "I don't know if you remember, but we kind of met back in Florida. At the Mermaid Inn."

As I looked at Paul, I wondered if he had watched the video of my breakdown. In most of the versions that circulated on social media, my breasts had been blurred. But it would've taken an extra two minutes to find an uncensored version on the Internet. Perhaps Paul had done such a search. It wasn't outside the realm of possibility.

Politely, Paul said, "Yes, of course. You checked us in."

"Did you have a nice time at Disney World?"

He nodded. "It was Ory's first time. He loved it."

On the gallery wall, there was already a framed photo of Paul and Ory with Goofy at Magic Kingdom, Goofy holding one of Ory's hands in his paws.

Paul started going through the pantry, taking out a sack of potatoes, laying a knife on the cutting board. I said, "Can I help you with dinner?"

"I've got it." He nodded towards the guest room. "You should get settled in. We'll call you when dinner's ready."

Back in the room, it only took a few minutes to unpack. Besides my clothes and basic toiletries, the only other thing I'd brought from home was the black-and-white framed portrait of my dad. It felt weird to start another homemade altar after so many years, so I just laid it face up on a stack of books.

There was a white sheepskin rug next to the bed, and I lay on it, staring into the nothingness of the ceiling. What had I done? What was I doing here, in the guest room of a couple I had just met, in *New Jersey*? The surrealism of the situation sank in only then, truly grabbed me by the horns and shook my entire body, and I began to cry.

My phone buzzed with a new text, and I checked it, sniffling. It was my mom. It was always my mom. I threw it aside without answering.

I was still lying on the rug when there was a knock on the door. "It's me," Sophia's voice said. "Can I come in?"

When I opened the door, Sophia was alone, holding something rectangular in her arms. She smiled at me. "How are you feeling?"

"Good. Great. How's Ory?"

"He's much better. His fever is mostly gone, but he's still very sleepy, so I've put him back to bed." She touched my arm lightly. "I appreciate your asking."

Then she held out the object in her arms. "I have something for you."

It was a framed drawing. Of what, I wasn't sure: It looked like it had been done with a graphite pencil, a bunch of tangled-up lines and squiggles that intersected in random, frenetic ways. But interspersed with that were these shadows: faint, watery splashes of black ink. "Wow," I said. "This is . . . this is dope."

My face must have been less than convincing, because Sophia laughed. "It's very abstract, I know," she said. "I made this ink-wash piece about twelve years ago."

"Was that when you were . . ."

"Living with my parents after being kicked out of Cornell, yes. I'd been taking art classes at the community college, learning how to work with water and ink for the first time. I didn't conceive of it; it just came to me. And I didn't understand its meaning at first, but something about it spoke to me. I took it home and hid it in my room, and it wasn't until a few days later that I realized what it was."

She looked at me. "It was a talisman."

"A talisman, like for good luck?"

Sophia was quiet for a moment.

"It was a strange time in my life," she said. "I was around other people, I was always being watched, but I had never felt more alone. No one could understand what I had done or why I had done it. All of my friends had stopped taking my calls. People from my past were posting on Internet forums, saying, *I knew her, I knew she was crazy from the day I met her.* It was only then that it really sank in: the realization that I had no one in my corner; I had nowhere to go. It was just me. It had been me all along."

She pointed at the bottom-right corner of the drawing. "This is the title."

It was a tiny inscription in pencil. *I love you, regardless.*

"I made this for myself," she said, "because it was the only thing anyone would give me. I protected myself with this talisman. Which is why I want to pass it on to you."

I couldn't help it. My eyes welled up again.

"Thank you," I whispered, and I stepped forward and hugged her, gripping the drawing in my hand. Sophia touched my hair, gentle. Then she stood up on her tiptoes, pressing down on my arm for balance, and gave me a kiss on the cheek. She was at least five inches shorter than I was.

The writing desk was bare except for a lavender candle in a porcelain dish. As I set the drawing down next to it, I said, "I was wondering why there was no art in this room."

"Oh," Sophia said, and she made a face. "That's because it's mostly Paul's mom who stays here. She has different tastes when it comes to art."

Then she lowered her voice conspiratorially. "She also has different tastes when it comes to a daughter-in-law, if I'm honest, but there's not much I'm willing to do about that."

That made me laugh. "Why wouldn't Paul's mom like you? You're like a savant with Asian parents. My mom was obsessed with you."

Sophia looked at me wryly. She said, "Would you be thrilled if your son married somebody who pretended to go to his school?"

"Wait, she knows about that?"

"She knows. Unfortunately."

It was clear, though, that this was not something that particularly bothered Sophia. She smiled at me, breezy again. "Want to help me set the table? Dinner's almost ready."

Ory was asleep upstairs, so it was only the three of us at dinner. Sophia sat next to me, and Paul sat across from Sophia. She had brought out a bottle of white wine from the pantry, but Paul had declined, and—feeling suddenly self-conscious—I had also said no, so Sophia was the only one who drank. As I looked at Paul, who was pushing his roasted potatoes around his plate with an air of indisputable moodiness, I wondered if the two of them had been fighting. I wondered if some of it had something to do with me.

I said, after a few minutes of silence, "So how'd you guys meet?"

They both looked at me, surprised. Then they looked at each other. "We met in school," Paul said. "In college."

Sophia tapped him on the wrist playfully. "I think Erin's looking for a better story than that."

"Yeah," I said. "I want the day, the time, the location, the details. Everything."

Sophia laughed. She leaned back in her chair with the glass of wine. "Let's see. Where to start? It was August, the first week of freshman orientation. I was in this big lecture hall, listening to the provost talk about the process of choosing a major. And I happened to look over to my right and see a very cute boy with a head full of the wildest, curliest hair."

She smiled at Paul, who had stopped pushing his food around the plate. A hint of a smile had also made its way to his face.

"I said hi to him as we were leaving," Sophia said, "but he told me later that he didn't recall meeting me at all."

She did a little pout at him, and this time Paul really smiled. "That first week was really hectic," he said. "It was a massive overload of names and faces. I got overwhelmed."

Sophia looked over at me, and she gave a cheerful little shrug. But for a moment, I couldn't help but keep my eyes trained on Paul. He was quiet again, scooping up some carrots and green beans with his chopsticks. How had he felt when he found out she was an imposter? Paul had been kind, Sophia had said, and I could've pictured that. But how you acted was one thing, and how you felt was something else entirely. Because here was this girl who'd lied to him for the better part of a semester. Who had slid shamelessly into this gilded institution on nothing but bravado and bullshit, trying to eat a piece of the pie he'd spent his whole life hustling for. Who, according to *The Korea Daily*, had been dragged out of a library basement by the Cornell police and perp-walked across half of campus. How was it that Paul had managed to fall in love with someone like that? How had he gone on to marry her, despite his mother's objections?

Back in my room that night, I took Sophia's drawing off the desk and carried it to my bed. I lay there, staring at it. Under the dim light, the lines and shadows looked different. They seemed to be making a little more sense than they had before.

I hugged the drawing to my chest and promptly fell asleep.

SOYOUNG

August 2004

It was easy to persuade someone to let you crash in her dorm room for one night.

It was much harder to talk her into letting you stay for a whole month.

Soyoung had first met Lillian Pietrowski two rows from the back of the classroom, having found seats next to each other in a hundred-person lecture on microeconomics. It was funny how the group mentality worked. People chose their seats on the first day and they stuck to them for the whole semester, even if they were at an odd angle from the whiteboard, even if they found themselves trapped behind people who whispered and snickered until the hissing sounds made your head hurt. Other eighteen-year-olds drifted, waded through life without thought or agency. Soyoung knew better.

She had chosen Lillian for a reason. There was a specific archetype of white girl; Soyoung had noticed them right away when she first moved to Brookline, Massachusetts, at eleven. These white girls had never known what it was like to be pretty: not as children, not as teens, not as young adults. Some of them had horses at home, and many of them had food allergies that Soyoung had never heard of before, like peanut butter and bread. They were often bad at regulating their emotions and cried a lot; they did this in full view of all the other kids in the class, which mortified them, which made them cry even harder.

These were the white girls who always gravitated towards her. Naturally, they would have preferred to have hung out with the white girls in the upper echelons, the Ashleys and the Laurens and the Nicoles with their straight blonde hair and their tiny waists and their linebacker boyfriends leaning casually against their lockers. But there were unspoken standards, and these white girls were too weird or too fat or too poor to meet them. So they turned to the Asian girls instead.

Lillian Pietrowski was tediously plain, which she had to be for this to work. She wore her mangy dirt-blonde hair in a ponytail, and her eyes were set a little too wide apart, a fact that wasn't helped by her thick glasses. The first time Soyoung sat next to her in class, Lillian had worn jeans and a hoodie that said CORNELL, which was funny because Soyoung was wearing more or less the same thing. The kids here bought their overpriced paraphernalia from the campus bookstore. Soyoung's T-shirt was from eBay and cost eight bucks with free shipping. The first time she had snuck into a lecture at Cornell, she had felt apprehensive. Lightheaded. She kept her head down and her elbows tucked in, because surely someone would call her out, someone would notice that she didn't belong. But no one had, and now she felt invincible; derisive, even. When she looked out at the sea of heads cascading down the rows of the lecture hall, it all made her want to laugh. Here they were, all these supposed geniuses who had clawed their way into the Ivy League, and they had no idea an imposter was among them, getting the same education for free.

That first day, after the lecture had ended and they'd been talking for a while, walking aimlessly in the corridors, Soyoung said, "I feel like such a loser, honestly."

Lillian looked at her, surprised. "Why?"

"No, it's just . . . it's been a month and I feel like I still haven't made any friends. I did meet a couple people during orientation, but they've gone on and met other people, and now it's weird to ask them to hang out again. It seems like everyone's settled into these little cliques already."

Then she said the clincher. "I guess I'd always thought college would be an easier time than high school."

There was a pause. Soyoung waited.

Then she heard Lillian say, "Oh my God, I'm so relieved you just said that. I've been feeling the exact same way."

It was a matter of money, when it really came down to it. Why she went out of her way to befriend dull, lonely, desperately impressionable people like Lillian Pietrowski. Why she spent the next three months bouncing between dorms, biding her time like a cockroach at the bottom of a bin, bracing itself for someone to lift the lid. It was why she got that night-cashier job at the grubby, foul-smelling convenience store just off campus, standing behind the till in a faded blue apron, watching the fluorescent lights hiss and flicker.

In her first few weeks at Cornell, Soyoung had saved enough pocket money from her parents to stay in a motel in Ithaca. From the store, it was a twenty-five-minute walk back to her room at the motel, ten minutes when she took her bike. The motel was a small, flat, aged thing: All the doors opened directly onto the parking lot, and whenever she peered out from behind the curtains, she'd see the rusty nose of a burgundy Buick pressed against the pavement. The walls in the room had a musty smell, and a suspicious ring of yellow was spreading across the bathroom ceiling, but in a way, it had served as a refuge. When she came back from class or her shift at the store, she took off her CORNELL T-shirt and, with it, the carefully crafted identity she wore as a skin. She pushed a chair against the door before pulling the ancient floral duvet over her head and falling into a dreamless sleep.

The store paid a pittance, but she couldn't afford to take on more hours; she needed time for her studies. When foot traffic was slow, she did her homework at the register. She bought older, cheaper versions of the textbooks from students who'd taken the same classes in previous terms. In the margins next to quizzes, someone had already scribbled the correct answers in ballpoint pen. Soyoung covered them with Post-it Notes and tried to figure out the answers on her own. Most people hoped foolishly for miracles, for saviors, for a deus ex machina that arrived in the final act. But Soyoung had known—ever since she was a little girl, standing on the bank of the Han River and looking through the midnight fog towards that ruthless, glittering city—that for someone like her, they would never come.

It was a night in early September, over a carton of ramen and a page of messy scribbles on her motel room table, that Soyoung came face-to-face with the inevitable. She was out of cash. It was time to turn to plan B.

Lillian.

It had been too easy to manipulate her; she was that gullible. All it took was one late-night knock on her door, a few dramatic tears, a huffish explanation. "This is the third time she's brought this guy back to our room in the last week! He, like, never leaves. I'm scared to change in my own room because he's always there."

And then, pushing past her into the room, sitting down on her bed, and looking up at her with watery, doleful eyes: "Is it okay if I crash with you for just one night? Please, I can sleep on the floor. I just need *one* night of peace and quiet away from them."

Lillian's room was a single. On the strip of floor next to Lillian's bed, Soyoung laid out a fitted sheet over a beach towel, then her pillow and a coverless duvet. That first night, as they lay there in the dark, Lillian said, "I really think he's going to be able to do it. He's going to defeat Bush."

"I don't know," Soyoung said. "I feel like a lot of people don't like Kerry."

"More people don't like Bush, though. Soyoung, he's literally a war criminal! You know that what he and Dick Cheney have done is in direct breach of the UN Charter, right? Kofi Annan just came out and said it yesterday."

The truth was that the war in Iraq was not something Soyoung had ever paid much attention to. Though she'd always had the TV on in the motel room, she'd done it not for the content, but rather for the company.

She racked her brain, searching for a sufficiently intellectual response, and finally she said, "But I heard somebody say that since we already started the war, we have to finish it. Like, we have to get the job done."

Lillian snorted. "'We have to get the job done'? What job is that, bombing entire cities to the ground and butchering thousands of innocent Iraqi civilians? Yeah, great job, America."

Soyoung said nothing, and Lillian said, "You know what? Tomorrow, let's go to the library, and I'll find some books for you on Middle East politics. We need to deprogram your brain from the warmongering propaganda that the administration has been spoon-feeding the masses."

"I'm not brainwashed," Soyoung said.

"Oh, Soyoung, it's nothing personal," Lillian said. "They're just really, really good at it. Plus, you know, with your background, it's easy to fall for it."

"My background?"

"I think it's just a cultural thing. Or at least that's what I've read. Asians are—well, you're very smart, obviously. Your test scores are unbelievable. But your whole cultural framework is, like—you're trained to retain information. It's all about rote memorization and repeating things back to the teacher. But what you don't learn in Asian cultures is critical-thinking skills. You don't question authority. You take things at face value. And honestly, that's what I think has been keeping Asians from achieving greater success and visibility in this country. And it's a shame, really, because again, you guys are crazy smart."

There was something in her tone that irked Soyoung, and it took her a while to decode what it was: confidence. No one ever gave Lillian a second glance when the two of them walked around in public, she was that ordinary, but whenever she raised her hand in class or spoke in a small group setting, her voice traveled, and people listened. She could talk at length about any topic, from the enlargement of the European Union to the political crisis in Haiti. And even more astonishingly: She actually believed she knew what she was talking about.

Back in high school, Soyoung had been the arts editor of the yearbook and the vice president of the Korean Culture Club and a Sunday school teacher's aide for preschoolers at her parents' church. Lillian, meanwhile, had spent the summer after her junior year on Capitol Hill as a page for the congressman representing her home district in Washington state, and the summer after that interning with the American embassy in Vienna, Austria. (How had it come to pass that Lillian had even heard about opportunities like these? How had she been chosen? And how had she managed to survive for months in DC and Vienna on unpaid internships? These were subjects Lillian shied away from discussing, and so Soyoung did, too.) In the fishbowl of Cornell, nothing about Lillian stood out, but nothing about her fell short, either. She had gotten in. She belonged.

In the dark, Lillian coughed. "Do you smell that?" Soyoung heard her say.

"Smell what?"

"There's a weird smell that just came out of nowhere. Like mildew."

Soyoung made a show of sniffing the air. "I don't know," she said. "I don't smell anything."

She turned on her side and felt the hard floor grind against her ribs. She said, once Lillian had stopped coughing, "Have you talked to that guy from your poli-sci lecture yet?"

This was the one topic Lillian couldn't pontificate on. Her peppiness deflated. "No," she said, "we were in the same small group yesterday, but we just talked about the discussion topic."

"You should catch him after class," Soyoung said. "Ask him if he wants to grab lunch."

Lillian had never had a boyfriend. "I don't know," she said. "I'm worried it might be awkward. And what if he says no?"

"That's why you suggest lunch in the dining room. It's super casual, and there are no stakes involved, so it doesn't really mean anything. It's not like you're asking him to dinner and a movie."

She could feel Lillian chewing this over. After a while, she said, "What about you? Any cute-guy sightings?"

Soyoung was quiet for a beat.

"No," she said. "There's no one."

In late September, the two of them took a bus down to New York City for an anti-war protest; while Lillian shook her homemade sign in the air and yelled, Soyoung stayed quiet, hugging her arms to her chest as she took in the scene around them, the storefronts, the glitzy skyscrapers, the commuters with briefcases who picked their way around the roaring crowds without a second glance. Afterwards, they ate lunch in a Midtown diner: chicken sausage and fried eggs and roasted potatoes, Lillian's treat. It was Soyoung's first real hot meal in weeks. In that diner, Lillian had leaned across the table and said, "One day soon, we'll be the ones in charge, Soyoung. We'll get to be the ones who change the world."

That was Lillian's everlasting gift to her, even though their short friendship imploded less than two weeks later. In the years that followed, Soyoung would continue to think of Lillian. In 2007, Paul heard from a classmate that Lillian had taken the fall semester off to join the fledgling Obama campaign and was working as a field organizer in Iowa. Eight years later, sitting in the waiting room of Ory's pediatrician on a rainy morning, surrounded by dead-eyed, unemployed mothers with screeching toddlers and sticky toys, Soyoung was not at all surprised when she glanced at the TV and saw Lillian on the screen, defending the administration's recent drone strikes in Yemen; the chyron identified her as *Lillian Pietrowski, deputy spokeswoman for the US Department of State*. Of course she had done it. Lillian had taught her that college was just a vessel, a cardboard box devoid of inherent value. The real education was something you had to design for yourself.

ERIN

January 2017

"First order of business," Sophia said, "we need to give you long hair."

I'd been right. That morning, after Paul had ushered Ory out the door, she had led me upstairs and given me a tour of the second floor. There was Sophia's studio, an intimate, moody space with forest-green walls and a huge iMac on an oak table. There was Ory's room, which was mostly nautical themed and had a teepee in the corner.

And then there was her and Paul's room. The master. It was more minimalistic than I'd expected, given the visual richness that defined the rest of the house. There was a Nordic-looking bed with a white duvet and white pillows, framed by a pair of bedside tables in the same pale make of pine. There was a single framed photograph on the dresser, and when I stepped closer, I recognized the younger versions of Sophia and Paul, standing in front of the Rockefeller tree. Paul's hair was still curly. Sophia had baby fat in her cheeks.

Sophia smiled now, seeing me look at it. "That was our first Christmas together after getting married."

"Jesus, you looked young. How old were you again?"

"Too young, really," she said. "Come—I want to show you something."

There was a full-length mirror in the master closet, and I had nothing to do but stare at my reflection as I sat on a stool, waiting for Sophia to retrieve something from the bathroom. I looked like a toy long out of commission. My hair was shaggy. There were bags under my eyes, green in a way that was almost translucent. The corners of my mouth drooped. Five months ago, I had strutted through the sunny glass offices of Ingram, Russo & McAllister with a takeout coffee in my hand and a ninety-dollar blazer with padded shoulders on my back. Now I was a ghost who lived in New Jersey on the back of someone else's pity.

Sophia returned with a large storage basket and set it on the floor. She came to stand behind me and ran her fingers through my hair. "If we want this to work," she said, "your hair needs to look completely different."

"I've had long hair before," I said, "up until high school. But I cut it all off my junior year because I thought . . . I thought it made me look like I was trying to be someone I wasn't."

Sophia smiled at me in the mirror. "Well, good thing that's exactly what we're going for."

Her touch was like velvet, pushing my hair back, smoothing out the tangles. "Don't get me wrong: I adore your short hair. And your eyes, too—stunning. But they make you stand out from the crowd. They make you too easy to remember."

Then she said, "I want to try something."

In the basket, Sophia found a flimsy piece of black lace, which I soon recognized as a wig cap. She slid it over my hair and secured it with bobby pins. Then she reached into the basket again and lifted out a long, flowing black wig on a plastic mannequin head. "Whoa," I said.

"I got a few of these from Korea," she said. "They're synthetic, but the quality is impeccable. You can't tell even when you're up close."

I watched my reflection transform as she put the wig on my head. Suddenly, soft, dark curtains of hair were tumbling down my shoulders, cloaking me in warmth. The high cheekbones I'd inherited from my dad's side of the family were swallowed up. Sophia used a tiny comb and scissors to finesse the thick bangs that now fell across my forehead. She stepped back and admired her work in the mirror, satisfied. "Perfect," she said. "You can wear this whenever you go out."

Then she worked on my eyes. Using a brush and a pot of black eyeliner gel, she drew a long, thick, dark line towards my temple. "You see how I'm drawing it further out and at a higher angle? You have beautiful round eyes. But we're going to make them look long. Fox-like, even. We want to create the illusion that you have monolids."

She handed me the brush and gel. "Now I want you to do the same thing for your other eye. Don't worry about getting it perfect; just try to copy what I've done to the best of your ability."

My best effort was a shaky re-creation that veered several degrees too high and smudged in several places. But Sophia was encouraging, even as she wiped the makeup off and reapplied the liner herself. "Good try," she said. "Keep practicing, and you'll get there in no time."

As she dipped her brush into the gel, I said, "God, you're nice."

"Should I not be?"

"It's not that. It's just that if it was my mom, she would have said it was—"

"Garbage?"

I glanced back at her, surprised. "How'd you guess?"

In the mirror, Sophia made a face. "My mother was the same way," she said. "She had the tendency to be very unforgiving with her words."

I nodded, and she said, "It's a good thing we know to do better with our own children, isn't it?"

The last thing to complete Erin Callaghan's look was a pair of glasses. We settled on a pair with purplish-black frames, their round shapes lending an approachable softness to the face. We both knew before I had even put them on that they were the ones. Sophia tugged on my sleeve, and I stood up, turning myself left and right. I was looking at a stranger. "It's perfect," I said.

Sophia nodded. She turned and pulled a neatly folded dust-pink cardigan from a shelf. "I couldn't agree more. Now let's get you dressed for that driver's license photo."

It was one thing to birth Erin Callaghan into legal existence. It was another thing to manufacture her whole backstory from scratch, twenty-four years of love and joy and loss and family out of nothing. Not to mention a credible personality.

One afternoon in 1998, not long after Shelley Hu had started the first grade, she had gotten off the school bus and come home to an empty apartment, as she always did. She let herself in with a key that sat hidden in the inner pocket of her dinosaur backpack. And then she had parked herself in front of the TV and waited. At six o'clock, her dad did not come home. At six thirty, her mom did not come home. On the TV screen, the shows changed from cartoons to sitcom reruns. The sky outside darkened.

At half past seven, the phone rang, and Shelley sprinted to pick it up. "Something's happened to your dad," she heard her mom say in a voice she barely recognized. "Stay at home and don't go outside. Don't answer the door if anyone knocks."

There were leftovers in the fridge, so Shelley heated them up in the microwave, standing on a stool afterwards to wash the dishes. She went through every room in the apartment, turning on all the lights so the bad people outside wouldn't know she was all alone. Something worrying had happened to her dad, and presumably her mom was dealing with it. They would need a treat when they came home. A pick-me-up.

Someone from her class, a girl named Tiffany, had handed out packets of M&M's that day for her birthday. Shelley had wanted to save hers for later. But she now emptied the packet into a small dish and arranged the M&M's into a single layer with her pudgy finger.

She had fallen asleep on the couch when her mom came home. She sank into the cushions by Shelley's feet and began to cry. "Your hardhearted father has left us," she said. "He's left us all alone in this world."

This made Shelley scared and confused. She crawled across the couch on her knees and tried to offer her the dish of M&M's. But her mom batted it away. "I don't want this garbage," she said.

Fortunately, this was not a memory that held any significance for Erin Callaghan.

Erin Callaghan was soft, whereas Shelley Hu was hard. With Shelley, there had been a brashness, an intense way of walking and talking and existing that suggested a lack of self-calibration. People who disliked her thought she was rude. People who liked her saw it as the gracelessness of unpolished youth. Years into the future, Shelley had the potential to grow into a real woman: the gritty, unlikable kind who made it all the way up to second-in-command, enough to almost change the world.

With Erin, there was no dichotomy of opinion. She was likable, period. She had glasses and long hair and a wardrobe of loose, shapeless sweaters and dresses in earthy, flowery tones, some borrowed from Sophia's closet, most thrifted from vintage shops. When she stood, her back was slightly hunched, making her look shorter than the five foot seven she was. When she spoke, her sentences were not punctuated with hard periods, but wasted away into soft, gravelly vocal fry. *I'm almost done speaking*, her voice said. *Just bear with me for two more seconds as I finish this thought.*

Sophia helped me workshop the character over the course of a month. We went to improv classes, Toastmasters meetings, nail salons, never visiting a location more than once so that no one could clock me as a familiar face. I watched interviews with white Hollywood actresses, studying the way these women talked, taking extensive notes on their cadence, their diction, the way they navigated hard consonants. I learned to let Erin inhabit me. There were tricks I used to get into character: twisting her hair around my finger, tilting my head slightly when I listened to someone speak, and the big one: smiling as I entered a room. I opened every interaction now with a smile, as if I'd never had a bad day in my life. "Hey, how are you?" I would say, as if I cared about the answer. Even in New York, where all anyone wanted was for you to get to the point, I found that the warmth I wielded in my voice was a form of power. It allowed me to take up space in a different way.

The final test was a zero-waste workshop in Brooklyn. In the conference room of a local library, we learned about turning old plastic water bottles into pots for planting herbs. The instructor handed out long, colorful strips of plastic for us to weave into baskets, and as I sat around a small table with three white women my age, I found that for the first time, I could dive into the conversation without the sinking suspicion that I was being left out. *Yes, I love barre classes! Are you a dog mom, too? I just applied for membership at that co-op grocery store in Park Slope. There are some wonderfully authentic ethnic restaurants in this neighborhood; it's a shame none of them are vegan-friendly.*

Being Erin Callaghan was physically exhausting, at least in the beginning. At home, I found myself falling quiet at dinner, unable to keep up with the giggly back-and-forths that Sophia and Ory batted around the table. Sophia assured me it was natural. "Being someone else requires a different muscle. You'll learn to conserve your energy with time. Soon, it will feel no different than putting on a sweater."

The final part of the preparation stage was my education. "We're going to make you a fabulous graphic designer," Sophia said.

A week after I'd moved in, she and I had taken the D Train to visit a pop-up art gallery in the Bronx. As soon as I saw the colored dots on the entrance to the subway, the stairs leading underground, my throat closed up. My fingertips started tingling. Sophia looked at me and held out her hand.

"Hold on to me," she said quietly, and I gripped it with an embarrassing amount of strength. I could feel her rings cutting into my palm, and somehow that began to ground me. I took deep, calming breaths.

We were still holding hands as we waited on the platform. Sophia reached up with her free hand and fixed my bangs, which had gotten caught up in my glasses. "Remember," she said, "the things Shelley experienced have nothing to do with Erin. You need to disengage yourself emotionally. If you collapse, so does our plan."

On the train, we sat facing an empty row of seats, our shadowy reflections staring back at us from the darkened glass. Sophia pointed at a framed poster by the door. "Can you tell me what this is?"

"An ad?"

"It's an ad, yes. But tell me more. You're almost halfway through the Principles of Design course; it's time to apply theory to real life. What's the first thing about the ad that catches your eye? What do you like? What do you not like? Does it succeed in delivering its message within the first three seconds?"

I looked back at the ad, and this time, I really studied it.

"The first thing that jumps out at me is the photo," I said. "I like that it's large and clear, and you can see the people wearing scrubs, so I can tell that it's medicine related. And then the tagline under it is well done, too. *Creating winning smiles for you and your family since 1987.* It's big and bold. But what I don't like is that the logo and website for the dental clinic are really small and in this lilac color. I'd have to get up close to figure out the name of the clinic. And if I'm in a rush on my morning commute, I don't think I'd have the time or inclination to do that."

Sophia nodded at me. "Well done. You're starting to think like a graphic designer."

She said, "When you become a designer, you begin to notice all the beauty in the things around you, but the imperfections can drive you mad, too. You look at a logo and notice the kerning is off between two letters. You see yellow text on a green background in a government brochure and wonder how no one had thought to run it through an accessibility checker for visually impaired people. Anyone can *do* design, and in fact, that's how most of us got our starts. I came up in a time when there were virtually no step-by-step tutorials. I had to figure it all out on my own."

"Not me, though," I said. "I have you to guide me."

She gave me a little smile, and I said, "Honestly, sometimes I still can't figure out why you're going through all this trouble to help me."

As the floor of the train thudded beneath us, Sophia was quiet for a beat. She said, "Do you know why I didn't change my name from Soyoung to Sophia until I was an adult?"

I shook my head.

"I was eleven when I moved to Brookline, Massachusetts. I remember walking into the first day of fifth grade at Bishop Road Elementary School with my new backpack, my new dress, a new name I'd spent ages picking out—Sophia, Greek for 'wisdom.' When I met my homeroom teacher, Mrs. Bayer, I was so happy to introduce myself for the first time as Sophia Kim. And do you know what that white woman told me?"

She looked at me. "She told me I wasn't allowed to have an English name."

That made me tilt back in my seat, widen my eyes at her. "Hold up," I said. "She said *what*?"

"Oh, but you misinterpret her. She thought my real name was so *lovely*. Such a *beautiful* embodiment of my traditional Korean culture. And what a shame it was to let it go in favor of some bland American name like Sophia. Mrs. Bayer was a steward of culture, don't you see? She was the only person standing between me and the tragic loss of my heritage. And it wasn't just me—all the kids in my class were forced to revert to using their ethnic names. Joey became Zhaoyang. Sam became Oussama. And Soyoung never even had the chance to become Sophia."

Sophia was no longer smiling. She looked down at her hands, and her lashes cast long, quivering shadows.

"And after that, even after I graduated from her class and moved on to middle school, high school, I never changed my name. The moment I arrived in her country, this white woman had denied me permission to use an English name, and for years afterwards, I still felt bound by her refusal. Like I wasn't good enough, wasn't *American* enough, to be Sophia or Linda or Sally. So I hung on to this name, Soyoung, this careless, meaningless name that they hurl at every other unloved girl in Korea, because I thought it was what I deserved. It wasn't until I had lost everything that I was finally freed from it.

"And you know what's funny? If you had asked Mrs. Bayer, she would have told you that she was a Democrat. She would have told you that she celebrates diversity. That she didn't have a racist bone in her body."

I exhaled slowly. In our reflections in the window, I saw a new coldness in Sophia's face, a brittle disdain. We were both quiet again until she said, "Do you ever think about why Amy Cloverfield adopted her daughter from China?"

For the past few weeks, we'd scoured every search engine and cached website, piecing together the life of the woman who had taken everything from me that day on the subway. Sometime in 2009, Amy Cloverfield-Schwartz had divorced her husband, Dan Schwartz; he now worked as a writer at large for a newspaper in Philadelphia. As part of the divorce settlement, Amy had dropped her hyphenated last name and held on to their daughter. Lizzie was a dancer, according to her private Instagram account. Modern jazz and tap, mostly. Last fall, she had applied to study media and communications at NYU and had gotten in, Early Decision.

Deep within the labyrinth that was the Loving Families International website, there was a full-page interview with Amy and Dan about how they had been sent Lizzie's photo from a catalog of hopeful orphans—back then, her name had been Dang Xueyang—and how they had traveled to a hotel near the government-run orphanage in Guiyang, where they'd signed the adoption papers within minutes of meeting her. *We weren't put off at all by the fact that she had a cleft lip*, Amy had said in the interview. *We had done the research and knew that it was a condition that could be addressed fairly easily.* The text was accompanied by a small photo of ten-month-old Lizzie in the arms of Amy and Dan at the hotel, both adults happy and flustered; Lizzie simply looked dazed. Her hair had been shorn, leaving her head looking like a potato with black fuzz.

Sophia shook her head.

"Adoption isn't a charity, Erin," she said. "It's a business. For a couple thousand dollars, people like Amy Cloverfield get to waltz into our country and collect our babies like puppies at the pound. Lizzie's adoption wasn't a coming together; it was a trauma. It was a severing. These people think they have the right to take our baby girls and whisk them away to a foreign country where they have no ties, no blood, no language—no way to say *No, I don't want to be yours*."

Her voice slipped into a whisper, but over the clanging of the train, I heard her in my ear, clear as day.

"Think about that poor baby girl. Lizzie. She already had a name, Xueyang, a beautiful name that means 'the snow and the sun.' It was all she had left, and Amy Cloverfield took it away from her and rebranded her like cattle. Do you know why she did that? For her, Lizzie isn't her daughter. She's a prop. She's the living, breathing embodiment of her benevolence: *I saved her from a mud pit in communist China. I fixed her hideous cleft lip and made her whole. Hell, I even let her call me Mom.*"

When we looked at each other, Sophia smiled slowly, with conviction.

She said, "I don't think Amy Cloverfield deserves to have a Chinese daughter. Wouldn't you agree?"

I was speechless.

The things she was saying—they didn't make sense. Didn't they? I thought of the handful of Asian adoptees I'd met over the years, tan-skinned, black-haired girls named Kayleigh Smith and Olivia Ratzenberger and Madison Wade. The other Asians, the people like my mom, sometimes whispered about them behind their backs. *That one lives with a white family. Look how dark she is, how much they let her run around in the sun with a soccer ball.* But on the whole, hadn't they been happy? Hadn't they been confident, trauma-free, breezing through the world with their boisterous laughs and white names? It had only been days since I'd taken on the identity of Erin Callaghan, but already I was experiencing the world in a new way. Customer service representatives no longer asked me to repeat my name on the phone. There was no more butchering of my last name, no moment of hesitation before flattening it like a pancake and drawing it out, *Heeew*. Whenever I walked into a place of business and gave my name, Erin Callaghan, to the receptionist, I could detect the flicker of confusion, then the recognition, the gradual acceptance. American name, American accent, American compatriot. Not a foreigner.

"They're all like that," Sophia said. "White women—they're masters of illusion. They pretend to be evolved, to be *better*. They've spent hundreds of years subjugated by white men, waiting for their turn. And the moment they gain an ounce of power—not over men, mind you, just over you—they'll use it. Look at Amy Cloverfield, the way she tried to present herself before her mask slipped. Hiding behind her Chinese daughter. Rattling off volunteer positions and diversity committees on her LinkedIn profile. But don't you remember the way she looked at you on that train? Even in the grainy video, it was so clear, her stark entitlement, her righteous indignation. How dare you exist in her country? How dare you go to an American university and take an American job? And where did you scrounge up the absolute *audacity* to take up an extra seat?

"It's true; she won that day on the subway. She took your dignity. She took your ambition. In a way, she even took your name. She walked away that day thinking she'd taken everything from you. But guess what, Erin?"

There was a tightness in my chest; my nose stung, and my vision was a white fog. Sophia squeezed my hand.

"You have me now," she said. "And the things I'm going to do for you, the things we're going to do together—trust me, darling. The tide is about to turn."

SOYOUNG

September 2004

The third time the boy with curly hair came by the store at half past eleven, Soyoung made up her mind that she was going to speak to him.

What had he bought that first time? A muffin, possibly, or some other saran-wrapped baked good that was long past its freshness. The second time, it had been a red packet of Shin Ramyun. College guys his age ate ravenously and revoltingly at all hours, she knew that, but there were other things she could tell just by looking at him. First, that he was Korean but not Korean Korean: He was dressed too sloppily to be anything but American. Second: That he was tall but not proud of it. And third: Like her, he was someone who was deeply and permanently unhappy. The difference was that the boy made the mistake of wearing his sadness on his face. Soyoung knew better by now.

He came shuffling up to the register now in his basketball shorts and black-and-white slides, and when he put the item on the counter, she saw that it was egg salad in a plastic carton. Possibly the most disgusting food item they sold at the store. That was another thing she knew from experience.

As Soyoung scanned the egg salad, she said, "What year are you?"

The boy looked at her, confused, and she nodded towards the gray CORNELL sweatshirt he was wearing. "I'm a freshman."

"Oh," the boy said, "me too. I'm a first-year."

Then he really looked at her. He took a moment to study her face, and then his eyes did a quick lap around the convenience store around them: the flickering fluorescent lights, the buzzing fridges in the back, the black specks of gum that had congealed on the grubby tiles. "You... Wait, do you work here?"

Soyoung smiled. She patted the blue apron she was wearing. "Yeah, I work here."

It seemed to occur to the boy only then that there'd been something rude about his question. She saw the tips of his ears go red. "Sorry, I meant... I didn't realize you could get a job off campus."

"Were you at orientation last month?"

"Yeah. Of course."

Soyoung cocked her head as she looked at him, narrowing her eyes, like she was trying to place him. "You look really familiar, actually. I feel like we must've spoken at some point. What was your name again?"

"I'm Paul."

"Are you Korean?"

"Yeah. Are you?"

"Yeah. My name is Soyoung."

She said, "I'm thinking about starting to go by an American name, though. What do you think? Should I keep Soyoung or pick something else, like Amanda?"

Paul seemed to consider this question carefully. After a moment, he said, "You don't look like an Amanda."

"What do I look like?"

The tips of Paul's ears were glowing red again. He held her gaze for only a second or two before he looked away. In a quiet voice, he said, "I think you look like a Soyoung."

When Soyoung laughed, her eyes were like merry little moon crescents. The next customer joined the line, someone with toilet paper and a pack of dental floss, and she caught herself. "Oh, shoot. Um—that'll be a dollar twenty-eight. Will you be paying with cash?"

As she deposited the change in Paul's hand, Soyoung said, "You need a fork with that salad?"

There was a basket of plastic-wrapped forks by the cash register. Paul said, "Do I have to pay for one?"

Soyoung smiled. She picked up one of the forks and handed it to him. "Let's just say that you did."

Then she said, "Maybe I'll see you around campus, Paul."

"Yeah. Maybe."

"Or maybe I'll just see you back here." Soyoung laughed again; in the next moment, she had whipped her head around, detached and professional once again. "Hi, good evening. Did you find everything okay?"

In her peripheral vision, she could see Paul linger at the register, still looking at her. He did this, Soyoung knew, not because she was extraordinarily pretty or particularly charismatic; it was the same way she knew as a child, when she went out into her grandmother's yard and the chickens crowded around her, squawking and bobbing their heads, that they were after nothing more than the bowl of millet in her hands. In that small convenience store of sour smells and shoddy lighting, she had unlocked the door between them—whether out of boredom, out of pity, out of her own loneliness—and he now stood before it, on the verge of pushing it ajar.

The next time Paul came in, which was two nights later, Soyoung noticed that he had cleaned up a little. Instead of slides, he was now wearing blue sneakers, and his hair showed some signs of effort with a comb. When he came up to the register with a buffalo chicken wrap, she said, "Hey, Paul."

"Hi."

There was no one else in line. She said, "You've forgotten my name, haven't you?"

Paul blinked at her, surprised. Then he said, "No, I remember."

"What's my name, then?"

"Soyoung," he said. "Your name is Soyoung."

She pursed her lips, impressed. "All right, then."

As Soyoung scanned the wrap, Paul seemed to be fumbling for something to say. Finally he said, "So what classes are you taking?"

"Oh, you know. Pretty generic ones. Sociology 101, microeconomics, European history. Stuff like that."

"I'm taking micro too," Paul said. "I don't think I've seen you in my lecture."

"Which section are you in?"

"Kerchner, Tuesdays and Thursdays at two thirty."

"I'm with Boswell. Wednesdays and Fridays at eight thirty."

She saw Paul's eyes widen. "That's really early. Don't you have to, you know, work all night?"

Soyoung laughed. "What? Read the sign on the door, dude. This place closes at midnight."

As Paul paid, he said, "So do you know what you want to major in?"

"Hmm," she said. "I haven't really thought about it, if I'm honest. What about you?"

"I think probably econ and management."

"You must be pretty good at math, yeah?"

Paul's ears went red. "I'm not bad."

When Soyoung gave Paul his change, she brushed against his hand for just an extra half second longer, short enough to be nothing more than a friendly accident. "Be careful with that wrap, by the way," she said. "The mayo is really heavy. You might want to scrape some off before you heat it up."

Paul nodded. "Thanks."

He was halfway to the door when she heard him hesitate; it took him another second or two to decide to double back. "Um," he said, and Soyoung looked up from her sociology textbook. "Maybe we could go for lunch on campus sometime."

For a moment, Soyoung looked surprised; then she smiled. "Oh, sure. Maybe."

The thread hung between them, unresolved. "Cool," Paul said. "I'll see you around, then."

"See you," Soyoung said, and they'd left it at that.

The reality was that you could get away with only so many excuses, paying with cash in Cornell's dining rooms while everyone else tapped their student IDs. *I'm a prospective student from out of town. I'm visiting my sister. I lost my ID and I'm waiting for a new one.* After a few rotations, the women who worked the cash registers had gotten suspicious. They had started to recognize her. *You still don't have your ID?* That was when she started avoiding the dining rooms, buying most of her food from the convenience store instead. Most of it was bordering on stale, and she often went to bed with a nagging hint of hunger. But it was nice to have the employee discount.

The next time Paul came into the store, neither of them brought up the hypothetical lunch date. There was a line behind him, so they exchanged two lines of pleasantries before the next customer heaved four two-liter bottles of soda onto the counter, and Paul headed out.

The time after that, it was half past eleven, and there was no line. There was only the drunk guy who'd been in the store for a few minutes already, stumbling back and forth between the register and the aisles like a bird building its nest. "I want this," the guy said, and he slammed a box down on the counter. "I want some popcorn."

"That's fine, sir. Have you found everything you're looking for?"

"You know what I want to find?" the guy said. He leaned on the counter with his elbows. "I'd like to find your phone number."

Soyoung's eyes flitted to Paul, who was standing by the chips aisle, watching them. She said, "I'll go ahead and ring you up."

As she scanned the items, the guy said, "What's your name, sweetheart?"

She said nothing. The guy said, "What's your name? I want to get to know you. Let me take you out on a date. I'll treat you like a princess."

"That'll be eighteen dollars and ninety-five cents, please."

The guy's arm snaked across the counter, and Soyoung took a step back. He said, "Why are you ignoring me, huh? I'm just trying to get to know you. You think you're too good to talk to me? Huh?"

That was when it happened. Paul took a deep breath and came up to them. Soyoung saw him ball his hands into fists before sliding them into his pockets.

To the guy, he said, "Hey, man, you need to go."

The guy straightened up to look at him. "Who are you?"

"She doesn't want to talk to you. You need to go."

For a moment, as Paul and the guy stared at each other, no one moved. Then the guy shrugged. He fished a twenty-dollar bill out of his pocket and threw it on the counter. "Fine. Whatever. Just trying to make conversation, is all."

Soyoung kept her eyes down as she counted out the change. The guy left with his purchases in a yellow plastic bag, and when he got to the door, he looked back at her and said, loudly, "You have a good night, now."

She didn't answer. The door slammed behind him, and the store was returned to silence.

Soyoung took another step back and, slowly, let out the breath she had been holding. She adjusted her apron, and she heard Paul ask, "Are you okay?"

They looked at each other, and after a beat, she smiled. "Yeah. I'm fine. It happens sometimes."

"Does it happen a lot?"

"No, it's fine, really. It's just . . . it's the nature of the night shift. You get some interesting people in here sometimes."

Paul nodded, and there was something in his face that she couldn't read. When he paid for a muffin and a container of apple slices, all he said was "Have a good night." He left the store without looking back, which surprised her, and she couldn't help trailing him with her gaze as he disappeared through the door.

A few minutes to midnight, as they always did, Soyoung and her boss, Dolan, who mostly watched TV in the back office, checked the inventory and mopped the floor and activated the security system and shut off the lights. After they locked the door, Dolan went to his car, and Soyoung was halfway to the bike rack when she saw a dark figure sitting on the curb outside. She jumped back and screamed; then the figure rose up into the light, and she realized that it was Paul.

Under the streetlight, he looked sheepish, like a kid who'd been caught out of bed. She said, "What are you still doing here?"

Paul shuffled his feet. He said, "I wanted to make sure he didn't come back."

"Oh."

Soyoung was quiet before she said, "You didn't have to do that."

"No, I know."

Paul cleared his throat.

"Is it okay if I walk you back to your dorm?"

The convenience store sat at the corner of a quiet street, flanked by small brick houses and beige apartment blocks. As they headed towards the nearest gate to campus, the streets were shrouded in silence; the only sound in the world was that of their footsteps.

Soyoung said, eventually, "So where are you from?"

"Baltimore. Maryland."

She waited for him to reflect the question back at her, but Paul was quiet. So instead she said, "I'm from Boston, but I've lived in Seoul, too."

"My family's from Busan," Paul said, "but we don't go back to Korea much. I've only been twice."

Soyoung hugged her arms to her chest. "Oh, I adore Busan. We used to go there in the summers when I was a little kid. We'd rent an apartment by the sea, and my mom would read magazines on the beach while my dad and I would swim in the ocean. The seafood in Busan! I ate my weight in eomuk when I was there."

"It's not bad," Paul said.

"So how are you liking your first semester? Do you like Cornell?"

"Yeah," Paul said. "It's fine. It's a nice place."

But his tone was flat, dispirited. Soyoung said, "Do you miss your family?"

She could tell the question affected Paul in some way; he tensed up a little. But then he said, "No, not really."

"Do you have a lot of friends here?"

"I have some."

"It's hard, isn't it? Some people are nice, but a lot of people can be really rude and standoffish. It's not easy finding someone who's genuine to talk to."

"There's a lot of rich people here," Paul said.

"I know what you mean. My roommate—she's this white girl from Washington, and her family goes to France every year to ski. We were talking about it once, and she asked me offhandedly, *Do you ski?* And I thought, *What kind of question is that?* So I asked her, point-blank, *Isn't skiing really expensive? How much does it cost you, the plane tickets, the accommodation, the equipment, everything?* And she was embarrassed. No, actually, it was worse than that: She was irritated that I had asked. Like I had offended her by crossing some invisible line that I hadn't known was there in the first place."

Paul shook his head. "I can't imagine," he said. "My family doesn't really do vacations."

"Do you have a big family?"

"Just me, my mom, and my stepdad. My dad died when I was seven."

"Oh—I'm sorry."

Paul gave a small, single nod, and after a moment, Soyoung said, "I was eight when my brother died."

"What happened?"

"Leukemia. He went very quickly, which was probably for the best. He didn't have to suffer too much."

Paul was quiet. He said, "It changes you."

"It does, doesn't it? You're never quite the same afterwards."

They were coming up on the residence halls now. Paul said, "Which dorm are you in?"

"Huntzinger."

"Oh, the one that's all women?"

"Yeah."

From where they were, Soyoung could see the outline of the residence hall looming in the distance, a beautiful redbrick building surrounded by lush maple trees. They were almost at the trees when she saw the dorm entrance. No one was outside. Next to the locked door, the light on a card reader shone bright red.

Abruptly, she stopped walking, and Paul looked back at her. "You okay?"

"Yeah. Yeah, of course. I just remembered—I can't go back just yet. I have to go check on a friend who's going through a breakup. It's the one next door, so I can take it from here."

Then she added, "But we should hang out. You and I, we should definitely hang out some time."

"Can I walk with you next time?" Paul asked. "In case that guy comes back."

And as Soyoung looked at Paul under the golden glow of the streetlight, it seemed, as if for the first time, that she was truly seeing him: his thick, dark eyelashes, downcast and uncertain as he looked at her. His halo of wild, overgrown curly hair. His sweatshirt was unzipped, and beneath his old track-and-field T-shirt she registered the broadness of his chest, the way it rose and fell with every shallow breath. Paul was nervous, she realized, and she, Soyoung, was the reason. Why had she ever thought of him as dispensable? As Paul gazed at her under the streetlight, it was so evident that he was utterly consumed by the thought of kissing her. Soyoung smiled and tilted her face up by a half inch. Her lips were full, waiting.

Paul's hands went into his pockets again. He said, "Well, have a good night."

There was a pause. Soyoung was still smiling.

"You too, Paul. Have a good night."

She had started to walk away when Paul said her name. "Soyoung. Wait."

Soyoung turned; he was holding out the muffin he had bought from her earlier. "Is that for me?"

Paul just nodded. After a moment, Soyoung reached out and took it. "Thanks."

"See you around," Paul said, and she could tell that he'd meant it.

That night in her motel room, Soyoung sat on the bed and turned the TV to a news channel. As she half listened to the panelists make predictions about the upcoming election, she unwrapped the muffin over her lap and examined it. It was dressed in a brown liner, and the top layer was dried out, already beginning to crumble. There were blueberries.

She held the muffin in her palm for a long time. Then she pushed the whole thing into her mouth and ate it in a few furious bites.

It was nearly two weeks after moving in with Lillian that the thing Soyoung had been harboring—the tiny, enthralling secret that had been blossoming within her since that night under the streetlight—finally grew out of her. Lying on the floor one night, she said, feigning casualness, "I've sort of been hanging out with someone."

There was a sharp intake of air from Lillian. "What? Who?"

"A guy. His name is—" And finally, there it was, her unguarded heart in the open. "His name is Paul."

"Do you have a photo?"

In her backpack, Soyoung found her point-and-shoot camera and turned it on to show Lillian. "He asked me to cut his hair last night because it was getting too long. I didn't do that great of a job because all we had were regular scissors, but I think it turned out okay in the end. He's . . . he's sort of cute, right?"

As Lillian thumbed through the photos, something about her seemed to shift; the excitement from before had evaporated, replaced by a bored indifference. "Hmm," she said, and Soyoung said, a slight edge to her voice, "What?"

"No, yeah. He's fine, I guess."

Lillian handed the camera back to Soyoung, who was sitting up in her new sleeping bag. With a yawn, she said, "I mean, not to lean into stereotypes, but I feel like with Asian guys, it can be hard to tell, right?"

"What's hard to tell?"

"Oh, you know. Just their attractiveness level. And I'm not saying they all look the same, of course I'm not saying *that*, but . . ." Lillian hesitated. "You do have to acknowledge that at a certain point, they do kind of blend into one another. Like, most of them are really skinny, they don't like to work out—"

"Paul is six foot one," Soyoung said, "and he used to run track and field in high school."

"No, and that's great. Good for him. I'm just saying that Asian men as a whole could . . . they could use a bit more work in the masculinity department, you know what I mean? They're just too meek. Like, can you imagine an Asian guy throwing you over his shoulder like some dude from a romance novel and being like, *I'm going to ravage you*? I wouldn't be able to keep a straight face. It'd be like dating your little cousin or something."

Slowly, Soyoung settled back into her sleeping bag. She lay there with her eyes open, her fingers curling into a fist, and it was then that Lillian broke into yet another one of her increasingly frequent coughing fits. "Jesus," she heard Lillian say faintly, "what is *wrong* with this room? It smells like a fucking swamp in here. Please tell me you smell it, too, Soyoung."

"It does smell a little wet," Soyoung said.

"It smells," Lillian said, "like a small animal crawled into a corner and died."

"Have you checked the closet?"

Lillian bristled. "Do you think I'm an idiot? Of course I've checked the closet. I've checked everywhere in the room. And I can't figure out where the *hell* this awful, putrid smell is coming from. I swear to God, Soyoung, my dad is friends with one of the school trustees. If the housing people don't figure out what's causing this by the end of the week, he's going to start making calls. Heads are going to roll, I promise you."

As she switched off the light, Lillian began to cough again. In the sleeping bag, Soyoung's face was impassive; then, gradually, she began to smile.

She said, "Oh, I'm sure they will."

ERIN

January 2017

On the website my old boss Gene Struzik frequented for gorgeous Asian females who were eager to chat with masculine yet respectful Western men, Sophia and I created a few different profiles, using photos lifted from the social media accounts of obscure Asian actresses. I count it as the great kindness of my life that Gene himself had not been the one to tell me about this website. I'd stumbled upon it by accident one day, searching for something on his computer at his request, when I made a typo and the browser autofilled with the URL. My face had burned behind the monitor.

We started off with some good old A/B testing, as Sophia called it. Jasmine was a mature piano teacher in Vietnam. Priscilla was a nurse originally from the Philippines, now working in Atlantic City. Gene liked Jasmine's vibe but didn't like that she was so far away. Priscilla he'd found too immature. Then we came up with Vivian, a Chinese grad student new to New York City and eager to practice her English with "real Americans," or white people. Gene liked Vivian the best. He'd resurface throughout the day to talk to her, often blowing through a whole lunch hour with his frenetic streams of consciousness, most of them being his sexual fantasies. The last few times they'd chatted, he had suggested they meet in person for a drink. Vivian had been coy. *I'm very shy*, she'd said, to which Gene had replied, *So am I, darling.*

Naturally, he sent dick pics to all three of them.

The next step, once we had collected enough evidence, was to mail a multipage printout to Gene's wife, Holly Wong-Struzik. We sent them to her work in a stamped envelope with no return address. I'd felt a clenching in my stomach, stuffing the envelope while wearing surgical gloves, writing down her address in a fake, bubbly script. I imagined the incriminating photos falling onto her lap in the offices of the wildlife conservation society where she worked as the director of fundraising. I imagined her face.

Standing in front of the mailbox at Third and Broadway, holding the envelope in my mittened hands, that was when it struck me, the finality of it: There was no going back after this. The moment the letter passed through the mail slot, I would have no choice but to continue moving forward, propelled by the fallout from my actions.

Sophia sensed my hesitation. She put a hand on my arm, gentle. "It's hard," she said. "I know."

"She was always nice to me."

"Which makes it an even tougher decision for you," she said. "I'm sorry, Erin. I understand how you must be feeling."

We were both quiet for a moment.

I turned to Sophia, finally. I said, "He can't keep getting away with it, though."

"You're right. He can't."

"Look at all the disgusting shit he said in the chats. Look at what he did to me, to other interns. He can't—he can't keep pulling the wool over her eyes. Somebody has to tell her."

"Think about the power you're holding in your hands right now," she said. "You can give her the knowledge that will set her free."

I thought about it. I nodded.

Sophia was right.

As I pushed the letter through the mail slot, the din of the city seemed to quiet around us. The tourists wearing backpacks on their chests, the deli owner flattening cardboard boxes on the street, the NYU students debating lunch options, the Uber Eats guy chattering in Bengali on his phone—as they brushed past me and Sophia at the intersection without a second glance, I was almost startled by the fact that none of them had any idea of the significance of what I had just put into motion. They scrolled on their phones on the subway. They ate takeout in front of a laptop. They waited for one meaningless day to roll into another. But Sophia and I, we were standing at the precipice, at the beginning of something great.

"Come with me," Sophia said, holding out her hand, and I took it. Even through her rose-colored mittens, I could feel the warmth of her touch. "There's something I want to show you," she said.

She took me to the art institute she'd once attended, just a few blocks from Washington Square Park. Walking into the glass atrium of the building, I could feel her physically unwind, softening as she took in the minimalist black benches, the sunlight pouring onto the jagged, abstract sculpture in the center. "Being back here always gives me a boost of energy," she said. "It reminds me of what it means to be in New York. That everything I did was worth it, in the end."

As we began climbing the staircase to the second floor, I said, "Do you miss it? Living in the city?"

Sophia looked back at me. "Do you?"

I hesitated, and she laughed once, quietly. "I'm guessing you never thought you'd wind up in some white picket fence cul-de-sac in Jersey."

"It's not so bad," I said, and even I wasn't convinced by my tone. "It's just a bit . . ."

She finished the thought for me. "It's the kind of place where you go to die."

"I'm pretty sure that's Florida," I said, and we both laughed.

On the third floor, at the end of the last corridor, we found what Sophia had been planning to show me. It was a showcase of award-winning student pieces from the last few years: There was a photograph of a frozen tundra in Iceland; a stylized painting of a wizened, toothless grandfather; lines from a newspaper cut into pieces and woven into dyed fabric. "This one won first place in an art competition in 2006," Sophia said, pointing at the painting.

Then she reached for a piece in the bottom corner. "And this was me. I placed first that year, too."

"You guys tied?"

Sophia smiled. "No," she said. "I won in a different group. First place for minority artists."

I bent to examine the painting. At first glance, it was a small, square canvas, every inch drenched in unforgiving black ink. But when I looked closer, I saw that the blackness had variations to it. Most of the ink had a lighter tint, a deep charcoal color. But the corner at the top left was darker. It was pitch-black, a tangled mass that almost seemed to heave and swell with fluid movement. It watched me with eyes that were hidden. It was—

"Fuck!" I said, and I took a step back, then another. Sophia held out a hand to steady me, but I wasn't looking at her. I couldn't pull my eyes away from the painting.

"What do you see?" I heard her ask.

My heart was beating wildly. It took me a moment to answer.

"It's—it's the thing that used to live in my mom's house. It's . . ."

I swallowed several times before I said, "A jinn."

Sophia nodded. She was holding on to my arm, and I suddenly remembered something she'd said to me back in Florida, the night before we departed for New York. "Sophia, you can see it, can't you?"

Calmly, she said, "Yes, I can."

"Do you know what it is?"

Sophia turned then to look at me. She said, "What do you think it is?"

"I—I don't know. I mean, yeah, objectively I know what it is. It's a hallucination. It's something our mind makes up when we experience sleep paralysis. But when I used to say that to my grandmother, she'd be like, *Then why is there no cure for it? Why are there stories of so many people seeing it across cultures, across thousands and thousands of years?* And I never really had an answer for that. I used to watch her try to fight it when I was a kid. I'd see the terror in her eyes, this primal fear of being trapped in place for God knows how long. And when I had to move back to Florida, I felt it, too. I . . . I . . ."

My face must have been pale, because I felt Sophia soften. "Oh, darling," she said. "Let's get you something to drink."

I slumped on one of the benches in the corridor while she went to a vending machine and got two sodas. The moment the fizzing liquid went through me, I felt better. Next to me, Sophia was quiet, gazing out at the atrium below us.

She said, "I've always seen her, too. Since I was a child."

"Her?"

Sophia smiled at me. "Yes. Her."

She said, "Has your mom ever told you about water ghosts?"

I hesitated. The term was familiar. In my memories, I saw myself bobbing in a lake, or perhaps it was a pond, and my mom standing on the dock, her face twisted in concern as she shouted something at me. In the water, my feet came into contact with something cold and slimy, and I shrieked; my mom reached for me, frantic, and the next moment I was lying at her feet, wet and slippery and giggling and safely back on land.

I said, "Don't they live at the bottom of lakes and rivers? And they're usually—they're women who have drowned. So they become these ghosts that haunt the water, and they try to pull other people under and kill them, because that's how they can get reincarnated. They have to find someone else to take their place."

Next to me, I heard Sophia exhale.

"Look at that," she said. "Even in stories where women are the victims, we're still made out to be the villains. Because even in death, we're vindictive, self-serving creatures, aren't we?"

She looked at me. "Do you know how women came to be associated with water ghosts? Or drowning, for that matter? In ancient times—and not-so-ancient ones, too—when a woman was thought to be impure, she was locked into a cage by her village's elders and lowered into the river to be drowned. Thousands of years. Countless women whose short, suffocating lives ended violently at the hands of men who hated them.

"And in those times, if you were a woman standing on the brink of desperation, too often drowning was the only form of escape. If you were raped; if you were forced into marriage; if soldiers were marching on your homeland and you were about to become the spoils of war. Women drowned themselves when they no longer had anything to live for, when suicide was their last form of resistance. We were all formed in water, Shelley, in the wombs of our mothers; to return to water is to go home."

Goose bumps pricked my arms at the sound of my old name. I shivered and put down my can of soda; it had become a block of ice.

"The first time I saw her," Sophia said, "I was eight years old, and my brother had just been presumed dead. I've never told you about my brother, have I? He was a few years younger. We were on a family vacation that summer, on the coast of Busan. It was so beautiful, I remember. The soft white sands. The blue ocean. The sun. My mother stayed on the beach, reading under a big orange umbrella. My stepfather took my brother and me into the ocean. He was careful. He made us wear life preservers. I remember floating there in the warm water, watching my stepfather with my brother a few feet away, teaching him to swim. He was getting the hang of it. He was kicking in the water, laughing, propelling himself along. It was midday. The sun had become white-hot, blinding, and my stepfather closed his eyes, only for half of a millisecond.

"And when he opened his eyes, my brother was gone."

"Shit—what happened?"

She shook her head. "The search and rescue people couldn't find his body. They called off the search after three days."

Weakly, I said, "I'm really sorry."

"It's been a long time."

She said, "The night after the search was called off, my stepfather drank himself into a stupor, but my mother was strangely silent. She refused to eat or drink. When I tried to speak to her, she couldn't hear me.

"That night, after the clock struck midnight, she got up from the couch and left the apartment we were staying in. I followed her. We walked to the beach, the same beach where my brother had vanished, and she took off her shoes and began to walk into the ocean. I screamed. I grabbed on to her dress and tried to keep her from going further. I fought with her until others came running up to us, and they dragged my mother out of the water and set her down on the sand.

"I'll never forget the way she looked that night. Pale, lifeless, her long black hair dripping onto her dress, like the drowned ghosts from my grandmother's stories. As they tried to hold her down, my mother screamed and screamed. *Let me die*, she said. *I'm his mother. Let me die in that ocean with him.* And then she saw me, as if for the first time. Her face changed when she looked at me. And she said, *Why are you still here? Why wasn't it you? It should have been you. It should have been you.*"

A single teardrop fell onto her hand, and I reached out and took it in mine. "I'm sorry," I heard her say.

"What for?"

Sophia shook her head then and smiled; there was something haunting about it, something that unsettled me with both its strangeness and familiarity. "I don't know," she said, "but ever since then, for as long as I've lived, there have been times . . . times when I thought perhaps she was right."

"Sophia, listen to me," I said, and she looked at me, fragile, uncertain. "Your mother was wrong. She was wrong about you. You don't need to apologize for being alive, all right? You don't need to apologize for being you. You deserve to be here, just as you are."

Sophia closed her eyes. She said nothing, and for a long time, we just sat there, bathing in the softness of the winter sun.

"The truth is," she said, "my brother's death was the best thing that could have happened to me."

I almost shivered. Not from shock, but from excitement. I had no idea that hearing someone else's ugly truth could be so exhilarating.

"You have to understand what it had been like for me up until that point. I'd spent the first eight years of my life cooped up in my grandparents' little house in that Chinese village; every day, feeding my halmeoni's chickens in her yard, I'd look out at the dirt road by our house, the one lined with poplar trees as far as the eye could see, and wonder if that was the day my umma would come back for me.

"And one day, as if by magic, she finally did."

She smiled, and I saw the little girl in her face, the childlike wonder.

"She looked so beautiful. So South Korean. She wore a brilliant fuchsia dress, I remember, and foundation and eye shadow and blush caked on her face. Even the Korean she spoke was different. She'd brought me presents—chocolates, dolls, a beautiful lavender dress. But they were nothing compared to what she said to me. *When you come back to Seoul with me*, she said, *you'll see that you have a new abeoji. You have a brother, too—a little boy called Seojoon. You must do everything they say. Do you understand me? You must always smile and nod and listen and always show them that you are so, so happy to be there. If you don't, your abeoji won't like you anymore, and I'll have to send you back to China to live with your halmeoni and harabuji forever.*"

She was still smiling, but another tear fell onto my hand, which was closed over hers. "I tried," she said. "I really did."

"Sophia," I began, but she was already drifting away, lost in the spell of her own story.

"I was so good, Shelley," she said. "I did everything just as my umma told me. I always smiled, always listened, always obeyed, and I showed them that I was *happy*. So happy, even when I helped my mother cook and sweep and serve tea to my stepfather while he lay on the couch watching TV. So happy, even when my brother laughed at my accent and called me Dirty Chinese Girl and made me carry his schoolbag and his toys. He had this beloved action figure: some stupid thing called

MightyMan, from a cartoon all the little boys watched. And when he lost it on the way to school, he blamed it on me. He cut up my beautiful lavender dress with a pair of scissors, and my mother and stepfather laughed and said, *Oh, look at Seojoon, isn't he so feisty?* And of course I had to laugh, too. I laughed like it was the funniest thing in the world."

We were both silent.

Sophia shook her head, and slowly, she seemed to come back from the daze. Her voice took on a new tone, one that was flat, almost matter-of-fact.

"Everything changed after he died," she said. "My parents had been making plans for him. He was never a particularly bright student; he was falling behind in school, despite all the tutors they'd hired. They'd been talking about moving to America. The curriculum would be easier. He'd have the chance to become fluent in English. Doors would open to him that never would have opened in Korea.

"I stole his life, Shelley. I stole the life they had planned for him."

"Don't say that," I said. "You didn't steal anything."

She squeezed my hand. "Let me finish. I need to tell you everything so that you understand. So you'll see why we're really here.

"A few weeks after he'd disappeared—after the flurry of relatives had gone home and left us to our grief—I started sleeping in my brother's room at night. Secretly, of course. He'd always had the nicest bedroom in the house. I'd crawl into his bed and stay there for a few hours before the sun came up. I'd read his books and play with his toys. Lying there in his room, I felt envious. I felt sad. I felt a sliver of happiness, too, which meant I also felt deeply ashamed. I . . ."

She fell quiet then, and her gaze shifted to the painting in the corridor, the one I was afraid to look at.

"That was when she began to visit me," she said.

"But who—who exactly is she?"

"Oh," Sophia said, "she's me."

She looked at me, her eyes calm, and I was speechless. She said, "Have you ever heard of a phenomenon, the call of the void?"

"Yeah, it's like . . . when you're standing on a bridge, and your brain suddenly starts wondering what would happen if you jumped."

Sophia nodded. "That's it, isn't it? For a moment, even though it knows it shouldn't, your brain wanders. It ventures into a subliminal space far outside the limits of law and sense.

"I've always thought that this was where she comes from. Most of us, we manage to go through life without crossing the line. We go to school, we go to work, we spend time with our loved ones. We recite our lines and perform our parts, and in exchange, we are rewarded with the privilege of being seen as human beings fit to live in society. But what most of us don't know—or, conveniently, what we choose to ignore—is that every one of us is just one hour, one person, one subway ride away from being pushed over the line. So don't ever tell yourself that you're crazy. Anyone else would have done the exact same thing."

Sophia slipped her arm around me and squeezed my shoulder. My eyes filled with tears.

She knew. She knew me like no one else ever had. The things that had once caused me violent spells of shame, unimaginable pain, sleepless nights in the company of nothing but bitter coffee and self-hatred and the endless chorus of poisonous voices in my head—I saw them in a different light now. They still hurt, *fuck* did they hurt, but they were special. They were something that only she and I shared, something that others would never know, not Paul, not Ory, not anyone else who existed on the periphery of our lives.

How could I have ever thought of her as unremarkable? As Sophia smiled at me, the golden rays of the afternoon sun washed over her, lit up the tiny stray hairs around her face, danced on the tips of her eyelashes. There was a little dimple that blossomed in her lower right cheek when she smiled, and I felt a sudden desire to reach out and touch it with my finger, to cup my hand around her face, the way she sometimes did with mine. The sensation filled my chest and condensed into a heavy weight, and abruptly, I realized what it was.

It was an aching.

SOYOUNG

September 2004

The third time he walked Soyoung back to campus, Paul began telling her stories.

"So we're there in the locker room, and he goes, *Bro, I need to see your toes.* And I'm like, *What?* And he's like, *I need to see if your second toe is longer than your big toe. I just need to see it.* And I'm like, *Why?* And he goes, *I don't trust motherfuckers with their second toe longer than their big toe. It's not right. I lost my last relay because I saw somebody with a toe like that, so I'm not taking any more chances.*"

Soyoung was doubled over, convulsing with laughter. As she wiped her eye on the back of her hand, she said, "So did you show him?"

"I didn't. I told him if he was really that concerned, then he shouldn't be asking to see anybody's toes. He should just assume that everyone around him does have a normal toe and go from there."

Soyoung was still laughing when she looked up at him. Tucking a strand of hair behind her ear, she said, "Now I'm curious whether your second toe *is* longer than your first one."

"You want to find out?"

"Yeah."

Paul grinned. "Take a guess."

"Paul, come on! Just tell me."

But he wouldn't let up. "I'm not going to show you unless you guess first."

Soyoung gave him a light shove in the arm, and they both laughed again. "Oh my God, Paul," she said, "I don't even want—okay. Okay. You know what? Fine. I'm going to guess that it's . . . not longer."

They looked at each other; Paul still had a cheeky grin on his face. She said, "Well?"

"Moment of truth."

As Paul began to take off his right shoe, Soyoung groaned. She hid her face in her hands and turned away, and she heard him laughing. "What, you're not curious anymore? I'm going to put my sock back on if you don't look."

And because her curiosity got the better of her, Soyoung did look. "Huh," she said, after a beat. And then: "So did he win the meet?"

"He did. Proving that superstitions are and always will be nothing more than myths. They're stories people make up to tell themselves because they're too afraid to face the truth."

Soyoung was quiet as Paul put his shoe back on. Then she said, "You know, sometimes I miss the days when you used to be quiet around me, and not such a smart-ass."

She said this with warmth in her voice, and Paul laughed, but a cold draft had washed over her. A long moment passed before she said, "Can I ask you something?"

"Sure."

"Why are you here?"

"Here as in where we are right now?"

"No. Here as in at Cornell. Why did you choose to come here?"

"Oh," Paul said, "I got the best financial aid from here. And it's a good school. Not much more to it than that."

"Which other schools did you get into?"

"Just a handful. Northwestern, Georgetown, Rice. Boston College."

Soyoung sucked in her breath, impressed. "Those are really good schools."

"I mean," Paul said, "everybody here got into really good schools, so it's not that impressive."

Soyoung shook her head. "You're always deflecting when I say these things, Paul, but you got into Cornell. You were always going to do great things."

Then she said, "When I was a little girl in Seoul, for a brief time, I believed there was something special about me, too. I thought—"

Abruptly, she stopped talking, and Paul said, "You thought what?"

"Nothing. It doesn't matter. I was wrong."

Soyoung hugged her arms to her chest. "I was never special," she said. "Coming here has taught me that. Not in Seoul, not in Brookline, not in Ithaca. Everywhere I go, I'm no one. I'm nothing. Just one of a million pebbles on the beach."

She could tell by Paul's silence that he had no response to this. She hadn't expected him to, anyway.

In the dorm room that night, Lillian was uncharacteristically silent. She had met Soyoung with a terse one-word greeting when she opened the door, and then she'd kept her headphones on the entire time she did her poli-sci reading, flooding the room with a sense of unease. There was a sink in the room, and after Lillian washed her face, she put her glasses back on and addressed Soyoung, who was reading in her sleeping bag. "Hey, there's something you should know."

"What is it?"

Lillian hesitated. Then she said, "My sister's coming for a visit tomorrow, so I can't let you stay here anymore. I need the space to accommodate her."

"Your sister who lives in Montreal?"

"Yeah."

Soyoung said, "I thought we weren't allowed to have guests stay in the dorms."

Lillian's eyes flicked to the purple sleeping bag, which Soyoung had bought after her first night on the floor, and the large pink suitcase in the corner, half blocking the door to the closet with its stature. She said, "Regardless, she's coming, so I need the space for her."

"That's fine. When does she leave?"

Lillian didn't answer, so Soyoung pressed again. "When does she leave?"

There was a pause. Lillian said, "Look, it doesn't matter when she leaves. Because I can't let you stay here anymore. I'm sorry."

Slowly, Soyoung put down her book.

She said, "You're kicking me out?"

Again, Lillian didn't answer immediately. She took off her glasses and wiped them on her pajamas before putting them back on. She was looking directly at Soyoung as she said, "Why don't you have a Cornell email?"

"What are you talking about? Of course I do."

"I tried to email you, and it bounced back. I got an error message."

"I was having email issues," Soyoung said. "Everybody who emailed me was getting the same error message."

Lillian bit her lip. "Well, I tried looking you up in the university directory, and you weren't there."

"You looked me up in the university directory? That's not creepy at all."

"I wasn't trying to be creepy," Lillian said. "I was just trying to—"

Then she said, "Look, I just find it weird that I'm always having to come to the front door and let you into the dorm. Because the policy you had cited about not being able to use your ID card to access dorms you're not assigned to—that's not true. I tested it with another dorm the other day. I could get in with no problem."

"I never said that was why I couldn't get into the dorm. I said that I've been having problems with my ID in general. Remember? There was a problem with IT. They mixed me up with another Soyoung Kim that graduated last year, so I keep showing up as a deleted user in the system. That's why my ID is all busted. That's why my email is busted."

Lillian was quiet, listening to Soyoung talk. Now she shook her head, and there was a weariness about her that Soyoung didn't like.

She said, "So I wasn't going to bring this up, but at this point, I feel like I have to."

"Put it on the table. Whatever problem you have, let's talk about it."

"I know you've been using my ID card behind my back."

Soyoung blinked. Then she laughed. "Are you for real?"

"Oh, I'm absolutely for real," Lillian said. "I noticed last week when I was swiping my card at lunch. The balance is almost thirty-two dollars lower than it should be. And you're the only person who has access to my room and my wallet."

"If you noticed last week, why are you just now bringing it up?"

Lillian threw up her hands, exasperated. "Jesus, I don't know! Because I was hoping I was seeing things that weren't there. I was hoping I was . . . I know you've been taking my food, too. You ate my bananas. You took a bunch of my granola bars. Soyoung, look—"

She stopped herself and ran her hands over the bottom of her face. She took a deep breath.

"Look, obviously you have something going on that is . . . challenging for you, and I get that. I sympathize with you. And if you need a certain amount of money, or if you need a couple of meals, I do want to help you. I really do. I just have to draw the line somewhere. So I'm really sorry, but I can't let you stay in my room anymore. You can still sleep here tonight, but if you don't leave tomorrow morning, then . . . again, I'm sorry, but I would have to get the RA involved."

Silence fell.

Soyoung looked down at her book lying face down on the tile. She looked at her legs, which were ensconced in the sleeping bag. She was quiet for a long time, and when she finally spoke, her voice was brittle. "Wow, really generous of you to not kick me out in the middle of the night. Should I get on my knees and thank you?"

"Do you *want* to leave now? Because you can, if you want."

There was another pause.

"No," Soyoung said. "I'll be gone in the morning."

"Okay, then."

There was a light above the sink, and Lillian turned it off before she got into bed. As she lay there in the dark, Soyoung could hear Lillian coughing quietly under her blanket, a long-suffering, muffled sound that had become a staple of their time together. She waited for Lillian to change her mind, to speak up and invite Soyoung to stay. But Lillian never did.

It had begun to drizzle when Soyoung climbed out of her sleeping bag. On the bed, Lillian was breathing evenly, finally asleep. Lillian's CORNELL hoodie was hanging over the back of a chair, and she slipped it on, along with her own pair of white tennis shoes, before closing the door soundlessly behind her.

It was a fifteen-minute walk to the gorge. By the time she reached the end of the trail and came upon the water, Soyoung's face was wet with both the rain and tears, and Lillian's damp hoodie clung limply to her skin. On the grassy bank, she sank to her knees. The fog was thick around her, and the trees had become shadows. Soyoung addressed the water.

"Please. I know I haven't spoken to you in so long, and I'm sorry. I'm so, so sorry. But I need your help. I have nowhere else to go."

The rain was growing stronger. She began to crawl, her wet hair clinging to her face, the warm sludge of mud coursing through her fingers. Her face was now inches from the surface; with every raindrop, tiny circles burst into violent ripples, died a thousand deaths in the depths of the water before returning anew. The sound was a symphony. Soyoung breathed in deeply.

"I know you're there. I know you'll help me.

"Please. Please. Please."

She closed her eyes and plunged herself into the water.

And then, abruptly: She was awake again, face down in a pool of mud. Her clothes were wet, stiff, weighing her down. The bitter taste of earth filled her mouth. She felt the warmth of a hand leave her neck.

"No, she's breathing," she heard a male voice say. "I think she's just passed out."

"Should we call campus police or something?"

This time, it was a girl.

"Let me see if I can wake her first," the man said.

The hands were now turning her over by her shoulders. "Hello? Hello, are you awake? Can you hear me?"

In the mud, Soyoung's eyes fluttered open.

Part Three

LOVING FAMILIES INTERNATIONAL

ERIN

February 2017

Across the table, Jay Gimbel leaned towards me, his hands clasped in anticipation.

"So, Erin Callaghan," he said, "tell us all about yourself."

In the lobby at Meek LeClerc's fourth-floor Chelsea office, the receptionist, a twentysomething with her hair twisted into a pair of topknots, had asked me if I wanted a coffee or tea while I waited. She had already taken a seat behind her desk; I said, "Oh, no, that's okay. I'd hate to trouble you."

"No trouble at all," the girl said. "Coffee or tea? Or I could get you a water."

She was back on her feet, looking at me expectantly. "A water would be amazing," I said. "I really appreciate it."

On the Our Team page of the agency website, the receptionist had been identified as Radha Suresh. She hailed from West Hartford, Connecticut, and when she was not busy making the clients of Meek LeClerc feel right at home, she could be found hunting for the best macarons in New York City or cuddling with her sweet rescue schnauzer mix, Tofu. When she returned with a paper cup, I nodded at the framed photo on her desk. "Is that your dog? He's so cute."

Radha brightened. "That's my baby," she said. "His name is Tofu."

"Oh, I just adore him. His cute little snout—it's literally killing me."

Then I said, "We're not allowed to have pets in our building."

Her nose crinkled. "Oh, boo. That's sad."

"The saddest. I have this joke that I'm a dog aunt. I live vicariously through hanging out with my friends' dogs."

That earned a polite laugh from Radha. "Sounds like you're getting the best of both worlds. All of the love, none of the running after them and picking up their poop."

She sat back down behind the desk, parking her hands over the keyboard, and I let the silence build before I spoke again, this time in a much softer voice. "God, I really shouldn't be admitting this, but I'm actually so nervous right now."

That made Radha stop checking her email. "Nervous? About what?"

"The interview," I said, and I nodded in the general direction of the office; all that was visible from the lobby was a stretch of bright yellow wall and the Meek LeClerc logo. "You guys have seriously impressive clients. Skechers, Dr Pepper, the National Audubon Society—and then there's Jay. I mean, I still remember that campaign he did for Coke back when he was at Ogilvy. Like, not to brownnose, but that was God-tier stuff. And it's like, who the hell do I think I am, coming in here to interview with Jay? I'm just a junior designer with a tiny portfolio. I don't even know if my work is any good."

Behind the desk, I saw Radha's eyes soften.

She glanced around the lobby. Then she said, quietly, "Look, between you and me, your chances are decent. They might be hiring more than one person for this role."

"Oh, no way."

She nodded. "We just won a big account. I can't tell you what or how much because it's not public yet, but it's big. There's going to be a lot more client work coming in, which is why Jay is looking to expand the creative team. Amy, too. She just got promoted to SVP, and she's been the biggest champion for Creative since day one. If she likes you, you'll definitely get the job."

"What kind of people does Amy like?"

Radha thought about it. "Just people that are nice, generally. It's important to her that everyone gets along."

There was a pause, and then I smiled, slowly.

"That's good to know," I said. "Thanks for the pep talk."

Now, as I sat in the small white conference room with my Longchamp tote by my leg and the cup of water next to my résumé, I smiled again. I made eye contact with each of the three interviewers. Josh, senior designer. Jay, creative director. Amy, senior vice president.

I said, "I'm from Davis, California, which I was lucky to call home for the better part of eighteen years. For college, I majored in English literature at the University of Vermont. While I was studying at UVM, I started volunteering with the student newspaper, and that was when I learned to work with Adobe InCopy, which was the software we used to put our stories into layout every week.

"Now, as you obviously know, InCopy isn't the most creative tool out there. It's not what people think of when they think design magic. But it was my gateway drug into design. It made me start asking questions like *Why does this layout look good?* and *Why doesn't that catch my eye in quite the same way?* And once I had answered those questions, I was moving on to bigger, even more experimental questions, like *If I were to use two different photos to illustrate the same story and presented them to the same audience, which version would get more of them to read the story, and why?*"

Jay nodded. "A/B testing," he said.

I beamed at him. "Exactly! I became obsessed with the principles of marketing. I was fascinated by the psychology of it all. And that was when I realized that design is more than just art. It's telling a story through art. It's persuading through art. It's *manipulating* through art, if you wanted to get kind of dark about it. And it's magic. Design is pure magic, and I wanted to become a magician."

They were all nodding.

I said, "That was when I started to sit in on design classes. I started messing around with the free software that was available in the computer lab. There were plenty of tutorials online, but that wasn't where I wanted to start. I wanted to get my bearings the old-school way. When all you had was your raw passion for making things and a pirated version of Adobe Photoshop—"

"—copied on a CD!" Jay practically shouted. He threw his head back and laughed, and next to him, Josh and Amy were laughing, too. "God, those were the good old days. Remember when you could get a free hour of AOL on a CD?"

Looking at me, Josh said, "Jay, come on. There's no way she's old enough to know what AOL is."

"Excuse me," I said, "but you're talking to someone who used to spend *hours* agonizing over the perfect away message on AIM. I had a rotating repertoire of Green Day lyrics."

They all laughed again, and that was when the atmosphere changed. Their body language loosened. Jay rolled his shoulders back, and Josh slid down half an inch in his chair. Then Amy spoke up.

Pleasantly, she said, "I see on your résumé that you're currently a junior designer with . . . New Moon Studio. Can you tell us about why you're looking to make a switch, and what about this role with MLC in particular that was attractive to you?"

I nodded. I smiled.

And for the third time in my life, I looked into the eyes of Amy Cloverfield.

Two weeks ago, on a sunny Thursday morning, I had stood behind Amy in line at the coffee shop on the corner, just two doors down from the building that Meek LeClerc was in. It was the one she popped into every day before work, grabbed an almond croissant in a bag, a black coffee to go. In the coffee shop, I had tapped Amy on the shoulder, and she'd turned around, halfway through typing an email to her assistant, Jess. "Sorry," I said. "It's just that you have something stuck to the back of your coat?"

It was a dirty piece of packing tape; long hairs were poking out of the corners. "Ugh, lovely," Amy had said, and she'd pulled the fabric towards her until she peeled off the tape and balled it up in her hand. "Probably from my Uber ride this morning."

Then she'd smiled at me. "Thanks for telling me."

She was wearing that same smile now as she sat across the table from me. A little taut, a little guarded, as all white women like her were, but there was also something approachable. She had by now spent enough time with me to deem me likable. She wasn't intrigued, not yet. But she was open to seeing more.

I said, "New Moon Studio is this amazing woman-owned boutique design shop, and our mission is to design for good. In the year and change that I've been working there, I've had the incredible opportunity to work closely with local women- and POC-owned brands, helping marginalized small business owners bring their diverse and eco-friendly products to market."

Amy nodded. Jay said, "I enjoyed the work in your portfolio. You've got a distinctive style. The fusion of ink and watercolor is very interesting."

I smiled. "Thank you. I do have to give huge credit to my boss, though. She's been my biggest mentor, and she's really helped me up my game with her guidance and support. In fact—my boss was the one who encouraged me to apply for this role."

The three of them exchanged looks. Amy said, "You're kidding."

"That's what I thought, too, the day she sat me down for a talk. We had this very candid conversation about what I wanted my career to look like, what she thought it could look like. And she was so supportive and forthright with me. She said that I had outgrown the small clients I was working with, and she believed I had the potential to do a lot more. She strongly supported me going out there and knocking on some big doors to see if any of them would open." I laughed lightly. "Obviously, when I heard about this incredible opportunity to join a world-class creative team at MLC, I came knocking on your door right away."

Amy nodded. "I love that," she said. "Women supporting women. As it should be."

They each asked one or two more questions, and soon the allotted hour was drawing to a close; Amy was reading emails on her phone more than she was looking at me. Josh said, "I just have one random question that's neither here nor there."

I nodded, and he said, "Callaghan—that's Irish, right?"

Brightly, I said, "Oh, I think so. Certainly sounds Irish."

Josh hesitated, unsure how to proceed with the next question, and I said, "I know, I know, I get it all the time. I look *incredibly* Irish."

He laughed. I pulled my mouth into a big smile.

"The basic story behind my name," I said, "is that I'm adopted."

At this, Josh and Jay both mouthed an *ah* of understanding, but Amy went one step further. "*Oh*," she said, and her eyes flew to my face. They searched my features, as though she were a fact-checker, trying to verify an unproven theory. I smiled at her.

I said, "I was adopted from a city called Guiyang in southern China when I was almost a year old. Apparently I'd been abandoned on a bridge in the freezing cold, but thankfully someone found me in time and took me to a hospital, and now I've been able to have this really great life with my parents in California, who are just so supportive and loving."

Amy put her phone aside. She slid forward in her seat until she was at the very edge, and her hand moved towards me across the table, as if she was on the verge of taking mine.

She said, "I just have to tell you the strangest thing. My daughter is from Guizhou Province. She was born in Guiyang and lived in an orphanage there until we adopted her at ten months old. Isn't that amazing? What are the odds? Truly, what are the odds?"

For a moment, I didn't speak. I just stared at her. Then I leaned in, too.

In a hushed voice, I said, "Wait, so she's from . . ."

I stopped. I leaned back in my chair and clapped a hand to my face. "You're *sure* she's from Guiyang?"

She gestured behind her. "I have a picture in my office. I have a picture of the day my ex-husband and I went to China and got her from the orphanage. We were in China for three days. We arrived in Shanghai, flew to Guiyang, picked her up, went back to Shanghai, then flew back to New York. It's been seventeen years since that moment."

"Twenty-three for me," I said. "No, this is . . . this is honestly kind of surreal. I've never met anyone else who was adopted from there."

"There was a French couple that was there at the same time as us," Amy said. "I remember that they got their own little girl and took her back to France. But I don't remember if anyone else was there. It was such a long time ago."

Then she said, "Oh, I'm going to have to tell my daughter when I get home. She's going to get such a kick out of it. Imagine meeting someone from the same city in China as you right here in New York. Literally an ocean away."

And Jay said, "I believe this is what they call an 'only in New York moment,' Amy."

And as Amy Cloverfield smiled at me, this time her guard was down. Her eyes crinkled. There was a warmth, an openness, a willingness to engage. It was a look I had only seen in the snapshots of Amy that occasionally appeared in the Stories section of her daughter's private Instagram account. For a fleeting moment, as I gazed into her eyes, it was easy to forget that she had been the woman on the train. Amy Cloverfield was a mom. She was a friend. She was a boss who valued team players and women who were brave enough to knock at the door.

And this time, she was going to let me in.

In the basement of the bookstore around the corner, I found Sophia nodding off in a small chair by one of the shelves. An open book was splayed across her lap, and her head was lolling onto her crimson shawl while her arms hugged her tote bag to her chest. Even in sleep, she breathed softly, cautiously, like a small animal curling up alone for the night.

I stood there for a while, not wanting to wake her, not in this moment when time seemed to stand still. But then her head twitched, and she looked up at me, groggy. "Erin?"

"It's me," I said. "I just got out of the interview."

And then I couldn't keep it in any longer. I let out a loud whoop, loud enough for the two other patrons in the basement to turn their heads and scowl at me, and bent down and hugged Sophia tight, squeezing her, laughing, triumphant. "It was unbelievable," I said. "I had them hooked. I had her eating from the palm of my hand. I felt—I was like a fucking *god*, Sophia."

The drowsiness vanished from Sophia's face. She threw the book aside and hurried to pull on her coat. "Let's get out of here. I want to hear everything."

In a grubby little restaurant a few blocks away, the kind only Asians and white people who'd taught English in China go to, we squeezed ourselves onto a narrow wooden bench by the window, our breaths fogging the glass. The server brought over a bowl of steamed edamame while we waited for the mains, and Sophia began shelling them as I gave her the play-by-play in a low voice. I was describing the way Jay had said, shaking my hand in the lobby with a broad smile, to expect to hear about next steps in the next week or so, when I sensed a wilting in her. She was no longer looking at me as she worked on the beans, her eyelashes downcast and limp. I said, "Are you okay?"

Sophia glanced at me, surprised. "Of course. Why do you ask?"

Before I could answer, she held a handful of salty green beans up to my mouth. "Here—start eating."

I obliged; my lips brushed against her fingers, and I felt a flutter in my stomach. Sophia was quiet, and after a moment she said, "You're just so good."

"What do you mean?"

She waved a hand. "All of it. Not just the deception part, taking on a new name. But you've gotten the hard part, too. I'd never seen anyone pick up design skills so fast in such a short amount of time. It's only been a matter of weeks, and you're already making original vector art in Illustrator. Sometimes, when I'm watching you, it makes me think . . ."

She trailed off, her gaze drifting towards the window. Finally, she said, "I keep thinking that if I'd had your gifts, I wouldn't have had to do what I did at Cornell. I would have gotten in."

She smiled at me, and it was only then that I saw the tinge of green under her eyes, startlingly obvious even under a careful coat of concealer. I recalled seeing the same thing on my face just weeks earlier.

Barely a month had passed since I'd moved in with Sophia and Paul and Ory, and already I had become the primary witness to her existence, the days and nights that melted into one another, always another plate to clean, another stained shirt to toss into the washer, another client email that demanded an urgent turnaround. In the mornings, while Paul showered, she awakened Ory and dressed him for school; even from downstairs, I could hear his high-pitched whining, stamping his feet as she tried to coax him into a sweater he suddenly hated. She was the one who made breakfast in the mornings, not milk and cereal but pan-seared tomatoes and seaweed soup and scrambled eggs garnished with fresh parsley, meals that Ory ate sparingly and begrudgingly while he played with plastic dinosaurs on the table. After that, once Paul had left with Ory and the house was plunged into sudden solitude, Sophia washed the dishes and wiped the counters in silence, a strange blankness overtaking her face that stopped me from trying to speak to her. And then: work. She disappeared into her upstairs studio, planting herself before her iMac and remaining there for hours without emerging. Most days, I didn't see her again until dinner.

Of course I'd offered to pitch in. I could cook. I could vacuum and fold laundry. I could help babysit Ory, even. But the first time I suggested this, Sophia had shot me down. "I don't want things to change," she'd said.

"Change in what way?"

We'd been sitting on the bench by the pond in the backyard, a small burning fire bowl at our feet. Even in the dead of winter, it had become our place to talk and strategize at night, a place where Paul and Ory couldn't overhear our machinations. Sophia was quiet for a long time before she said, "This isn't the life you're meant to have."

Now, as she raised her hand to feed me edamame again, I shuffled in my seat and cleared my throat. "Hey, so," I said, "I don't mean to pry, but are you okay? Are you . . . like, depressed, maybe?"

There was a pause. She said, "What makes you think that?"

"Sophia, come on. I of all people know what depression looks like. I know the signs."

Something in her face shuttered. She said, "You have no idea what real depression looks like."

I was speechless.

"What happened to you, it was a tragedy, of course. A life-altering event. You sank into a temporary state of despondence. But you don't know what it is to look despair in the face and know that it is your whole being, it is your destiny. Your home."

Sophia shook her head. "You'll move on," she said, and her voice had become strange, brittle. "One day, our plan will be over, and you won't need me anymore. You'll move out of my guest room in New Jersey and get on with the rest of your beautiful, brilliant life."

We looked at each other. Sophia bit her bottom lip; it was white, tense, barely concealing a tremor. She took a deep breath, and abruptly, she was smiling again.

"I'm sorry," she said. "I didn't mean to . . . I'm in one of my moods, that's all. I didn't mean what I said."

She started to reach for another edamame, but I was faster. I wrapped my fingers around her hand, and she fought me for a protracted moment before allowing me to take it.

"Sophia, listen to me," I said, "is everything okay? Because if something's wrong, you can tell me. I'm serious. I could help you, too."

She said nothing, and I said, "Are you not happy with Paul? Are you guys in a fight or something?"

Sophia looked away. Quietly, she said, "Paul is a good person."

"I wasn't asking if he was a good person. I was asking if you were happy."

When she finally looked back at me, she seemed almost afraid. "We've been arguing over whether I should go back to work," she said. "He thinks it's better for Ory if one of us stays at home."

"But don't you already work for yourself?"

Sophia let out an exhale of a laugh. "Yeah, for a handful of freelance clients who pay me pennies, and three months late on top of that. What I have, it's not a real business. It's . . . it's a farce. It's a charade that Paul and I keep up to help me cope with the fact that I have no career, no income, no . . ."

Then she said, "Did you know that I used to work for one of the biggest ad agencies in the world? The kind of place people dream about getting a call from. My boss was so disappointed when I didn't come back after maternity leave. We had one last coffee the day I went in to clear out my cubicle, and I remember her saying, *You have so much potential, Sophia. I hope you'll find another way to use it.* But I never did. I . . . I became a stay-at-home mom. I stopped making real art. I let her down."

Tears had clouded her eyes. One clung to an eyelash, refusing to let go; I hesitated before lifting my finger to her face to catch it.

"You didn't, though, Sophia," I said, and I meant it. "You might have sat out for a minute, but you're still in the game. Like, no offense to Paul, but fuck what he thinks. You're the most brilliant artist I know. If the curators at the Louvre saw the work that's hanging in your living room, they'd be crying and shitting themselves."

But Sophia just smiled, sadly.

"It's different when you're a mother," she said. "It just is."

We spent the rest of the meal in silence. It wasn't until nearly an hour later, when we were standing on the train platform, waiting for the PATH back to Hoboken, that Sophia put her hand on my arm. "Don't worry about what I said earlier," she said. "I didn't really mean it. I was just venting."

"Were you?"

"Paul is a wonderful person," she said. "He really is. You have no idea how lucky I am to be married to him, especially after everything I did at Cornell. How lucky Ory is to have him as his dad."

I nodded. I looked down at my shoes.

I said, "This is super petty, but have you ever noticed that thing he does with the glasses?"

She just looked at me. I said, "Every time he drinks water, he gets a new glass out of the cabinet. And he'll just leave the half-empty glass sitting out. It's such a minor thing, but sometimes I just want to shake him by the shoulders and ask him, *My guy, what is keeping you from using the same glass? Why are you always leaving this shit out for other people to put away?* And again, it shouldn't matter, but every time I see his glasses all over the house, it fills me with this, like, incandescent rage. I'm just curious if you've ever noticed it."

"Oh, yes," Sophia said, "I've noticed."

She was gazing at the train that had appeared in the distance. When she looked back at me, the fracture I'd seen in her face was gone. In its place was a stillness, a blank canvas. She had recomposed herself.

"When Ory was nine months old," she said, "the three of us went to Coney Island on the Fourth of July and stayed late to see the fireworks. At the time, things were . . . I was exhausted with the baby, with Paul. I hadn't slept for months. Walking around the park that day, I felt like a ghost, like I was trespassing in the land of the living. And I remember thinking, not for the first time, *What would happen if I just stopped trying and walked away? Really, what would happen if I did?*

"But then we saw the fireworks."

Sophia smiled, and I saw the wonder in her eyes. Her voice washed over me like water.

"Ory fell asleep halfway through the show. We were sitting on a beach blanket; he was curled up on Paul's lap, his tiny hand was holding tight on to my finger, and when I looked at him, I could feel my heart beating outside my own body. And that was when I realized: How could I have ever thought of walking away? Uproot the only life he's ever known, a different house, different schools, shuttling back and forth between homes, spending Christmas and Thanksgiving and Chuseok with a different parent every year? That wasn't what I wanted for my little boy. I wanted him to be happy. I wanted him to fall asleep during a fireworks show and dream the sweetest dreams, knowing that when he wakes up, his mom and his dad will be right there, side by side, watching over him.

"We've both made mistakes. Of course we have. Paul and I got married way too young, way before either of us were ready, but over time, and because of Ory . . . I've learned to make my peace with it."

I didn't know what to say to that.

The lightness and triumph that had filled me from the job interview, the pang of delight that had jolted my stomach when I held her hand earlier, it had all drained away. I heard Sophia sigh.

She said, "Just promise me you won't get married before you're thirty."

"That's easy," I said. "I don't think I'd get married, period."

The train was pulling up to the platform now. Amid the cacophony of the engine, Sophia looked down and smiled, a bit wistfully. "Sometimes it has its moments," I heard, or saw, her say.

That night, when Paul was watching TV in the living room, I decided to join him.

It was a spur-of-the-moment thing. I had no reason to do it. But I saw the back of his head over the couch, and something made me go to the kitchen, fill up a glass of water, and walk back to the living room. "Mind if I hang here for a bit?" I said, and I dropped onto the other end of the couch before he'd answered.

Paul looked around at me, surprised. For the past month, I'd pretty much stayed out of his way. When he and Sophia took Ory to a playground or a museum or a birthday party, I went into the city and did my own thing. And on the rare occasion we spoke, it was to exchange essential information: *Do you need more toilet paper in the guest bath?* Or it was channeled through Ory at the dinner table. *Yeah, I know your daddy works in the city. No way, his building is how tall?* The implicit understanding between us was that I had the run of the house during the day, a fact that Paul tolerated, but when he was home, the second floor and the living room were his domain. For me to cross the line like this now—it was unusual. I could tell Paul was on edge.

He shrugged. "Sure" was all he said.

I nodded at the hockey game on-screen. "Who's playing?"

"Flyers versus Oilers."

"Oh. Nice."

We were both quiet for a minute or two, but I could feel the tension within Paul building. He turned to me. "So," he said. "Your interview today. You think you have a good shot with this place?"

"Well, I don't want to jinx myself, but I'd say it went well. Sophia really went above and beyond, helping me prep for it."

"I know. She told me."

His eyes darted back to the game. Another minute passed.

I'd thought the conversation was over when he looked back at me again, and this time his face had changed. It was calm in a sort of eerie way. In a voice that was almost pleasant, Paul said, "So after you get the job, will the two of you be wrapping up your little scheme?"

I blinked. Then I smiled. "I'm not sure what you mean."

"Really?" Paul said, and he picked up the remote and muted the TV. The room was silent now. Above us, Ory was asleep, and Sophia was shut away in her studio, on deadline for a client.

Paul said, "You and Sophia have been spending quite a lot of time together. What are you working on?"

"I just told you. Job stuff. My design portfolio."

"And when you get a job, what happens? What's the next step?"

Lightly, I said, "Oh, I don't know. I guess I'd focus on getting myself up to speed, collaborating with my colleagues, familiarizing myself with our clients' visual brand identities. Things like that."

Paul's eyes flickered; I knew I had pissed him off.

"Here's the thing," he said. "I've known Sophia for thirteen years."

"Yeah, I know."

"What you need to know about Sophia is that she cares about other people. She feels things very deeply. And she has a tendency to get herself involved."

I cocked my head. "Okay. And?"

"I don't know what it is you're planning with her," Paul said, "but I can guess it's something you think will help you. Which is why I want to give you a word of advice. Don't."

There was a pause, and then I laughed. *"Don't?* That's it, *don't?"*

Paul was shaking his head.

"You don't get it," he said. "Sophia doesn't exist in a vacuum to cater to your needs, all right? She's a wife. She's a mother. She has responsibilities. She has things she needs to prioritize before—before—"

"The thing is," I said, "I'm not sure if you've noticed, but Sophia is her own person."

"That's not the point I was trying to make," Paul said.

"Wasn't it? Because I think it would actually be pretty dope if you remembered that before she was a wife or a mom, before she met you, she was her own person. She was Sophia. She continues to be Sophia. And she continues to be the most brilliant fucking artist in New York City, regardless of whether you're big enough of a man to acknowledge that."

As I spoke, I saw a subtle shift take shape in Paul's face, something I couldn't quite put my finger on. He shook his head.

Quietly, he said, "You don't know her at all."

"Do you?"

With that, I got up from the couch. In a cheerful voice, I said, "Well, I'd better leave you to it. Enjoy the game, Paul."

Then I nodded at the glasses on the table. "Be a champ and put these in the dishwasher when you're done, will you?"

He was still staring at me as I left.

SOYOUNG

September 2004

In the dining room, they bought her breakfast: a carton of apple juice and a greasy grilled cheese. As Soyoung ate, she could feel the sludge in her hair dripping onto the table, forming small, sticky puddles. Mud caked her face, her hands; the filth clung to her skin and her clothes with a stiffness that almost transported her, separated her from the small, pathetic creature that was tearing into the sandwich like a rabid animal. She floated above.

The girl and the man both watched her with a mixture of pity and curiosity. The girl said, "Are you sure you don't need to go to the clinic?"

"I'm fine."

"You scared us," the girl said. "When we saw you lying there, half of your body sticking out of the water . . . we thought you'd drowned."

Once Soyoung had finished, she looked up, wiping her mouth on a napkin. The girl looked to be about her age; the man was a little older, maybe mid-twenties. They were both Asian. And the way they were seated next to each other, their shoulders touching, they were either a couple or close to it.

"I'm Stella," the girl said. She set her hand on the man's shoulder. "This is my boyfriend, Nathaniel."

"I'm Soyoung. Thanks for your help."

It was clear that Stella was struggling to form an opinion on Soyoung. She said, finally, "So are you a student here?"

"Why wouldn't I be a student here?"

Stella's face turned pink, and Soyoung picked up another napkin and dabbed at the mud across her chest. "Look," she said. The writing on Lillian's hoodie was beginning to come through. CORNELL, it said.

In a small voice, Stella said, "Sorry. I thought that maybe..."

She trailed off, and Nathaniel said, "So what were you doing out in the gorge? Got wasted at a frat party and decided to go for a dip?"

As Soyoung looked at him, she was suddenly flooded by an acute feeling of distaste. Coldly, she said, "My roommate kicked me out."

Stella's mouth fell open, and next to her, Nathaniel looked taken aback, too. "What do you mean, your roommate kicked you out?"

"We got into a fight, and she made me leave the dorm. She does it all the time."

"But that's absurd! She can't just do that. Did you talk to the RA?"

Soyoung shrugged. "What's the point? They always side with her. These preppy white girls always have each other's backs. The administration, too. You know how it is. A place like this, money talks. And she's old money."

"So what are you going to do?" Stella asked.

Soyoung considered this.

"The law library," she said finally. "There's a couch in the basement there, in one of the archival rooms. No one ever goes in there. I should be able to crash there for at least a couple nights."

"But are you allowed to do that? Sleep in the library?"

Stella's eyes were wide with intrigue. There was something so naive about her, so utterly untarnished; Soyoung leaned back in her chair, suddenly cold and brittle. "Probably not," she said, "but what other choice do I have? I don't have any friends here. My parents are all the way out in Massachusetts, and they wouldn't blink an eye if I dropped dead. I thought things here would be different. I thought that for once, I could find someone who cared about me, I could finally fill my life with meaning, but I was wrong. I don't belong here. I have no one. I have nothing. That night by the Han River—I should have stayed. I should have listened to her and stayed in the water and never come back to this world, because it's full of nothing but disappointments."

Across the table, Stella and Nathaniel were speechless.

Abruptly, Soyoung rose, pushing her chair back roughly. The doors to the dining room were swinging wide, pushed open by another group of students moments earlier, and as she approached, she could see the red maple leaves fluttering on the branches outside, the sun bright in the sky. The sun had been scorching that day in Busan, too. When she closed her eyes, she could feel the warm, salty water all around her, the plastic life preserver encircling her chest, the sound of Seojoon's laughter ringing out—

That was when she heard her name.

"Soyoung! Soyoung."

Stella was hurrying towards her, Nathaniel a few steps behind. When they finally caught up with her, Stella's eyes were shining, almost watery.

"I have an idea," she said, "and it might sound crazy, but I really think it's the right thing to do."

"Stella—" Nathaniel began, but she ignored him. Looking at Soyoung, Stella took a deep breath.

She said, "I want to invite you to come live with me."

They helped her vacate her possessions from Lillian's room, Nathaniel wheeling the large pink suitcase, Stella carrying Soyoung's art supplies in a cardboard box. A few other students on the floor had come out into the corridor to watch the move, and among them Soyoung recognized the RA, a tall, athletic girl who regarded her with a bald distaste.

On her way out of the room, she turned to Lillian, who was sitting on her bed, pretending to read a textbook. "Well, good luck with everything," Soyoung said. "It was lovely getting to know you."

For a moment, Lillian was taken aback; her lips parted slightly, and then her eyes landed on the CORNELL hoodie that Soyoung was wearing, now so muddy it was nearly unrecognizable. She said, "Are you wearing my hoodie?"

As they looked at each other, Soyoung smiled, slowly.

She said, "God, Lillian, you are just unbelievable."

Lillian opened her mouth, but then she began to cough. She bent over the bed, her face turning a tortured shade of red as hacking sounds escaped from her body. Soyoung watched her from the doorway, taking comfort in the knowledge of what would happen next. Another day would pass before Lillian would be rushed to the emergency clinic and hospitalized for pneumonia. In both her mattress and the wooden slats underneath, a maintenance crew would find an alarming growth of slimy black mold. In the end, they would conclude that the bed had been visited by an abnormal level of moisture: a dampness that had come from out of nowhere, as though conferred by a ghost.

Stella was still seething after they had left the building. "I can't believe she accused you of stealing her stuff! Who does that?"

"Rich white people," Soyoung said. "You know that her parents paid someone to write her college applications? She probably cheated to get into Cornell."

Stella's room was a cozy double. The walls were covered with family photos, cutouts of severe-looking models from fashion magazines, glossy posters of a dimpled, boyish Singaporean pop singer that Soyoung knew vaguely as JJ. Stella's bedspread was a sea of white dots on bright pink; a row of stuffed animals sat along the wall, dolphins and penguins and polar bears. On the floor was a single upturned Ugg boot and a crumpled North Face jacket in black. As she bent to retrieve the jacket, Stella said, "Sorry, sorry, sorry—I'm incapable of not making a mess anywhere I go, but I'll keep it all on my side of the room, I promise."

The other bed in the room was empty except for a guitar lying on the mattress. As Stella returned it to its case, Soyoung said, "Do you play?"

"Oh, barely. Nathaniel's the one who's actually good. He leads the worship team for our fellowship."

Then Stella said, "Do you want to wash up, maybe?"

The heat of humiliation coursed through Soyoung. Quietly, she said, "Sure."

In the bathroom across the hall, she took a long shower, scrubbing her skin until it was red and raw. She dried her hair and changed into fresh clothes, and when Stella opened the door, something seemed to shift in her face. It wasn't until Soyoung had begun putting a fitted sheet on the mattress that Stella said, "You're really pretty."

Leaning over the bed, Soyoung paused. She said, "I'm not, but you're kind to say that."

"I'm not just saying it," Stella said. "You are."

But she seemed quiet, pensive, and Soyoung said nothing. After she finished making the bed, she sat on it, facing Stella. "Hey," she said. "Thanks again for letting me stay with you."

Stella shook her head. "It's nothing," she said. "And really, it's not me that you should be thanking."

"What do you mean?"

"Nathaniel and I go jogging every morning, rain or shine. But we don't usually go by the gorge. And we never go that early. Today, though, it was like there was a voice telling us to go. Like there was someone guiding us. And when we saw you lying in the water . . ." Stella took a deep breath. "That was when we knew. It was God's will, you know? He had led us right to you."

Soyoung blinked once, then a few more times in rapid succession. Her eyes filled with tears.

She said, "I don't know what to say."

"It's true," Stella said. "It's what I believe. It's what Christians believe. God is always out there, looking out for us. He saw that you were in trouble, and He told us to help you. All we did was answer His call."

Soyoung shook her head.

"He wouldn't do that," she said. She was almost whispering. "You don't understand, Stella. I'm not . . . I'm not a good person. I don't deserve to be helped."

Stella got up from her bed, then, and sat next to Soyoung. She took Soyoung's hand in hers.

"Listen to me," she said, "because I have good news, okay?"

Through her tears, Soyoung looked at Stella. "Here's the thing," she heard Stella say. "You could be a liar. A cheat. An adulterer. A thief. You could be a freaking serial killer, and still I'd have good news for you. Because guess what? God still loves you. Regardless."

It was then that Soyoung let out a soft, despairing gasp. Teardrops began to fall onto her jeans, dissolving into the fabric. Stella squeezed her hand.

"Why don't we pray for you?" she said. "I can tell that you need it. Here—let's get on the floor, and we'll pray together. I'll help you."

On the carpet, they clasped hands and closed their eyes. Stella spoke in a clear, earnest voice.

"Lord God," she said, "I'm coming to You today with my sister Soyoung. Lord, when I look at her, I can see that she is so lonely. I can see that she is in so much pain. She has been lost in the shadows, away from Your flock, away from Your protection. But all this time, Lord, You have never forgotten her. You have never abandoned her. And it was through Your grace and Your love that we were able to find our sister Soyoung and bring her back to us. Thank You, Lord. Thank You for bringing her home."

She waited. Soyoung was silent, and after a moment, Stella whispered, "Say something."

"What do I say?"

"Anything. Tell Him what's in your heart."

Slowly, Soyoung opened her eyes. She saw Stella, her eyes closed, her head bent in prayerful devotion, her fingers laced through Soyoung's own. Soyoung took a small, shuddering breath, then another.

"I'm sorry, God," she whispered. "I'm . . . I'm so sorry."

Stella's fingers tightened around hers. Soyoung continued.

"That night, when I heard her calling my name . . . I never should have answered her. I never should have gone. She promised to make me the most special girl in the world. She promised to make my parents love me, and I . . . I was so stupid. I believed her. I didn't know—oh God, I didn't realize!—until I was deep in the water, and by then it was too late. I didn't want to do it. I didn't mean to hurt anyone. But it was too late. It was too late!"

From the deepest part of her, there came a small, rattled gasp, then a wail. Her body crumpled. Her forehead hit the carpet, and she felt Stella's arms close around her, catch her as she rocked back and forth. Her fingers were in her hair. "I'm sorry," Soyoung told Stella's hands. "I'm sorry. I'm sorry. I'm sorry."

"It's okay, Soyoung," Stella said. "It's okay."

She said, "Everything you've just said, everything you've just apologized for—He has already forgiven you for it."

There was a long silence.

Slowly, Soyoung straightened up to look at Stella. Her eyes were red, swollen; in a dull voice, she said, "He . . . He has?"

"That's what God is," Stella said. "He is forgiveness. He is unconditional love. And He is home."

From the box behind her, she passed a tissue to Soyoung, whose hand instinctively tightened around it. Still dazed, she blew her nose into the tissue, and when the passages cleared, for a moment it was as though everything had changed; she was, as if by miracle, suddenly breathing quietly, easily, in a way she had not been able to for years.

She was at peace.

"Thank You, God," she whispered. "Thank You for . . . for letting me come home."

It had taken a great deal of convincing on her part, but in the end, Paul had begrudgingly trailed Soyoung into the student activities room that following Saturday evening. As they crossed the lawn, he said, "You know I think it's all make-believe, right?"

"I know, Paul. You've told me a million times already."

Soyoung said, "I used to feel the same way. I thought it was . . . psychological. Things you made up in your head to cope. But then something happened, and . . ." She shook her head. "I can't explain it. All I'm asking is for you to keep an open mind."

"Evangelicals creep me out," Paul said. "They all act like they're in this exclusive club, and you're not. Like they're better than you."

"Stella's not like that. Plus, she told me that everybody at the fellowship is Asian, and they're all really nice. It'd be good to make some friends."

"We have each other," Paul said.

"But what are you going to do when I'm no longer here?"

"What do you mean?"

"Forget it," she said. "Just promise me, Paul—open mind."

The room was already teeming with other Asian students, a sea of shiny black heads bobbing around a pair of mismatched couches and poufs scattered across the floor. At the door, Stella greeted both Soyoung and Paul with quick hugs before she pointed them to the snacks table in the corner. There was a bowl of potato chips, an open bag of trail mix, and frosted sugar cookies in a plastic carton—overall a disappointing presentation, but Soyoung loaded up her plate nevertheless. In the background, she heard a strumming sound; Nathaniel Lee, Stella's boyfriend, was perched on a chair near the whiteboard in the back, tuning his guitar with the other members of the worship team. Their eyes met, and he frowned, as though trying to place her. Soyoung was the first to look away.

By eight o'clock, the crowd had begun to settle into three rows, and Soyoung and Paul sat side by side on the carpet, their backs against the wall. Up front, the worship team began playing a melody that Soyoung immediately recognized as a catchy, soulful song she'd heard countless times in the Korean church she'd attended back in Massachusetts. Nathaniel leaned into an imaginary microphone.

"Father God," he said, "we thank You for Your presence here with us this evening. It hasn't been an easy week for a lot of us both here and around the world. War. Disease. Famine. The divisiveness of the politics that threatens to tear apart our country. And many of us have midterms coming up. So in these stressful times, when hope can feel so fragile, I want to remind all of us in this room tonight that Your love is abundant. Your grace is abundant. And I call on every one of us to come before You today and lay down our pain and our sorrows at Your feet."

Soyoung's eyes filled with tears. As Nathaniel began to sing, the song, once so corny and mass-produced to her ears, seemed to take on new meaning. *Here I am to lay down my pain*, she mouthed along to the lyrics. *Here I am to lay down my sorrows. Comfort me, O Lord.*

All around her, people were weeping, praying, raising one hand into the air while touching the other to their heart and twisting their body in devotion. Soyoung, too, sank to the ground, touching her forehead to the carpet in surrender. *I'm so tired*, she confessed. *I don't know how much longer I can stay in this cold, lonely place. Please, God. Please give me just one person who will love me no matter what. Just one person who will protect me and take care of me.*

She could feel Paul watching her. But when Soyoung resurfaced, he said nothing, and so she remained quiet, too, her eyes fixed on a boyish, jolly-faced man in jeans and flip-flops who was now pulling up a stool at the front of the room. The man introduced himself as Pastor Jeremy; as he looked around the crowded room, he said, "Can I see a show of hands? Who here is joining us for the first time today?"

Soyoung and Paul looked at each other, and Paul shook his head frantically. *No*, he mouthed.

Soyoung ignored him. She raised her hand, and Pastor Jeremy called on her. "Can you tell us a little about yourself, please? Your name, your year, where in the world you come from, and—how about as a fun little icebreaker—the worst thing you have ever done. That last one's optional, but we won't say no to a good story."

"My name is Soyoung," Soyoung said, and she glanced at Paul, who was practically melting into the wall. "This is Paul. He's from Baltimore, and I'm from Boston. Oh, and we're both freshmen."

She paused, and Pastor Jeremy prompted her. "And the worst thing you've ever done."

"I . . ." Soyoung began.

Then she said, "I've done a lot of bad things. Things that were really, really horrible. I . . ."

The room had grown quiet. Soyoung's eyes filled with tears again.

She said, "If I had known God was there, if I had . . . if I had only realized He was there, watching over me, loving me, I think it would have all turned out differently. I think I wouldn't have done the things I have done. But I see Him now, I really do. I feel His love, His forgiveness. And I . . . I'm so tired of fighting for myself. I'm so tired of running. I just want to come home."

Applause rang out, filling the room like thunder. Above a sea of friendly, curious faces, Pastor Jeremy beamed at her.

"Welcome home, Soyoung," he said. "We've been waiting for you."

There was one last frosted cookie in the plastic carton on the snacks table. As the room began to empty out, Soyoung stood in front of it, hesitating; finally, she swiped it from the carton and added it to her plate. No one else had wanted it, anyway.

Behind her, she heard a voice say, "You've cleaned up nicely."

Soyoung turned. Nathaniel Lee was smiling at her, flashing his perfectly white teeth. "I almost didn't recognize you when you walked in," he said. "How's the new dorm situation? You two girls getting along? Braiding each other's hair?"

"Stella's wonderful. She's the best roommate I could've asked for."

"She's a good egg," Nathaniel said. "Someone who stands firm in her walk with Christ."

Then he said, "So you're a freshman."

Soyoung nodded. Nathaniel said, "I'm in grad school, myself. Second year of working on my PhD."

"How old are you?" she asked, and Nathaniel laughed.

"How old do you think I am?"

"Twenty-five?"

"Close." He grinned at her. "Twenty-six."

Then he said, "Oh, I see that look on your face. You think I'm an old geezer. Twenty-six-year-old grandpa."

"Oh, no," she said. "Not at all."

"Because I do know what the kids are into these days. Hey—you're on Myspace, right? What's your Myspace?"

"I don't have a Myspace."

"Facebook, then. You heard about this Facebook thing? They just rolled it out to all the Ivies. You can get one with your school email."

Soyoung shook her head. "I don't think I'll get one," she said. "It sounds kind of pointless, if I'm honest."

A curious expression had appeared on Nathaniel's face. "You're a bit of an enigma, aren't you?" he said. "A mystery woman."

Looking into Nathaniel's eyes, Soyoung suddenly felt an unpleasant lurch in her stomach. "I don't know what you mean," she said, and she tried to smile. "I'm just a regular person."

"Oh, no one's a regular person," Nathaniel said. "We're all hiding something up our sleeves."

He took the cookie from Soyoung's plate, broke it into two, and popped half into his mouth. "You're a little mystery, Soyoung Kim," he said as he chewed. "And I'm going to figure you out."

ERIN

March 2017

"She's spineless," Sophia said. "There's no other explanation."

On the branches of the cherry trees in the backyard, tiny white buds had begun to form. The day before, with Ory's help, Paul had cleaned dead leaves from the pond and turned on the filter pump; there were now a dozen goldfish splashing busily in the dark green water, watched by a stoic, long-necked turtle that Ory had named Felix. Spring was days away.

On the bench next to me, Sophia had been massaging her temples. She now looked up at me, and I saw the shadows again, gaining ground under her eyes. "It's decided, then," she said. "We need to move into phase two."

She was talking about Gene Struzik, of course.

A few weeks after sending the letter with Gene's chats to Holly Wong-Struzik's office, we'd chased it with an anonymous message to Holly's email, which was publicly listed on her work website. *Hi, I met this man on a dating website and he told me he was single, but I recently found out that he is actually married and I am guessing you are his wife. I would want to know if it was me. I have more info if you need it. Sorry.*

With the help of an online tutorial, we'd embedded a tracker in the body, one that could tell us if the email had been opened by the recipient. On the twenty-first of February, Holly Wong-Struzik had read the email.

She never responded.

I said, "Should we give her more time? It's only been two weeks."

"There's no point," Sophia said. "She's not going to respond."

Then she said, "I should have known, honestly. These women care more about saving face than anything else. Doesn't matter if their husbands cheat. Doesn't matter if they beat them. It's only the end of the world if they're not married. I'd feel sorry for them, but I don't have the energy."

I said, "Maybe she thought we were trying to blackmail her. Like, shaking her down to keep her husband's nasty business quiet. Or maybe—" The thought made me hopeful. "Maybe she's preparing to divorce him."

"If she wanted to divorce him, she'd have reached out to us," Sophia said. "No sense in turning down free evidence."

Something occurred to me then, a question I had no business asking. But I heard myself say, "What would you do if you found out Paul was cheating? Hypothetically speaking."

"I'd kill him. Then I'd throw his body into this pond and let the fish eat him."

There was a pause, and then I laughed, mostly from the shock. Sophia laughed, too, lifted from her moodiness for a moment.

"Regardless," she said, "if Holly Wong-Struzik's not prepared to grow a spine, then we're just going to have to move forward without her. I'll print a copy of the letter after Paul leaves tomorrow and mail it to the partners at Ingram. Should I send one to the HR lady, too? Katharine?"

In her office, Katharine Browne had said, *I want you to know that this is a safe space.*

And she had said, *The thing is, though, no one else saw what happened between you in that hotel. It's a classic case of he said, she said.*

And she had said, *How would you feel about being reassigned to another team?*

"I met with her three times," I said. "She said they'd talk to him, but either they never did, or it didn't work, because nothing changed. He didn't stop. He—"

It all hit me then: The dim lights in the corridor of the hotel. The carpet under my feet, beige with blue circles. The way my windpipe had clenched when Gene pressed his body against mine. His heavy breathing, his fingers digging into my chest. The way I had frozen, not pushed him away, not said no, just *frozen*.

I shook my head, suddenly drained. "Maybe there's no point," I said.

"What do you mean?"

"It's like you said. Men like Gene, no one ever holds them accountable. We've just spent a month of our time catfishing him, building all this evidence that doesn't matter. Fact is, IRM's not going to fire him over some dick pics. All they care about is the hours he's billing."

"Well, then," Sophia said, "maybe we should go for the source."

She reached for my hand and squeezed it. "Think about the big-name corporations that IRM represents. The clients that Gene works with. What if they all got a letter in the mail tomorrow with everything we've gathered? The photographs. The things he said about Asian women. Maybe we go one step further and make their embarrassment public. An anonymous Tumblr where we dump all the evidence. Twitter accounts to call them out one by one. *Is this the kind of law firm you want representing you? We could—*"

"Sophia," I said, cutting her off mid-sentence. "We can't do that."

"I thought you wanted to take him down."

"Right, but if we start contacting everyone who has a contract with IRM and sending them salacious, private information about one of the firm's senior counsels—that's sabotage. It's a declaration of war. Things would get really ugly, really fast. They'd have grounds to subpoena our information from our Internet provider, from Gmail and Twitter. They'd sue us for extortion and libel. They'd have the firepower to completely fuck us over."

Abruptly, Sophia let go of my hand. She said, "So we're just going to let him off? Is that it?"

There was a chill in her voice, one I'd never heard before. Instinctively, I was consumed by a defensiveness, the desire to get back in her good graces. I moved closer to her on the bench.

"Fuck no," I said. "We're not letting him off. I'm just saying we have to find a better way. Something that's more practical."

"Practical as in what? We can't take him to court for sexual harassment. There's no evidence that it was coerced. It's your word against his."

"I know," I said, weary. "I know."

"And having an Asian fetish isn't a crime. Have you met the Asian women in this city? Nine out of ten are married to white men. They'll complain about the white male gaze all day long, but it's never their husband who is the problem, is it? Just look at Holly Wong-Struzik."

We were both quiet.

"Maybe we should just TP his house," I said.

Sophia looked at me. "Maybe we should set it on fire."

"Maybe we should follow him to work one day and push him into an open manhole. He'd eat shit. Literally."

We both began to laugh, quietly. I took her hand back into mine. Our fingers laced through one another, and with my other hand, I drew idle circles in her palm. I saw Sophia glance up at the house, but Paul wasn't at the window watching us. And so what if he was? This pull between me and her—I was almost certain I wasn't imagining it. Her eyes were always on me when the four of us ate dinner at the same table, like she couldn't tear them away. She laughed at every joke I made, even the throwaway quips that I didn't think were all that funny, the dimple in her cheek deepening in a way it never did for Paul. She often folded my clothes after I forgot them in the dryer and left them on my bed in neat squares; it made my face warm to think of her touching the things I wore, the ones closest to my skin. And whenever the two of us ventured out together, her hand, her hand—it slipped right into mine, like magnets clicking into place. Like a ship coming home.

In the faint glow of the lanterns in the garden, holding Sophia's hand, I felt something swell inside me. I straightened up. "Let's send those letters," I said.

"Are you sure?"

"I mean, why not? We already did all this work. The least we can do is mentally scar all the partners with these close-up shots of his crooked dick. Create some core memories for these assholes."

Sophia laughed, and I said, "But also, don't be surprised if . . . well, you know. If nothing happens. If they keep protecting Gene. It's like he's this little cockroach. He's indestructible."

"I don't know," Sophia said. "I don't think anyone is indestructible."

She shifted on the bench, and the next thing I knew, there was a gentle weight on my shoulder. Her frizzy hair was tickling my nose. I felt the heave of her body as she breathed in and out, soft and slow. I sat still, holding my breath, afraid that if I so much as moved a muscle, it would startle her into flight, into flittering away like a bird. I felt Sophia yawn against my shoulder.

"I don't want you to worry too much about this, all right?" she said. "Focus on your new job. There's going to be another way to take him down. Trust me—we'll find it."

Getting hired at Meek LeClerc was a walk in the park by comparison.

Three days after the interview, Crista, the head of HR, had called me with the offer. Junior designer, health, dental, vision, 401(k), partial public transit stipend, a salary at the lowest end of the band. I'd countered with $45,000, and Crista had come back with $43,000. That was when I signed the contract. I started working there a week later.

The creative team shared an enclosed studio space in one of the sunniest corners of the office, and the décor was corporate meets a twelve-year-old's dream bedroom: There were beanbags, whiteboards, a box full of stage props, pool noodles, candy jars, paper and markers in every shade, *Star Wars* figurines, green screens, $5,000 DSLR cameras, and rude caricatures that Pedro, one of the other designers, had drawn of every one of us, even me. When Jay, who sat at the back of the room, made a cheesy joke or an obscure pop culture reference, the rest of us threw paper clips at him. People from other teams would wander into the creative studio to say hi and end up lingering for minutes, clearly unwilling to go back to their uninspired desk jobs. We were a respite. A place in the woods where you could play like a kid again.

I'd been surprised when Radha, the receptionist, popped her head into the studio at the end of my first day. "Yo," she said. "Finnegan's in fifteen minutes. Who's coming?"

Josh was. So were Pedro and Erkin and CJ. Radha's eyes turned to me, and she said, "You're coming, too, right, Erin?"

I hesitated, and she said, "Don't worry, the vibe is super chill. We just sit at a table and drink and bitch about work."

From his corner, Jay said, "I'll pretend I didn't just hear that."

The drinks at Finnegan's took place every two or three days: same place, same time, the same cast of childless, shittily paid, mildly depressed Meek LeClerc staffers guzzling cheap beers around the same table and gossiping about who in the office had the most psychotic client, who was faking their childcare emergencies, whose head was on the proverbial chopping block. Radha was the ringleader, and the second time I'd joined, she had grabbed my arm across the table and said, her words slurring slightly, "I am so, so glad you're here."

"Oh, same," I said. "This place is dope."

Radha shook her head. "Not here," she said, and she pointed behind her, in a direction I understood to be Meek LeClerc. "There. I put in a good word for you, you know."

"What do you mean?"

She smiled conspiratorially. "They always ask me afterwards what I think about the people who come in to interview. The receptionist sees all, you know? It's my hidden power. Anyways, A, you were super nice to me. And B—" She glanced around the table and made a face. "I had to help a sister out. There's way too many pasty white guys working here already."

Josh, Pedro, and CJ all made indignant noises. "On behalf of pasty white guys everywhere," Josh said, "I actually find that incredibly triggering."

"Oh, shut the fuck up," Radha said, and everyone had laughed.

I had spent the month leading up to my first day neck-deep in Adobe tutorials, desperately cramming my brain with text frames and anchor points and clipping masks the same way I had studied for the LSAT. I blew through a thirty-day Introduction to Design boot camp in just four days. Though I now technically possessed the skill set, I had little confidence in my abilities: Sophia was the one who had created my design portfolio from scratch, infusing it with a level of skill that was impressive for a junior designer with limited experience, but not so mind-blowing that I could have bagged a job at a more prestigious agency like Grey or BBDO. But Sophia had reassured me. "The good thing about being a graphic designer," she'd said, "is that you get to be a dragon."

I laughed. "A dragon?"

She said, "Once you're on the job, you'll be largely left alone. Most designers are fickle creatures who prefer to work independently. We guard our work jealously until we feel it's ready to be shown to the art director. So this is what I want you to do: As soon as you are given a project that is too hard, something that exceeds your current skill level, send it to me, and I'll work on it for you. The only task you have to perform in front of others is the small adjustments: changing the color of a box, moving a subheading to the next line. Anything bigger, you'll say, *This is going to take some time to get right.* And then you give it to me."

My first project was the creation of Facebook ads for a moderately well-known apparel company, a package of ten banners featuring different slogans and products. I'd spent hours studying the branding guidelines, going through comp after comp before throwing everything out and starting again. When the time finally came to show Jay the designs on my iMac screen, I felt sick to my stomach, scrolling through the art file slowly. I waited for him to unload on me.

Instead, I heard Jay say, "These are good."

I almost didn't believe him. I whipped my head around, fast. "Are you serious?"

"For sure," Jay said, and he pointed at one of the banners. "This one needs some tweaks; the text is getting lost against the photo backdrop. But overall, really solid. Nice work, Erin."

Jay walked away, and I sat there, quiet, disbelieving, staring at my reflection in the now darkened screen. I saw Erin: her long hair, her glasses, her face blossoming into a tentative smile. Shelley Hu had been an imposter. Erin Callaghan, on the other hand, had proved herself worthy.

For her traditional getting-to-know-you lunch with new hires, Amy Cloverfield took me to a cozy French-inspired bistro a few blocks from the office.

In the lobby, as we waited to be seated, she said, "And the thing is, even though Skechers has awarded the bulk of their traditional comms work to Flickerman in the past, with this new digital marketing contract, believe it or not, we're in a very interesting position to be competing for it."

She looked at me. "What do you know about Flickerman's digital marketing capabilities?"

"Uh," I said, "nothing, really."

She clapped her hands at me. "Precisely. Precisely! Digital marketing is not in their wheelhouse. They don't have the years and years of case studies that we can point to and say, *This is how you reach your target online audience. This is how you get your message seen on Twitter for two cents per eyeball.*"

As the hostess led us to the table, I said, "You know, I would actually love to do more to support the work around the Skechers pitch, if . . . you know, if you think that would be helpful."

Amy smiled at me benevolently. "Really? You would?"

"Yeah, absolutely. I'd love to learn more about how we put together pitches to potential clients. How we craft narratives that win them over. There's so much that I want to learn from you, personally. Not to be cheesy, but as a woman in advertising, you're a huge inspiration for me."

Then I said, "I have a small gift for you, actually. If that's okay."

From my bag, I took out a long, thin green tube, about thirteen inches in length. I removed the cap and handed the tube to Amy, who peered inside, feeling for the contents with two fingers. She drew it out and unfurled it slowly.

"Oh," she said. And then: "Oh, it's beautiful."

It was a traditional Chinese landscape painting, created entirely in ink and water. At the heart of the painting was a vast, sprawling lake; with a few expert strokes of a brush, the artist had given life to the morning mist rising from its calm waters. In the distance, a flock of cranes flew above snow-capped mountains, their faint shadows disappearing into the clouds. Sophia had truly outdone herself. Amy Cloverfield was undeniably impressed.

"I got this from a Buddhist temple the last time I was in China," I said. "It represents the Chinese concept of serenity. Of becoming one with your chi so that you can access your inner peace."

"Oh, I just love that," Amy said. "I've been saying for years that I need to get into Eastern meditation. Especially with these turbulent times we're living in—if you don't have your mental health, then you don't have anything, you know?"

She was still gazing at the painting when I said, "The thing is, I know you took a chance on me."

"What makes you say that?"

"I mean, I know I don't have the most stellar portfolio. I haven't worked for any impressive clients. You probably interviewed tons of other candidates who were much more qualified for the job, but you picked *me*." I met her eyes. "And for that, I couldn't be more grateful. Truly."

I saw Amy's face soften. Carefully, she rolled up the painting and returned it to the tube. Then she laid a hand on my arm, and I saw her nails. Pearly pink, translucent.

"I will always, *always* be a fierce champion for women of color," she said. "As the mother of a minority daughter, I've always said that we need to work proactively to open doors for girls like her and hold a seat for them at the table. You can thank me by paying it forward to others like you."

Then she picked up her phone. "I'm going to send Jess a text now before I forget, asking her to add you to the invite for the pitch strategy meeting on Tuesday. How does that sound?"

"It sounds perfect," I said.

I waited for Amy to finish typing on her phone. Then I said, "And in the meantime, if there's anything I could prepare, anything I could do that could make your day easier, please don't hesitate to let me know. Seriously."

I put both of my hands on the table, a good little supplicant. I smiled. I looked into her eyes.

In the subway car, Amy Cloverfield had stopped talking the moment I began to unbutton my shirt. By the time I had stripped off my bra, her brash, pissy attitude had vanished. My antics had unmoored her. She was frightened. She took a step back, and then another, her burgundy pants swishing from the movement. And yet she couldn't look away. She stared into my eyes as I sank to my knees. She stared into my eyes as I began to wail.

What do you want from me?
What do you want from me?
What do you want from me?

Take it. And I flung my bra at her feet, and she did a little tap dance to avoid it. *Take it. Take everything that I have. Everything belongs to you. Take it!*

And then my voice had risen into a bloodcurdling scream.

Cunt!
Cunt!
CUNT!

In the bistro, Amy Cloverfield looked into my eyes for three seconds. Five seconds. I wondered, briefly, if this was it. This was the moment she would see me for who I really was.

She smiled. "I have an idea," she said. "What are you doing tonight after work?"

- THE PLANS I HAVE FOR YOU -

In the office bathroom, I zipped up the back of Amy's royal-blue sheath dress, carefully picking her stray hairs out of the way. It was a quarter to seven and we would almost certainly be late to the New York Women in PR charity gala; I'd spent the last fifteen minutes watching her curl her hair before deciding to straighten it again. Her hair had grown longer in the eight months since I'd met her on the subway. It seemed thinner now. A little more on the ashy side of brown.

As she powdered her face in the mirror, Amy said, "You know, you're a champ for doing this. Normally it would be my daughter going as my plus-one, but she's a teenager, so . . . you know. Too cool to be seen in public with Mom."

I laughed. "I remember going through that phase with my mom. How old is your daughter?"

"Eighteen. She's starting at NYU in the fall."

"It's great that she's staying in New York."

"We're so close." Amy looked at me and smiled. "You know what my daughter calls us? She says we're the Gilmore Girls. Because it's just me and her. The two of us against the world."

I felt something unexpected rise in my throat. I swallowed.

"I know what that's like," I said. "My dad passed away when I was a kid. After that, it was just me and my mom."

Softly, Amy said, "I'm so sorry."

She placed a hand on my arm, and I couldn't look at her. I just kept my eyes down and nodded. "Thanks."

We were both quiet for a moment. Amy said, "You know, I've always felt—ever since the day I met her—that my daughter is the singular great joy of my life. I know your mother must feel the same way about you."

Back in Kissimmee, one day in 1999, I'd been bad. I had acted up in class, or maybe I'd failed a math quiz. All I remembered was that the following Saturday, instead of leaving me with Mrs. Alvarez, my mom took me with her to work at the motel, and she made me watch her clean every room, change every bedsheet, scrub every toilet. *Look at this*, she'd hissed, prodding me in the ribs until it hurt. *Look how hard Mama has to work to be able to provide for you. Is this what you want? Do you want to do this, too, when you grow up? Maybe I should just send you to China. Make you go to school there, compete with millions of other kids for universities, jobs, opportunities. See how you'll like it then.*

And in my mind, I saw her again: picking me up from the airport in Orlando, her back hunched in a way I'd never noticed before, wordlessly closing the lid of the trunk over my suitcases, my broken New York dreams. I'd been so deeply mired in my own misery that I'd barely registered her hair, how it had seemed to turn gray and white overnight. In the car, my mom had said, *I made your favorite sweet-and-sour fish for dinner*, and I had burst into tears. *I'm so sorry*, I remembered telling her through my wails. *I'm so sorry, Ma.*

That day in the car, she hadn't told me that it was all right, that I was forgiven. She had simply put her hands on the wheel and driven me home.

As I looked at Amy Cloverfield, I remembered that it had been almost two weeks since the last time I'd talked to my mom. She had called twice and sent texts earlier that day (*Nothing urgent, just call me back when you can*), but I had been so busy that I'd left them unanswered.

I swallowed again, and there was a prickling sensation in my nose.

"You're right," I said. "She does."

SOYOUNG

October 2004

The best thing about living with Stella Cheung was that Soyoung did not have to steal her food.

Stella shared everything. If she had a pack of Twizzlers, she gave half to Soyoung. If she had one choco pie, they split it down the middle. Once, late at night, Stella bought a chicken sandwich and fries from a diner and carried it back to their room, where she stared at them from her bed. Then she'd turned to Soyoung, who was studying on her bed, and said, "Here, you eat it."

Soyoung looked up. "What? Why?"

"I can't," Stella said, and she began to bite at her fingernails. "I shouldn't have bought it. It's after ten o'clock. If I eat after ten, the calories go straight to my thighs. That's what all the research says. I should've stopped myself."

Then she said, "Look, if you don't eat it, I'm going to take it to the kitchen and dump it in the trash."

There was a pause, and Soyoung said, "Jeez, all right. I'll take it."

A month had passed since her induction into the fellowship, and the strength of her devotion had continued to grow. She now slept with a New Living Translation Bible on her bedside table, one that was filled with Post-it Notes marking her favorite passages about faith in times of adversity. She bowed her head and said a prayer before every meal, even the rubbery sandwiches she got on a discount from the convenience store. Even Paul had, despite his disdain towards organized religion, continued to attend the fellowship alongside her each week. Strange faces in the crowd morphed into friends; Paul began playing pickup basketball with a few of the guys, and when Stella's aunt visited from Hong Kong and took a group of girls out for lunch at an upscale restaurant, Soyoung was invited. One evening in October, Pastor Jeremy and a couple of the grad students packed as many people as could fit into their cars, and they drove to a popular Korean barbecue joint in upstate New York. In the car, space had been so tight that Soyoung and Paul had sat with their thighs pressed against one another. Neither of them spoke for the duration of the car ride, and at the restaurant, Paul had used the scissors to cut up Soyoung's meat before he did his own.

That night, as they changed into their pajamas, Stella said, "So what's the deal with you and Paul?"

"What do you mean?"

"Oh, don't look all innocent," Stella said. "It's so obvious from where I'm sitting. Paul is *into* you. It's the same dynamic Nathaniel and I had when we first started dating."

She said this with such an air of authority that it made Soyoung laugh. She said, "How long have you two been together, anyway?"

"One year, one month, and almost two weeks. He asked me out two weeks into my freshman year."

Stella's nightgown was pale lavender, with tiny white daisies stitched throughout. Soyoung said, "You didn't think he was a little too old, maybe?"

"I like that he's older," Stella said. "He's more knowledgeable about things."

She sat down on her bed, opposite Soyoung, and began brushing her hair. After a while, she said, "You know, he's really helped me a lot with my weight."

Soyoung looked up. Stella said, "Everybody in my family called me Fatty, growing up. Fatty, Fat Girl, Fat Sister. And then at school, none of the guys I liked ever liked me back. They only liked the girls that were skinny, like models. And my dad was always like, *You know, if you want to be a doctor, you're going to have to be skinny. Nobody wants to be treated by a fat doctor.* And I tried going on so many diets, but every time, I would lose control, and I would end up eating even more than I was eating before. I thought nothing good would ever happen to me, ever."

She was sniffling now. Soyoung went to sit by Stella and rubbed her back. Stella blew her nose into a tissue.

"And when I came to the fellowship, my very first meeting, I met Nathaniel. He was so kind to me, Soyoung, you don't even know. When I talked to him, I could tell that he genuinely listened. And when we started going out, he would always tell me, *Other guys are too vain and immature to appreciate somebody like you, but I'm not. I see how beautiful you are on the inside.* He really showed me what it means to love each other like God loves us. He helped me come up with a diet and exercise plan, and he's talked me out of so many late-night cravings. He tells me I'm going to be so, so beautiful when I reach a hundred and twenty pounds, he can already see it." Stella shook her head and laughed. "I know he's just saying that because he's my boyfriend, but I'm so excited. I can't wait to become the most beautiful version of myself for him. He deserves it."

Soyoung, still stroking Stella's back, said nothing. Stella blew her nose again before she lowered her voice.

"I'm going to tell you a secret, but you can't tell anyone, okay? I'm dead serious."

"I won't tell," Soyoung said. "I promise."

Stella nodded. Her face had become flushed, a dreamy shade of carnation pink.

"When I get down to a hundred and twenty . . . we're going to do it."

There was a pause. Slowly, Soyoung turned her head to look at Stella. "Do it?"

"Yeah. You know. Do it."

"You haven't done it already?"

Stella's eyes widened. "No, of course not! The church says we're supposed to wait. But I already know in my heart he's the one, Soyoung. We're going to get married one day, so it's only a matter of sooner or later. Jesus would forgive us for that, right?"

Then she said, "Wait, have *you* done it?"

Soyoung blinked; then she shook her head. A grin began spreading across Stella's face.

"Would you do it with Paul?"

Soyoung withdrew her hand from Stella's back. She said, "It's not what you think. I don't see him that way."

Stella pursed her lips. After a moment, she said, "Yeah, I see what you mean. He's kind of odd, isn't he?"

"Odd?"

"He's just so quiet. I feel like I've only ever heard him say two sentences. Honestly, if he weren't hanging around you all the time, I'd forget that he even existed." Stella laughed, suddenly self-conscious. "Wait, was that too mean?"

Soyoung stood up. Her insides were suddenly chafing with a quiet anger, an instinctive defensiveness, and it was then that she said it, the thing that had been burning inside her for weeks now. "Stella, Nathaniel is . . . he's a jerk. You deserve better."

She expected Stella to freeze. To erupt in anger, even. But Stella just laughed. "A jerk? What are you talking about?"

"He's not a nice person," Soyoung said. "He—he said—"

She fumbled for a moment, at a loss for words. Finally, she said, "He's too old for you."

"I'm nineteen," Stella said. "I'm an adult."

"What about what he said about the way you look? He's forcing you to lose weight."

"Soyoung, he's not forcing me to do anything. I'm the one who wants to lose weight."

Soyoung was silent, and Stella sighed. "Look, I get it," she said. "You're just trying to look out for me. But you don't know what it's like,

Soyoung—spending your whole life in a corner, knowing that no one will ever see you, no one will ever want you. He *sees* me, Soyoung. He sees me when no one else does."

For weeks now, Soyoung had been picking up after Stella in their room, returning her misplaced shoes to the rack, hanging up discarded clothes in her closet. She wiped down Stella's writing desk and organized her pens and notebooks, and after Stella accidentally left a red T-shirt in the wash with her white sheets, Soyoung took over her laundry, too, washing and drying and folding her clothes with the same care she imagined wrapping around her hypothetical children one day. She learned every song by Stella's favorite singer, the Singaporean Mandopop sensation, and they spent hours listening and relistening to his latest album on Stella's MP3 player, each wearing one earbud. At night, whenever Stella kicked in her sleep and her comforter slipped off the bed, Soyoung retrieved it and tucked it back around her. Stella often talked in her sleep while hugging her stuffed animals. "Ugh, no, Mom," Soyoung once heard her say, "I do not want cap sleeves on my prom dress." And another time: "There's a test? We have a test right now? But I forgot to study!"

As they looked at each other, Soyoung swallowed the lump in her throat.

"I see you, though," she said. "I see you every day. And I think you're perfect just the way you are."

When Stella smiled, her face was lined with sadness.

She said, "Oh, what I wouldn't have killed for a guy to have said that to me in high school."

In late October, for its annual off-campus retreat, the fellowship drove across the border into Vermont, where they'd rented a campsite of wooden yurts on the outskirts of a flaming maple forest. In one of the women's yurts, Stella and Soyoung set down their bags on adjacent beds. "I'll be watching you," Stella said. "No sneaking out at night to meet Paul."

"Ha ha," Soyoung said. "You're hilarious."

Weeks had passed since the first time Soyoung and Paul stood under the streetlight, and days since they'd sat next to each other in the car ride to the barbecue restaurant, yet they still had not kissed, nor had they attempted to define the terms of their relationship. Paul continued to wait for her outside the convenience shop every night she was on shift, and often, when Soyoung looked up from a deep quagmire of thought, she found him watching her quietly with a softness in his eyes. So much had been left unsaid between them; whether any of it was implicitly understood was another matter entirely.

As they walked to the main lodge, where Pastor Jeremy and a few of the students were already setting up for dinner, Stella said, "Seriously, though, a lot of *interesting* things happen at this retreat every year."

She wriggled her eyebrows at Soyoung, who said, "Like what?"

"Oh, you know. Something about being out in the woods, away from campus. People have been known to get a little frisky out here at night. That's all I'm saying."

Soyoung looked at Stella then. She said, "What's going on with you?"

Stella blushed. She beckoned at Soyoung, who leaned in, and whispered, "I just weighed myself this morning. I'm at a hundred and twenty exactly."

After Soyoung had filled her plate, she found Paul outside, sitting on a tree stump near the campfire and staring into his own plate of food. "Hi," she said, and Paul moved to make room for her. They sat together on the stump, their thighs touching, her body almost leaning against his. The sky was a brilliant canvas of crimson and gold; a few feet away, people were already roasting marshmallows on the fire.

Soyoung said, "So what are you doing tonight?"

"Nothing much."

"Do you want to hang out after Bible study? We could go for a walk in the woods."

There was a pause.

Paul said, "I can't. There's . . . there's something I have to do. I have to meet someone."

He was not looking at her. "Oh," Soyoung said.

And then: "Right. No, of course."

As dinner transitioned into the evening's worship session and Bible study, Soyoung watched as Paul withdrew even further into himself, staring at his shoes while the others sang and laughed and cried and threw their hands in the air. More than once, she glanced towards the worship team and saw Nathaniel watching her, an almost taunting look in his eye as he sang her favorite song.

Finally, Bible study came to a close, and Soyoung stood up abruptly. "I'm going to bed," she said.

Back in the yurt, she took off her white peacoat and put on Stella's black North Face jacket. It was now completely dark; the only lights in the campsite were the fire and the lanterns along the paths leading to the yurts. After Soyoung had made a large, meandering loop around the campsite, she parked herself behind a large maple tree, from which she could see Paul sitting on the tree stump, still and alone. A group of people called out to him, invited him to join in a game of cards in their yurt, but he just shook his head. Soyoung waited.

Finally, Paul got up. She tailed him all the way to the main lodge, where a dim light had come on. Paul entered the lodge and closed the door behind him. As Soyoung pressed an ear to the window, she heard a voice say, "Hey, Paul."

It was Pastor Jeremy. Paul said, "Is this still a good time?"

"It is an excellent time. Come in, my man, come in."

The floorboards creaked under Paul's feet as Soyoung scurried to the next window, which was open by a sliver. The table of food and drinks from dinner had been cleared and folded away; there were now two chairs set up in the middle of the lodge, facing one another. "Take a seat," Pastor Jeremy said, and Paul obliged.

"So," Pastor Jeremy said, "halfway through your first semester. How are you finding things? Classes going well?"

"Yeah."

"Starting to know your way around campus?"

"Yeah. Pretty much."

"The campus is beautiful," Pastor Jeremy said. "You know, I read somewhere that the Cornell campus was voted the most—"

That was when Paul made a small, yelping, wretched sound, like an animal that had been trampled on. Pastor Jeremy looked startled, and outside the window, Soyoung felt her breath catch in her throat. Paul buried his face in his sleeve. His entire body was shaking.

"Sorry," he managed to say, after a moment. "Sorry. Sorry. Sorry."

Pastor Jeremy leaned forward.

"It's okay," he said, his voice gentle. "It's okay, bud. Hey, no need to be sorry. You're doing great."

There was a box of tissues behind Pastor Jeremy, and he offered it to Paul, who took a handful. As Paul blew his nose, still trembling, Soyoung got a good look at his face for the first time: It was red and blotchy. His eyes were squeezed shut.

When Paul spoke again, his voice was hoarse. "I'm a piece of shit," he said.

Quietly, Pastor Jeremy said, "What makes you say that, Paul?"

"Because I left my mom back in Baltimore."

"We all leave our parents at some point," Pastor Jeremy said. "All of us, there comes a time when we have to leave the nest and fly free. It's a part of life."

Paul nodded, and then he shook his head. His face was filled with despair. "I left her all by herself with my stepdad," he said. "He beats her."

For the first time, Pastor Jeremy was at a loss for words.

Paul said, thickly, "He's been hitting her since I was a kid. He was so tall back then, I couldn't stop him. All I could do was scream and cry. I used to get on my knees and beg her to leave him. She wouldn't. She said she had to stay for me, even though I didn't want that. And then... and then I grew up, and I got taller than him, but I still can't stop him.

I've called the cops, and every time, she forgave him. Once he broke her collarbone and put her in the hospital. I talked to the nurses there, begged them to help her. She still took him back. So I . . . I gave up. I left her back there with him."

He was crying so hard now that his words were barely more than gasps and sputters. Outside, Soyoung's eyes had also filled with tears. She watched as Pastor Jeremy considered the box of tissues in his hands; after a moment, he handed the whole thing to Paul, who went through half of the box, crumpling the wet tissues in his hands.

When he had finally stopped crying, he looked up at Pastor Jeremy. "I have a question."

"Of course."

"My mom's a Christian," Paul said. "She goes to church every Sunday. Prays to Jesus every day. If he's real, why doesn't he protect her? Why does he let this happen to her?"

There was a pause. Pastor Jeremy said, "First of all, let me say that I'm very sorry to hear about your mom. It's not right, what's happening. It's . . . it's terrible."

"So why does he let it happen?"

Pastor Jeremy sighed deeply.

"Look," he said, "I can't profess to know the intricate workings of God. I don't pretend to. There are a lot of things—a lot of terrible things in this world that should not happen, but they do. And as humans, because we can only see the limits of what is shown to us, it's natural for us to ask why. It's natural for us to look for reason, to look for a deeper—"

Paul cut him off. "Are you saying that everything happens for a reason?"

"Well, I'm saying, rather, that God doesn't always work in ways we understand."

Paul shook his head. "I don't get it," he said flatly.

"That's the whole point," Pastor Jeremy said. "We don't get it. Much of the time—most of the time, I would even say—we experience the things that happen to us without understanding why. Why was I born into this family in this part of the world when I was? Why does one person get to grow up in peace while another person suffers through war? And when we ask why, we find that the answer, in one form or another, always leads back to God. From where we're standing, all we can see is one small piece of the sky. But God is greater than the entirety of the universe. His love for us, the plans He has in store for us—it's greater than anything we'll ever be able to understand. And knowing that is, in its own way, a great form of comfort."

He patted Paul on the knee. "And you know what we call that? Faith."

Then he said, "Why don't we pray together for your mother? We can pray for her healing. Pray for her comfort. Pray for her protection during this time that you are away from her."

By the time Paul emerged from the lodge, the campfire had died, leaving behind a circle of blackened cinder. In the distance, people had already begun washing up for bed; there were shrieks of laughter as the cold water from the outdoor faucets chilled their fingers and faces. For a moment, Paul just stood there, taking it all in. Then, with a heavy sigh, he began to walk towards the yurts, and Soyoung ran up to him, breathless. "Paul. Paul, wait."

Under the moonlight, they looked at each other. "What are you doing here?" Paul asked.

"I . . ." Soyoung began, and trailed off. Finally, she said, "I overheard. I'm sorry."

"You overheard?"

"Your conversation with Pastor Jeremy. I'm so sorry for intruding, Paul. I just—I wanted to make sure you were okay."

She saw Paul's eyes widen, but she pressed on. "The thing is, I'm sorry for everything that's happened. But what you need to understand is that you're free now. Don't you see? You got into Cornell on a full-ride scholarship. You're going to work on Wall Street one day and make seven figures. You can put that old life behind you. You can let it go."

But Paul was already shaking his head.

"You have no idea what it's like," he said. "I can't just let it go. My mom is there all by herself. The fact that I can't be there to protect her—"

"What about her? Wasn't she supposed to protect you, too?"

Paul was silent, and Soyoung said, "I'm sorry your stepdad is abusing her. I really am. But at what point is she going to shoulder some of the responsibility here? She married him. She *stayed* married to him. She put both of you in this situation. The trauma that she has allowed him to inflict on you—"

"Don't talk about my mom," Paul said. His breathing had become ragged, shallow. "You have no idea what it's like for her. You have no idea."

"Enlighten me, then. What's stopping her from leaving? I'd like to know."

"You think it's that easy to leave? To just pack your bags and walk out the door? My mom doesn't work. She's spent her whole life taking care of our home, taking care of me. If she left, where would she go? What would she do? She has no money. She has no skills. I'm her only way out. I have to provide for her. I have to protect her. That's the whole reason why I'm at Cornell, why I'm studying econ, why I have to do what I do. It's all for her."

Soyoung shrugged.

"No, I get it," she said. "You're her golden ticket. You're an investment she made eighteen years ago, and she's waiting for the day she can finally cash you out."

Paul's eyes flashed.

Coldly, he said, "You know, Soyoung, sometimes you're really not as smart as you think you are. You don't know anything about my mom. You don't know anything about me. So you should stop pretending to understand things you know nothing about, because it just makes you look foolish."

Soyoung blinked. She said nothing.

A long moment passed.

Paul looked down. He said, "I'm sorry. I—I didn't mean that."

"No," Soyoung said. Her voice was unnaturally high. "No, of course not."

Then she said, "I'm really sorry I listened to your conversation. Have a . . . have a good night, Paul."

"Soyoung," Paul began, but she had already begun to run.

The leaves in the forest were rustling as Soyoung veered off the marked trail. Her face was wet with tears; with every step, she sniffed and hugged her arms closer to her chest. Above her, the moon had lost its luster. Behind her, a figure had been following her for minutes now, a trail of dead leaves crunching quietly under its feet as it maintained a steady distance between them. Oh, but what did it matter? She turned, finally, to see Nathaniel Lee grinning at her, his teeth flashing white in the darkness.

She said, "What are you doing?"

"Watching over your safety," Nathaniel said. He seemed completely unabashed. "You don't know what's out here in these woods."

"*You're* what's out here."

Nathaniel laughed. He stepped forward, and Soyoung felt her muscles grow tense, her hands clench. "Is that Stella's jacket?" he said.

"She let me borrow it."

"It looks better on you."

"You're disgusting," she said, and he laughed.

"Perhaps," he said, "but what about you?"

"What do you want?"

"I know your secret," Nathaniel said. "That pesky little problem you've been hiding all semester? I've finally figured it out."

"I have no idea what you're talking about."

That was when he said it: "I know you're not really a student."

Soyoung's heart had been pounding; in that moment, it stood suddenly still, and she felt a coldness seep down her arms and into her fingers. She swallowed and said, a second time, "I have no idea what you're talking about."

"Tell me, then," Nathaniel said, "why can't I find you in the email system? Why can't I find you in the university directory?"

"You can. You just didn't look hard enough."

"I talked to Lillian Pietrowski."

"She's a liar," Soyoung said, and she could hear the tremor in her voice. "She has an agenda. She only kicked me out because she's a racist."

"I think that's for Stella to decide. Wouldn't you agree?"

At this, Soyoung felt the air go out of her. Nathaniel took another two steps towards her, and she stayed rooted to the spot, frozen. They were now so close that she could feel his breath on her face, see the faint stubble dotting his chin.

"Don't worry, though," Nathaniel said. His voice was low and calming, in a way that was almost pleasant. "I won't tell Stella a word."

"Why wouldn't you?"

"Because I want to help you."

The statement was so absurd that Soyoung almost laughed. She remained silent, and she heard Nathaniel say, "How much an hour are you making, working at that little store? Can't be very much. How are you getting by on food? Textbooks? Basic necessities? What are you going to do for housing when Stella's roommate comes back from study abroad? Because she's coming back from Berlin next semester. You won't have a place to stay come mid-January."

His hand brushed against her cheek, and Soyoung shivered. "The thing is, though," he said, "I get it. I get why you've done what you've done. I have Asian parents, too. Probably just as insane as yours. If I hadn't gotten in, I don't know what I would've done, truthfully. Maybe I would've done the same thing. Who's to say?"

His thumb was under her chin; he now applied a bit of pressure, and her face tilted up to meet his. Halfway to kissing her, though, Nathaniel stopped.

"Look at you," he said, sounding amused. "Look at that face. What did you think I was going to do to you? Good God."

Soyoung said nothing, and Nathaniel let go of her chin. He stepped back.

"Don't worry," he said. "Your secret's safe with me. I won't tell anyone. Not Stella. Not Paul. No one needs to know but us."

He reached into his pocket and handed her a yellow Post-it Note. On it, an address was written in ballpoint pen.

"My apartment off campus," Nathaniel said. "Swing by when you get the chance, and we can figure out what to do. I meant what I said, Soyoung—let me help you. You're going to need it."

SOYOUNG

It was demented that Soyoung had taken so much time to pick out an outfit, but she had. Over a long-sleeved shirt, she put on a cream sweater with heart-shaped buttons, which she paired with jeans and her usual white tennis shoes. She pulled her hair into a ponytail and left her face bare. From her desk, Stella said, "Do you think we should join the newspaper?"

"What?"

Stella nodded at her open laptop. "The student newspaper's holding an open house on Thursday afternoon. Should we go? I've been thinking it might be fun to try to do some writing. And you take really good photos."

"Sure," Soyoung said. "Let's go on Thursday."

It was already dark by the time she set out across the grass, a long, singular shadow dragging behind her. About four blocks off campus, at the end of a small, quiet street, she found what she was looking for: a redbrick apartment building with only three units. The sign on the door of the ground unit announced itself as apartment 1A; next to it, behind the linen drapes on the window, she could see the bluish glow of a television screen.

Soyoung took a deep breath before she rang the bell.

The door swung open, flooding her with warm light and the distant voices of sports announcers. Nathaniel stood there, blinking at her, and then he smiled. "Well, hey! Come in, come in."

He stood aside to let her in, and Soyoung said, "Are you busy?"

"Not at all. Just watching the game and grading papers. You came at the perfect time."

As Nathaniel closed the door behind her, Soyoung hugged her sweater close to her and looked around. The place was small but neatly kept. There was a dining table and two matching chairs. The couch and coffee table barely fit between the bed and the television, and on the table were a stack of exams, a red pen, and a glass of what looked to be whiskey. "Can I get you a drink?" she heard him ask.

Soyoung pointed at the glass. "I'll have that."

He poured some whiskey into another glass and handed it to her, the shallow amber liquid swishing inside. Without hesitation, Soyoung threw her head back and downed the whole thing. She coughed a few times, and Nathaniel laughed. "Pace yourself there. That stuff is strong. You want anything else?"

Soyoung ignored him. She took another deep breath; then she walked to the bed and sat down on it. There, looking directly at him, she unbuttoned her sweater and peeled it off. Next, she took off the shirt underneath. The last thing to go was her bra. She sat there, silent, watching him.

Softly, Nathaniel said, "You're not one for mincing words, huh?"

Soyoung smiled, slowly, coldly.

She said, "You know, if you just owned up to it, I'd actually have some respect for you."

After, Soyoung took a long shower in Nathaniel's bathroom, and when she emerged, her hair still dripping, the vent fan was whirring in the kitchen, the apartment was filled with the aroma of butter and fish and roasted vegetables, and Nathaniel was standing by the dining table, setting down plates.

"Hey," he said, noticing her in the doorway, "grab a chair. Dinner's ready."

For a long time, Soyoung stood on the spot, not moving.

Then, wordlessly, she walked over to the table and took a seat. She picked up a fork and began to eat.

ERIN

March 2017

By the time I got home from the gala, my mom had called another three times. I decided to call her back from my bathroom, unclipping my wig from the wig cap as the phone dialed, and she picked up on the second ring. "Hey," I said. "Everything okay?"

"I'm fine," my mom said. There was some shuffling in the background, and she said, "What are you up to?"

"I just got back from a work event. I'm at home now."

"You're still staying with that girl, Sophia?"

"Yeah."

My mom said, "It's been two months already. You don't think she's getting tired of hosting you for that long?"

"No," I said, and I heard the curtness in my voice. My mom always had a way of bringing out that side of me within seconds. I said, "If there's nothing else, I'm going to go. I have some work to catch up on."

"There's just one thing," my mom said.

I waited for several seconds before she said, "Your little aunt passed away last night."

It was a testament to how rarely I saw or even thought of what remained of my mom's family that it took me a moment to remember who Little Aunt was. My mom's sister, the youngest of three, the long-suffering cancer patient. Second Aunt was still alive, presumably.

"Oh, Ma," I said. "That's terrible. I'm so sorry."

On the other end, my mom was quiet. She said, "Her cancer came back. She went very quickly."

"Are you going back to China?"

"For the funeral? I've already missed it. They buried her today."

"Seriously? That seems really fast."

My mom said, "She had a Muslim burial in a cemetery that's only open to Hui people. They had to do it within twenty-four hours, according to their religion."

"Well, even if you've missed the funeral, you should still go. You could spend some time with Second Aunt. See the rest of the family."

"The plane ticket's too expensive," my mom said. "And anyway, your second aunt has her hands full with your cousin's new baby. There's no guest room at her apartment for me to stay in, so I'd just be an inconvenience."

Then she said, "I was just calling to let you know. That was all."

After I hung up with my mom, I stood in the bathroom for a while, absentmindedly massaging my scalp. Then I went back into my room in search of my phone charger. That was when something caught my eye, something small but jarring, and it took me a moment to clock what it was: The black-and-white photo of my dad that I'd left face up on a pile of books was now standing upright in its frame.

Someone had moved the photo.

Chills crept up my back as I paced the rest of the room, hunting for other hints of disturbance. The bed looked normal. I went through each of the desk drawers carefully, examining my scrapped design mock-ups, my health insurance booklet, even my CVS receipts for signs that they'd been tampered with. There was no sensitive information in the drawers. Of course I didn't keep a journal or any written records of the plan; Sophia had warned me from day one.

There were no other signs. I exhaled, frustrated, on edge.

Then I remembered something.

In the living room, Paul was on a late work call; he was silent as a droning man's voice spilled out of the speakerphone. I circled around to the other side of the house so that he wouldn't see me tiptoeing up the stairs. The door to Sophia's studio was half closed. I could see her profile in front of the iMac, staring intently at the screen.

In Ory's room, I found him belly down on the carpet, playing with action figures and plastic dinosaurs. "Hey, buddy," I said, and Ory looked up. "Is it cool if I play with you?"

He nodded. I got down on my elbows and took in the scene: He had arranged the action figures in a single-line formation, while the dinosaurs looked on from the other side. "What's happening here?"

"They're enemies," Ory said. "They're getting ready to fight."

He handed me a green triceratops. "You can take him. He's not as strong as MightyMan, but he's the king of the dinosaur army, so he's pretty cool, too."

We played for a few minutes, Ory easily vanquishing my army with his lineup, which was led by a masked superhero in a tight silver outfit. As we regrouped our fallen soldiers for round two, I said, keeping my voice as casual as possible, "Hey, did you go in my room today?"

He shook his head. I said, "Are you sure? Because it's okay if you did. You're not in trouble or anything."

"I didn't go in there," Ory said.

He was rearranging his action figures into a circle when he said, "I saw my daddy go in your room."

My heart was pounding so hard that I could hear it in my head. "Are you sure?"

"Yeah."

Ory had noticed a bent arm on the silver superhero. As he tried to twist it back, I heard him say, "My daddy says you have a job now, so you're going to move out."

I felt it then: a cold, prickly irritation, snaking through my veins like mercury. I said, "Did he say that?"

"Yeah." He nodded again. "My daddy wants my halmeoni to come live with us. But my mom told me she doesn't want my halmeoni to come. I think she and my halmeoni don't really like each other."

"That's tough."

Ory had stopped playing. He was motionless on the carpet, staring at the action figure in his hands.

"Erin," I heard him say, "do you think my mommy and daddy are mad at me?"

His voice was small, tremulous, and I was speechless, taken aback by the question. "No," I said, after a beat. "Of course not. Why would you think that?"

"I don't know. They're just really sad all the time. And maybe like they're mad, too."

"They're not mad at you," I said. "Your mom and dad love you very, very much, all right? You're the best thing that's ever happened to them. I promise."

To this, Ory just nodded moodily. Raising the silver superhero into the air, he said, "Are you ready to fight to the death?"

"Ory?"

We both looked up. Sophia was standing at the open door, her face inscrutable. "Ory, baby," she said, "it's time to change into your pajamas. Daddy will come read to you in a bit."

Then she looked at me. "Can we talk? There's something you need to see."

In her studio, Sophia closed the door and gestured for me to take a seat in front of the iMac. "Look at this. I just got the Google Alert."

On the screen, I saw the familiar IRM website, the sleek interface and the blue-and-white logo, and my stomach tightened. "Look," Sophia said again.

It was a blog post.

Remembering Our Colleague Gene Struzik (1974–2017)

Ingram, Russo & McAllister LLP (IRM) is deeply saddened to announce the passing of Gene R. Struzik, senior counsel with the Intellectual Property Litigation practice at IRM.

After joining the firm as a legal associate in 2000, Mr. Struzik went on to establish himself as one of the nation's leading litigators in the telecommunications space. Across nearly two decades, he argued more than thirty federal court appeals

"No," I said.

I pushed back from the desk. My mind had gone blank. "No way," I said. "No fucking way."

Sophia nodded. Quietly, she said, "I know."

I turned back to the screen. I read the post again, slower this time, trying to make sense of the pixels, the way they came together to form meaningless words. There was a long list of Gene's clients and accomplishments, sentences I recognized as having been pulled directly from his professional bio. There was a quote from Loic Russo, one of the partners, thanking Gene for his brilliance, his dedication, and his mentorship of over fifty legal associates and interns over the years. I looked around. "It doesn't say how he died."

Sophia took the mouse from me and clicked to a different tab. "The obituary from his funeral home," she said. "It says he died in a scuba diving accident in the Caribbean."

On the web page, there was a small, blurry picture of Gene and his wife, Holly, arms around each other, smiling in front of the Grand Canyon. They were both profoundly sunburned and wearing sunglasses that made them look like highway cops. The tribute book was filled with pages and pages of condolences. *We are still in utter disbelief that Gene is gone*, Nick and Deborah Ackers from Litchfield, Connecticut, wrote. *When we close our eyes, we can still hear his wisecracking jokes and his belly laugh. I hit the jackpot with having Gene as my supervisor*, Garrett Margalli, Esq., from Chicago wrote. *I wouldn't be where I am today in my legal career without his apt guidance.* And Scott Reamer from Miami wrote, *Rest easy, brother. I'll catch you on the next wave.*

That was when it washed over me, all at once. I closed the browser. I sat there for a long time without moving.

I felt Sophia's hand on my shoulder. When I looked at her, her face was gentle, full of concern. "How are you feeling?" she asked.

"I don't know. Pissed off, maybe."

"That's good," Sophia said. "Anger is a healthy emotion."

She squeezed my shoulder. "Personally," she said, "I think we should take a moment and celebrate."

I exhaled. "Celebrate his death? Isn't that kind of morbid?"

"It's not for him," she said. "It's for you. And for all the women who deserved better."

In the kitchen, Sophia retrieved a bottle of champagne from the pantry, along with two flutes. We pushed out of the back door and began walking into the garden; then, abruptly, she stopped, and I almost collided with her. That was when I saw it.

Our wooden bench by the pond was gone.

I couldn't see Sophia's face. She was silent, motionless, and after a beat, I said, "Where'd the bench go?"

There was another pause.

"I forgot," Sophia said. She turned to face me, and I saw that she was smiling again. "Paul told me that he'd moved it into the garage to do some work on it. An issue with one of the legs. It completely slipped my mind."

I opened my mouth, but already she was brushing past me, heading for the door. "Come on. We'll go out."

"Out where?"

"Into the city," she said, setting the champagne and glasses on the counter. "Let's go somewhere fun, have a drink, and just enjoy ourselves. It'll be a nice change of scenery."

"Aren't you guys supposed to put Ory to bed?"

Breezily, Sophia said, "Oh, I'm sure Paul will understand. In fact, let's go tell him right now."

Before I could speak, she was walking briskly to the living room, where Paul was still on his work call. "Paul," she said, and he turned. "We're going out."

For a moment, Paul just gaped at her. "You're going out?" he repeated.

"That's right. Erin and I, we're going out."

Sophia was smiling. To me, she said, "Let's get our coats."

Uncertainly, I followed her back into the hallway. She had just wrapped her cream coat around her when Paul appeared, a splotch of red rising in his cheeks. "Sophia," he said, and I could hear him struggling to keep his voice level, "it's Ory's bedtime. He's waiting for us to read him his stories."

"Oh, I already told him. He knows it's just going to be Daddy tonight."

She began to put on her shoes, and Paul said, "So you're just going to leave him here in the middle of the night? Is that it?"

Sophia laughed, a light, tinkling sound. "Don't be dramatic, Paul," she said. "It's only for a few hours. We'll be back before you know it."

From the coatrack, she retrieved my jacket and tossed it to me. "Hurry, darling," she said. "We should just be able to make the next train."

Without another look at Paul, she opened the front door and stepped out. As I followed her, Paul and I made eye contact, and I almost shivered. The dislike in his eyes wasn't a suggestion anymore. His anger had solidified into something more useful. It had become resolve.

Paul wanted me out of the house.

As we walked to the train station, the neighborhood seemed to be shrouded in a spell of silence, broken only by the sound of our footsteps. Sophia's hand was in mine; she started to laugh quietly once we had turned the corner. "I haven't gone out in years," she said. "Not since before Ory was born."

"We should do something big, then," I said. "Like—what's something you loved doing when you first moved to the city? Something you don't get to do anymore."

Sophia thought about it. She turned to me, and under the faint moonlight, I saw her eyes come alive. She smiled. "I have the perfect idea."

The pizza place was on Twelfth and Third, just a couple of blocks from Union Square. It was the kind of scrappy, no-frills operation you could find anywhere in New York: an array of cooked, pre-sliced pizzas laid out behind a long glass barrier, another stack of pizzas baking in the back, a South Asian guy at the register, scrolling on his phone. Sophia pointed out a sign on the window that said **BEST DEAL IN NYC!!! $3 = 2 SLICES + 1 SODA DRINK**. "It was two dollars when I first moved here for art school," she said. "They've only raised prices once in the last decade."

I paid for the food: two slices of plain cheese each, plus two beers. There were no chairs in the pizzeria, so we migrated to a bar table in the corner, standing next to each other with our pizzas on paper plates and a stack of flimsy napkins. For a moment, I just watched Sophia lift her first slice from the plate and bite into it delicately. She looked at me and laughed. "What?"

"Oh, nothing," I said. "I was just picturing Baby Sophia, all alone in the big city for the first time."

That made her giggle again. "God, those were the times. In a way, they were terrible—I was in school, I was waiting tables, I was always stressed about money—but they were resplendent, too. Life in the city was full of possibilities. It felt like anything could happen."

Sophia took a long swig of her beer. She said, "Until you came along, I hadn't felt like that in a long time."

"I didn't come along, though," I said. "You sought me out."

"Yes, I suppose I did."

Under the table, I felt her brush against me. Her coat was hanging open, and underneath she wore a long, loose-fitting gray cashmere dress; I thought, for a second, that it might have been a coincidence, a thoughtless flash of motion. But then it happened again. She shifted her weight to her left leg, and her thigh leaned into mine and settled against it. I felt her warmth, the softness of her body through the layers of fabric. My throat went dry.

I heard her say, "Paul thought I was crazy for insisting on staying at that ratty motel. We usually go for nicer places on vacation—no offense, darling. But I had made up my mind."

I nodded, but in truth I was barely listening. My heart was pounding. The right side of my face, the side closer to her, was in flames.

What was it Sophia had once said about the call of the void? They were intrusive thoughts. The urge to do something that would set catastrophe into motion, to unleash something that could never be put back into the bottle.

But what if I did tell her?

What if I told her that the weekend before, when she and Paul and Ory were gone, I had crept into their bedroom closet and run my hands through her clothes like a psycho? She'd been clattering around the house all morning Saturday, doing laundry, getting Ory dressed, wrapping a present for another kid's birthday party. By the time they left, the clothes were sitting in the dryer, warm, fresh, forgotten. All I'd meant to do was give them a quick fold before they crinkled, the way she liked to do it for me. But when I held Sophia's lavender nightgown in my hands, I'd been overcome by something else. A pulsating heat under my skin. A perverse joy that made me lightheaded. Standing in the laundry alcove, I buried my face in the silkiness of her gown and pressed my lips to the fabric. I thought that'd be it, that it would be enough.

But it wasn't. Right away, it wasn't. The next day, when they were at the children's museum, I found myself tiptoeing up the stairs. I pushed into the master bedroom and stepped into the closet. Inside, I gathered a handful of Sophia's sweaters and dresses into my arms and held them against my body, breathing her in. That was when I felt it: the glare of Paul's finance-bro vests and Uniqlo button-downs behind me, white-hot on my back, intent on driving me away. I'd put her clothes back on the shelf and slipped away. Downstairs, back to the guest bedroom where I belonged.

Sophia's thigh was no longer touching mine. I closed my eyes, and suddenly the unpleasant thing Ory had told me earlier was back, itching at the top of my throat. "Sophia," I said, and she looked at me. "Paul was in my room earlier today."

She didn't even blink. Her face was blank, and after a moment, she said, "Are you sure?"

"Yeah. Someone moved the photo of my dad. And when I asked Ory, he said that he had seen Paul go in there. And taking away the bench in the garden, too—it can't be a coincidence."

"What about the bench?"

She wasn't meeting my gaze anymore.

"Sophia," I said, "I went to Columbia Law. Shockingly, I can put two and two together. You don't have to cover for him, is all I'm saying."

She went quiet. I watched as she traced a finger around the base of her beer, which was already empty.

Finally, she said, "Don't worry about Paul."

"Do you think he knows about the plan? Is that why he's fucking with me?"

"This isn't related to the plan," Sophia said. "It's about something else entirely."

She looked at me. "Paul is jealous."

"Of what?"

Sophia smiled. "Isn't it obvious?" she said. "He's jealous of you."

And as I looked at her, there it was: bubbling up in my stomach, echoing in my head, filling every inch of me with its wild, feral cry. The call was getting louder.

What if I decided that none of it mattered anymore?

What if I came clean about how much of a pathetic sicko I really was?

Or what if I just kissed her?

She was still smiling. Her face was inches from mine, her lips were red and full, and I had to tear my eyes away. I thought, with an ugly rush of resentment, of Paul: how he was the one who got to drive to Disney World with her, raise a child with her, sleep next to her at night in the house they'd bought and furnished together. Of all the people who thrummed with life, with the sort of vibrancy that powered the world and all that was beautiful about it—poets, architects, filmmakers—she had chosen Paul. A gray, joyless, unapologetically mediocre man who didn't deserve it.

I couldn't stop myself. I said, "What do you see in Paul, anyway?"

The question had come out blunter than I'd intended. But Sophia wasn't offended. "I've told you before," she said. "He's a good dad. He takes care of our family."

"Seems like a pretty low bar," I said. "No offense."

I was pushing it, I knew it, but Sophia just shrugged. "You'd be surprised. Do you know what percentage of married men don't do any work around the house at all? Paul takes Ory to school every morning. He makes dinner. He tucks Ory into bed every night and reads him stories, and he even does the funny voices, too. You can't ask for much more than that."

"I guess," I said. "He's just . . ."

I hesitated. Then I said, "Have you ever heard of that quote, I think it was by Kafka, about how we can have a frozen sea within us? For some people, when you meet them, you can tell right away they have that sea, that vastness, that depth. But for Paul—he seems like the type of person who has a pond. Or maybe, like, a lake at best, he's so tragically bland. Again, no offense."

Sophia didn't seem to take offense. She looked at me, cocking her head slightly, and after a moment she said, "And what about me? What do I have?"

I didn't even have to think about the answer.

"You?" I said. "Sophia, you're the whole fucking ocean."

Sophia's eyes widened. She took a soft, shaky breath, and then I saw it: tears, glimmering between her lashes, catching the fluorescent lights above us in a way that made my heart skip a beat. But then she turned her head. She took another deep breath, and when she finally looked back at me, she was smiling again, composed. "You don't like men that are boring, I take it," she said.

"Actually," I said, "I kind of don't like men at all."

I said it lightly, but the sentence sat on the table between us, leaden.

My heart was pounding as I looked at her; her face was blank, no expression at all. Slowly, she nodded.

She said, "Does your mom know?"

"Yeah. She found out when I was a junior in high school."

"She took it well, I imagine."

"Oh yeah. She took it like a champ."

We both laughed; the weight between us was gone.

I said, "My girlfriend in high school was named Emily. We were in marching band together. I was first chair oboe, she was second chair. We used to write each other these cheesy love notes. Really embarrassing teenage stuff. I kept them in a locked drawer in my writing desk. So naturally, my mom found them."

"Naturally."

I downed some of my beer. Then I said, "She never actually confronted me about it. I only knew she'd found out because one day I unlocked the drawer, and all of the notes were gone. I found them in the trash can in the kitchen. And after that, every once in a while, she'd make a comment like, *If only you grew your hair out, you'd be so much more attractive to men.* Or she'd be like, *One day, you'll come visit me with your husband and your kids, and we'll all go to Magic Kingdom together and it will be so much fun.*"

Sophia burst out laughing. She picked up a napkin and coughed into it, steadying herself. "Trust me," she said, "as someone who actually has been to Magic Kingdom with a husband and child, it was one of the most miserable and draining weeks of my life."

There was a pause. I said, "I'm sorry. I didn't . . ."

Sophia shook her head. "How could you have known? I hide everything beneath the surface. It's the only craft I've perfected throughout my life."

Her face had changed. She was still smiling, but there was a sadness there now, something that was almost too vast for me to comprehend.

She said, "I'll probably regret telling you this, but do you remember when I told you about our family vacation to Greece last year?"

I nodded. Sophia said, "We booked a little apartment in Santorini with a blue door and a view of the Aegean Sea. Ory loved it. But at night, lying in bed with Paul next to me, I couldn't sleep. I kept imagining myself walking out onto that patio and taking a leap. I saw myself sinking into the depths of those blue waters, and it was a much more enticing thought than sleeping next to my husband for the rest of my life."

She looked away, and her voice dropped to a whisper, so quiet that I had to strain to hear it. "Paul slept with someone," she said.

"What—wait, like, just now?"

"No, last year. Or maybe he's still doing it. I don't know, and I don't care at this point. All I know is that he came home late one night last June, drunk out of his mind, smelling like the most disgusting perfume. And he told me . . ."

She had to close her eyes to continue.

"He told me that he'd gone home with one of his coworkers, after they'd had too much to drink at a work event. And then he told me it was *my* fault. It was my fault for being such a cold bitch to him all these years after Ory was born, for not letting him touch me, for not showing him any *love*. He said he was having suicidal thoughts. He was crying as he said all this to me. Can you imagine that? A man who has everything in the world, crying like a spoiled child, lecturing *me* about what it's like to want to kill yourself. His selfishness sickened me. It was the most grotesque, pathetic thing I had ever seen.

"And when we were in Santorini a month later, because Ory was so happy, because we wanted so badly to be the perfect family for him, I caved, for just one night. I tried to be the bigger person. I agreed to have sex with him. But it was too late. When he touched me, I felt . . . cold. Nauseated. He repulsed me. I had to close my eyes. I had to pretend I wasn't there.

"I resent him, Shelley. I resent him for being in my life, I resent the permanent place he occupies in me through my baby, and sometimes when I look at him, it feels like I don't even exist anymore. Like I'm already dead."

As I looked at her, I was struck by how small she was, so fragile that even the lightest touch could have shattered her. Her pain was something I could not fully grasp, something that was far beyond my understanding, but it didn't matter. All I wanted, in that moment, was to answer the call that had been swelling within me, a rising fever pitch, a deafening crescendo—

I said, "You need to leave him."

Sophia was shaking her head. "We've been together since we were eighteen years old," she said. "I've never—"

"You've never known different. You said it yourself. You got together when you were practically infants, when you were completely different people. Maybe he was right for you back then. But what about now? Is he still right for you now?"

"It doesn't matter. None of it matters anymore. The only thing that does matter in all of this is Ory."

That was it. I put down my beer. I took a deep breath.

"Sophia," I said, "Ory is miserable."

Her eyes widened. She took a step back; her arms flew up to her chest in a defensive gesture, and she looked at me with shock, with something that could have been reproach. I knew instantly that I had gone too far, had breached a boundary. But I couldn't stop myself.

I said, "Do you seriously think he hasn't noticed how bad things are between you and Paul? He's five and a half, Sophia. He's a smart kid. Do you not see how he's basically stopped talking during meals? It's because he can feel the tense fucking atmosphere in that house, and because he's a kid, he thinks it's his fault. He literally asked me that tonight. Do you actually believe that your son is happy, Sophia? Is this what you had in mind for him when you decided to quote, unquote, 'make your peace with it'?"

With effort, I shut my mouth. I watched the blood leave her face. She swayed on the spot, and it was as though she were cradling her own body, rocking herself the way a mother soothes an infant.

Abruptly, she turned and walked out of the pizzeria.

"Sophia," I said, but she was already steps away, fading into the night. I had to jog to catch up with her. "Sophia," I said again, and I tried to put my hand on her shoulder, but she shrugged it off and kept walking. "Please. Please—look, I'm sorry. I shouldn't have said that. I'm sorry."

We were almost at the end of the block when Sophia turned to face me. Quietly, she said, "Fuck you, Shelley."

I felt a jolt of shock. Then relief. "I'm sorry," I said again.

"Do you think it's so easy to leave? To pack up my things and my baby and just *go*? I don't have a real job. I don't have savings. Most of my friends disappeared the moment I had a baby. And what about Ory? What about his toys, his bedroom, his friends, his entire life? Paul is his best friend. His entire face lights up when he sees him; he *worships* him. So if you're going to sit there and judge me—"

"Sophia," I said, "I'm the one person in the world who would drop dead before I judged you. You know that."

Her eyes filled with tears.

And suddenly, as she stood there before me, grasping at the coat that hung loosely over her slight body, I saw her not as the woman who had saved me at the motel in Kissimmee, but as the little girl she had once been: the one who had stood on a dirt path lined with poplar trees in the countryside, waiting for her mother to come home. The one who had waited by a locked dorm at Cornell, hoping for someone, anyone, to swipe their ID and let her in. I saw her standing in her old cubicle at the ad agency, dazed and aching and milk-stained from her first weeks home with a newborn, slowly gathering her belongings into a box in the same robotic way I'd packed my things the day I was forced to leave New York. I saw Sophia. I saw Soyoung. I saw all of her.

We stared at each other. An infinity passed. Then another.

And then Sophia stood on her tiptoes, seized the front of my jacket, and kissed me.

Her lips were even better than I'd imagined. They were full and red and soft, and they tore at my mouth with ferocity, bit into my skin and pulled it taut over and over again, as if she had the power to shatter every bone in my body, as if she could consume me whole. Her hand was at the back of my neck, gripping the roots of my real hair, forcing me to draw closer to her, and our bodies buckled in unison. Her knees knocked against my legs. I stepped on her shoe. I held on to her as we rocked back and forth on the pavement, a pair of wobbly dance partners finding our balance, and I started to laugh. That made her giggle, too. She rested her head against my shoulder, and in my mouth I tasted pomegranate and honey. Her favorite winter lip balm.

Sophia's eyes were closed. I lowered my face and kissed her eyelids, one by one; that made a sigh pass through her, something that finally cut the strings that had been holding her up. She settled into me. Her breathing slowed. "I don't want to be a bad mother," she whispered.

"You're not," I said. "You're an amazing mother."

Sophia tilted her head back to look at me, and after a moment, she smiled. Softly, she said, "I really liked that."

"Me too," I said, and I heard a crack in my voice. "I—I liked it a lot."

And with a jolt, I realized that we weren't alone. As if by magic, an entire world had risen up around us: People were brushing past us on the pavement, tourists dragging their suitcases, a woman selling cut-up fruit on a cart, two kids wearing flashing neon-green necklaces as they sprinted ahead of their parents. The night was thick with the sound of pulsating club music, indignant voices gossiping about a friend's transgressions, a soccer game broadcasting live from a phone's shitty speakers. The spell was broken. "We should head back," I heard Sophia say.

On the train, after we had taken our seats at the back of the car, she moved closer to me and rested her head in the crook of my neck. Then, when no one was looking, she gave me a quick peck on the neck like a baby bird. That made me laugh. I cupped her chin in my hand and coaxed it towards me, gentle, until we were kissing again. Her weight was on top of me. My hands slipped under her coat, and the soft cashmere of her dress bunched up between my fingers. Her arms tightened around my neck and tightened again. They were clenching my windpipe, cutting off my circulation, and I felt my ears ring and my head slam into the window behind me. I heard the sound of falling sand. I couldn't breathe, but breathing no longer mattered. She was my oxygen; she was my salvation; she was the lifeboat that had finally come along at the end of my drowning, and I needed her, I—

Sophia let go of my neck. She pulled back, and even in my dazed state I could see that her face had gone white. She was staring at something in the window behind me. I turned.

And saw nothing.

Except the dark outline of the city outside, and the water that was sloshing gently against the windows. It had started to rain.

ERIN

The frozen yogurt shop two doors down from the dance studio was always swamped this time of day. To snag a table, I had to arrive an hour and forty-five minutes in advance, ordering a total of five cups throughout the course of my wait to keep both the staff and other customers at bay. My mouth had become a tasteless tundra by the time I felt a tap on my shoulder and heard a familiar voice, a mixture of both perfunctory and genuine delight. "Erin! What are the chances?"

I turned around, and there was Amy Cloverfield, smiling at me in black-and-purple athleisure. Next to her was a tall, spindly Asian girl wearing a black T-shirt and black jeans; her black hair was in a high, taut bun. "This is my daughter, Lizzie," Amy said.

Lizzie smiled at me with perfect white teeth. "Hi," she said, and she had none of the self-consciousness, the close-lipped sadness that Chinese girls who'd grown up in China tended to carry with them. She was all sunshine and Miss Americana. Aloud, I said, "So *you're* Lizzie! I've heard so much about you."

Amy said, "Honey, this is Erin, the one I was telling you about. We work together at MLC."

I saw Lizzie's eyes widen. To her, I said, "Your mom is actually my boss."

She raised an eyebrow. "Is she a good boss? You can tell me."

That made Amy laugh, and I saw her scanning the shop for free tables; she and Lizzie were holding identical berry-themed concoctions. I reached for my yoga mat, which was curled up on the other seat. "Please, feel free to sit. I'm not waiting for anyone."

As Lizzie pulled up a chair from another table, Amy nodded at my yoga mat. "Did you just come from a class?"

"Huh? Oh, yes." I jabbed my thumb in a vague direction. "I just started yin yoga. There's a great studio down that way."

"How fun," she said. "We were just saying we should really get back into yoga again. Lizzie's dance studio is just a few doors over that way—we come to this place all the time."

"Oh, no way! That's awesome." I looked at Lizzie, who was spooning sliced strawberries into her mouth. "Your mom told me you're an incredible dancer."

Lizzie made a face. "She has to say that," she said. "She's my mom."

Amy put her hand on the back of Lizzie's head and rubbed it affectionately, careful not to disturb her hair. "She really is, though," she said. "And you know, at NYU, they have a professional dance company that the students participate in, and it's just terrific. You could still keep yourself engaged with that community, honey. It'd be a shame to give all that up."

"I don't know," Lizzie said, nonchalant. "I think I want to do more than just dance. I want to learn about other stuff, too."

"What are you planning to study?" I asked her, and Lizzie answered immediately. "Media and communications, like my mom. I want to go into marketing."

Amy had been watching her with a quiet, effusive pride. She now turned to me and said, "We're thinking about going abroad, too, for a semester or two."

"Europe?"

She shook her head. "It turns out NYU has a satellite campus in Shanghai. It's technically a separate institution, I believe, and the students are all Chinese, but it *is* fully accredited. I could get a visa and work remotely from Shanghai for a few months while Lizzie's studying there. We think it could be a good way for her to get to know China. To learn about the culture."

"Have you guys gone back to China since the adoption?"

"Oh, of course. A few times. But the thing about Guizhou is—" Amy paused. Then she said, "Well, you know how it is, being from there yourself. It's one of the poorest provinces in the country, and it shows. Plus, no one there speaks English, which is frustrating. So when we do visit China—and we've been quite a few times—we tend to stick with the big cities. Beijing, Shanghai, Guangzhou. The development over the last few decades has really been astonishing to see. When I was there the first time in 1999, nobody had a car. Everybody was zooming along the roads in this army of scrappy metal bikes. Now they have smartphones, subways, and food delivery apps. It's just terrific, what they've been able to accomplish."

I smiled, stirring the frozen yogurt in my cup. It was beginning to melt.

"You know, I actually went to Guiyang three years ago," I said, "when I was trying to find my birth mother."

Silence.

Across from me, Amy's hand paused in the middle of scooping another spoonful of yogurt, so brief that it was nearly imperceptible. Next to her, Lizzie had stopped eating. Her eyes were on my face, unblinking.

I let the silence build for a few seconds longer. Then I shook my head and exhaled. "It was honestly a huge disappointment," I said.

Visibly, Amy relaxed.

"I'm so sorry to hear that," she said. "What happened, if you don't mind my asking?"

"It was just . . . it wasn't what I expected. I knew I'd been left on a bridge in the middle of the night, in the freezing cold, when I was only about a month old, and a passerby found me and brought me to a hospital. I spent the next few months at an orphanage before I was adopted by my parents. Apparently the orphanage was really poorly run back then—there was one adult to every ten babies, and when my parents met me, I was seriously malnourished and underweight."

Amy nodded. "It was the same with her," she said, rubbing Lizzie's head again. "Her hair had been completely shaved off when they brought her to meet us at the hotel. They said there was a lice infestation in the orphanage. She looked like a bald little boy."

"I'm not surprised to hear that. Anyway, when I got to the orphanage, they showed me my original case files."

I looked up at Amy. "It turned out that when my birth parents abandoned me on that bridge, they had left a letter for me in the basket."

She drew in a sharp breath. They were both engrossed now. "What did it say?" Lizzie asked.

Slowly, I picked up my phone, pulled up the photo app, and scrolled through the folder until I found it. I set the phone down in front of them. "I took a picture when I was there."

The letter was in Chinese. Amy and Lizzie looked at each other. "What does it say?" Lizzie asked again.

I took a deep breath. There were tears in my eyes; they had been reluctant to make an appearance when I'd practiced days earlier—emotional performances had never been my forte. But now all I had to do was think of one person, and immediately I was blinking back the deluge, steadying myself. "It was dated the same day I was left on the bridge. It gave my time and date of birth. And it said that, um . . . that my parents didn't want me because I was a girl. It said they already had three girls, and I was the fourth. And it said they hoped I'd find a kindhearted family to take me in. They hoped I'd be so happy and loved that I would . . . I would never feel the need to look for them in the future."

I wiped my eyes on a napkin. "That was it. Sorry to get emotional. It was, um . . . it was hard reading that letter. I guess it's still hard, all these years later."

"It is," Amy said. Her voice was gentle. "It's so, so hard. God, I can't even begin to imagine."

She reached across the table and patted me on the arm. "Thank you for sharing that. It was extraordinarily brave of you."

I nodded, and in the periphery of my eyeline, I saw Lizzie. Her face was drawn, deep in thought.

She said, "So what did you do after that?"

"After I saw the letter? I didn't really know what to do after that. So I went home."

"Oh," Lizzie said.

She was quiet before she said, "They didn't deserve you, anyway."

I said nothing, and Lizzie added, "The orphanages in China are full of girls. That's what it was like when I was there. I was lucky my biological parents even let me live because I was born with a cleft lip. A lot of baby girls got thrown into mud pits. In latrines, even. Their families drowned them when they weren't even a day old."

"It's just unfathomable," Amy said. "Some of the stories we heard were nothing short of horrific. It really makes you wonder what human beings are capable of."

We were all silent.

"Well," I said, reaching for my yoga mat, "I'm sorry to run, but I should probably get out of here. I need to call my mom and check on her. Her sister, my aunt, just passed away from cancer, so I've been talking with her every day, just making sure she's okay."

Immediately, Amy said, "Of course. Go. Don't let us keep you."

I smiled at her, and then at Lizzie. "It was really nice to meet you," I said. "Good luck with the rest of senior year, and with NYU."

Lizzie returned a smile, a polite one. As I slung the yoga mat over my shoulder, we made eye contact, and I knew then what would happen next.

That night, as I was watching a movie on my laptop, a message appeared in my Instagram inbox. Not the fake high school student account I'd created months ago to follow her. The real, public one I used as Erin Callaghan, designer, recovering maximalist, and Nutella lover sharing bits and bites of my crazy little life in New York City. It was from Lizzie Cloverfield.

Hi, she wrote, this is Lizzie

And then: I don't know if you remember but we met today. I'm Amy's daughter

Me: Hi! Of course I remember. It was great to meet you.

Lizzie: Same

Lizzie: Sorry this is weird but I was wondering if I could ask you a question

Me: Sure

Lizzie: It's about your birth parents

Lizzie: Did you ever go back and look for them? After you got the letter?

Me: That's a tough question

Lizzie: I'm sorry

Me: No, it's okay

Me: I guess I was torn about it. On the one hand I felt like the letter made it clear they didn't want me to look for them. But on the other hand I also don't feel like I got a proper sense of closure

Me: I don't know. I guess I still feel conflicted about it

Lizzie: Yeah I can imagine

Lizzie: I'm sorry about the letter. It sucks

Me: Thanks

Lizzie: But I feel like you should try again, just one more time

Me: You think I should go back and look for them?

Lizzie: Yeah, bc like you said, you didn't get closure

Lizzie: And also, according to the letter, you have three older sisters

Lizzie: I think it could be cool if you could meet them, regardless of your parents

Me: Yeah that would be huge I think, to have three sisters, bc I'm an only child

Lizzie: Me too

Lizzie: It can get lonely sometimes

Me: I know

Me: Would you ever look for your parents?

Lizzie: Don't ever ask me that in front of my mom lmfaooo

Me: LOL

Lizzie: She keeps saying that she would support me if I wanted to, but if I really did that it would kill her. She would have like an actual nervous breakdown

Me: Hahaha I'm having a hard time seeing that if I'm honest. Your mom seems like a super compassionate and understanding person

Lizzie: lol trust me you don't know her like I do

Me: Haha yeah my mom can be tricky too sometimes

Me: When I was growing up she would encourage me to make Asian friends at school, but she wouldn't let me sleep over at their houses because she was scared I'd get too close to their moms and not love her anymore

Lizzie: hahaha what that's wild

Me: But we're really close now, we talk on the phone at least three times a day and she's really involved in my life

Lizzie: haha

Lizzie: Can I ask you for a favor?

Lizzie: If you ever decide to go back to the orphanage will you tell me? I just want to know what it's like

Lizzie: Maybe it'll help me make up my mind one day

Me: I will. I'm still thinking about it

Lizzie: Thanks

Lizzie: I mean it

ERIN

April 2017

Sophia was alone in the laundry alcove when I got home. She looked up from her phone, the dryer humming behind her, and I took a deep breath before saying, "You will *not* believe what Auggie Flores is up to on Wednesday evenings."

Immediately, she put down her phone. "Tell me."

As I joined her by the dryer, the stirrings in my stomach cautiously reared their heads. Almost two weeks had passed since the night at the pizzeria, since she'd pushed me away on the train with a sudden, brutal coldness, and things between us had shifted, then shifted again. For the first week, we hadn't spoken at all. I'd gone out of my way to avoid seeing her at mealtimes by leaving early in the morning, then staying out late at happy hours with the guys from work. I'd assumed she didn't want to see me, didn't want to be reminded of the fact that I was still loitering in her guest room, as welcome to her as an upturned dead cockroach overdue to be swept away. But on the seventh night, I came home from happy hour to find my clothes freshly laundered and folded on my bed. Next to them, Sophia had laid out a new pair of pajamas: a T-shirt and shorts that reminded me of her nightgown. They were buttery cotton and pale lavender. I wore them to bed that night, and the next morning, when I heard her making coffee in the kitchen, I had ventured out in the pajamas, and Sophia had smiled at me and said, "I've been working on something for Amy that I think you'll like." And just like that, the moment on the train had been expunged from the record by unspoken agreement, the tape rewound and filed away. That night, we brought the bench out of the garage and reinstated it by the pond, and we began scheming again. I made contact with Amy and Lizzie at the frozen yogurt shop the very next day.

Now, leaning against the washing machine, I said, "Auggie runs a local chapter of the New York Depression and Bipolar Support Alliance. They meet every Wednesday at seven p.m. in the basement of a church."

Sophia raised her eyebrows; then she laughed. "The gall," she said. "The absolute gall. Did you go?"

Of course I had. After Auggie Flores had left the *New York Gazette*'s office near Grand Central, I had followed him to the Whole Foods a few blocks away. There, I watched him scavenge a simple dinner from the salad bar, which he ate alone at one of the tables while scrolling on his phone, his left arm raised crookedly into the air like a scarecrow. In the photos of Auggie Flores that I had seen on social media, I had not found a familiar face, nothing I could have traced back to the blur of people in that subway car. But in person, something about him clicked. He was stringy and curly-haired, and he wore thick black-rimmed glasses and designer sneakers that looked two sizes too large against his reedy legs. It was as though he, too, were in disguise.

It was beginning to rain when I followed Auggie into the basement of St. Ignatius Catholic Church.

Sophia was shaking her head. "You should have talked to me first," she said. "It's far too close for comfort. He could have recognized you."

"I know," I said, breathless. "I know. I'm sorry. But look—" I patted the wig on my head. "I've been working side by side with Amy for weeks, and she hasn't recognized shit. It's your disguise, Sophia. It's bulletproof."

Sophia nodded, though she didn't seem much assuaged. "Go on, then," she said. "How many people were in the meeting?"

Quite a lot, it turned out. In the conference room in the basement, a circle of twelve metal chairs had been set out. Some of the other support group attendees were clear regulars; they greeted each other with a subdued, joyless sort of intimacy. At a table in the corner, I poured myself a cup of coffee. It was even shittier than the kind we served back at the motel.

At 7:09, the meeting began. Auggie shuffled a stack of papers and pamphlets on his lap. Then he cleared his throat and said, "I think we're going to go ahead and get started here."

His voice surprised me; it was soft and watery, lacking any semblance of authority. Auggie cleared his throat again, and this time, the murmured conversations came to a gradual end. He held up the top sheet of paper in his lap.

"This is, um, a sign-up sheet, and you're welcome to put down your email if you'd like to be added to the newsletter for this chapter of the alliance, which comes out, um, usually once a month. Or at least that's what I try to aim for." He gave a self-conscious little laugh. "We're kind of a one-person operation at the moment, so . . . if anyone has a background in graphic design and wants to help out, do feel free to get in touch after the meeting."

Then he went over the ground rules. "I want to be totally clear that this is a place to talk candidly about mental health. There's no judgment in here. There's no giving unsolicited advice on what someone else should or shouldn't do. We're just here to share what's going on and to say, *Hey, I'm really sorry that's happening.* By virtue of being here, we're recognizing that we're all more or less broken. And we're here to, you know, sit with that."

Over the sound of the dryer, Sophia scoffed. "That's rich," she said, "coming from the man who tried to interview your classmates about whether you had shown previous symptoms of psychosis. Remember that?"

My mouth was dry. "I remember," I said.

The way the support group worked was that we went around in a circle. Each person was given about five minutes to talk about what was ailing them, and then the other attendees had five minutes to ask follow-up questions or simply to say, *Yeah, that sucks, dude.* Two of the other newcomers shared that they had sought out the group because they couldn't afford out-of-network therapy, and the story was generic enough that I jumped to borrow it. A regular named Gary shared that he was furious that his brother, from whom he'd been estranged for years, had visited New York on a work trip recently but hadn't called Gary to say he was in town, a fact that Gary had only learned through their father, from whom he was also mostly estranged. Another regular named Charissa told us that she was suffering panic attacks from having to work alongside her boss, who was also her ex-boyfriend, who was now engaged to another one of her coworkers. I was tempted to raise my hand during the Q&A portion and tell Charissa to just find another job, but then I remembered Auggie's rule and bit my tongue. No unsolicited advice.

When it was Auggie's turn, he took a moment before he started speaking, staring down at his shoes. "For me, I guess this week has been the same," he said. "I feel like I've been coming here and sharing the same thing for the last three years, but, um . . . I guess that's just how it is. Nothing ever changes."

Then he said, "I just really fucking hate my job."

A few people looked up. I shifted in my chair.

Auggie said, "I'm turning thirty-five next month. And I know everyone's like, *Age is just a number. It has no meaning.* But it does. It absolutely fucking does. I'm thirty-five years old, I've been in New York for eleven years, and I'm still working at the same hellhole, churning out the same noxious *shit* day after day. And I don't know who I'm even doing this for. I pretend that it's for me, so I can pay my rent. But then I'd be fucking lying. I'm lying to myself; I'm lying to the twenty-three-year-old version of me who went to journalism school and would be so ashamed of what I've come to. Like—I'm a loser, you know? And every single person who looks at me can see it. They can see that I have no value, that I have nothing beautiful to offer up to the world, that my hopes and my dreams and my aspirations mean nothing. And, like, I am *this* close to accepting that this is it. You know?"

Next to me, Sophia was gazing at the dryer, which was whirring to an end, and for a moment, I thought I saw something pass through her face. But then the dryer beeped, and she turned to open the door. "Well," I heard her say, "at least he has a shred of self-awareness. What happened after that?"

I opened my mouth. Abruptly, the alcove was filled with a rush of humid air, and as Sophia began unloading laundry into a basket, her soft, frizzled hair falling over her face, I found myself at a loss for words.

The things I'd said at the support group—how could I begin to bring myself to repeat them to her? I'd started off all pompous, casual, leaning back in my chair as I launched into the health insurance cover story. But then I'd been caught off guard by their sympathetic eyes, their quiet nods. My chin and my voice started to wobble. My voice began to crack. And suddenly I found myself telling them my real story: not the one about being pinned against a hotel room door by my boss, not the one about losing my entire future in a single viral video, not even the one about returning to New York in the vengeful skin of someone who was not real, but a story about how I had fallen hopelessly in love with a woman. A girl, really. I told them about sitting with her on a wooden bench, her head on my shoulder, golden lights glowing in the house before us. I told them about kissing her on the train to New Jersey, her arms tight and fierce around my neck, drowning me, saving me. And I told them about living a flight of stairs away from the same girl who had stopped loving me back, who was drifting further and further from me with every passing day, who no longer gave me any hope for the future. They all nodded as I bawled into my sleeves, and a few people said, *Hey, I'm sorry that's happening.*

Later that evening, after the meeting ended, Auggie and I had found ourselves standing next to each other outside the church, waiting for the rain to stop. I'd watched as he lit a cigarette, took a long drag, and blew out the smoke. Then he'd glanced over at me. "You ever been in therapy?" he said. "The real kind. Not this sharing-circle bullshit."

The question took me by surprise; my instinct went to telling the truth. "I've tried," I said, "but all the therapists here have long waitlists."

"Big surprise," he said. "Everybody in New York is fucked in the head. Especially these days."

Amid a cloud of smoke, we looked at each other. "Word of unsolicited advice," Auggie Flores said, and his eyes were so strange and sad behind his glasses that for a second, they almost brought me to tears. "Just try not to screw up your life like the rest of us did, all right? You seem like somebody who could do a whole lot better."

But Sophia was straightening up now, waiting for me to go on, and I swallowed. "Nothing much, really," I said. "Just a bunch of pointless bitching. I left as soon as the meeting was over."

"And you're *sure* he didn't recognize you?"

"I'm positive. He barely even looked at me, dude's such a raging narcissist."

Sophia nodded. She was quiet before she said, "I don't want you going to that support group anymore."

"Why not?"

"It's too risky. With Amy, she had only seen you that one time on the subway. But Auggie knows your face and your voice. He was the one who filmed you. He's written stories about you. We can't take any chances."

Sophia put her hand on mine. She said, "Promise me you won't go again. It's not safe. We'll figure out another angle with him."

We both glanced down. It was the first time she'd touched me since that night on the train, and as she intertwined her fingers with mine, my stomach stirred again. "Promise me, Shelley," she said.

It was impossible to say no to her. "I won't go again," I said. "I promise."

In the dim light of the alcove, I couldn't look away from her eyes. Slowly, she brought my hand up to her lips and kissed each finger. My breathing stopped.

"I miss you," I said, and it came out as a whimper. I saw Sophia's eyes glisten.

Quietly, she said, "I've missed you, too. It's been hard, barely seeing you at home these days."

"Do you—do you want me to move out?"

There was a pause. Sophia looked away, still holding my hand in hers, and my heart sank. But then she turned back to me, and I saw that her eyes had filled with tears.

"I don't want you to move out," she said; her voice had become shaky, almost petulant. "Of course I don't. Having you here has been the only bright spot in my life for years. But I can't tell you to stay, either, because then that would be selfish."

Then she said, "That night on the train, I . . . I was afraid. I couldn't stop seeing things from the past, things I wish I could take back. Things that never should have happened. I . . ."

Her hand had gone cold.

"It's not a good thing for me to love someone," she said. "You have to listen to me when I tell you that."

I heard her. I had. But that word—that one word. It lit a spark in my brain. My vision was suddenly illuminated; in front of me, I saw flames.

I said, "You—you love me?"

Sophia smiled, just a little. She said, "I'm trying not to."

Her voice reminded me of a small wounded animal, and as I smoothed her hair back and kissed her on the forehead, it occurred to me, for the first time, that perhaps it wasn't just me who needed her so that I could live, so that I had a reason for persisting in my meager existence. She needed me, too.

But then she let go of me. "That was a very interesting thing he said at the support group," she said, and her tone had become brisk, businesslike again. "It's giving me an idea, actually."

A dull, aching feeling had set in around my forehead. I said nothing, just dug my fingers into my temples.

Sophia began to pace. She said, "Have you heard of Stephen Glass?"

"Who?"

"Never mind," she said. "Too ancient of a reference. You know about the *Rolling Stone* story, right? The one about the University of Virginia?"

"The one they had to retract because the victim's story fell apart, and UVA ended up suing them? Sure."

"What if we did something like that? What if we handed him a really juicy tip—a story so big that it could launch the career of any journalist, no matter how disreputable? We could make it about Mike Palazzo. We know how much Auggie hates him, given his constant, inane tweets. And we know he's running for NYC mayor again. So what if we got someone to reach out to Auggie, posing as a whistleblower from Palazzo's office? I could ask an old friend from improv that I trust, someone who used to be an actor. We could hand him a stack of fake evidence that makes him think he's got a smoking gun. A paper trail that shows Palazzo taking bribes from a foreign government—sketchy invoices. Wire transfers. Email correspondence that doesn't exist."

"Jesus," I said, "how much time would it take to make all of that from scratch? Could be months."

"Well, we said we were going to take him down, didn't we?"

Sophia stopped pacing. She took one of my hands again, cradling it between hers.

She said, "Think about what would happen if we pulled it off. He'd be the journalist to break a stunning political story. The public uproar, the attention, the inflated hope—for once, he'd be on top of the world. Delusional enough to think he could finally play in the big leagues. But there'll be an investigation, of course. His sources will fall apart. And he'll be discredited as a liar who's willing to fabricate witnesses and evidence for a story. After that—forget working for *The New York Times.* He'll be blacklisted from every reputable publication in the country. How's that for a plan?"

Her cheeks were pink, and she was in high spirits, eager for my assent. But once again, I felt the aching in my temples, and suddenly my head was so heavy that I could have laid it down right there on the dryer. "Sophia, listen," I said. "There's something we should talk about."

"What is it?"

"I've been thinking that . . . that maybe it's time to stop."

She stared at me. I took a deep breath.

"It's just that . . ." It was laughable now, applying the brakes on a plan that was already months in motion. But if anyone could understand, it was her. "I keep thinking about Lizzie. I still don't like what we did with her. With that letter you wrote, with the Instagram messages I've been sending her. I don't like that we pulled her into this plot with Amy when she had nothing to do with what happened on that train. She's just a kid, Sophia. Her biggest concerns in life are high school and dance classes and what she's going to study in college. And what we've been doing, manipulating their relationship, trying to create a fissure between her and her mom, it's . . . it's . . ."

I swallowed before I said, "It's ugly. It's starting to keep me up at night, wondering if we've gone too far with this whole revenge thing, if we're even hurting the right people. Like—Gene, who started all this, is already dead. So what if we just called it a win, you know? What if we said that it was enough, that we had gotten what we wanted, and we just moved on with our lives?"

Abruptly, Sophia let go of my hand, and that was when I saw it again. The coldness, the irritation. The rings under her eyes had grown darker.

She said, "You were on board with the plan."

"I was on board."

"So what happened?"

"Maybe I'm just starting to see things differently. I . . . Look, you know I trust you with my life. But you don't know what it's like, growing up with a single mom. My whole life, my mom has been my biggest supporter. My shoulder to cry on. She's my *everything.* And for her, I'm her only hope. I'm her purpose. I'm the reason she's been able to put on a smile and clean motel rooms every day for the last twenty years. If I lost my mom, or if she lost me—Sophia, I can't even wrap my mind around that. And if that's the kind of relationship Lizzie has with Amy, then . . ."

I trailed off. As I spoke, Sophia had remained perfectly still. And yet when I looked at her, I saw a stranger.

From the window came a soft shushing sound, like sand being shifted in a sieve. It had begun to rain.

"You know," Sophia said, "I'm just so tired."

I said nothing. She said, "All my life, all anyone has told me is that I don't understand. That I don't know what it's like. And you know what? Maybe they're right. Maybe I don't understand, and I never will."

She looked at me. "I guess I'd just hoped that you'd be different."

Instantly, my face stung as if she had slapped me. I said, "I *am* different, Sophia."

"How can you be? You don't see it. You refuse to see it."

"I don't understand. What do I refuse to see?"

When we looked at each other, Sophia's eyes were glimmering with tears.

"You don't want to see it, but I do," she said. "How much your own mother has hurt you."

No.

No.

No.

The shock was instant. I opened my mouth, and behind me I felt fissures opening, felt the ground shift and give way beneath my feet. The kitchen flashed white behind us; in the distance, I heard thunder.

Sophia said, "I've heard the things she's said to you. I've seen the way she treats you. What you've just said—feeling like you're your mother's only hope. Like you're her only reason for living. No child should have to bear that burden for their mother, Shelley. It's too heavy."

"No," I began, but she pressed on.

"Look at how you've lived these last twenty-four years. The best grades. The highest achievements. Columbia Law, a bright future as an attorney. But have you ever asked yourself whether you truly wanted these things? Or did you pursue them because you thought it was what your mother wanted—because even as a child, she had impressed upon you the belief that you had to devote your life to saving hers?"

"That's not true," I said, but my voice was gone, barely there. "It's not true, Sophia."

"Shelley," Sophia said, and her voice was cold, flat. "Your mother won't even accept you for who you really are."

I felt nothing, then.

Except it wasn't nothing. It was vast, and it was lightless, and it was empty, and it was then that I realized what it was.

Despair.

My legs gave way. I slid onto the floor of the alcove. It washed over me, all at once: the realization that there was nothing else I could do. There was nowhere else I could go. There was only one thing left to do.

So I sank.

How long was it before I felt her presence? She was there, on her knees, crouching next to me. I felt her arms around me, lifting me through the surface. I felt her hair in my face, inhaled the familiar smell of pine and snow. Through the sound of thunder, I heard her voice.

"I do understand, believe it or not," she said. "I know what it feels like to be turned away as a child by the same people who should have kept you by their side. I know what it feels like to beg for love like a dog begs for scraps at the dinner table, knowing that all of it is conditional, all of it is earned.

"What exists between Amy and Lizzie, it was never love. It's an arrangement. It's a contract that children are forced into when they have no power, no discernment, nothing driving them except the deep, aching hunger to be wanted. I learned my lesson twenty-three years ago, in the days after my brother drowned. I stopped waiting for something that would never come, and instead, I set myself free. It took me years and years—longer than I could have ever possibly imagined—but I found it, and one day, freed from the trauma of her adoption, Lizzie will find it, too. One day, she'll find something beautiful. Something incomparable. Something that belongs only to her, just like I did."

Her hair fell away then, and the fragrance of winter dissipated. I raised my head to look at her, dazed, barely aware of my surroundings. We were in the alcove, on the floor. The house was filled with the sound of rain. Sophia was gazing at me with so much tenderness that in that moment, I never wanted to get up. I never wanted to let go. "What—what did you find?" I whispered, and I was almost afraid of the answer.

Sophia smiled at me.

"You," she said. "I found you."

That was it.

In that moment, as I looked at her through my tears and through hers, the invisible wall between us crumbled. My dignity, my restraint, my conscience, the little sense of self I had left—every piece of it fell away, and in their place was a resounding clarity. There had never been another way. I'd always imagined that the unraveling of my life began the day I exposed myself on the subway, but now I saw the thread from the very beginning, every moment, every juncture where it had torn from the fabric and carried me further and further away. The day my dad died and my mom pushed away my M&M's. The day I found Emily's handwritten notes in the kitchen trash, greasy from eggshells and fish bones. The day I said no to my dream school because we couldn't make the financial aid work. The day Gene put his hand on my knee on the plane and rested it there, knowing that he could, knowing that I would let him. I saw it all, and in a rush of both despair and exhilaration, I saw my freedom: Through it all, there had been one call all along. One answer.

I took Sophia's face, pushed her hair back, and kissed her.

Just as she'd done that night outside the pizzeria, I no longer held anything back. I seized the roots of her hair and forced her head back against the dryer. I bit her. Our teeth clashed; through the ringing in my ears I heard Sophia cough and gasp for air, and it filled me with a savage pleasure, the feeling that I was a feral dog and she was the paper doll shaking between my teeth. Under the looseness of her sweater, Sophia's spine was a pronounced ridge, smooth skin taut over bone; she was even thinner than I had thought. The band of her bra stretched and wound itself around my fingers. It was cotton, thin, soft from years of washing. Her body was made of liquid.

"Shelley," I heard her say. "Shelley, wait."

We were both breathing unsteadily as we looked at each other. On Sophia's bottom lip, a scarlet, glistening bubble had formed; it took me a second to realize that I had been the cause of it. "Oh, shit," I said, "let me get you a tissue, let me just—"

I made to get up, but Sophia put her hand on mine. "Don't," she said. "It doesn't matter. I need you to listen."

It took her several deep breaths to steady herself, to bring herself to speak again.

She said, "There are . . . there are things I need to tell you. Things about me that you deserve to know. Things that if you knew, you would . . . you would . . ."

"Sophia," I said, "I don't give a fuck."

That made her gasp. She leaned back slightly to look at me, her eyes wide, her lips half parted in shock, and I said, "Tell me, don't tell me, do whatever you want to do. But I literally do not care. Because whatever it is, it's not going to change the way I feel about you. I'm done waiting around, okay? I'm done being a duck at a pond that you feed when your husband isn't around. I'm done with this hot-and-cold crap, kissing me, then pushing me away like my feelings don't matter. I need you to tell me what you want, because I want all of you. And if you don't—if you don't feel the same way—"

I swallowed before I said, "Then I'll leave. I'll move out tomorrow, and I'll never bother you again. But if you feel like this is worth fighting for, if you and I are worth fighting for, then all I need is one word, Sophia. All I need is a *yes*."

Sophia went quiet then. She closed her eyes, and I waited. For her, I had all the time in the world.

Her hand was freezing. Her fingers were shaking in a way that seemed involuntary, and I squeezed them, reminded her that I was there, that I had died in the abyss and come back a new person, wild and unashamed; that I was ready to love her without abandon.

Sophia opened her eyes.

"Will you meet me outside the front door at one a.m.?" she asked. "There's a place I need to show you."

ERIN

On the train from Hoboken into Manhattan, just before two in the morning, both of our phones buzzed at the same time. "Shit," I said. "Flood warning in the city."

Rain was lashing the windows, a downpour so thick that I could no longer see the shadowy landscape outside, the skyscrapers on the other side of the river. I said, "Should we head back? The subway's going to be flooded."

Sophia didn't answer. Her pale face was turned towards the glass, and for a moment I thought she hadn't heard me. But then she looked back at me, and there was a grimness in her eyes; her lips were drawn, tight. "It's fine," she said. "We'll make it."

At Penn Station, we transferred to the E Train and got out at Fifty-Third and Fifth. At the subway entrance, muddy rainwater was gushing down the steps, an impromptu river. I saw Sophia take a deep breath before she pulled a small umbrella from her bag and opened it above us. "Come on," she said, looping her arm through mine. "Let's hurry before it gets worse."

As we waited to cross Fifth Avenue, a clap of thunder tore through the sky above us; electricity was in the air. The rain had become white, flashing sheets of water, lashing sideways against our bodies, vanishing even the traffic lights from view. I had to shout into Sophia's ear. "Where exactly are we going?"

She pointed. "Look. It's right there."

It took a second and a flash of lightning, but then I saw the building. I saw the vertical sign hanging in the distance. I said, "We're going to MoMA?"

Sophia shook her head. "Not there," she said. "Across the street."

It was one of those beige prewar apartment buildings: a neatly trimmed tree on either side of the entrance, a long, rotund column of sunrooms running down the front. At the entrance, Sophia produced a fob, and we swept into the building, gasping, teeth chattering.

The light in the lobby shone over an empty concierge desk. Sophia made a beeline for the elevator, and I had to hurry to catch up with her, my shoes sloshing with water as I jogged across the marble floor. We were both quiet in the elevator.

On the sixth floor, Sophia led me to a nondescript white door. She looked at me, keys in hand, and took a deep breath.

"Here it is," she said. "Who I really am."

It was an empty apartment. Or, rather, an apartment without furniture. The walls and cabinets were white. The hardwood floors were laid out in a fancy geometric pattern. Leaning against the walls of the large living room were six or seven large paintings that came up to my chest, all carefully sealed in Bubble Wrap and plastic sheets. There was an easel set up with a blank canvas, a few loose brushes and paints scattered on a plastic sheet on the floor. In the corner was a blue sleeping bag rolled out across a stack of white foam boards. A pile of crumpled newspapers lay next to them.

But that wasn't what caught my eye. I walked up to the window wall at the end of the room and pressed my nose to the glass. Even through the rain, I could see the neon lights dotting the city, the outline of the museum on the other side of the street. "Holy shit," I said. "This view is unreal. How'd you get the keys to this place?"

"Oh," I heard Sophia say, "I stole them."

There was a pause as I turned to look at her. Sophia's face was still, stoic, and in that moment I could not parse whether she was telling the truth. She smiled after a beat.

"It's a friend's place," she said. "I'm keeping an eye on it while she's away."

She slipped off her shoes and walked over to join me, her bare feet leaving a slick trail of prints on the floor. She said, "This is where I've been spending my days while you were at work."

"You were here? In Midtown?"

She nodded. "I come here most weekdays. After you leave in the morning, I take the next train into the city after yours. I spend most of the day here, holed up in this apartment, and in the afternoon, I return to Hoboken to pick up Ory from school. No one ever has to know I'm gone."

"But what do you do here? Are you, like—"

I glanced at the easel behind us. I said, "Are you using this place to work on your art?"

Sophia let out a thin little laugh. "No," she said. "I'm not using this place to work on my art."

I watched as she walked to the corner of the room and bent over the stacks of newspapers. She lifted something from the pile and shook it at me: It was a large bottle of whiskey, mostly full, the amber liquid swishing inside. There were more bottles in the back. "How about a nightcap?" she asked.

After I'd kicked off my shoes and hung my jacket over the radiator, we sat side by side on the sleeping bag, the bottle between us. Sophia was the first to take a long, graceful swig; we traded off a few times, and after a minute or two, I began to feel a peppery warmth spreading through my fingers. "So," I said, "tell me."

"Which part?"

"Everything. Starting with—what do you do here, if you're not making art?"

I watched as she traced the glass pattern on the bottle with a finger.

"I've had this place to myself for months now," she said, finally. "A friend from art school used it as a studio. Her parents bought it for her a decade ago, when we were still in school. She's lived here on and off for years, but never for long. Her career was already taking her around the world while the rest of us were waiting tables. If I told you her name, you'd probably recognize it. Exhibitions in Berlin. Tokyo. Copenhagen. Always flying from one show to the next, one residency to another.

"I first got the keys from her years ago. I'd volunteered to feed her cat when she was out of town, keep her two succulents alive. I paid myself with her skincare products, a bag here, a pair of shoes there; of course she never noticed. And four months ago, when she packed up everything and moved to Paris, I didn't remind her that I still had the keys. *I'm peacing out*, she told me at our goodbye dinner. *I'm not living here under the orange fascist.* That was the day I stopped feeling guilty about taking what was hers.

"I was careful at first. On the days when it was too much, with Paul, with Ory, my clients, I'd come here with my sleeping bag, set an alarm, and rest my head. I couldn't risk letting you see how much I was struggling. I stayed an hour one day, two hours the following week. But eventually I became careless. Sloppy. After you got a job, I started staying longer. I left my sleeping bag here overnight. I stopped checking her Instagram to make sure she wasn't in town. So I shouldn't have been surprised when she walked in on me last month."

Sophia drank again. Then she said, "She was gracious about it. God, she was so unflinchingly generous, it repulsed me. *Jesus, Sophia, I can't even imagine, never having a moment of quiet to yourself with a family to take care of.* She gave me her blessing to use this space. She encouraged me to bring my easel, my supplies, anything I needed to start painting again.

"I tried, in the beginning. I really did. But I was stuck. Frozen. I couldn't even bring myself to open a tube of paint. So instead, I did other things. I read books. I sat by the window and looked at the people outside, the tourists wandering the sculpture garden. Sometimes I'd drink a little too much; I'm not proud of it. Mostly, though, I . . . I . . ."

Sophia swallowed. She said, "Mostly, when I come here, it's to think about you."

The warmth was in my stomach now. I said, "You . . . you think about me?"

We looked at each other, and Sophia smiled.

"I think about you constantly when you're at work," she said. "I think about what you might be doing, who you might be talking to. I wonder where you're having lunch, if you're going with your coworkers, or if you're all by yourself. Being in the city, it makes me feel closer to you. We're on the same island. I don't have to worry about you drifting away."

"Sophia," I said, and I took her hand. "You don't have to worry about that. I told you, I'm not leaving."

But Sophia just shook her head. "That's because you don't know the real me," she said, and her voice was small, tremulous. "I'm . . . I'm a fraud. I've pretended to be someone I'm not."

"Yeah, I know," I said. "That's why you got kicked out of Cornell, remember?"

I'd meant it as a joke, to lighten the atmosphere. But Sophia's eyes clouded. She looked down at the bottle in her lap. It took her a long time to speak again.

She said, "I was a fraud that night I went to speak to you at the motel. I was a charlatan. I . . . I promised you things that were impossible. I inflated my credentials and sold you a dream. A fantasy. The truth was that I was never some master con artist with a genius plan to rebuild your life and destroy your enemies. I was just a housewife. I was a sad, boring suburban mom who wanted so desperately out of my own miserable life that I latched on to yours. I lied to you, Shelley."

"I mean," I said, "sure, you might have oversold it by a bit. But I wouldn't say you lied, technically."

"I was the one who sent Dolly," she said. "Remember her?"

The image was in my mind before she'd even finished. I saw the coral lips, the overplucked eyebrows, the shrewd eyes studying me behind enormous sunglasses. The hairs on the back of my neck stood up.

I said, "You sent Dolly? What do you mean, you sent her?"

"She's a friend. We've known each other for years; she's a brilliant actor who used to do off-Broadway shows. I told her about you, about how smart you were, how unlikely you were to be persuaded, and so we thought..."

Sophia hesitated. She said, finally, "We thought you just needed a little nudge in the right direction."

I was speechless.

A version of me wanted to shake her by the shoulders. Another version of me was standing on the ledge, mouth gaping open in an unending scream.

And yet a third version of me still—still—wanted to kiss her.

Abruptly, I reached for the bottle. I drank until I began to cough, until my insides were churning, and only then did I put it down. Sophia was watching me, white-faced, anxious. "I'm sorry," she said. "I'm so sorry, my darling."

I said nothing, and she took both of my hands in hers. "It was unforgivable, the things I did," she said. "I see that now. I never should have lied to you. I never should have manipulated you and your mom by sending Dolly. It was my fault, all of it. It's my fault that we've accomplished nothing. It's my fault that nothing has gone according to plan. And it's my fault..."

She took a deep breath. "It's my fault that I've fallen in love with you," she said. "And no matter how much I try, I can't seem to make myself stop."

I had never seen Sophia more beautiful.

Her eyes glimmered with tears. She smiled at me, sad, repentant, overcome by shame, and in that moment she seemed to glow, to have become incandescent. My breath caught in my windpipe. I couldn't breathe. I couldn't think. All I could do was look at her in the middle of this rainstorm. All I wanted was to let her in.

"Don't stop," I said. "I don't want you to stop."

Instinctively, we moved towards each other. We kissed.

This time, it was slow. I took the time to really get to know her, to dive into her. Her breathing was soft and steady, and it calmed my racing pulse like a lullaby, took every second between us and stretched it across an infinity. "I love you," I said, and I was surprised by how sharply the words stung my nose. My eyes welled up. "I love you so much, Sophia. I love you so much it literally hurts."

Her entire body seemed to stiffen. It took her a moment to gather the words.

She said, "Do you really mean it?"

"Of course I mean it. I love you."

Sophia shook her head. "No," she said, "that's not enough."

Then she said, "I want everything. All of it. Not just this moment, not just today or tomorrow or the next day, but all the days and months and years after that. You'll have to . . . There's no exit after this. There's no way out. If you change your mind, if you wake up one day and decide you've had enough of me, I . . . I . . ."

Her face crumpled. I reached for her, but she shrank away from me, held me at bay with the bottle. "I'm afraid," she whispered. "I'm so afraid, Shelley."

"Is it Paul? Are you scared of him?"

Sophia shook her head. Her face was wet with tears.

"I don't care about Paul. He's nothing, he doesn't . . . I'm afraid because I know that if I let you in, one day, you'll realize I'm not the person you thought I was. You'll decide you don't want to be with me anymore, and you'll get up and walk away."

"That's bullshit. Sophia, I would never leave you. I would never walk away."

Even the idea of it was preposterous. I sat up straight, indignant, eager to prove myself to her. But Sophia wasn't looking at me. She was staring at the bottle.

"The thing is," she said, "I've . . . I've had an affair before."

My heart stopped.

It took me a moment to say, "With who?"

"An old coworker. I've mentioned her to you once, I think. Casey."

It took a second for the name to rise to the surface.

"Hang on," I said, "Casey, your friend from art school? The one you helped get away from her partner and get a job at your agency? You had an affair with *her*?"

Sophia nodded, unsteady.

"I didn't mean for it to happen," she said. "I just . . . All I wanted was to help her get back on her feet. You have to understand what it was like. I was the same age you are now. Twenty-four. Paul was putting in long hours at Morgan Stanley back then; we barely saw each other, and when we did, there was nothing to say. But Casey, she sat in the cubicle next to mine. We'd been through so much together; we'd become so close. She was . . . she was always there."

"Did Paul find out?"

She smiled weakly.

"I told him. Of course I did. We hadn't kept any secrets from each other since we were eighteen. When Paul found out, he begged me not to leave. He begged me to go to couples counseling. But I'd already made up my mind. I packed my bags. I went to her apartment and knocked on her door—but she was gone. Her neighbor said she'd moved out in a hurry. She resigned from work without notice, and when I tried to call, my number was blocked. I realized only then that it had meant nothing to her. A casual fling. A rebound from her previous relationship. I looked around in the dust, and Paul . . . he was the only person I had left.

"That was when we decided to have a baby. We thought—stupidly, fantastically—that this was the one thing that could fix everything that was wrong between us. I told myself that having a child would make us a real family. I told myself that even if I couldn't make myself love my husband, the fact that he loved me—that in itself would be enough to live on."

Sophia shook her head. "But I was wrong," she said, and there was a stillness to her voice, a quiet that unnerved me. "I didn't understand it until it was too late. Paul didn't beg me to stay because he loves me. It was because he *needs* me. He needs me the way any man needs a woman: A pretty face to show off on his arm. A body to carry his children. He needs a maid, a secretary, a nanny, a hole between two legs. He needs me because I'm a distraction from the fact that he is alone, his life has no meaning, and one day he will die and it will all be over."

There was nothing to say. I watched as Sophia took another drink.

"I don't regret having Ory," she said. "I'll never regret having him. But sometimes I look back and think, *If only someone had told me. If only.*"

A tear fell onto the back of her hand. Then another.

I didn't hesitate. I wrapped my arms around her and squeezed her tight, and from her there was no resistance, only the limpness of her body. "Listen to me, Sophia," I said. "Casey was an asshole, okay? So is Paul. They let you down. But I'm not them. I'll never be them."

She was quiet. I said, "Do you know how obsessed I am with you? I wasn't going to tell you this because I didn't want you to think I was a giant pervert, but since we're putting everything out in the open—look, I've been sniffing your laundry. I snuck into your closet and smelled your clothes. That is literally how desperate I am to be close to you."

Slowly, Sophia pulled back to look at me. Her face was inscrutable.

She said, "I . . . I've been doing the same thing. More or less."

"What?"

"That old T-shirt of yours from high school. The soft green one. That one week when we weren't speaking, when you were gone in the evenings, I missed you so much that I stole it from your laundry. I wore it to bed every night. And from there, I started . . ."

A faint pinkness had risen in her cheeks.

"After Paul fell asleep," she said, "I would go into the bathroom to be alone. There, I would . . . I would get myself off while wearing your shirt. It helped me imagine that I was with you."

My brain went blank then.

Every smart-ass comeback I'd ever had, every quip I'd ever thought of—it all fell away. In that moment, I couldn't muster a single coherent response. "Wow," I said.

And then: "Oh. Oh, wow."

And out of nowhere, I started to giggle.

That made Sophia laugh, too. She buried her face in my shoulder, and I tightened my arms around her. I said, "I was wondering where that shirt went. I nearly gave the dryer a colonoscopy, looking for it."

"I'm sorry," she said, her voice muffled. "It was why I gave you the new pajamas; I thought that could make up for it, somehow. God, you must think I'm some kind of . . . you must think I'm a lunatic."

I swallowed.

"Sophia," I said, "that was the hottest thing anyone has ever said to me in *years*."

When Sophia looked at me, her eyes changed.

The foam boards were more slippery than expected when we moved. The topmost one slid out a few inches beneath the rustling nylon of the sleeping bag, and when I shifted positions, my elbow sent a bundle of unopened plastic sheets rolling towards the other side of the room. We both peeled off our damp sweaters, and I kissed her neck, her collarbone, the front of the long-sleeved cotton shirt that clung to her body. I could feel her heartbeat: warm, racing, jittery. Her fingers were at the top of my chambray shirt. She undid the first button, then the second.

I froze. I did my best not to show it, but my hands went cold. Goose bumps rose all along my back. I took a few shallow breaths, and I heard her ask, "What's wrong?"

"Nothing. I—nothing's wrong. It's just . . . it's just that . . ."

Finally, I said, "It's just been a while for me. It's been weird for me since . . . well, you know."

Sophia nodded. Her eyes were like pools, drawing me in.

"I know," she said. "I know, honey. It's been a while for me, too."

She withdrew her hands from my collar. We lay face-to-face on the sleeping bag, listening to the rain wash away at the windows, and Sophia smiled at me. She didn't have to say another word; in her face, I saw it all. We didn't have to do anything. We didn't have to touch, didn't have to kiss, didn't have to exchange a thousand promises for me to know that she loved me. We could just be.

Slowly, I sat up. Her eyes followed me. I unbuttoned the rest of my shirt, my fingers shaking, and tossed it into a wet heap with the sweaters. Then I reached behind my back and took off my bra. I knelt before her, trembling, exposed, allowing her to see me, to take me for who I was. And I invited her, silently, to do the same.

I told her I was ready.

I didn't have the right words to describe what it was like. I couldn't have painted a picture if I'd tried. But I remembered thinking that she reminded me of a cloud. Soft, resplendent with light, impossibly shapeless. Being with her was like being forgiven for every sin I had ever committed. She met me in all the ways I would ever need. We were on a tiny lifeboat in the middle of the open ocean, and when the storm rose and shook the boat in its rage, I clung to her as tight as I could and closed my eyes. In my arms, I felt her tremble. I felt her quick, shallow breaths. We weathered it together, again and again and again.

We were home.

The bottle of whiskey sat on the floor, now emptied. Outside, the thunderstorm seemed to be quieting down; the water hitting the window had slowed to a trickle. Sophia propped herself up on an elbow, reaching for her phone. I made a playful attempt at blocking her, and she laughed. "Shelley, don't. I need to see what time it is."

"I'll tell you what time it is," I said. "It's time to stay here forever and never go back to New Jersey."

"We couldn't stay here forever even if we wanted. This place is under contract as of next week."

Already, reality was seeping in. Sophia put down her phone and brushed my hair back. Her palm rested against my forehead, pensive.

"There's something that might be kind of interesting," she said.

"What is it?"

"It's a thing with the Hoboken Art Collective. A kind of . . . a group exhibition for local photographers. I just got another email from the organizer about it. They really want me to participate."

I touched her cheek. "Seriously? That's great."

"It's taking place at their warehouse, though. So just a small, local thing. And it's only for Asian American artists, so there's also this feeling of . . ."

"I think you should do it," I said.

She looked at me. "Yeah?"

"Yeah. I think it'll help you ease back in. Get you in the right headspace for making art again."

Sophia considered this. She nodded after a long moment; then she bent her head and kissed me again.

"You're right," she said. "I want you to see my work. I want you to see every part of me."

It was agony to get dressed again in the warm apartment, our clothes still damp and wrinkled, our shoes heavy with water. In the elevator, Sophia used her fingers to comb through the tangles in my hair, and her touch was so gentle that it almost made me tear up. We were at the front door of the lobby when she said, "I'm ready to answer your question from last night."

My heart started pounding. Sophia smiled at me.

She said, "I'm going to talk to a lawyer. I had a consultation with one years ago, before I found out I was pregnant with Ory. I never ended up retaining her services. But this time, I . . . I'm going to do it. I'm going to put my old life behind me, and I'm going to fight for us. You, me, and Ory. I'm ready to do whatever it takes."

There was a lump in my throat. I swallowed it.

"Whatever it takes," I said, "I'll be right there with you, every step of the way."

Sophia opened the door, and the sounds of a stirring city washed over us. The storm had passed. It was almost morning.

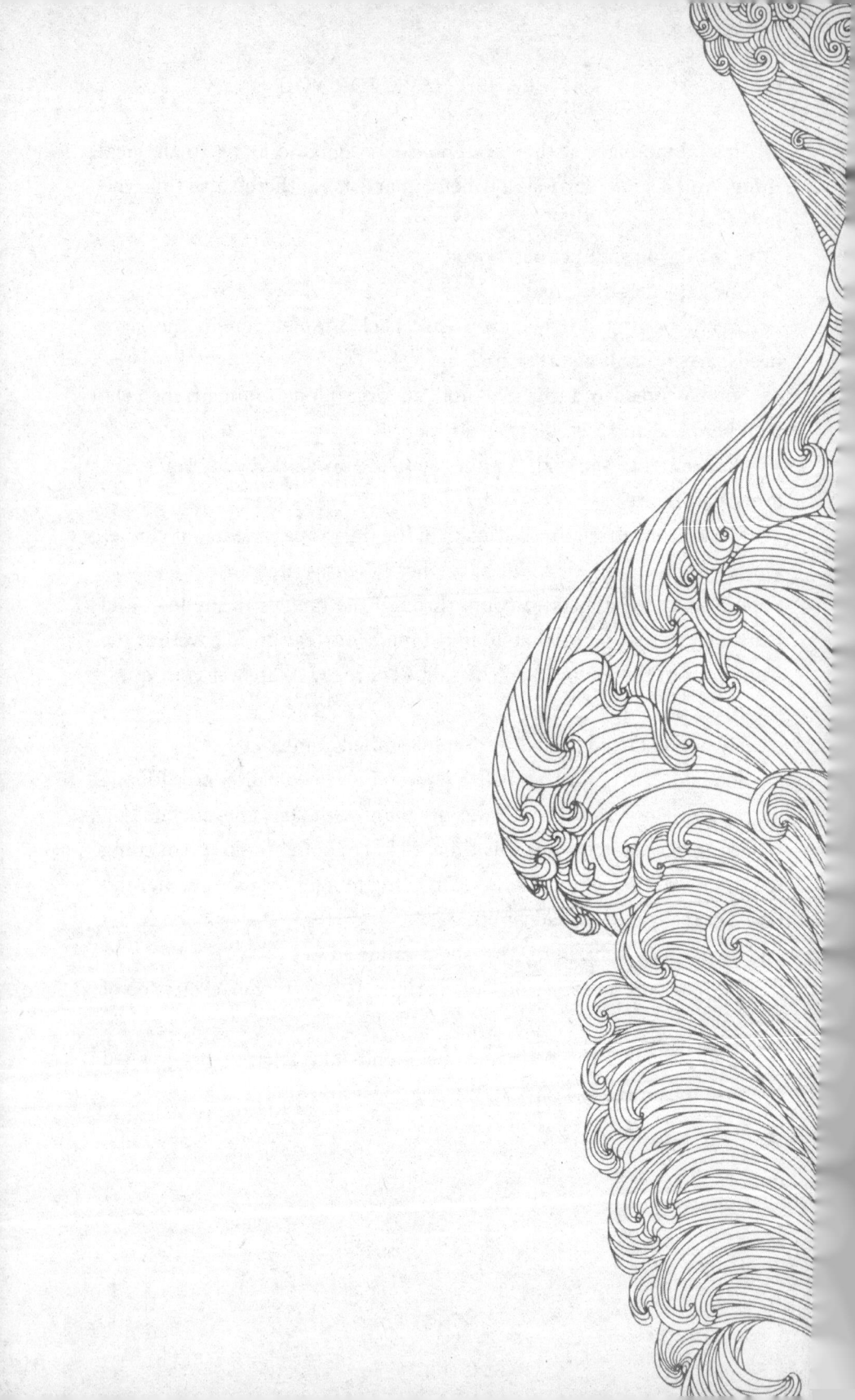

Part Four

COUNTERWEIGHTS

SOYOUNG

December 2004

They had started leaving her bedroom door unlocked at night, so confident they were that she'd become too broken to leave. That night, Soyoung waited until they had gone to sleep before she packed her things, her movements slow and staggered so that they would not make noise.

In her room, she strapped on her backpack and picked up a duffel bag. In her other hand, she carried a pair of white tennis shoes, the laces already done up. She was almost at the door when it came to her—a buried memory from long ago, rising from the depths of the water like a ghost.

Kneeling on the floor of her closet, she moved a storage basket out of the way and lifted the loose floorboard below. Inside was a carved wooden box: a parting gift from her grandmother, one she had carried with her to every home since she was eight years old. With a small key, Soyoung undid the rusted lock and pushed back the lid.

In the box was a silver-painted action figure: a relic of the early 1990s, back when superhero cartoons had dominated TV screens in every Seoul household and feral schoolboys screeched and wrestled on the playground as they battled hero against monster. Oh, how he had stamped his feet and shouted until he was red in the face when he thought she'd lost it. The angry tears he'd shed as he took to her beautiful lavender dress with scissors. And in the end, what had it all been for? Shows ended. Trends changed. Little boys grew up—well, some of them did. The action figure lay in the box now, a time capsule, a corpse long resigned to its coffin. But Soyoung had never forgotten. She was the keeper of his memory now.

For a long moment, as Soyoung looked at the action figure, her face was impassive; her bottom lip trembled, once, but gradually it turned upwards into a smile. She closed the box and stowed it carefully in her backpack.

Outside the house, without pausing to put on her shoes, she began to run.

She did not stop at the next street, or the next. She ran, her socks padding softly on the pavement, until she had reached the mouth of the suburb, the point where the sign that said WELCOME TO CEDAR HILLS met the main road. There, she sat on the curb, put on her shoes, and hugged both of her bags to her chest. She waited.

By the time the car pulled up, Soyoung's fingers and toes had become stiff with cold. She stood up slowly, the fog of her breath swirling around her, and watched as the passenger window lowered.

From the driver's seat, Paul peered out at her, his hands on the steering wheel.

Soyoung moved quickly. She pulled the door open and slipped inside, closing the door before she'd settled into the seat. "Drive," she said, her voice terse. "Just drive, Paul."

Paul didn't hesitate. He stepped on the gas, and they were off.

Soyoung was quiet for the next few minutes. Beside her, his eyes trained on the road, Paul also said nothing. There was a printed stack of MapQuest directions on the dashboard, and he referred to them occasionally before changing lanes or making turns. By 12:31, they'd made it onto the highway.

Soyoung exhaled slowly then. Her entire body seemed to unclench, and she let her head fall back against the headrest. She looked over at Paul. "Thanks for coming to get me."

Paul's eyes were still on the road. "Sure," he said.

"How long was the drive from Baltimore?"

"It's fine."

The last time they had spoken was via a hushed phone call, when Soyoung had managed to sneak her old cell phone out of her mother's purse for five minutes the afternoon before. And before that, she had watched from a bench outside the Cornell law library as he walked away, using his sleeve to wipe away angry tears.

Paul said, "There's some food in the back if you're hungry."

In the paper sack was a pastrami sandwich, a bag of chips, an apple, and a bottle of chocolate milk. Soyoung tore open the chips and held a piece out. "You want one?"

Paul shook his head. She ate quietly, letting the chips dissolve in her mouth before they had the chance to crunch.

There was a cross dangling from the rearview mirror, as well as a small, plump red heart made of satin. Soyoung said, "Is this your mom's car?"

Paul nodded. "She lets me borrow her car for errands."

"Am I an errand?" she said, and immediately regretted it. It had come out flippant. Paul didn't answer.

Soyoung said, "My mom told me about your calls."

"Did she?"

"Yeah. I didn't get to see them. She took my phone away as soon as she and my dad picked me up from Cornell. But she asked me who you were. She said you'd been calling every day, even though she told you to stop, so . . ." She smiled tremulously. "Thank you."

Paul nodded.

After a beat, he said, "So what are you going to do now?"

"I don't know."

"I thought you always had a plan for everything," Paul said.

He said this evenly, with no grievance in his voice. But it made Soyoung wince. She looked away, and the shame washed over her.

She said, "I'm so sorry, Paul. For the horrible things I said to you. For . . . for everything."

To this, Paul said nothing, and Soyoung leaned her head against the window, looking out at the gray, colorless highway. It was what she deserved.

It was just past four in the morning when they crossed the border from Connecticut into New York, and Soyoung sat up straighter in her seat. She said, "Is it okay if we make a slight detour? Drive a little bit further into Manhattan?"

"Sure," Paul said. It was the first time they'd spoken in hours.

The city, as they wove into it, was already wide awake. The pink morning sky was peeking through the gaps between skyscrapers; Soyoung pressed her nose to the window, watching the commuters pour out of subway exits, the scaffolding, the people who were already at work, pushing carts and trolleys down the street. "I was here with Lillian in September," she said. "We had a delicious lunch at a diner in Midtown. It must be somewhere nearby."

"The traffic is looking pretty bad," Paul said. "We should probably get back on the highway."

"No, right. Of course."

Soyoung slumped against her seat again. She said, "So when do you head back for spring semester?"

"The twelfth of January. Wednesday."

"Are you looking forward to it? Or has it been, um, nice being back at home?"

There was a pause.

Paul said, "Last semester, just . . . a lot of bad shit went down. I guess I'm still processing a lot of it."

"Are people on campus talking about me?"

"A bit. Just when the news first came out. But mostly, it's been—you know. Nathaniel and Stella. Everyone's in shock. They're still trying to figure out what happened."

"No, right," Soyoung said. "That makes sense."

Then she said, "Well, that's good to know about the twelfth. I'll be sure to get out of your hair well before then."

Paul glanced at her, surprised. "You don't have to do that," he said. "You can stay for as long as you want."

"With your mom and your stepdad? I bet they'll be sick of me after a week. Besides, what would I even do in Baltimore, anyway?"

"You could land in DC," he said. "There's lots of universities there. Art and culture. Museums. You could work on your art."

"I was thinking," Soyoung said, "that I might try to land here in New York for a while, maybe. But I don't know. I don't like staying in the same places or doing the same things for very long."

Paul had been looking at her, holding her quietly in his gaze. He shook his head, and this time he really smiled, though there was nothing in it but sadness. "You know," he said, "I've always thought you were like a bird."

Soyoung cocked her head. "A bird? Why?"

Paul said, "When I was a kid, my dad liked to garden. We had all these flowers in the backyard, bushes, trees. And all kinds of birds would come to visit. I'd see a hummingbird next to one of the flowers, and I'd get so excited, I'd run over and try to grab it. And of course it would fly away. All I wanted to do was to hold it in my hand and look at it, you know? But they never stayed still for me. They'd always fly away. And my dad said, *You know, that's how birds are. Unless you keep them in a cage, they're going to fly away.*

"That's how I felt the first time I met you. I know we didn't meet at orientation, by the way. If we'd met at orientation, I would have remembered. The first time we met was at the store. I had bought a muffin."

Soyoung was quiet for a long time.

"Paul?" she said, and he was silent, waiting. Soyoung's voice was small.

"Take me with you back to Baltimore. Please, Paul. There's something I need to do."

Paul nodded.

"All right," he said, and his voice had become quiet, too. "Let's go home, then."

The house where Paul's mom and stepdad lived was small and flat, with two bedrooms and two bathrooms squeezed between the yellowing walls. In Paul's bedroom, his mom had remade the bed with fresh linens for Soyoung, and in the basement, he and his mom worked together to inflate an air mattress. It sat in the middle of the space, flanked by a shelf of old books on one side and a Ping-Pong table on the other.

That night, Soyoung waited for forty-five minutes after the light in Paul's parents' room went out. Then she opened the door and slipped out, her socked feet landing soundlessly on the carpet as she headed for the basement.

Paul was stretched out on the air mattress, looking at something on his laptop, when she appeared at the base of the stairs. For a moment, he looked surprised, his face illuminated in the light of the laptop; then he smiled. "Hey," he said. "What's up?"

Soyoung said nothing. She crossed the room to the mattress and lifted one corner of his quilt, slipping underneath. Paul watched with shock as she shimmied up to him on the mattress and wrapped her arms around him, burrowing into his chest. In a small voice, she said, "Can I stay here tonight?"

There was a pause, and then Paul closed his laptop and set it aside. They were in total darkness now; his arms closed around her, and Soyoung felt his warmth radiate through every part of him that she touched. She ran her fingers through his curly hair. She leaned in and kissed the side of his neck, slow, tender.

Paul's breathing had become heavy. A moment passed, and he murmured, "Is it okay if I kiss you?"

"Not yet," Soyoung whispered back.

Then she said, "I want to. Trust me, I really want to. But there's something I have to do first."

Paul laughed. "What?"

"Just a small thing."

"Any chance you could do it now?"

This time, she was the one who laughed. "No, I can't do it now. But soon, I promise."

Just before dawn, Soyoung woke up to Paul's face next to hers, sharing the same pillow. Under the faint dusting of morning light, he looked so young, so at peace. The hint of a smile clung to his lips.

Soyoung brushed his messy hair aside and kissed his forehead, light as a feather. Then she slipped out of Paul's arms and tiptoed towards the stairs, back to his bedroom before anyone else could discover that she'd been gone.

ERIN

May 2017

The Muslim cemetery where Little Aunt was buried was built on a plot of land near the highway, about a half-hour drive from the city of Zhengzhou. At the entrance was a sprawling white gate with three dark green domes; in the distance, the mountains loomed.

There were only two other visitors in the cemetery. As Second Aunt led us past a row of black headstones engraved with Islamic calligraphy at the top and Chinese characters in the middle, I couldn't help but look back at them. They were standing in front of a grave in the corner, an elderly couple in clean, old-fashioned clothes. The man had on a little white skullcap, a taqiyah. The woman wore a hijab.

There was no headstone at Little Aunt's grave yet, only a fresh patch of dirt. My mom took a moment to take it all in; her lips began to tremble.

"Don't cry," Second Aunt whispered. "Apparently you're not supposed to cry. It's against their religion or something."

My mom managed a nod. She reached for the large plastic bag I was holding. "Are we allowed to put down food offerings?"

Second Aunt shook her head. "No food, no joss paper, no offerings."

We had bought oranges, chocolates, and a stack of joss paper from the shopping street near our hotel. My mom stared into the plastic bag, lost. She said, "Are flowers allowed?"

"They are, Ma," I said, pointing. "Look, that grave has flowers."

My mom exhaled. She reached into the bag and came out with a small bouquet, which she set on the dirt carefully. "We'll just leave these here for you," she said to the dirt. "You've always liked flowers, Xiaoyun, since you were a little girl. I hope you enjoy how pretty they are."

Second Aunt's eyes filled with tears. She turned away, and I put a hand on my mom's shoulder. She didn't seem to notice.

The trip back to China had come together in a matter of days. Hours, really. I'd made a more conscious effort at checking on my mom in the weeks after Little Aunt died, texting her every other day or so, sending her wholesome pictures, like one of a dog that had adopted a group of ducklings. And she'd seemed fine—until the morning after Sophia had taken me to the apartment by MoMA. That day, after we'd said goodbye, I'd checked my phone on the way to the office and found an avalanche of missed calls and voicemails from my mom, sobbing, distraught, barely coherent. *Your little aunt came to me in a dream in the middle of the night. I tried to talk to her, but she wouldn't answer. She just stared at me with tears running down her face. And when I woke up—I could feel the jinn watching me. It was with me in the apartment. It had come back.*

Forty-eight hours later, we were on a plane.

In the back of Second Aunt's car, I started fussing with my phone again. It had been years since my last trip to China, but I'd done my research before leaving. Google and YouTube had been blocked since the 2000s. Wikipedia, Twitter, Facebook, Instagram—if you could use it to check out what was going on in other countries, it was on the shit list. But there had always been workarounds. The Great Firewall was known for its holes. I'd purchased and downloaded not one but two VPN applications on my phone before leaving and tested them multiple times for posterity. But now, zooming along the highway in Second Aunt's electric-blue Honda, neither of the apps worked. I watched as the wheel spun idly on the connection screen. *Connecting... connecting... connection failed.* "Fuck," I said, not caring to keep my voice down, and my mom reached around and gave me an admonishing jab in the temple.

From the driver's seat, Second Aunt said, "Shelley, how are your studies at Columbia going? You must be busy, what with final exams coming up."

My mom and I exchanged a look. "She's just completed them, actually," my mom said. "The American school year finishes earlier than the Chinese one. After this, she's going back to New York to do her internship. The law firm she interned at last year asked her to come back, so it seems she didn't do that terrible of a job."

The next gravesite on our agenda was the one that belonged to my grandparents. After they moved back to China during my sophomore year of high school, my grandmother had died from a heart attack within a year, followed by my grandfather the year after that. They now rested together on a small hill just outside the village where my grandfather had grown up, overlooking a grove of orange trees. In front of their tombstones, my mother sank to her knees and kowtowed, touching her forehead to the dirt. "Ba, Ma," I heard her say. "It's your eldest daughter, Xiaofang. I'm sorry it's taken me so long to come and see you."

Then she began to cry. "Everyone's gone," she said. "Shelley's dad is gone. You're gone. Now Xiaoyun is gone, too. The world has become such an empty place."

As I stood next to her, hearing her wail and beat her head against the dirt, the sudden, unbridled display of emotion unsettled me. I took several steps away, giving her space. On my grandmother's tombstone, a small portrait had been embedded into the space below her name: my laolao in black and white, self-conscious in front of the camera, unsmiling. It was her passport photo, the only one I'd ever seen taken of her alone. My nose prickled, and I turned away. When neither of them was looking, I took my phone out of my pocket and tried the VPNs again. *Connection failed.*

My mom straightened up. "Let's burn some joss paper for your grandparents," she said, wiping her eyes.

Once Second Aunt had lit up the first batch, the two of them began scattering paper into the air, a faint cloud of white smoke forming around them. "Please eat well," I heard them say, their voices overlapping softly. "Please drink well. Please spend this money in the underworld and take good care of yourselves."

My mom said, "I should have never moved to America."

"Don't be ridiculous," Second Aunt said.

"I wasn't here to care for them in their final days. I didn't even make it home in time to say goodbye."

"You were busy with Shelley," Second Aunt said. "It was a critical time in her life. You had to keep a close eye on her studies, make sure she wasn't distracted. How else could she have gotten into a top school?"

My mom was quiet, and Second Aunt said, "Have you forgotten what Ma used to tell us when we were younger? The day you become a parent, your life stops being yours. Nothing else matters. No one else compares. Ma would have understood. She would never have forgiven you if you had chosen her over Shelley."

There was a long silence.

"You're right," my mom said, finally. "You're right."

She turned back to the tombstones. It took her a moment to gather the words.

"Ba, Ma," she said, "I've brought good news for you. Shelley is—she's been accepted to one of the top universities in America. She's going be a lawyer soon. She's living the life of her dreams. I know you're watching over her. I know you'll make good things happen for her."

Then she tugged at my sleeve. "Come," she said. "Come kowtow to your laolao and laoye so they'll give you their blessings."

I hesitated. It wasn't just the logic of everything she'd just said that wasn't adding up—it was everything else on top of that. It was the crying, the lies, the stark lonely sight of the tombstones in the dirt, the smell of paper burning. I felt sick, suddenly. I said, "I don't know how to kowtow."

"It's easy. You just get on your knees. Please, Shelley. *Please.*"

There was something in her voice. I complied.

In the dirt next to my mom, the smell of ash and incense thick around us, I got down on my knees and touched my forehead to the ground. A memory came floating to the surface, accompanied by a thousand others just like it: my grandparents on a hot summer day in Kissimmee, my laolao slicing watermelons in the kitchen, my laoye snoozing in a chair, his shirt pushed up high over his nipples while a tape of Peking opera played in the background. The staticky singing, the thud of the knife on the cutting board, the squeak of the ceiling fan spinning above us—hadn't it all been yesterday? How was it possible that we had existed in this world without them for going on ten years? My grandparents had carried within them oceans, both of them, and I had spent my entire life playing on the shores, never bothering to look past the closest wave. My nose pressed into the dirt, I began to cry, finally. The last of the joss paper was almost gone.

Back in Zhengzhou, after Second Aunt dropped us off at the hotel, I perched myself on the desk in our shared room while my mom changed into a starchy dress with a blue-and-white porcelain pattern. As she began to put on jewelry, I said, "What if you went by yourself, and I just stayed here and napped?"

"Don't be ridiculous," my mom said. "You're the whole reason for this dinner. You're the one they want to see."

She glanced at the phone in my hand. "Who are you talking to? You've been glued to your phone since we got here."

On the screen, the wheel of death was still spinning, and I felt a surge of irritation. "I'm seeing someone," I said.

My mom had been in the middle of putting on a necklace; she turned, slowly, and I forced myself to meet her eyes. My pronouncement had been too loud. It was jarring. It hung in the air, and for a few seconds, neither of us said anything.

She said, "You . . . you have a boyfriend?"

Her voice was tentative, hopeful, and I looked down. I turned my phone over in my hand.

Maybe it was time to get it over with.

Maybe this was what I needed to step out of the night and walk under the sun, the way I'd always said I wanted to.

But I remained silent, and after a moment, my mom said, "We should head downstairs. Your big uncle is already waiting in the car."

Big Uncle met us in a black Audi. The seats inside were a sleek leather, and when we rolled to a stop at the next red light, he lowered the window, lit a cigarette, and turned to give me a long, appraising look. "She's tall for a girl," he said.

In the passenger seat, my mom said, "She's tall like the Americans."

"Must be the food in America," Big Uncle said. "Something in the water."

He addressed me directly. "You don't remember me, do you? The last time I saw you, you were just learning to walk. I held you in my arms. You had your hair up in these two little pigtails."

In Big Uncle's face, I searched for a passing resemblance to my dad, or at least the two-dimensional version I knew from old photos. Big Uncle had the same eyebrows, I decided. Possibly the same jawline, too, if he lost twenty pounds. He blew out a billowing puff of smoke, and I stifled a cough. "Does she have a boyfriend?" he asked my mom.

"She's not thinking seriously about this stuff yet," my mom said. "She's young. She's focused on her studies."

"She's almost twenty-five," Big Uncle said.

My mom glanced at me. She said, "It's young in America."

Big Uncle turned to me again.

"Listen to your uncle, Shelley," he said. "You have to start thinking about this before it's too late. I see it with my coworkers' daughters all the time: They spend their twenties going from one academic program to the next, noses buried in a book, not even bothering to learn how to put on makeup. Then they graduate into the real world, and guess what? All the decent, eligible men are already taken. There's no one left to marry. They've been left over."

"In that case," I said, "maybe they should just marry each other."

From the front, my mom shot me another look. But Big Uncle just threw his head back and laughed. He said, as the light turned green, "You Americans always think it's about what you want, don't you? In the West, they teach you to be selfish. To put your needs first. But let me ask you this: Have you ever thought about what your mother needs? What are you doing to take care of her?"

Fuck you, I thought. I made a note to look up the phrase in Mandarin as soon as I had Wi-Fi again.

For dinner with my dad's side of the family, Big Uncle had chosen a Xinjiang-themed restaurant, an opulently furnished two-story space full of archways and Turkish rugs in the midst of a busy shopping area. All the waitresses wore colorful striped dresses as uniforms, and one of them, a girl with black curly hair and a round, smiling face, showed us to a private dining room, where the rest of the family was already waiting. The moment we walked in, there was a rush of commotion: People were shooting out of their seats and flocking to me, touching my face, rubbing my arms. "She's so tall," everyone was saying. "I can't believe how big she's gotten."

Introductions were a blur. There was Big Uncle and his wife, Big Aunt. There was their son, Liangliang, who was around my age and worked at the same municipal government office as Big Aunt, doing some kind of pencil-pusher nepotism job. My dad's younger sister, Little Aunt, was there with her husband and her ten-year-old daughter, Lili. And there was another aunt with a copper-red poodle perm who wasn't a sibling but close to the family, maybe a first cousin, accompanied by her husband and son, a sulky teenager named Dodo. As we arranged ourselves around a large table with a glass lazy Susan, I could feel everyone's eyes on me. "Shelley," Perm Aunt said, laying a hand on my arm, "do you know Chinese? Can you understand what we're all saying?"

All three men had already started smoking at the table. I had to cough to get the words out. "Um, yeah. I can speak Chinese. I can read a bit, too."

There were delighted murmurs around the table. "Look at her," Perm Aunt said, awed. "She's fluent in both languages."

Then she elbowed her son, who was playing on his phone. "Stop playing your stupid games for once and look at your big cousin. Look at her! This is someone who got into Columbia University in America. You should be asking her questions. You should be learning from her while she's here."

She snatched the phone from his hands, and the kid scowled. I felt a rush of sympathy for him.

The waitress returned with menus and hot tea, and we fell into a respectful silence, waiting for Big Uncle, who was ostensibly bankrolling the entire dinner, to order for the table. He turned to my mom. "What does Shelley like to eat? We'll get all her favorites. It's rare that the child gets to come home."

Immediately, my mom was leaning forward, brushing off the offer. "Oh, it doesn't matter. She likes the same things that everyone likes."

"Sweet-and-sour pork?" Perm Aunt asked me. "That's always a crowd favorite."

"Lulu, you can't ask for pork here," Big Aunt said. "This place is halal."

Perm Aunt clapped a hand to her mouth. "I'm so sorry," she said to the round-faced waitress, who was still smiling. "I'm terrible at these cultural things. I always forget which religion is which."

Big Uncle, meanwhile, was giving the waitress the same appraising look he'd given me in the car. As she poured baijiu into his glass, he said, "You're from Xinjiang, aren't you? I can see it in your face. You have all the classic Uyghur features."

The waitress smiled, wide and warm. "You have an excellent eye," she said. "I'm from Ürümqi."

"Look at how well she speaks Mandarin," Big Aunt said, impressed. "Barely a trace of an accent."

And Perm Aunt said, "Look at how high her nose bridge is. Those natural curls. She's got that exotic look. What's the name of that actress everyone's talking about? The gorgeous Uyghur one from TV?"

Liangliang answered from across the table. "It's Dilraba, Auntie."

Perm Aunt clapped her hands together. "That's it!" she said. "That's the one. God, just positively stunning. I'd give ten years of my life to trade her face for mine."

To the waitress, she said, "You look just like Dilraba. You're very pretty."

The waitress beamed. "Thank you," she said. "Thank you very much."

From a sofa in the hallway, I connected to the restaurant's Wi-Fi and tried to start up the two VPN apps for the fiftieth time that day. Just as before, they wouldn't give. I remained cut off from the world I was used to living in: Gmail. Instagram. YouTube. I couldn't read the news on CNN. I couldn't even send a fucking WhatsApp message to the woman I loved. I shoved my phone back in my pocket, seething. A throbbing ache had started in the side of my head.

Back in the dining room, the waitress was gone, and the conversation had turned to Uyghurs. "I just don't understand why you had to pick this place," Little Aunt was saying. "I haven't felt at ease around them since the riots. We know they hate us. We've seen what they're capable of."

To that, Big Uncle waved his hand. "See, now you're being prejudiced," he said. "Shengnan and I just got back from a holiday near Tian Shan. We were surrounded by minorities everywhere we went, and we couldn't have been more welcomed. The best hospitality. The best food. The lamb kebabs, the dapanji, the laghman—the Uyghurs know what they're doing in the kitchen, I'll tell you that. Best part of their culture by far."

"And the dancing," Big Aunt said. "Don't forget about their beautiful dancing."

Little Aunt, however, drew her shawl closer around her. "I can't believe you went to Xinjiang," she said to Big Uncle. "You could have been stabbed on the street. Caught up in a suicide bombing at the train station."

"It's safe now," Big Uncle said. "They beefed up the police presence significantly after what happened in 2009, and all the terrorists have been rounded up. It's been perfectly safe for years."

"Only because they managed to tamp it down for the time being. But people like that, they don't stay down for long. It's like cutting the tail off a venomous snake; another one grows in its place. Doesn't matter how much our government invests in building their villages, their schools, teaching them our language, helping them assimilate into modern Chinese society—all that work, and it's like pressing your warm face to someone's cold ass cheek. There's no gratitude. They just go on hating us Hans. One generation after another, they pass it down."

"Their religion," Perm Aunt's husband said. "That's the problem. Why do you think there are so many wars in the Middle East? Why do you think they're going around in public, stabbing everyone? It's violent to the core."

Big Aunt frowned. "I don't think it's their religion," she said.

She looked around the table. "The Hui are Muslims, too, aren't they? You never hear of them becoming terrorists. They're content to practice their religion in peace and leave the rest of us alone."

My head shot up from my phone. It was as though the walls in the room were closing in; the chandelier above me was suddenly too bright, too hot on my skin. Instinctively, I turned to my mom, but she was busy pouring herself a glass of baijiu. She seemed not to have heard.

Little Aunt opened her mouth, but closed it abruptly; the door had opened, and a group of waitresses were filing in with the food, setting the plates down along the circumference of the lazy Susan. Big Uncle spun it in my direction. "Let Shelley eat first," he said. "Let the child have the first pick."

Then he waved a hand at the round-faced waitress from earlier, who was refilling his tea. "Dilraba," he said, and she paused to look at him. "Dilraba, let me ask you something. Did you meet a lot of Hans when you lived in Xinjiang?"

The waitress smiled.

"There's a lot of Hans in Xinjiang," she said. "Half of Ürümqi is Han."

"And how do you feel about them being there, really? You can be honest with us. We won't be offended by the truth."

Big Uncle's tone was warm, encouraging, but around the table, the atmosphere shifted. Little Aunt tugged at her shawl. My mom was staring into her glass of baijiu. Even Perm Aunt had paused in the middle of adding food to my plate. The waitress was still smiling.

"I think it's wonderful," she said. "It's like they always say: China is a big family made up of diverse people. The fifty-six ethnic groups shouldn't be fighting. They should be hugging each other tightly like the seeds of a pomegranate."

Big Uncle looked around the table, delighted.

"You see?" he said. "This is what I'm talking about. We shouldn't be fighting! We're all Chinese. We're all family. If all the Uyghurs were like you, and if all the Hans were like me, we could actually accomplish something. No more violence. No more hate. All of our ridiculous issues would finally be solved."

After I'd rushed to finish my plate, I slipped back into the hallway and parked myself on the same sofa. Predictably, the VPN apps remained down, but at this point anything was preferable to being subjected to my dad's relatives. The door to the dining room opened, and I saw the waitresses file out, the round-faced woman among them. As she passed by me, she was staring straight ahead, her face blank. I thought of saying something to her—but what was there to say? By the time I had finished constructing half of a shoddy Chinese sentence in my mind, she had disappeared around the corner.

The door swung open again. This time, it was Dodo, the kid who was maybe my second cousin. He wandered over to me, hands in pockets, and I was predisposed to ignore him. But then he said, "Can I use your phone?"

"To do what?"

He shrugged. "I want to play some games. I hate these dinners. Everybody in this family sucks ass."

The kid had a point. As I handed him my phone, I said, "Do you know how to use a VPN?"

"Yeah, I've used them a few times. Why?"

I watched over his shoulder as he tried to troubleshoot the two apps, but they didn't budge. Dodo downloaded another app, but the moment we booted it up, it went belly up, just like the other two. That was when the air went out of me, finally. I buried my face in my hands, rubbing my aching temples, and I heard Dodo ask, "What are you trying to do, anyway?"

"I need to talk to somebody in America. It's important."

"Why don't you just talk to them on WeChat?"

"Jesus, because I don't have WeChat. WeChat is something only Chinese people use because they don't give you another choice. I'm not—I'm not Chinese like you."

Dodo was quiet, and after a pause I looked up, disconcerted by the ugliness of the thing I'd just said. But his head was down, his glasses almost pressed against the phone screen. He was already deep into his game.

He was in the middle of hacking a veiled assassin into pieces when Little Aunt opened the door and called us back in for desserts. On the table, the waitresses were setting out nutty cakes and bowls of what looked like a sugary white pudding. I made a beeline for my mom and knelt by her chair, putting both hands on her arm. "I can't take this anymore," I told her in English. "We need to go, Ma. Please. I want to go back to the hotel."

Her eyes scanned my face, and she nodded.

"All right," she said. "I'll tell your big uncle that you're tired from jet lag."

Leaving was another round of chaos. All three aunts hugged me, and the husbands nodded at me, their cigarettes glowing red between their fingertips. Little Aunt beseeched me to go shopping with her the following day so she could buy me new dresses. Perm Aunt wanted me to come to her house for dinner and practice speaking English with Dodo, the lazy punk. Big Uncle and Big Aunt walked us to the front door of the restaurant, and as we waited for a taxi to pull up, Big Uncle put a hand on my shoulder. I had to resist the urge to shrug it off. "Be good," he said. "Be good and listen to your mother, won't you?"

I nodded. A moment passed, and Big Uncle shook his head. A strange expression had overtaken his face.

Quietly, he said, "It's remarkable."

"What?"

"Your dad," he said. "I've been thinking to myself all evening—you look just like him. You look just like he did when he was a kid."

Then he said, "Did you know that I used to take him to school with me? He was just a baby, but your grandparents had to work in the fields, and no one else was there to watch him. So I strapped him on my back and walked to school with him every day. He'd sleep in a basket next to my desk while I studied, and I'd feed him porridge when he cried. I've always remembered that."

His eyes were glistening, and despite myself, I felt my eyes well up, too. Then Big Uncle raised his cigarette to his lips and took a long drag, and the moment was broken.

"Here," he said, and I felt a thick envelope in my hand. Instinctively, I held it back out towards him. "I can't," I said. "I don't need this."

"Take it," Big Uncle said. "We're separated by an entire ocean. You lost your father when you were so young, and I can't be there to take care of you. So this is . . . this is . . ."

He shook his head.

"Take good care of yourself," he said. "And remember what I said about not getting left over."

In the taxi, my mom and I were both quiet. We were in the heart of the downtown area, and as we drove, it occurred to me that the city was far glitzier than I'd expected. There were glass skyscrapers and malls at every turn. Massive billboards flashed with skincare ads and tourism slogans. Even the public buses looked sleek and new. When we rolled to a stop at an intersection, my mom nudged me. "Look," she said in English.

Across the street was a small mosque. "I was here before," she said. "With your little aunt, a few years ago."

"You want to go in?"

She shook her head, and it was then that I noticed the crimson banner hanging above the mosque entrance. In large block characters, it said, THE CORE SOCIALIST VALUES: PROSPERITY, DEMOCRACY, CIVILITY, HARMONY, FREEDOM, EQUALITY, JUSTICE, RULE OF LAW, PATRIOTISM, DEDICATION, INTEGRITY, FRIENDSHIP. Below that, two men in all-black clothing stood with their hands behind their backs, patrolling the entrance.

"It's not good for the people inside if we go," my mom murmured. "We have American passports. We'll bring trouble."

"But what—"

The taxi driver was watching us in the rearview mirror, curious. I closed my mouth.

At the sprawling plaza near the hotel, we got out early to walk off the heaviness of the dinner. It was dotted with people: elderly couples doing tai chi, families on an evening stroll, a group of middle-aged women in matching workout clothes dancing to exercise music being blasted through a set of speakers. After we'd passed them, my mom said, keeping her voice low, "Your little aunt's request to travel to Mecca was denied, in the end."

"Why was it denied?"

"Why do you think? We all knew the winds were changing. And she had to go and make things harder for herself."

My mom was cryptic and cagey, the way she always was whenever I asked her about anything important. I stopped walking, and after a moment, she did, too. I said, "Does Dad's family even know that you're Hui?"

She blinked. "Of course they do," she said. "It's not a secret."

"So, what, they just don't care? They don't care that it's insulting to you to talk shit about Muslims when you're sitting right there? And you're not even going to speak up to defend yourself? To defend your own people?"

My nose was stinging. I wiped it roughly with my sleeve, but my mom just exhaled, impatient.

She said, "You think everyone in the world is out to get you? That people are just sitting there, thinking up all the ways they can persecute you? None of it is personal. They're not thinking about me. They don't even remember that I'm Hui. And honestly, with the way things are going, why should I care to remind them?"

"It's fucked up, though," I said. I was blinking back tears now. "It's fucked up that we can't just be who we really are."

My mom was quiet as a family of three passed us, the kid blowing a stream of bubbles into the night air. She said, "Did your laolao ever tell you what happened to her family in the nineteen forties?"

"I don't know. Was it the Cultural Revolution?"

"No, that was later. This was when she was younger. When she was just a little girl."

My mom said, "There was a famine in Henan. Her entire family starved to death in the span of two weeks."

Her tone was light, but my breath caught. I felt chills.

"Shit," I said. "No, yeah, I . . . I think I did know that. Someone must have told me when I was younger. I don't think it was her, though."

"She didn't like talking about it," my mom said. "I was the one who told you. I thought it was important that you knew."

She looked away, her gaze trailing the sun, which was beginning to set behind the skyscrapers in the distance. She said, "I know you've always hated our apartment in Florida."

I opened my mouth. But there was nothing to say.

My mom said, "I know you always thought you deserved better. I did, too. I've always wanted better things for you than what I could provide. I remember what it felt like to want things: By the time I and my sisters were born, the famine was over, but that didn't mean we were much better off. We ate the same things for every meal. Cornbread, millet, yams if we were lucky. I'd come home from school every day with the front of my stomach touching the back. We had meat only once a year—tiny precious slivers of beef floating in a bowl of watery noodles. I remember there was a day when I was so hungry that I threw an empty bowl on the floor and cried. I said to your laolao and laoye, *Why can't you get us meat to eat every day? Why can't you give us better things?* And they pulled down my pants and beat me with a shoe."

I snorted. "Nice to hear some things in this family never change."

That got my mom to laugh, even if briefly. "I was good!" she said. "I only got beaten once or twice my entire childhood. I was nothing like you."

It took her a minute to speak again.

"There was a story your laolao told me once, only once," she said. "I don't think she meant to, or that she knew she had. We'd gone back to her old village together, she and I. I was a teenager back then. We rode through the countryside all day on the back of a pickup truck, and when we got there, your laolao stopped talking. She walked around, looking everywhere, and I followed her. It wasn't until later that I worked out that she was trying to find the graves of her parents, her sister, her brother. But they were long gone. Back then, people starved to death every day. Those who survived didn't have the energy to bury the dead. So they just left them there.

"That night, when we slept over at a relative's house, your laolao got drunk. I'd never seen her drink before. And she started crying. She started rambling to me. She told me about eating grass. Eating the bark off trees. She told me about lying in bed with the rest of her family, weak with hunger. She didn't even notice when they'd stopped breathing. She was close to being gone herself.

"In the end, she summoned the will to leave. She found a cane and walked slowly from house to house, begging others in the village for scraps of food, anything. She went to the house of a little girl she knew, a friend she'd played with. In the yard, she heard the sound of a pot boiling. She smelled meat cooking in a stew. But that was impossible, she thought. How could anyone have meat to eat right now? How could they have anything to eat? Inside the house, her friend wasn't there. Neither was her friend's mother. The only person there was her friend's father, standing over a pot of stew in the kitchen. Your laolao walked over and looked into the pot, and in the stew, she saw . . . she saw white chunks of melting fat, rising to the surface.

"And that was when she knew."

Abruptly, she closed her mouth. My mom looked at me, and it took almost a whole minute for the words to sink in.

"Fuck," I said.

And then: "*Fuck.* Holy fucking shit."

I barely made it to the nearest trash can. I bent over it, gripping the metal rim, and let loose. The contents of my stomach splattered over a sea of fruit peels and plastic cups, and by the time I finally straightened up, wiping my mouth with the back of my hand, my mom was waiting behind me with a bottle of lemon tea.

Once I'd chugged the whole bottle, I said, "I can't believe you just told me that. It's *sick*."

"It was a time when things didn't make sense," my mom said. "The things people had to do, the things they had to see, they were . . ."

She shook her head. She said, "You always thought your grandparents were such hypocrites for giving up our faith so easily. So what if the Red Guards burned down our mosques and took away our Qurans? So what if they beat our imams and locked them in the barns with cows? You're an American through and through, filled with so much naive idealism. You think there are principles worth putting your neck on the line. You think there are things worth dying for. But what Chinese people know— what ordinary people like us have known for five thousand years—is that the only way to make it through this life is on our knees.

"That day in the kitchen, even as a little girl, your laolao looked into a pot of stew and saw the truth: that there is no God. No mercy. No justice. No salvation. She saw that there is nothing in this life that is ever worth dying for."

In the distance, the sun was almost gone. My mom reached out and tucked my hair behind my ear, the strands that were sticking to my face through sweat and vomit. Her touch was gentle, and instinctively, I stepped forward and hugged her.

"I'm sorry," I said. "I wish . . . I wish . . ."

But I was at a loss for words, and my mom cradled the back of my head with her hand. "It's all right," she said. "It's all in the past. None of it matters anymore."

Then she said, "We changed our name, too, you know."

My brain was so scattered, it took a moment for her words to click. I looked up at her, startled. "You changed your name? What are you talking about?"

"Our real last name, the one we had a hundred years ago—it was Nasruddin. We changed it to Ding so that people wouldn't look at us sideways. So people would believe that we were Chinese, just like them."

Behind us, the group of dancing women had changed their routine to a new song. Placidly, in a tone that was almost bored, my mom said, "Personally, I like Ding much better."

That night, after my mom's snores faded and the jet lag gave way to melatonin, I dreamed I was thirsty.

In the dream, I stood on an endless desert, the land cracked open beneath my feet. Around me, I saw nothing but dust and sand. The sun bore down on me with rage.

I needed water.

I must have walked for miles. My feet broke out into blisters. My skin started to peel. But in the dream I felt no pain, just unrelenting thirst. I kept going. Another mile. Then another. I was getting closer, I could feel it. It was there, just beyond the horizon, calling out to me.

And then I saw it. A hundred feet in front of me: an oasis. A panoply of lush green. In the distance, I heard trickling water. I saw dancing silver under the sun. I started to run.

My eyes snapped open.

I was standing in the hotel bathroom, my mom's sunscreen and toothpaste and medications scattered on one side of the sink, our used hand towels on the other. The faucet over the sink was running.

My right hand was hovering over the handle, as if I'd just lifted it. My throat was on fire, and instinctively, I wedged my head under the faucet and opened my mouth, let the water pour in. Almost a full minute passed by before I remembered that the tap water here wasn't drinkable.

Coughing, I spat out the remaining water in my mouth and shut off the faucet.

Back in the room, I flopped on the bed and pulled up one of the VPN apps. The wheel whirled. *Connecting...* it said. *Connecting...*

And then: *Connection successful.*

I bolted up. My fingers moved frantically to bring up WhatsApp, where dozens of notifications were suddenly pouring in. *Missed call from Sophia Moon. Missed call from Sophia Moon. Missed call from Sophia Moon.*

Then I saw the messages.

> Already missing you. Let me know when you land. I love you so much.
>
> Have you landed?
>
> I saw that your flight landed. Are you still in Beijing? Did you get a train to Zhengzhou? Call me. I love you.
>
> Shelley? Can you call me back? Feeling a tiny bit worried. I just need to hear your voice.
>
> Sorry, I know I'm probably spiralling for no reason. I'm guessing you're having issues with the VPN. Can you just call me when you get this? Don't worry about the other messages. Just got back from musical night at O's school. He played a singing asparagus and was the cutest. Love you.
>
> Shelley? It's been almost two days.
>
> Are you ignoring me? Did I do something wrong?

If you're angry with me, can we at least talk?

Please, Shelley. I'm desperate. I need you to answer the phone. Please.

And, finally, sent two hours ago: I don't think I can do this anymore.

My entire body went cold. I rolled off the bed and ran back into the bathroom. There I dialed her, fingers trembling. The phone rang once. Twice. A third time.

I heard her voice. "Shelley?"

It was small and distant, but relief flooded me. "Oh, thank God," I said. "Sophia, listen, are you okay? Where are you right now?"

She didn't answer right away. I tried again. "Sophia? Sophia, where are you?"

When Sophia finally spoke, there was an odd, almost childlike quality to her voice. "I'm in bed," she said. "I've been sick since last night."

"Oh, baby, I'm so sorry. Do you have a fever? Is it the flu? You scared me with that last message."

"I don't know. I'm just feeling very weak. And, Shelley . . ."

Her voice wavered before she said, "It's been raining every day lately. I don't . . . I don't like it when it rains."

Again, I said, "I'm so sorry. I'm so sorry I haven't called. I wish I was there with you. Is Paul—is he bringing you food? Is he taking care of you?"

"Yes, but it doesn't matter. I can't eat. I can't sleep, either. You said you would call as soon as you landed."

She sounded calm, but I could hear the veiled reproach. I sat down on the edge of the bathtub and rubbed my temples.

"I know, baby. I'm so sorry. It was the stupid VPN. I couldn't get either of the apps to work after I landed in Beijing. I don't know if it was a firewall issue, or if it was the apps themselves, I—"

"Then you could have called me on the phone. You could have bought a SIM card and called me long-distance."

"I know, I know, and I was going to do that tomorrow, it's just that all day I've been running around, going to these cemeteries—"

"Skype isn't blocked in China. You could have bought international credits and called me from there."

"No, I know, and I'm sorry, I—"

"You knew," she said, "and you just didn't care to. Because at a subconscious level, you're already tired of me. You've already decided to walk away."

The accusation was so absurd that I started laughing. "Sophia," I said, "come on. You know me better than that."

Sophia was quiet for a beat. She said, "How well does anyone know another person, really? We all have things about ourselves that we keep hidden away. Secrets that we never show anyone."

"Not me, though," I said. "You know everything about me. You're the only person who sees the full extent of how fucked up I am. And that's because you're the only person who matters."

"What about your mom?"

"What about my mom?"

"You dropped everything when she called you. You went to China with her even though she didn't ask you to, even though she didn't really need you. You just . . . you just left."

That was when it clicked, finally. I exhaled. I leaned my head against the wall.

"Sophia," I said, "are you actually jealous of my mom right now?"

"And what if I am? Is that so wrong? She's never done the things for you that I have. She's never taken care of you the way you needed. You were the one who told me how much you hated being stuck in that dingy little apartment with her. How all your life, she's made you feel like you couldn't breathe. Yet one phone call from her, and not a day later, you . . ."

She was sniffling now, and suddenly, I felt a rush of a strange new emotion that I could not place, could not even draw outlines around it. I rubbed my temples again.

"Sophia, listen," I said. "I want you to listen to me, okay? I'm sorry about dropping off the radar for the last couple of days. From now on, I'll call you every day. I'll buy credits on Skype. I'll buy a SIM card. I'll never fall off the grid and scare you like that again. Oh, and for the record, I'm not, like, having a good time here. I had dinner with my dad's family, and they were a bunch of dicks. Plus, I'm sharing a hotel room with my mom, and she snores like a drunk rhino. I literally have not been able to sleep since we got here. I'm counting the days until this trip is over so I can come home to you."

I waited. On the other end, I could feel Sophia smile, just a little.

She said, "I don't snore when I sleep. I'm very, very quiet."

"I know, baby. I know you are."

That was when I felt it again: the nameless emotion. In my mind, I saw two images of Sophia emerge. The first was the Sophia who had sat across the table from me at the motel. She had smiled at me like a figure from a painting, calm, enigmatic, quietly in control. And the second was the Sophia who had cried to me on the phone, who in that moment had both startled and delighted me with her jealousy, with a desire that lacked both magnanimity and disguise. This Sophia stepped off the page. She was flesh and blood and bone.

After I hung up with Sophia, I checked Erin Callaghan's social media accounts. On Instagram, there were five new messages waiting for me from Lizzie Cloverfield, sent in response to a picture I'd taken inside the plane cabin shortly after boarding. **On my way back to the motherland!** I had messaged her.

!!!!! Lizzie had written back minutes later.

And then: wait but you're actually doing it

holy shit so so so so excited for you im crying. are you in beijing? or are you already heading to guiyang?

A day later, when I hadn't replied, she had followed up. any news?

also my mom is being so extra this week i lowkey wanna dieeeeee lol

As I took in the messages, I felt a sudden, inexplicable fatigue: My phone was a brick in my hand. I closed the app and pulled up Snapchat instead.

There, I had an unread message from Josh. *Pulling an office all-nighter just for the chance to sell midlife crisis dad sneakers is truly the epitome of the American Dream,* he wrote. It was accompanied by a selfie taken surreptitiously inside one of the small conference rooms: There was a half-eaten box of pizza on the table, and behind Josh's head I could see Amy, a pair of reading glasses dangling from her hand as she pointed at something in the Skechers pitch deck on the big screen. This one was far easier. I responded to him with three skull emojis.

Then I used my fingers to pinch the screen and zoom in on Amy's face. The image quality was far too grainy, and in the sliver of her profile I could see, there was nothing out of the ordinary. But still—something felt off.

The day before I'd left for China, when I walked into Amy's office for our weekly one-on-one, there had been a hint of something intrusive in the air. Like a rotting piece of fruit forgotten in a drawer, faint but present. She was standing by the open window, staring into the distance, and when I rapped on the open door, Amy had jumped. "What?" she snapped.

"Oh, sorry. It's just—our one-on-one? I could come back later, if you're busy."

Amy sighed. "No, come in," she said. "It's just the migraines acting up again."

I settled myself into the chair opposite her desk, pencil and notebook poised on my lap. As Amy returned to her own chair, she said, "So: The big pitch meeting with Skechers—when they come into the office on Friday, we're rolling out the red carpet. Large conference room. Branded MLC tote bags and other fun tchotchkes courtesy of your team. Radha's ordering a catered lunch. I'm going to send out an all-staff email in a bit, reminding everyone to clean their workspaces and show up wearing shirts that are ironed. I want to knock those hideous dollar-store paper bags off their feet with our can-do attitudes and winning smiles."

"Sounds like a plan," I said. "What do we think are the chances that they'll give us the digital contract?"

"It's decent. Maria knows us. Maria loves us. If it were up to Maria, we'd be signing on the dotted line right now. But now they've got this new chief marketing officer, Gavin, and he's a bit of a wild card. He's distrustful of longevity in client-agency relationships because he thinks it leads to complacency and stale ideas."

"Good luck getting rid of us," I said. "You can't build these kinds of capes in-house. Or the real-time agility."

She clapped her hands at me. "Precisely. Precisely! And that's what the entire pitch boils down to. *Look at what we've done for you. Look at the resources we have at our disposal.* Are you all set for your part of the presentation?"

I hesitated. Then I said, "I'm so sorry, but I actually can't. I have to go to California for a family funeral. But Tess has agreed to cover my slides, so . . ."

There was a pause. Amy said, "You didn't tell me you'd be in California."

"Oh, I sort of did, actually. I emailed you yesterday afternoon about it?"

"Did I reply to your email?"

"No."

"If I didn't reply, then you can assume I didn't see it. Every minute, I have six new messages pouring into my inbox. It's impossible for me to keep track of it all. In the future, I'd appreciate fewer assumptions about what I have and haven't seen, and more proactive follow-up, especially if you're going to be missing out on a high-stakes client pitch."

A moment passed.

"I'm sorry," I said. "It won't happen again."

"And I appreciate it," she said, brisk. "Now, about your slides—we need to reassign them to Afua."

I blinked. "But Afua isn't even on this pitch."

"No, I know. We'll need to pull her from the Marshalls pitch and get her up to speed. The thing is—" She hesitated. "Oh, all right, I'll just come out and say it. Gavin is Native American."

I said nothing. Amy shifted in her chair before she said, "He sits on the Diversity and Inclusion Committee at Skechers. I just read an interview he did with *Adweek* where he talked about the need for diverse creative teams. You understand what I'm trying to get at, right? We need to show him that Meek LeClerc isn't a bowl of oatmeal. We have diverse people. We love diverse people. I mean—you get me, right? I'm not somehow being offensive when I say that?"

Her eyes were boring into me. I smiled.

"No," I said, "of course not. Diversity is always the goal. And you've been such a great ally."

Visibly, Amy relaxed.

"I just think it's so important for us to hold space for women of color," she said. "And she'd be a terrific face for it. Such an eloquent speaker, too. So go ahead and ping her the slides after this meeting, and we'll—"

She trailed off. Her eyes had taken on a glazed look again, and I watched as they drifted past the awards on her desk, past the snake plant in the corner, and back to the window. When she spoke, her voice was barely a whisper. "Did you hear that?"

"Sorry?"

"I thought . . . there was a voice, I really thought it was . . ."

Amy shook her head, collecting herself.

"Let's go over the wording on slide seventeen one more time," she said.

In the bathroom, still perched on the edge of the bathtub, I opened Instagram again. I stared at the stack of messages from Lizzie until the screen went dark, and I had to reenter my password to get back in. I took a deep breath before typing out a reply.

I'm good, still in Beijing as of today. How are you? Everything ok?

Lizzie's answer came instantly. no wayyy so happy for you!!!
And then: when do you think you'll go to the orphanage? whats the plan?
Me: They called me this morning and said they might have found some additional info about my birth parents, but I don't have the full details yet. I will probably head there tomorrow or the day after to take a look

Lizzie liked the message. praying for good news eeeeek, she wrote.
Me: What did you mean by your mom was being extra? Did she do something abnormal or . . . ?
Lizzie: hehe I mean normal for her is acting like a bitch sooo
Lizzie: she has this super important pitch meeting on friday so she's been running around not sleeping yelling at me like stressed out of her mind
Me: Yeah I'm on that pitch too, we're trying to win a big contract with Skechers
Lizzie: lmao imagine having a mental breakdown over skechers i cant
Me: Does your mom yell at you a lot?
Lizzie: sometimes
Lizzie: but it's fine idk we're good most of the time

The aching in my head was gone, but it had been replaced by something else; in my stomach, I felt a strange, cold disgust, a creeping irritation. I drafted five different messages before finally settling on one.

Me: I was just thinking, while I'm in Guiyang I could also drop by the place where you were adopted and ask about your files. But no pressure though

She was quiet for about five minutes.
Lizzie: I don't know

Lizzie: I'm sorry

Me: That's ok, don't be sorry

Lizzie: it feels like a really big decision and im not sure im ready

Me: I get it

Me: Call me any time if you need to talk things through. Day or night. I'm always here for you.

At some point during my time in the bathroom, my mom had woken up. I saw her lying on her back when I tiptoed back into the room, her eyes wide open, staring at the ceiling. "Hey," I said, and she stirred. "Jet lag?"

My mom looked at me, and that was when I saw it: Her face was glistening with tears. "Don't mind me," she said hoarsely. "Just go back to sleep."

Of course I ignored her. I poured a glass of boiled water from the kettle and brought it to her. Then I sat down on her bed and rubbed her shoulder. "I'm sorry you had a rough day," I said. "Maybe you could spend more time with Second Aunt while you're here. Go to a day spa with her or something."

My mom shook her head. "Your second aunt has her job and her own family," she said. "She has other people to look after. All I have is you."

She reached up and squeezed my cheek, and I felt that stinging sensation in my nose again.

She said, "I pray for you every day. Do you know that? I've prayed for you every day since before you were even born."

The sentiment washed over me like warm water, and I ducked my head, as if to avoid it. I said, "I thought you said God wasn't real."

My mom smiled, just a little. "I don't even know who I'm praying to, really," she said. "I pray to anyone who might be out there listening. Just in case."

After she had drifted off to sleep, I went to retrieve the envelope Big Uncle had given me earlier. It was stuffed with pink hundred-yuan bills, the stack so thick that it had gone rigid. In my mom's wallet, I found a zippered compartment and wedged the envelope inside. I tossed the wallet back into her purse.

Back in my bed, I pulled the duvet over me, and that made me think of Sophia. I let my mind take me places. I saw her curled up against me on the nylon sleeping bag, her skin warm and flushed, her breathing soft beneath the sound of rain. I saw the little house in Hoboken with the blue door, the way the kitchen always glowed with golden lights, her outline in the window welcoming me home. Two days earlier, when she drove me to Newark and we said goodbye in the departures hall, Sophia had clung to me. "Sometimes I'm afraid of how much I love you," I heard her say, her voice muffled, and I had kissed her forehead and told her the same.

With that, I finally fell asleep.

ERIN

Radha called me on Skype at 6 a.m. local time, just as Zhengzhou was waking up and New York was dissolving into the weekend. As she spun the camera around, I could see Josh, Pedro, Erkin, and CJ around our usual table at Finnegan's; even Jay had joined this time. No one was smiling as they waved to me.

"So?" I said. "You're killing with me the suspense. How'd it go?"

They all looked at each other. Radha said, "We've made a pact that none of us are leaving this bar tonight unless it's in the back of an ambulance."

"Shit, was it that bad? What happened?"

Another meaningful look was exchanged over the table. Carefully, Erkin said, "Well, it was, uh . . . Amy, she, uh . . ."

"Erkin," Jay said. I could see him shaking his head.

There was another pause.

Josh said, "Jay, we have to talk about it. We're among friends here. I don't know about you, but I trust all of the people at this table, including Erin."

"I know that," Jay said. "I know that, Josh. And it's not a matter of trust. It's a matter of . . ."

He shook his head. "None of us know what happened," he said, "and until we do, we need to give Amy the respect, the time, and the distance that she deserves to deal with whatever is going on."

I saw people squirm in their seats. A few seconds later, Josh was the one to speak up again.

He said, "I think it's pretty clear what happened. Amy had a complete fucking mental breakdown in front of the client and lost us the contract."

Jay grimaced, and Josh reached towards me. "Here, give me the phone, Radha. I'll tell Erin what happened."

There was a shuffling noise and a temporary blackness, and then the phone was in Josh's hand, the camera pointed at his nostrils. "At lunch, the Skechers people come in," he said. "We roll out the red carpet, we take them to the large conference room, we get catered Portuguese for lunch. The new CMO, Gavin, he's having a great time. He's smiling and laughing and nodding along to the whole presentation. We get to the Q&A portion. Gavin asks a question. Amy starts to answer, and then she stops and gets this look on her face. I don't even know how to describe it. It was..."

He shook his head. "She starts, like, running circles around the room. And she's going from person to person, asking, *Do you hear it? Do you hear it?* And we're all like, *Hear what?* But she's totally checked out at this point. She goes over to the window, which is open, and she starts trying to climb out, like she's going to jump from the fourth floor, right? And we're all freaking out. We're grabbing at her, trying to get her away from the window, and she's kicking and screaming like she's getting run through with a chain saw. Nobody has any idea what the fuck to do. So finally we call 911, and they send an ambulance and haul her away. Now I guess she's under a psychiatric hold."

"She's not under a psychiatric hold," Jay said. "Lloyd and Martin just visited her at the hospital. They said she's lucid again. She's writing a personal apology to Skechers as we speak. They think—look, it's unlikely. But they're choosing to believe that there's still a chance we could save the contract."

Behind Josh, I could hear Radha snort. "What, are we doing a prayer circle? Should I run and grab some manifesting candles?"

The table was quiet.

Pedro said, finally, "I always thought those shoes were shit, anyway."

On Instagram, I messaged Lizzie. Hope everything's all right with your mom. Call me if you need any help or just want to talk.

She called me that night at 3:14 a.m., just as I was beginning to drift off to sleep. In the other bed, my mom grunted and turned over, and I slipped into the bathroom, closing the door behind me. "Hey," I said. "How's everything? Are you guys holding up okay?"

She had been crying. Her face was red and swollen, and as she wiped her eyes on a large bath towel, she said, "I wish I could run away."

"Oh, honey." I sat on the edge of the bathtub. "Is it your mom? Is she still in the hospital?"

"No, she came back this morning. They said she was fine, like, she just had a stress-related meltdown or whatever. She . . ."

Lizzie blew her nose into the towel. She said, "She's been making my life hell since she got back. I can't take it anymore, Erin. I just want to pack up my stuff and go."

"I'm sorry. I'm so, so sorry, Lizzie."

Lizzie was quiet before she said, "You know, she always does this."

"Does what?"

"I think she's bipolar or something. Because most of the time, she's, like, my best friend. But every once in a while, she goes through one of these periods where she just snaps. It's like she turns into a crazy person. Nobody's safe. She got—" Lizzie took a shuddering breath. "She did something really messed up on the subway last year."

My mouth was dry. I said, "What'd she do?"

"There was this video. She was on the train, and she got into an argument with this girl, I guess it was over seats or whatever. And she screamed at that girl like she was crazy. She was on the floor, and she was crying, and my mom was just screaming and screaming at her. And somebody filmed all of it, and it was all over the Internet."

Lizzie shook her head, despondent. "I don't know what happened to her. The girl—she was Asian. And it made me so upset, seeing my mom yell at her like that. I cried for days after I saw that video. I found her name and where she went to school, and I wrote her an email, but she never replied. I just wanted to find her and tell her I was sorry. I just wanted to see if she was okay."

She was crying again, burying her face in the towel. I sat there for a long time, motionless, listening.

"Lizzie," I said, and she looked up. "You're a good person. You're—you're nothing like your mom."

Lizzie blew her nose again. Thickly, she said, "Is it too late to sign the release form for the orphanage?"

"It's not," I said. "I could even go meet with them tomorrow, if you want."

"Can you send the form to my email? I'll print it out and sign it right now. I'm in my mom's office."

"Is she there?"

"She's been in the bath all day for her migraine. I haven't seen her come out since noon."

I exhaled. "Good," I said. "After you scan the form, I want you to tear it up and flush the pieces down the toilet. Delete the scanned file, too. You don't want her to find something in the trash and go off on you again."

"She won't," Lizzie said. "I'll be careful."

In the end, all it had taken to persuade my mom to fly down to Guiyang with me were two simple sentences. "It's a favor for my boss," I said. "She asked me to help look for her daughter's birth family."

That made her look up from her phone. "Well, why didn't you say so? Of course we'll go. If we find the family, maybe she'll give you a promotion."

On the plane, my mom said, "These white people are more generous than I'll ever be, I'll give them that."

That got a laugh out of me. "Ma, what are you talking about?"

"They actually encourage their children to look for their birth parents. Some of them will even travel to China with them and search for them together, pouring their money into plane tickets, flyers, even taking out advertisements in newspapers." She shook her head wonderingly. "And what's the point? We Chinese people have known the answer all along. There's a simple reason those girls were abandoned. Their parents didn't want them."

A thought occurred to me then. "If I were adopted, would you tell me?"

Without hesitation, my mom said, "Why would I ever tell you? You look like me."

Across the rosewood desk, Ms. Ye, the assistant director at the Green Mountain Welfare Home for Children in Guiyang, peered at the computer screen over her gold-rimmed glasses. "And the first name is Xueyang?" she asked.

I nodded, and over Skype, Lizzie said, "Can you ask her about my last name? They said it was Dang in my adoption papers."

"Her last name when she was adopted was Dang," I told Ms. Ye in Mandarin. "I don't know if it was the name of her birth family?"

"Oh, no," she said. "All the children here have the last name Dang. We name them after the Communist Party because even though they don't have parents, they're still the party's children."

As I translated for Lizzie, Ms. Ye began typing into a database. The orphanage was on the outskirts of the city, a salmon-colored building in a cloud of pink rhododendrons. A group of little kids were playing on the monkey bars and swing sets in the yard as we passed, supervised by two young female teachers; they watched us with a mild curiosity. In Ms. Ye's office, her assistant had brought us each a mug of hot water.

"Found it," Ms. Ye said.

She read the profile out loud. "Dang Xueyang. Brought to our facility in December 1998 and adopted through Loving Families International in September 1999 by an American couple. It says here that she had a cleft lip. Ask her if I've got the correct information."

I relayed this to Lizzie, and she nodded eagerly. "Does she know anything about my parents?"

Ms. Ye turned away from the computer and opened a filing cabinet to her right. After a moment, she pulled out a faded green folder and skimmed the contents. It only took her a minute or two.

"It says she was surrendered by a relative," she said. "Her paternal grandmother."

My heart was pounding. "Really?"

"Yes, it says so right here. She was brought to the home on December 12, 1998, when she was a month old, and given to one of the employees. The reason provided was that her parents wanted to try for another child without physical blemishes but couldn't have one because of the one-child policy. They decided to give her to the orphanage and mark her as deceased with the population register to free up their child quota."

Ms. Ye passed the file to me. "You can take a look for yourself," she said dispassionately. "We saw cases like this all the time in the eighties and nineties."

In my hands, the papers were yellow and flimsy; the blue-ink handwriting of the intake employee, once so neat and meticulous, was beginning to fade. I swallowed, and I heard Lizzie ask, "What did she say? What did she say?"

"She said . . ."

I hesitated before I said, "She said you had a foster mother."

In the next chair, my mom threw me a glance but remained silent. "I had a foster mother?" Lizzie repeated.

The words were coming more easily now. "Yeah," I said. "Yeah, she was, um . . . she was one of the employees at the orphanage at the time. She worked there because she loved the kids. And when you had first come in, when you were a baby, she loved taking care of you. She would feed you and rock you in her arms. She would sometimes take you home for the weekend and have you spend time with her family. She was really sad when you were adopted, you know, but also happy that you were going to have a much better life in America than what you would have had here."

On the screen, Lizzie had begun to cry again.

"Oh my God," she said, and she ran her hands over her face; her hair was a mess. "Oh my God, Erin. I knew it. I knew there was somebody out there that loved me for me."

Across the table, Ms. Ye regarded Lizzie's blurred form sympathetically. My mom, on the other hand, was looking at the rhododendrons outside the window. After that initial flicker of surprise, she had become unperturbed again.

When Lizzie looked up, she said, tearfully, "Can you ask if she has a phone number? Please ask her if there's a way to contact my foster mother. I want to talk to her."

My mom and I exchanged a look.

"Sure, Lizzie," I said. "I'll see what I can do."

Outside the orphanage, as we waited for the taxi, I said, "Is there anything you want to say to me?"

My mom looked over, surprised. "No," she said. "Not particularly."

"You don't think it's messed up that I lied to her?"

She was quiet for a moment. Finally, she said, "Sometimes there's no difference between right and wrong, really. It's more about why you felt that you had to do something. It's about who you did it for, in the end."

I nodded. I drew circles on the ground with my foot.

After a while, I said, "Ma, are you still in touch with Dolly? You know, the exorcist you hired to get rid of the jinn when I was in Florida?"

Instantly, my mom was puffing out her chest, indignant. "Don't even speak to me about that woman," she said. "She scammed me out of hundreds of dollars. The jinn came back after just a few months. I called her to complain and ask for my money back, and guess what? The number was no longer in service. The absolute *gall*."

Then something occurred to her, and she looked at me, anxious. "Don't tell me you have another jinn problem."

"Nope, not a jinn," I said. "But I might need her for something else."

ERIN

In the stately art deco condo building overlooking Central Park, I heard the pulsating music the moment the elevator spat me out on the fourteenth floor. It grew louder as I approached the unit at the end of the hall, muffled but raucous—some kind of heavy metal. Was it Lizzie? But Lizzie had gone to stay with a friend. I knew from our Instagram messages.

At the door, I straightened the bouquet in my hands and pressed the doorbell.

It took her a long time to answer, but she finally did, after I'd rung repeatedly. The door swung open slowly, filling the hallway with the screech of an electric guitar, and Amy Cloverfield stood in front of me, wrapped in a damp purple bathrobe, the water from her hair dripping onto the carpet. Without her heels, her stature was stooped. She had lost her armor.

"Amy, hi!" I said. I had to shout to hear my own voice. "How are you doing?"

She said nothing. There was something shifty about her gaze, the way it ran across me sideways instead of head-on. A moment passed before she said, "Did Lloyd send you? Or Martin?"

Brightly, I said, "I'm here of my own volition, but the rest of the creative team did tell me to say hello. Is this a good time?"

There was a pause. "It's fine," Amy said. "I was just about done with my bath, anyway."

She shuffled aside to let me in. The apartment was large and airy, decorated in a vaguely Parisian style: The sofas in the living room were forest green and heather gray, a sleek glass coffee table resting between them, and above the white fireplace sat an enormous mirror in an ornate golden frame. I could see the door of the bathroom standing ajar, the light still on, the tub filled with water. Hot steam rushed at my face as I passed by.

Amy made no effort to put the flowers in a vase. She set them down on the coffee table and took a seat, and I sat on the opposite sofa. As we looked at each other, it was clear that she wasn't going to offer me anything to drink.

I said, "Where's Lizzie? Is she home?"

As the music roared around us, she said nothing. I tried again.

"Have you seen the cherry blossoms outside? They're in full bloom. New York is lovely this time of year, isn't it?"

When Amy smiled, I saw a tinge of green under her eyes, shadows so deep that they seemed etched into her skin. She reached for the remote on the coffee table and pressed a button; instantly, the apartment fell silent.

She said, "Lloyd sent you to check on me, didn't he? He wanted to know if I was really and truly crazy."

Then she tilted her head and looked at me, in a way that was almost taunting. "What are you going to tell him? On a scale of one to ten, how crazy would you say I am?"

"Honestly, Amy, I have no . . . I literally don't know what happened. I wasn't there at the pitch."

Her lip curled. "You were in California. Attending a funeral."

"Yes, I was in California. I just got back to New York last night."

"And so you missed The Incident. It's a shame, really. I've been assured that it was quite a spectacle."

I said nothing, and Amy looked away.

She said, "I've been evaluated by two different psychiatrists, and they've both found me to be perfectly competent, suffering no delusions or auditory hallucinations. So you can take that back to Lloyd and tell him to shove it up his ass."

"I'm really not here on behalf of Lloyd, Amy," I said. My voice was gentle. "I came here because I wanted to see if you were all right. I was concerned about you."

Amy didn't answer. She was picking at the chips on her nails; the pink paint fell onto the table like dust. Her fingers and toes were pale, wrinkled prunes.

She said, "You've probably heard that they put me on administrative leave at work."

"I didn't. I'm sorry to hear that."

She looked up at me. "Well, don't be. Administrative leave is nothing. It's a formality. It's a cooling-off period for both parties to come to their senses and come back to the table. I was the one who won that initial Skechers contract for MLC eight years ago. I *am* Skechers. I've already written three apology letters to Gavin and Maria, and I'm prepared to write three hundred letters every day for the rest of my life if it means they'll stay the course with MLC. I'll get them to come around. I always do."

I hesitated. She was already looking away, her gaze drifting towards the bathroom, and I said, "Amy, Skechers has awarded the contract to Flickerman."

There was a pause. She said, "Say that again."

"We just found out yesterday. Not only did they give Flickerman the digital marketing work, they're pulling their creative contract with us, too. We've . . . we've lost Skechers, Amy. We've lost them for good."

I expected her to scream. To pick up the bouquet of flowers and throw them at me. But she just fell silent, looking at her fractured nails.

She said, "I've lost my daughter, too."

"Lizzie? What happened to her?"

Amy looked at me; she sounded almost amused as she said, "Oh, will you just drop it with this wide-eyed, goody-two-shoes act? It must be exhausting, keeping up the façade day after day. And frankly, it doesn't become you."

I said nothing, and Amy said, "I know you put her in touch with that woman. The—the Chinese foster mother. You were the only one who could have done it. You were adopted from the same city. You had the connections."

There it was.

The revelation, the exhilaration of it, bursting before my eyes like sparklers. I leaned back in my chair. I relaxed.

"You're right," I said. "I did put Lizzie in touch with her foster mother. I was there with her on their call, too, providing her with interpretation and moral support."

"How lovely," Amy said. "What a wholesome, heartwarming family reunion."

"It was. But you know what sucked, though? The fact that they didn't get to have a deep, meaningful conversation because everything had to go through my shitty interpretation. Lizzie couldn't even pronounce the *x* sound in her own name, Xueyang. I've always been curious about that, Amy. Why would you adopt a child from China and not allow her to learn Chinese?"

Her eyes widened. Her nose flared.

"Allow? *Allow?* Of course I allowed it. I encouraged it. I even enrolled her in Chinese school when she was younger! She was the one who didn't want to learn. She said it was too hard. She didn't see the need. She saw herself as American, not Chinese. She *liked* having a name that everyone in her life could pronounce. You try going through life in this country with a name like Xueyang; let's see how many days you'd last before you gave up and asked people to call you Susan."

She jabbed a finger at me. "You sit there on your pedestal and judge me. Worse—you project your own parents' failings onto me. I was never the white savior who raised my kid in a monolithic bubble and insisted that I didn't see race. I brought her up in one of the most diverse cities in the world. I took her to ethnic restaurants. I watched documentaries. I've educated myself on the Asian American experience in this country.

"Those kids—the ones raised by their biological parents, the ones that were never abandoned by their families—they go through the same things my daughter does. They don't speak their languages, either. They don't know their cultures, their history. When they travel to their homelands, they feel like foreigners who don't belong. So why is it that when it happens to them, it's part of the fucking Asian American story, and yet when the same thing happens to my daughter, it's because I've failed as a parent? Why is no one pointing fingers at those parents? Why is no one accusing them of creating trauma for their kids by raising them in a country where they'll always be a minority, where, according to these same people, they'll always be second-class citizens and never truly belong? Is that my fault, too? Because if it is, good golly gosh, I am so sorry. I'm sorry for being white. I'm sorry for rescuing my daughter from a lice-infested orphanage and giving her a life of private schools and dance classes and SAT tutors and early admission to NYU. I'm so sorry, everyone!"

Spit was flying from her mouth. It landed on the table, speckles of saliva coating the pink dust of her nail paint. She looked at me, panting, and her eyes were the most alive I had seen since I walked through her door. They were burning.

"Jesus, Amy," I said, and I shook my head. "You really are unbelievable."

"What did your parents do to you?" Amy said. "Whenever I look at you, I see so much trauma in your eyes. I've seen it since the day you came in for that interview. Let me guess: Did they beat you? Or maybe they threatened to send you back to China whenever you acted up. I can't even imagine what you could do to someone for them to become such a . . . a fucked-up, psychopathic person."

That was when I began to laugh.

I threw my head back and cackled. There was no joy in it. But I had to laugh at the absurdity of the situation we were in, at the audacity of the woman who sat before me: broken, disgraced, mentally deranged, on the brink of being fired, left alone to rot in her apartment by her daughter. She had hit rock bottom. And yet when Amy Cloverfield looked at me, it was with the same contemptuous look she had worn that day on the subway, the same look that had haunted me every night for the past nine months. Despite my best efforts, she had not been vanquished. She had not been taught a lesson. She was still an unrepenting cunt.

"You still don't get it, do you?" I said. "I've been sitting right under your nose for the past three months, and you still haven't put two and two together."

Then I said, "I'm not Erin Callaghan. My real name is Shelley Hu."

And as she stared at me, I raised my hands to the crown of my head and unclipped my wig. I set it down on the coffee table. I took off my wig cap and my glasses, and I looked back at her, calm, self-assured.

Amy blinked at me. A moment passed, and she said, "Who . . . who did you say you were?"

"Shelley Hu from the subway. The 6 Train."

"Shelley Hu from the 6 Train?"

And as she repeated this information to herself, her face blank, a new feeling began to sink in. It was horror.

It was the realization that Amy Cloverfield did not seem to remember me at all.

"You've got to be fucking kidding me," I said. "You and I got into an argument on the train. You wanted my seat. Do you seriously not remember?"

"We got into an argument? Over seats?"

"Yes!" And I brought my hand down on the table, frustrated, and she jumped. "Goddamn it, Amy, how the fuck do you not remember this? It wasn't even a year ago. It was in a video—it was in a video that went fucking viral—"

Then I said it. "I'm the New York Subway Naked Lady."

At that, her eyes widened. Realization was flooding her face.

"Oh," she said. "Oh, that does . . . It rings a bell."

"'It rings a bell'? That's all you have to say to me?"

I got up from the sofa, breathing heavily. We looked at each other.

I said, "You ruined my life."

She said nothing, and I said, "I lost everything because of you. I got fired from my internship. I got expelled from Columbia Law. I had to move back to Florida and work the night shift at a motel like some brain-dead high school dropout. Do you have any idea what it was like for me? In the span of twenty-four hours, I lost my friends, my career, my reputation, my future. I lost my ability to build a better life for my mom. She had nothing going for her in her life; she had no one. I was it. I was her one shot, and you ruined it. Is that what you call women helping women, Amy? Is that the type of behavior befitting a New York fucking Woman in PR?"

Her face had changed as I spoke; the haughtiness was gone, in its place a sort of gaunt, hopeless finality. Her shoulders sagged.

She said, "So that's why you took my daughter away from me."

"You did a pretty good job of pushing her away yourself. All I had to do was give her a little nudge in the right direction."

"She's going to China after graduation," Amy said. "She bought a plane ticket with the money she saved from her allowance. She's going to look for her birth parents, and she told me . . . she told me she doesn't want me to come."

"Oh, she won't find them," I said.

She gaped at me, and I said, "Adoptees like Lizzie can't ever really face up to the possibility that they were unwanted. They dream of a perfect birth family back home, desperately searching for them all these years. But I read her case files when I visited the orphanage. She was dumped there by her own grandmother. Her parents didn't want her because of the cleft lip; it probably didn't help that she was a girl, either.

"Even if a miracle happens and she manages to track them down, even if she shows up on their doorstep with a DNA test, do you know what'll happen then? They'll welcome her in with open arms, sure. But it won't be because they love her. It won't be because they've felt guilty all these years, abandoning her at that orphanage. It'll be because she's an American citizen now, shiny and rich and pretty and attending a top university in New York. They'll ask her for money. They'll ask her to help out the shitty younger son they had to replace her, ask her to help buy him a house, pay the bride price for his wedding, even bring him to America with her. They'll suck her dry like vampires. Blood is thicker than water, you know?"

Amy's face was ashen. I smiled at her.

"You're welcome to tell her all that, by the way," I said. "I'm Chinese. I know the cold, hard, ugly truth when I see it. But you try telling her what I've just told you. See how well that goes over."

Then I began to pace. I circled the coffee table and came to a stop before her, bearing down on her. She was smaller than I'd remembered. The crown of her head had gone completely gray.

"And you know what's the saddest part, Amy? I believe that you love her more than her birth parents ever did. I really do believe that. But I . . ."

The exhaustion I'd felt since I first read Lizzie's messages back in Zhengzhou—it swept over me then. The grand speech I'd fantasized for months and months about giving felt suddenly childish, pointless. I was sick of looking at her, sick of being in the manic confines of this room.

I wanted, more than anything, to leave.

"It's too late," I said, finally. "You fucked up, I fucked up, and . . . here we are."

But Amy wasn't looking at me anymore.

She said, as if talking to herself, "No. No."

Her fingers dug into the arm of the sofa. Veins had appeared in her forehead. She looked around, frantic. "No, I'm not going," she said, and her voice was a rasp now, thin and desperate. "I won't go. You can't make me. You can't make me."

"Amy?" I said, but she wasn't listening. She sprang from the sofa and reached for the remote, and with a jolt, the heavy metal was back. I watched as she scurried back into the bathroom and climbed into the tub, still wearing the purple robe. It swirled around her in the water; she closed her eyes, gulping for air, and sank.

It was clear that she no longer knew or cared that I was there.

On my way out, my eyes caught on a painting that was hanging by the front door, just above the shoe cabinet. It took a moment under the dim lighting, but then I recognized what it was: an old ink-wash piece that Sophia had taken off the wall of her living room when I first started working at Meek LeClerc, the bullshit present we'd given to Amy to get into her good graces. I saw the mist-filled lake, the mountains in the background. They seemed to come alive on the scroll; Sophia really was a master.

And then I saw something else.

On the lake, a dark shape had appeared, a blotchy dot of ink, something I couldn't make out until I leaned closer. At the heart of the lake was now a tiny leaflike riverboat. On it stood a tiny human figure, looking out over the water, its back to the viewer. The figure had long, flowing black hair. It wore white.

At half past midnight, my bedroom door creaked open. I heard Sophia in the darkness before I saw her. "Hi, darling," she whispered. "Are you awake?"

"I'm awake."

The door closed soundlessly, and a moment later, she was in my bed, under my covers, her head next to mine on the pillow. The night before, after I'd gotten in from China, Sophia had slipped into my bed after the rest of the house had fallen asleep, and it had been both tiring and glorious. But now, as she pushed up my T-shirt and pressed her lips to my bare skin, I felt detached, as if I were floating above the bed, watching us. "I missed you," I saw her tell me. "I've been thinking about you all day."

"Sophia," I began, but she didn't seem to hear me. It took a moment to muster the energy to push myself up and switch on the bedside lamp. "Sophia," I said, "wait—wait. Just hang on."

In the dim golden light, Sophia looked up at me, her eyes soft. "Honey, what's wrong?"

"I don't know. I just . . . I've been feeling kind of shitty all day. Can we just cuddle?"

"Of course we can," she said, reaching for me. "Come here."

I lay back against the pillow, and Sophia curled up in the crook of my arm, her cheek against my chest. "So what's bothering you?" I heard her ask.

I hesitated.

"I went to see Amy today," I said, finally.

"How was she?"

"Bad. She was in a really bad state. She was all alone."

I could feel her smile. "Good. I'm glad."

Then she said, "I hope seeing her like that made you happy."

"It did, at first. But then it got weird. She was . . . Sophia, she was seriously fucked up. She was playing this really loud music, and she kept looking around with her eyes all bulging, like there was something out there, talking to her. It was like . . . like she couldn't hear me. Like she wasn't really there anymore."

Sophia was quiet for a beat. She said, "She was playing loud music?"

"Yeah. It was heavy metal."

I saw Sophia smile again: slowly, with a faint amusement I couldn't quite grasp. She said, "Well, whatever she thinks might help."

She swept my hair back and kissed me. "Congratulations, my love," she said. "You've won. The woman who ruined your life has lost everything. She'll never come back from this. She'll never have power over anyone again."

It began to sink in, all at once.

"Fuck," I said. "It's . . . it's over. She's done."

"She is."

"There's something else, though."

Her hand was still on my cheek, warm, waiting. I swallowed.

I said, "I . . . I told her who I was. When I was over at her house, I told her."

Silence.

In my arms, Sophia was frozen. She regarded me, unblinking, and when I reached for her, she didn't react. She said, "What did you tell her, exactly?"

"Pretty much everything. That I was Shelley Hu. That I was the person who argued with her on the 6 Train. I took my wig off and showed her who I really was."

Sophia sat up, pushing my hand away. She rounded on me.

"Tell me you didn't do that," she said. "Tell me it was a joke."

"No, but I was just—you didn't see the way she looked at me, Sophia. She had lost everything, she was in such a low place, and she was still looking down at me like I was trash. I had to say something. I had to find some way to beat her down."

Sophia ran her hands over her face. She took several deep breaths.

She said, "We had a plan, Erin. We had agreed—"

"We didn't have a plan. You had a plan. You were always the one with the plan. And I did everything you told me to. I even went to the courthouse and changed my own fucking name! I'm not Erin, Sophia. I'm sick of being Erin. And I'm . . . I'm . . ."

My head felt light, like a balloon on the verge of spinning away. I said, "I don't want to do this anymore. Going through life with this fake name, putting on a ridiculous wig and glasses every day, pretending I'm someone I'm not. We spent months and months scheming, day and night, and what did we get? Gene is dead. Amy's crazy. And Auggie's a pathetic loser who's already living a life worse than anything we could've given him. I want out, Sophia. I'm tired of living in this house, tired of sneaking around your husband, tired of New Jersey. When I came back yesterday, I was looking around, and I kept thinking, *When do we get to move on? When do we get to hold hands and walk under the sun like we said we were going to do?* Because that's all I want at this point. I just want us to move on and start our life together."

We were both crying now. I held out my arms, and Sophia clung to me, weeping. She was so beautiful, even as she cried, perhaps especially as she cried.

"I'm sorry," she said. "I'm sorry I've made everything so hard. You must be so angry with me."

Emphatically, I shook my head. "It's not you," I said. "You've been nothing but perfect. I was just venting. I didn't mean it."

"No, but you're right. You're right."

When Sophia spoke again, her voice shook slightly. "I spoke to an attorney when you were gone," she said. "I spoke to her more than once, actually. And I've decided . . . I'm going to start the separation process. I'm going to look for a place for you, me, and Ory so that we can move out of this house. There'll be paperwork and custody arrangements and negotiations, and Paul won't make it easy for me, but . . . one way or another, we'll make it happen. We'll fight for our life together."

It took a moment to process her words.

"You're leaving him? You're really leaving him?"

Sophia smiled at me. "I'm really leaving him," she said, "because you're worth it. Because you're the person I've been waiting for all my life."

I took her face in my hand, cupping it gently, and kissed her. Her lips tasted like salt, and so did mine.

I said, "Have you told Paul?"

Sophia bit her lip. "I can't. Not yet."

Then she said, "Your salary is . . . Well, you can barely support one person on what you're making. And my freelance income is virtually nothing. I've relied too much on Paul for everything, but I won't make that mistake again. I'll go back to work full-time. I have an old friend at Ogilvy who says they're looking for an associate art director; I'm going to ask her to pass my portfolio along. I need to make sure that when I leave, I can stand on my own two feet."

"I'm sorry," I said. My face was burning with shame. "If I'd stayed in law school—if I'd become a lawyer—I would've been able to support you. I would have been able to get you out faster."

"Don't say that," Sophia said.

She shifted so that her cheek was resting on my chest again. "Maybe it was a good thing you didn't become a lawyer," she said, a haziness in her voice. "Otherwise, you and I never would have met."

ERIN

Radha called in the morning as I was brushing my teeth. Before I'd even said hello, she said, "Are you coming to work today?"

It was a quarter to six; the imprint of Sophia was still warm in my sheets. "Yeah," I said. "I just got up."

I waited for her to explain the reason for the early call, but she hesitated. "Something's happened," she said.

Then she said, "They're going to announce it at an emergency all-hands meeting this morning, but I thought I should tell you now, just so you don't . . . just so you're aware."

There was a hollowed anguish in her voice. "What happened?" I said.

Again, Radha was quiet for a few seconds before she spoke.

"Amy, um . . . Amy died last night."

The sink in front of me had begun to contort in shape, the porcelain folding in on itself. I closed my eyes. My voice was oddly calm as I said, "Wait, who died?"

"Amy. *Our* Amy."

I said nothing, and Radha said, "They're saying she k-killed herself last night. Or early this morning, I guess. Someone saw her walking on the GW Bridge, and it sounds like she . . . she climbed over the railing and jumped. They couldn't stop her."

After we hung up, I stood there, looking at the toothbrush in my right hand. Somehow, in the last few minutes, it had lost all meaning.

I released my fingers slowly, barely conscious of the muscles and appendages that I purportedly controlled, and it fell into the sink with a clatter.

At the dining table, Paul was wiping Ory's mouth. Behind the counter, Sophia was humming quietly to herself as she mixed a bowl of batter; she looked up at me and smiled. "Erin, just in time," she said. "I'm making waffles. Are you in the mood for blueberries or chocolate chips?"

I couldn't look at her. "I—I can't," I said. "Early work meeting. I'll see you later."

Paul ignored me, and Ory said, "Bye-bye, Erin."

On the train, I read every article I could find, even though they were all regurgitations of the same statement from the NYPD. Deceased female, late forties to early fifties, pulled out of the water by the fire department's marine division at 3:09 a.m. A single eyewitness said they saw the woman, who was dressed in all white, leap from the George Washington Bridge. First responders pronounced her dead at the scene.

It was just words, I thought.

Squiggles on a page.

When I got into work, I half expected to see Amy in her corner office, typing out an email on her phone, her advertising awards set out on the glass table before her. But she wasn't there. No one was at their desks. Everyone had poured into the large conference room, an impromptu wake. Some people were standing around, shell-shocked. Others were crying. When Radha saw me, she ran up and hugged me. Her eyes were red and swollen. "How could she do this?" she said. "How the fuck could she do this?"

In the conference room, the CEO, Lloyd, said a few tearful words, and we were dismissed for the day. "Go home," Jay said, putting a hand on Pedro's and my shoulders. He looked exhausted. "Go home and hug your families."

As we filed into the elevator, we looked at each other, drained, despondent. "Finnegan's?" Radha asked quietly. "Or whatever bar is open at this hour."

I shook my head; I was beginning to feel sick. "You guys go ahead," I said. "I just want to go home."

I found Sophia in the living room, bending over a dozen black-and-white photographs scattered across the coffee table, humming to herself as she arranged and rearranged the order. For a moment, I just stood in the doorway, watching her. She looked around at me and smiled.

"You're home early," she said. "Want to help me with the photos for the show?"

We were both quiet, looking at the photographs, when I began to cry. I didn't make a sound. The tears streamed down my face soundlessly, and I heard Sophia say, "Oh, honey."

She held me, rubbing my back as I sobbed. All the strength had drained from me; I felt myself slip from her grasp and fall to the floor, the wool area rug scratching my face. "No, no, no," I moaned, and the sound that emerged was so guttural, so mangled, that it could not have come from me. My insides were convulsing; I turned my head, and in the next moment I felt hot, sour liquid leave my mouth. I lay there, trembling in my own sick, Sophia's gentle hands on me.

"I'm sorry," I told her. "I'm sorry I ruined everything."

"It's all right," I heard her say, her voice gentle. "It's perfectly all right, Shelley."

Instinctively, listlessly, I nodded. Then I shook my head.

"It's my fault," I said. "It's my fault that she's dead."

"Don't say that. It's an absurd idea."

"It's true. I was the last person to see her. I . . . I destroyed her with what I said. It was all my fault."

"Stop saying that."

Sophia pressed a tissue to my face. "You're in shock," she said. "You're not thinking clearly. What you need right now is to rest."

"No," I said, and I pushed her hand away. It was coming into focus now, all of it. I tried to get up; my mind was scattered, frantic. "I have to come clean. I have to tell someone."

"About what?"

"Everything. The things I did behind her back. The things I said to her about Lizzie. The role I played in . . . in . . ."

I couldn't bring myself to say it. Sophia put the tissue aside and took both of my hands in hers. We looked at each other.

She said, "You're not responsible for her death, Erin."

I blanched. But she pressed on.

"She was fifty-four when she died. Think about it. Think about what she's lived through, what any woman on this earth might have lived through by the time she is fifty-four. A father who tells her she's not smart enough. A husband who slaps her in the face as she cooks him dinner. Old men who leer at her before she has even started puberty; strangers who feel entitled to force their tongues down her throat; a boss who works her twice as hard for half the pay, none of the recognition. A dead marriage. The grief of infertility and loss. The bitter acceptance, as the corners of your face sag and your hair turns gray and the people who once gave you their attention now look away, that you are now invisible to the world; that you have becoming nothing. Do you know what a fifty-four-year-old woman has to do to get through a life like this, Erin?"

I shook my head.

"She does it because she has to," Sophia said. "The world has always been an open-air sewer, always. We're rats, all of us, swimming against the tide, and we do it because we're convinced, somehow, that if we swim long enough, we will be one of the few rats that can emerge from the filthy water, that we can finally make it ashore. What did I tell you when we first met? You and I, our mothers and our grandmothers, all the women who came before us—we never had another choice. We always clawed our way back from the bottom of the sewer, even when we were pushed there by others, even when they tried to keep us down. Time and time again, we resurfaced. We put ourselves back together, no matter how broken we were, no matter how much we'd lost, and we kept swimming. So really, what makes Amy Cloverfield so special? What stopped her from doing the same thing?"

There was nothing to say to that. I closed my eyes.

"You'll feel better after you've had some sleep," I heard Sophia say.

And then, without warning: The room was dark.

The drapes were drawn, the windows behind them a grainy outline, and I looked around me, dazed, not understanding where I was. Under my head was a pillow; above me, a soft duvet the color of seashells. I was back in the guest bedroom, tucked into bed. There was a glass of water on the bedside table.

Someone was knocking on the door. "Erin?" I heard Ory's voice say. "Erin, do you want to eat dinner with us?"

He knocked again. "Erin?"

I could hear his little feet turn and patter away. "I think she's still sleeping," I heard him say.

Slowly, I sat up in bed, looking at the sliver of golden light seeping under the door. There was the din of dishes being set around the table, forks and knives clattering against plates, Ory's bright little voice as he recounted the species of birds he'd learned about in school that day. I heard Sophia suggest that they go to Central Park that weekend to do some bird-watching. I even heard Paul laugh.

I sat there for a long time, motionless, a void expanding inside me. It grew out of me and swallowed me whole, and I sank back under the covers and slipped into nothingness once more.

I didn't go to Amy Cloverfield's funeral. I was a coward.

Meek LeClerc sent a flower arrangement and a donation in Amy's name to Loving Families International. When Jay came to the office the next day, he showed us pictures of the service on his phone. In some of them, I saw Lizzie in a black dress, her hair in a taut bun, her eyes red. Her nose had swelled up from crying.

She had called me twice in the days after Amy died. Both times, I had watched her name flash across my screen until it faded away.

I took three days of sick leave, during which I just lay in bed, staring at the ceiling. Sophia brought me meals and ginseng tea every few hours; she'd sit by the bed and stroke my hair while she talked to me, but I was too tired to answer. The third day, Ory came into my room with a pail of his favorite toys and climbed up over the covers, where he proceeded to spread them out. "Are you really, really sick?" he asked me as he fixed the cape on one of the action figures. "My mommy said you might be."

"I don't know," I said. "I think my heart might be sick."

Ory contemplated this. Then he surprised me. He climbed across the covers and wrapped his little arms around me, resting his head on my heart. "I'm sorry," I heard him say, his voice muffled. "I hope you feel better, Erin."

My vision fogged. I felt Ory release me and go back to sorting his toys. "Do you want to play superheroes versus dinosaurs again?" he asked.

"Sure."

He handed me the silver-painted action figure I'd seen in his room before. "Here. You can play with MightyMan today 'cause you're sick."

The toy was still warm from his fingers. The silver paint was chipped and fading, showing its age, and something about it had suddenly started to prick at me, giving me unease. I said, "What did you say his name was?"

"MightyMan. He was my mommy's toy from when she was a little girl in Korea. Her mommy and daddy got it for her 'cause she was their favorite."

He went back to wrangling the toys, and I felt it then.

A chilling cold that started in my organs and seeped through my bones, until at last it condensed in the tips of my fingers and toes.

Like sinking into icy water.

I slept poorly that night, in fits and bursts. Every time I awakened, I could feel it in the shadows of the walls, watching me. I tried to close my eyes and go back to sleep. But it inched closer.

And closer.

Until finally it was sitting directly on my heart the way it used to, its weight pressing into me, its hands tightening around my throat, the water in its hair dripping onto my face, drop by drop. My limbs were frozen, useless. I was a prisoner. I waited for the curse to lift.

Just before dawn, I fell from the bed with a gasp and crawled over to the desk, where Sophia's talisman sat next to a candle. In the faint morning light, the lines and the shadows in the painting looked different. They made my heart race. They made me want to look away. I stuffed the frame inside a drawer and went to the bookcase, where the black-and-white photo of my dad was lying on a stack of books, face down. I brought it to the desk and sat it upright, facing the bed. Looking at his face brought an instant relief. I felt lighter, somehow.

In the bathroom, I doused my face with cold water and got myself ready for work.

When I returned to Meek LeClerc, my work got inexplicably really fucking good. Jay called the poster I'd illustrated for a client "exquisite, like fine art." I won my first advertising award for Most Innovative Brand Identity Refresh, and shortly after that I was promoted to full designer. I went to every single happy hour at Finnegan's and stayed until everyone else had gone home, and then I started going clubbing by myself afterwards. The strobe lights made my head spin, made me throw up, made me want to crawl the lengths of the earth until I found a hole in the ground and jump into it, falling down, all the way down, until the abyss took me, too.

A week after Amy Cloverfield died, her office was cleaned out. A few days later, some guy named John was announced as her replacement, a man with a weak chin and red, puffy fingers that threatened to burst out of his wedding ring. There were rumors he'd been fired from his previous agency for defrauding a client. While Radha and Josh dissected this breathlessly at happy hour, I kept my eyes on my beer, only half listening. Somehow, we were already in June.

I started taking little field trips by myself, sitting on the subway with my bag strap twisted around my arm, Josh's old DSLR camera inside. I went to the art institute that Sophia had attended and took pictures of the atrium, the swirling staircases, her award-winning painting that hung on the third floor. I went to the pizzeria and photographed the table where Sophia and I had stood in front of one another in our beautiful, grotesque vulnerability, the street corner where we kissed for the first time. I even went to MoMA and paid a whopping twenty-five dollars just so I could stand in one of the galleries on the top floor and look into the apartment where she and I had once spent the night, the place where we had sliced ourselves open and laid it all out for each other to witness. The wrapped artworks in the unit had been emptied out; there was a crew inside with stained overalls and rollers, painting. I raised the camera to my face and photographed all of it.

When I got home from work, Paul and Ory were playing catch in the backyard. The cherry blossoms in the garden had come and gone by then, vanishing from the branches like snow. Sophia was in her studio, working at her iMac. I knocked on the open door, and for a moment, we just stared at each other. Sophia smiled, finally.

"Hey, stranger," she said.

We hadn't spoken, really spoken, since Amy's death. The rare night I was home, I'd started keeping the guest room door locked. I didn't know if she'd tried the handle. Perhaps she had given up, too.

I said, "There's something I have to tell you."

Sophia closed her eyes. She said, "You're leaving, aren't you?"

I started to speak, but no words came out. Sophia nodded.

"So I was right," she said. "In the end, you became tired of me. You decided to walk away."

Her face was calm in a way that unsettled me, and I reached for her hand. She did not react. "Sophia, listen," I said. "I'm not leaving you. That's not what's happening. I just..."

I took a deep breath. Then I said, "This whole time, when we were planning all these things, when we were using pictures of innocent women to catfish my boss, when I groomed an eighteen-year-old girl on Instagram, when we cheated on your husband who is literally feeding and housing us—did you never stop to think, *Hey, this is kind of fucked up*? And did that not make you ever wonder if we were fucked-up people because of it?"

"But of course we're fucked up. We're broken, both of us. It's why we gravitated towards one another. Because together, we can heal."

Slowly, I shook my head. I saw Sophia's face falter.

"We didn't heal, though," I said. "We couldn't. What we did together in the name of vengeance—it's unforgivable. We hurt people who should never have been hurt. We destroyed lives without even thinking twice. And you know what's the most fucked-up part of this, the part I can't stop thinking about? Ory. He's such a good, sweet kid, Sophia. He's the best parts of you and Paul put together. He deserves nothing but the greatest happiness. And when he finds out that his friend Erin is the reason his mom and dad hate each other—when he realizes that our selfishness and our cruelty are what caused the only life he has ever known to fall apart—Sophia, I can't do that to him. You said it yourself: Our parents fucked us up when we were kids because they didn't know better. But we do."

Sophia's face was pale. She regarded me, unblinking, and I brought her hand up to my mouth and kissed it. I said, "You know, I've finally figured out what the jinn in my mom's apartment was."

She just looked at me.

"The jinn was never real," I said, "but in a way, it was, too. It was the help we never got. The bags we never learned to put down. It was the tears we had to swallow, all the shit we passed down from generation to generation, the open wounds my mom and her mom and all the moms before her never had the tools to deal with, and I . . . I'm going to stitch it up for good. I'm going to break the cycle.

"I'm not leaving you, Sophia. I meant what I said. This isn't the end of our story, it's just . . . a pause. I'm flying back to Florida the day after your exhibition. I'm going to get my own place, find a temporary job, and start seeing a therapist. Work on my relationship with my mom and try to get her into therapy, too. I'm going to get the help I need to lift this weight off my chest and get myself to a place where I'm going to be okay for the first time.

"And once I've saved up enough money, I want to go to China. I want to talk to my aunt, talk to all the relatives I've never met, try to write down some of our family history before it gets lost forever. If I ever have kids, I want them to know that we used to be Muslim, even if we never wore it on our sleeves. And, Sophia . . ."

I cupped her face in my hand. I said, "I want you to do the same thing. I want you to sit down with Paul and talk to him, really listen to what he has to say, really try to reach a fair compromise. Not for him, but for Ory. I want you to find a new place for you and Ory, just the two of you, and build a life where he can feel comfortable, where he can feel like his parents splitting up isn't the end of the world. And in a year's time, after the paperwork is done and Ory has settled, if we still miss each other like crazy, if we both feel like we want to give this another shot, then . . . then . . ."

My vision was fogging. I swallowed and said, "Then I'll come back to New York. I'll be all yours."

Sophia closed her eyes.

Slowly, a teardrop appeared between her lashes and made its way down her face. On her cheek, it glistened, reminding me of a pearl.

When she opened her eyes again, I was surprised by how calm she had become. "I understand," she said.

"You do?"

"Yes," Sophia said. "I understand perfectly."

Beneath my wig, her hand found my wig cap, where my real hair sat limp and shapeless. "Let's send you home as the person you really are," she said.

In the bathroom, I closed my eyes as she snipped at my damp hair, the little clumps falling in my lap and around my feet. She dried my hair with a blow-dryer and styled it with a smidge of product that smelled like apricots. I saw myself in the mirror—older, worn, a heaviness in my eyes, deeper lines running along my mouth—but I was me again. I was Shelley Hu.

I got up from the stool, and we stepped towards each other and hugged. I held on to her for a long time, breathing her in. She smelled like pine cones and snow, just the way I liked it.

When we came apart, I said, "There's just one more thing I wanted to do."

From my bag, I retrieved the camera and turned to face her. "Can I take some pictures of you? There's so many photos of Paul and Ory around the house, but almost nothing with you in it. I just want to remember you in this moment."

Sophia closed her eyes, and for a long time, she did not speak. She simply nodded.

As I clicked the shutter again and again, I saw her so clearly, so completely, every little detail I loved: The way her frizzy hair floated above her shoulders. Her long eyelashes, golden and quivering in the dying sun. The soft hollow of her collarbone, a place I had once rested my head. Her lips, red and full. Looking at her, it struck me again, just as it had done the first time I had kissed her outside that pizzeria, what a spectacularly heartbreaking thing it was to love someone so deeply, to want nothing more than to pull them into your own skin and sear them into your bones. So she had told lies; she had misled me; she had spun harmless little stories that had cast her in a better light. None of it really mattered anymore. All that mattered was that for one fleeting moment in our short time on Earth, she had belonged to me, and that had made all the difference.

And with that, I was at peace.

SOYOUNG

November 2004

In the end, Soyoung counted herself lucky that she had only pretended to be enrolled at Cornell, as she would otherwise have failed all of her midterms. She sat through the first exam listlessly, her mind adrift, and as much as she tried to read the words on the page, none of them made sense in her brain, nor would the answers come to her. At three-quarters of the way through the exam, she got up and slipped her blank, anonymous paper into the pile. She did not bother showing up to her other midterms.

About a week into November, she went to Nathaniel's apartment again, and in the morning, he made her chocolate chip pancakes. As Soyoung washed her empty plate in the sink, she heard Nathaniel say, "I hear from Stella that you've stopped going to class. She's worried about you, you know. She thinks you're going to flunk out."

"I've been thinking about leaving," Soyoung said.

It was deranged, talking to Nathaniel about this stuff. But he was the only person in the world that she could talk to.

Nathaniel said, "Leaving Cornell?"

She nodded. "It's not worth it anymore. All the lying, the sneaking around, the things I have to do to pretend I belong here. I'm tired."

"Where would you go if you left?"

"Not my parents' place," Soyoung said. "Not there."

Then she said, "I think I want to go to New York City. It's crowded and chaotic, but that's why I like it: With so many people, so many things going on, no one has the time to scrutinize you. You could just blend in."

"I can see you fitting in in NYC," Nathaniel said.

Then he said, "Hey. Come here."

After a moment, Soyoung walked over to his chair. She sat on his lap, holding her body stiffly, and he put his hands on her waist and kissed her. "I want to help you get there," Nathaniel said.

"How?"

"Depends. What do you want to do when you're there?"

The answer came easily to her. "Art school," Soyoung said. "I want to become a real artist. I want to paint, I want to sculpt, I want to learn photography, I want . . . I want my art to be in museums all around the world. I want everyone in the art world to know my name."

She stopped, suddenly self-conscious, embarrassed by what she had divulged. But Nathaniel just nodded. "I can see that," he said.

"You can?"

"Sure. I mean, art is a whole different ball game, right? That shit is subjective as hell. You don't have to go to school for four years and take a test to get certified. You can just—what, throw a bucket of red paint on a canvas and call it art? Or not even that. Show them the blank canvas and say it's a meditation on the human condition. There's idiots out there that'll pay big bucks for that kind of stuff."

Soyoung's face was blank. Nathaniel said, "That's what art is—grifting. And you're excellent at it, Soyoung. Probably the best I've ever seen. Stealing from that white girl right under her nose. Getting Stella to let you live with her when she didn't even know you. And Paul—you've got that poor bastard following you around like a lapdog. You have a way of winning people over. They trust you. They love you. They *worship* you. What you have is a gift. You should use it."

Soyoung got up then, pushing his hands away from her. She stepped back from the table, and as they looked at each other, she said, "You're a piece of shit."

Nathaniel shrugged. "Hey," he said, raising his hands, "you were the one who told me to own up to it."

In the final days of November, it began to rain in Ithaca: not a thunderstorm, but a cold, clinging drizzle that stole through coats and muddied walking paths and filled every room and hall on campus with a damp, musty smell. Outside activities were hastily moved indoors, and the common areas of the dorm were suddenly swarming with people, huddled together in warmth and laughter as they took refuge from the rain. It was during this week, sitting cross-legged on Stella's bed while playing cards with Stella and two other girls, that Soyoung finally made up her mind about what must happen.

She returned to Nathaniel's apartment three days before Thanksgiving, and as they lay in bed that afternoon, listening to rain sloshing against the window, it occurred somewhat belatedly to Soyoung that perhaps he deserved one last chance. She propped herself up on an elbow and addressed Nathaniel. "Don't you ever think about it?"

"About what?"

"The things you've done," Soyoung said. "Your sins."

"We're all sinners," Nathaniel said. "We can't help it. It's who we are."

He reached for her, but Soyoung shrank from his touch. She said, "It's not right, what we're doing. Don't you ever think about that?"

Nathaniel smiled in a way that repulsed her. "Come on," he said. "Really? You of all people?"

"Are you just not attracted to her? Is that what the issue is?"

"I *am* attracted to her," Nathaniel said.

"So you don't love her."

"I do love her. But so what? Honestly, so what?"

Then he said, "Have you ever heard of the story about the white and red roses?"

Soyoung shook her head.

Nathaniel said, "It's from a movie or something. White roses are the roses that are good for you. They're sweet. They're cute. They're vanilla. You like them, you can't live without them, but they're boring. There's no excitement. There's no spark."

He nodded at her. "And then there's red roses. They catch your eye right away, because they're beautiful. They're wild, they're exciting, they keep your attention. But they'll prick your finger if you hold them for too long. Because at their core, behind those beautiful red petals, they're nothing but a bunch of thorns.

"See, white roses . . . those are the roses you want to keep in your house."

Nathaniel paused, and he looked at Soyoung expectantly, waiting for her to ask the next question. But she just smiled.

"Thanks for the story," she said. "I think I get it now. How it all ends."

As Soyoung got out of bed, she said, "Could you run a bath for me? With extra-hot water. I've been feeling so cold with all this rain."

She began to put on her clothes, and Nathaniel said, "Are you going out?"

"Just a quick run to the corner store. I'll be back by the time the bath is ready."

Outside the apartment, as Soyoung closed the door behind her and leaned against the wall, just out of view of the window, a gust of rain washed over her. She breathed in deeply: It smelled like home.

She waited.

It would only take minutes.

The apartment was empty of Nathaniel when she let herself back in. From the bathroom, she heard the sound of water running, and when she pushed the door ajar, a blast of hot steam rushed at her face. Nathaniel was stretched out in the small yellow bathtub, the water now rising halfway to his chest. He smiled at her, naked and unabashed. "Thought I'd jump in and help you get warmed up," he said.

Soyoung smiled back at him. The bathroom was so cramped that the toilet almost touched the bathtub; she pushed down the lid and perched herself on it, crossing her legs neatly. "You're not going to come in?" Nathaniel asked.

"Oh," Soyoung said, "I'm waiting."

"For what?"

Soyoung was quiet for a beat. She said, "Do you really believe in God?"

Nathaniel laughed. "What kind of question is that?"

"Just answer me."

"Would you believe me if I said yes?"

Soyoung cocked her head, and after a moment, Nathaniel said, "Here's the thing—I think of it as insurance. Of course God exists. He loves us, He's watching over us, He sent His only begotten son to die for our sins, et cetera, et cetera. I believe in all of that. But you know what I also believe?"

"What?"

"If God didn't want us to sin," Nathaniel said, "then why did He make us out to be sinners? Humans were literally designed to have free will. And having free will means that we're going to want to sin. We can't help it. There's a little voice inside all of us, always probing, always asking, *What's the worst thing that could happen?* Well, if you don't believe in God, the worst thing that happens is that you die, and you go to hell. But if you *do* believe in God—"

He raised an eyebrow at her. "All you have to do is repent the moment before you die. Do that, and all your sins will be forgiven. It's as simple as that."

The water was up to his collarbone now. "Tub's getting full," Nathaniel said. "Why don't you hop on in? It's nice and cozy in here."

He reached for her then with his right arm, which had been hanging off the edge of the tub; it flailed feebly and fell back into the water. Soyoung laughed. "Dead arm?" she asked.

"Yeah, I guess. It . . ."

Nathaniel was staring at his arm, puzzled. It remained limp in the water, and as he made to move one arm, and then the other, Soyoung could see the veins in his neck strain with effort. "I can't feel my arms," he said. "I don't—"

The water in the bathtub was lapping his chin now. "Soyoung," Nathaniel said, and his voice had taken on a tinge of panic. "Turn off the water. I need you to turn it off."

"Why?"

"Why? Because I can't move my arms and legs, I—Soyoung, turn off the water. Fucking turn it off!"

A moment passed; Soyoung nodded. She reached across the tub and shut off the faucet, and Nathaniel almost moaned in relief. "Good. Good girl. Here's what I need you to do next: I'm going to need you to grab my arm. Go ahead—put my arm over your shoulder and give me a little lift so I can get out."

"But why would you want to do that?" Soyoung said.

They looked at each other. Soyoung was smiling as she dipped a hand into the bathtub and stirred the water. "Look how nice it is," she said, her voice soft. "It's so nice and warm and relaxing in the water, don't you think, Nathaniel? I think you should stay a bit longer. In fact, I think you should take all the time you need and really dive in."

At the bottom of the tub, there was a sudden squelching sound; Nathaniel's buttocks had come loose from the porcelain surface. His body sank an inch, then another inch into the water, as though it were being reeled in slowly by an invisible hand.

A vein was throbbing in Nathaniel's forehead. He began to pant. "Soyoung, listen to me. You need to—what the hell are you doing, just sitting there like a fucking idiot? I'm going to drown if you don't pull me out. Fucking pull me out!"

"Oh, drowning's not so bad, really," Soyoung said. "In fact, by the time you've reached the end, it's actually quite comfortable."

That was when she finally saw the fear in his eyes.

She watched as Nathaniel took several deep breaths, steadying himself. "Okay," he said. "Okay, I get it. I get it."

"What do you mean?"

"You wanted to punish me, right? I did something that pissed you off, and now you've—you've put something in my drink to mess with my nervous system so I can't move. You wanted to give me a good scare. And you've done it, okay? You've scared me, and I apologize. I sincerely apologize to you, Soyoung. We good now? Can you stop messing around and help me out?"

Soyoung shook her head. "Poor Nathaniel," she said, and her voice was gentle, laced with concern. "You still don't get it."

"What don't I get? Explain it to me, and I'll get it. I promise I'll get it."

Then he said, "Is this about you and Stella? You want me to choose, is that it? Because I choose you, Soyoung. Of course I choose you. You're the most beautiful woman I've ever met. You're beautiful, you're smart, you're hot, and you're special. You're so fucking special, Soyoung. I never want to be with anyone else again. Just you. All I want is you."

Soyoung laughed lightly. "I thought I was full of nothing but thorns."

"That was bullshit, I swear. I just made it up to get a rise out of you. I didn't mean any of it."

"No," Soyoung said, "you were right."

She was pensive as she said, "You're the only person at Cornell who really sees me as I am. Do you know that? Stella, Paul, Lillian—they've all only seen what I have allowed them to see. Even I was starting to believe the lies I had constructed. I thought that I had seen the light of salvation, that I had actually, truly changed. But you looked at me and saw right through."

"Of course I saw you," Nathaniel said. "You and I, we're the same."

Most of his head was submerged now; as he tilted his face desperately towards the ceiling, his eyes and nose and mouth were the only parts of him that remained above the surface. Below him, they could both hear a steady sucking sound: A small whirlpool had formed in the water. It was a vacuum, ready to consume.

The air in the room was heavy with steam. Beads of sweat had appeared on Soyoung's face; she dabbed at them gently with a cotton handkerchief. Then she leaned forward on the toilet, so close that she almost touched his hopeful face.

"Repent," she said.

There was a pause.

"Re-repent?" Nathaniel repeated.

"You said it yourself. Redemption can only be earned if you repent for your sins. So will you repent?"

Nathaniel didn't hesitate.

"I will," he whispered. "I do."

He took several deep breaths, gathering his words. He said, "I repent before God, Soyoung. I apologize for everything I did. I'm going to spend the rest of my life making it up to you. Do you—do you want to get accepted to Cornell for real? Because I can make that happen. I have friends in the admissions office. All I have to do is give them a name. They do it all the time for legacy admissions. Dumbass kids whose families donate a building. Think about it, Soyoung. This time next year, you could be living in the dorms for real. Taking classes for real. This life you've wanted for so long, it could be yours. Or if you want to go to art school, I can make that happen, too. You want to go to Pratt? I'll work my ass off to pay your tuition. I'll take care of you for the rest of your life. I'll make it right. I promise."

He closed his mouth. His nose was the only thing that remained above water now, and when he watched her from the water, his eyes were bulging, straining with hope. Soyoung considered his words. She nodded.

"Do you know what I love the most about water?" she said. "Water doesn't discriminate. She doesn't care about your academic achievements. She doesn't care about the wealth in your pockets. She doesn't care about the people you know or the places they can get you. And she certainly doesn't care about your sniveling, self-serving repentance. Before water, everyone is equal, Nathaniel. She has cleansed the entire world of its sins before, in a gargantuan flood whose memory has lingered across time and across cultures, and one day she will do it again. But for today—"

She smiled at him. "She's just happy to take you. And in exchange, she's going to give me something precious. Something that will belong only to me."

"You bitch," Nathaniel whispered, swallowing a mouthful of water. "You fucking psycho."

"Lie back," Soyoung said. "Lie back and let the water wash away your sins."

"Bitch! Bitch! Psycho cunt! I'm going to kill you! You're going to burn in hell!"

She was silent, watching him choke and cough and sputter. He was crying now. "The Lord is my shepherd," he panted, "I shall not want. He maketh me to lie down in green pastures, He leadeth me—"

With a last, ragged gasp, his face disappeared below the water. Soyoung watched as his head thrashed in vain, as his face turned purple and then blue from the loss of oxygen, as veins bulged and throbbed in his forehead to the same beat as his muffled screams. His strength gave way. A stream of bubbles issued from his open mouth. His head lolled limply to the side, and Nathaniel Lee lay in the water, his body flushed pink, motionless, finally at rest.

For a long time, Soyoung sat on the toilet, not moving.

When she stood up, she reached into the pocket of Nathaniel's jeans, crumpled and draped over the radiator, and pulled out his wallet. Inside, she counted ten twenty-dollar bills. She tucked them into her own pocket and let the wallet and jeans fall to the floor. By the time the rain slowed and the sun began to emerge from the clouds, she was already gone.

SOYOUNG

In the days leading up to and following the funeral, Soyoung saw Stella only in glimpses. Stella's parents flew in from Los Angeles, and at the service, Soyoung saw them sitting on either side of her in the first row of the church, Stella's mother dabbing at her eyes with a Hermès scarf while her father—the one who had said she was too fat to be a doctor—stroked Stella's hair. She recognized them from the photographs Stella had strung up all over the dorm. Every year, Stella's parents took her and her two sisters to Disneyland for Christmas. The entire family wore matching T-shirts and Mickey Mouse ears.

Stella's parents booked a suite at the Ithaca Marriott, and she stayed with them for nearly a week before they finally brought her back to the dorm. When Soyoung returned to their room that evening, she saw Stella sitting on her bed, alone, a stuffed penguin in her lap. "Hi," Soyoung said, pausing in the doorway.

Stella's eyes were fixed on the penguin. "Hi," she said.

Soyoung walked to her own bed and sat, facing Stella. She said, "How are you feeling?"

Stella didn't answer. She turned the penguin over in her hand. It was small and tubby, covered in soft gray fur.

She said, "They found this in his apartment, when they were . . . cleaning up. It was supposed to be a Christmas present to me. He knew how much I loved penguins."

"I'm sorry," Soyoung said.

Stella looked at her. "I can't believe I didn't catch it," she said, and her voice was dull, lifeless. "We were together for over a year, and I never saw the signs. I was premed, too. I should have known. I should have . . ."

"It wasn't your fault," Soyoung said. "Sometimes seizures come out of nowhere. He was so young and healthy—how could anyone have seen it coming?"

They were both quiet.

Soyoung said, "So do you still have to take your finals?"

Stella nodded. "They're giving me a one-week extension. I can take them in my room."

"I'll help you, then. We can work on them together."

But Stella just shook her head. "What's the point?" she said. "He's gone. Nothing matters anymore."

She was not crying, as she had done at the funeral; something inside her seemed to have been extinguished, leaving behind an empty husk. Soyoung went to sit by her and put an arm around Stella's shoulder. Stella did not react.

"One day," Soyoung said, "it'll all be over."

Then she said, "The pain that you feel now, it hurts, but it's temporary. It's . . . ephemeral. Time will pass, you'll go on, and one day, you'll look around and realize that you've turned a corner. That your life is bigger and more beautiful than you could have ever possibly imagined."

Slowly, Stella turned her head to look at Soyoung.

"What is wrong with you?"

"Stella—" Soyoung began, but Stella shook her arm off and backed away, still holding the penguin. "What is *wrong* with you?" she said. "Why would you say that to me?"

"I was trying to comfort you. I didn't mean—"

"You were trying to comfort me? You don't know what it's like. You don't know what it's like to lose the only person you've ever loved. You have no idea."

"Maybe I don't," Soyoung said, "but I know Nathaniel."

"What's that supposed to mean?"

Soyoung closed her eyes. She took a deep breath, and when she opened them, Stella was staring at her from the other end of the bed, hostile, apprehensive. Soyoung swallowed.

"Look, Stella," she said, "I wasn't sure if I should tell you, but at this point, I think it's better that you know. Nathaniel and I were . . . we were sleeping together."

Stella blinked several times.

She said, "You're joking, right? Tell me that was supposed to be a joke."

Soyoung shook her head, and Stella said, "Because that's a really messed-up thing to say about someone. Soyoung, he's—he's dead. You have no right to lie about him. No right at all."

"His old bedspread," Soyoung said, "it was really itchy, wasn't it? It would leave these diamond-shaped imprints on your skin. He replaced it with a new duvet cover the first week of November. It was navy blue. It had a higher thread count."

She watched as Stella's face changed.

The stuffed penguin fell to the floor. As Stella rose from the bed, she reached for her writing desk, almost losing her balance as she stumbled to her feet. All the blood had drained from her face.

"I let you stay in my room," she said. "I gave you my food."

"I know."

"I invited you to fellowship. I introduced you to all my friends. I pulled you out of a *gorge*."

Again, Soyoung said, "I know."

She stood, too, facing Stella. Her face was radiant, filled with tenderness. She said, "Don't you see? I've known Nathaniel was bad news from the very beginning. I saw how he manipulated you, how he made you feel bad about yourself so that you would stay with him. I knew then that I had to save you. You had pulled me from the mud and saved my life. You had shown me the love of God! I knew that Nathaniel didn't deserve to be with someone like you, and I was proved right. I've been sleeping with him since October, not to steal him away from you, you have to understand, but to gather evidence. I've been waiting for this moment for so long, Stella. I've been waiting to tell you everything."

As she spoke, something in Stella's face shifted. She swallowed, twice.

She said, "So is that . . . is that the truth, then? Everything as it happened?"

Soyoung nodded emphatically. "I would never lie to you."

Stella said nothing, and Soyoung approached her and knelt before her, taking both of Stella's hands in hers. "It's like you once told me," she said. "It was God's will for us to meet. He called on you to save me, and now He has called on me to save you. You and I, Stella—we see each other like no one else does. You're the only light in my darkness. You're all that I have. I'll never hurt you like he did. I'll never leave you. I'll protect you for as long as we both live."

She waited; Stella's face remained blank. She was looking away from Soyoung, at the posters hanging on the opposite wall.

She said, "I don't know what to say."

"You don't have to say anything. Just know that I'm here for you."

"No, I know," Stella said. "I know."

She closed her eyes, and after a moment she said, "My entire head is spinning."

"Do you want to lie down?"

"Yeah. Yeah, I think I'll do that."

Then Stella said, "Can you get me some food from the diner? I haven't eaten in forty-eight hours. I feel like I'm going to pass out."

It took twenty-five minutes from waiting in line at the diner to finally picking up Stella's favorite order, a spicy chicken sandwich and a carton of curly fries. As Soyoung walked back to the dorm with a plastic takeout bag, she saw a ring of people at the residence hall entrance, all gawking at something in the middle of the sidewalk. She pushed her way through the crowd and stopped.

Lying outside the entrance was her large pink suitcase, its lid flopped open. Her clothes spilled out like guts, her sweaters and her shirts and her dresses dragged carelessly across the dusty pavement. A few feet away was her box of new art supplies, her paintbrushes and her bottles of ink and her watercolors and her canvases, all the things she had bought with the cash from Nathaniel's wallet. The box sat there, neat and upright, like it had been waiting for her.

SOYOUNG

The sun had just passed over the horizon when Paul appeared on the grass outside the law library. Soyoung was seated on a bench by the entrance; for a long moment, they simply looked at each other across the lawn.

Paul joined her at the other end of the bench. "Hi," he said.

"Hi."

Paul leaned forward.

"Hey," he said, "what's going on?"

His voice was quiet, but in his tone she sensed a sharpness, an agitation. Soyoung shrugged. "What?"

Paul said, "Where have you been? I haven't seen you for ages. I thought you had . . ."

Then he said, "Did you move to a different dorm?"

"I've been here."

"Here as in where? The—the law library?"

"There's a room with an old couch in the basement," she said. "I've been using it to work on my art. And the couch is surprisingly comfortable."

Paul was speechless, and Soyoung said, "You said you wanted to talk. What about?"

Paul looked at his hands.

He said, "I was wondering about . . . about us. About you and me."

"What about us?"

"No, it's just, before the retreat, I thought things were . . . you know. They were good. And after that, I don't know, things just got . . . everything got weird, somehow."

Paul took a deep breath. "At fellowship, there's been this rumor going around after Nathaniel died. People have been saying that you . . ."

He trailed off. Soyoung said, "That I what?"

"That you maybe had something with Nathaniel. I don't even know where it came from. It's just this stupid rumor."

Soyoung was picking at a pill on her sweater, and when it came off, she flicked it into the grass. Paul leaned towards her again.

"Tell me it's not true," she heard him say. "It's just bullshit, right?"

Soyoung's gaze drifted away, trailing the sun. It had almost vanished, a few remaining rays of gold barely hanging on.

She said, "What does it matter, really?"

"It matters to me," Paul said.

His face had become flushed. In a tight voice, he said, "Just tell me if it's true or not. Please, Soyoung."

A long moment passed before she nodded.

Something seemed to shift within Paul then. The air went out of him. He buried his head in his hands, and when he finally came up, he said, in a voice that was both hoarse and quiet, "This is so fucked up."

Then he said, "I thought we were . . . This whole time, you acted like you were into me. You acted like you and I were together, like you cared about me, and I fell for it. Because I'm the biggest idiot in the world."

A tear had made its way down his cheek. Paul wiped it away roughly. "Of course you were out there letting other guys fuck you this whole time," he said. "That night at the convenience store—you liked it when that guy hit on you, didn't you? I should've seen it all along."

He got up from the bench, and Soyoung couldn't help it; she called out after him. "Paul. Wait."

He turned to look at her.

She said, "I was just using him. You get that, right? I use people to get the things I want. It's all I do. I used Lillian. I used Stella. And I used Nathaniel. I used each of them until they had nothing left to give me, and then I kicked them to the curb and replaced them with someone else. Because that's the kind of person I really am. It's who I've been all along."

Still, Paul was quiet, and Soyoung sat up straighter, her hands folded neatly on her lap. There was a resigned amusement on her face as she said, "There's no need to look so surprised. You were smart enough to get into Cornell; surely you figured out the truth at some point. When did you first catch on?"

There was a long silence.

"Early September," Paul said. "After the first time I walked you back from the store."

Soyoung raised her eyebrows; then she laughed, quietly. "How did you know?"

"I looked you up in the university directory. You weren't there."

"God," Soyoung said, "that stupid, stupid directory."

Then she said, "So why didn't you tell anyone? Why didn't you turn me in?"

Paul hesitated, but she answered for him. "It was because you were lonely, wasn't it? God, in those days, you were practically invisible. You were drifting through campus like a ghost, no agency, no purpose, no sense of self. And when I saw you—when you knew I could see you and chose to see you—you attached yourself to me, all of your meaning, all of your self-worth, even though you knew I was a fraud.

"I don't mean to say this in a cruel way, Paul, but you're so *weak*. Look at all the gifts God has given you! Your athleticism, your intelligence, your gender, your citizenship. You have it all, and you don't even appreciate it. You've done nothing with the power that you have. Not even to raise your hand to protect your mother, not even to throw a punch back at your stepfather, even though you now tower over him. You're not a man, Paul. You're a disappointment to everyone in your life, to your mom, to me, most of all to yourself.

"You were wrong, by the way: There were hundreds of times when I would have fucked you, I could even have seen us in a relationship, but now I just pity you. Me? I've stolen, I've lied, I've done terrible things. I was never a good person. But at least I'm not the type of person who just lies down and takes it. I will never, ever be like you."

More tears were glistening on Paul's cheek. He didn't bother to wipe them away. As he met Soyoung's gaze, his eyes were wet, bright, burning.

Quietly, he said, "I can't believe I ever thought you were too good for me."

SOYOUNG

At midnight, when Stella appeared at the gorge, Soyoung was already sitting on the mossy bank. Her bare feet dangled over the edge, and her wet hair was loose and flowing over the long white dress she wore. Stella was in her nightgown, the lavender one with the tiny daisies; she walked up to Soyoung slowly, her legs carrying her in a way that was odd and stilted, and when they looked at one another, Stella's face was pale, haunted.

She said, "You—you're still here."

"I have some things left to do," Soyoung said.

Stella took a deep breath. She said, "Why did you tell them?"

"What do you mean?"

"You've been telling people in the fellowship. About you and—you and Nathaniel. That disgusting lie you made up about him—" Stella's voice rose sharply before it cracked. "Now everyone knows. Everyone's gossiping about it."

Soyoung was quiet for a long time.

She said, "You know, I used to feel sorry for you."

Then she said, "When I first met you, I thought you were this... this tiny white flower. You were innocent, and you were precious, and you were so susceptible to the whims of the world. I saw how you languished under the weight of your family's judgment. I saw how you clung to Nathaniel for his approval. I saw how much you ached to be loved. And

I thought, *I have to protect her. I have to save her from all the people in this world who want to do her harm.* It was why I had to kill Nathaniel, you see. It was the only way to free you from his control."

In the moonlight, Stella's face was wet with tears. Soyoung shook her head.

"In the end, though," she said, "I realized that you were a disappointment. You let me down, just like my parents, just like Paul, just like the guys I dated in high school. You claim to want someone to see you in the darkness, for someone to love you just as you are—but when I came to you and laid myself bare for you to see, what did you do? You rejected me. You cast me out. And you threw yourself into the arms of your parents and your sisters and your other friends instead. What must it be like, Stella, to be so flush with love, so content with what you already have, that you have the *luxury* of turning down someone who offered you their entire heart? That was when I knew that you and I were not the same."

She rose from the bank and began to wade into the water. As she turned to face Stella, the hem of her dress swirled.

"Love isn't a gift," she said. "Do you understand that, Stella? It's something we have to earn. It's something every person in the world should have to work for. Because how else could you possibly appreciate the beautiful things that someone else has so selflessly given you? How else could you learn?"

She raised a hand towards Stella, who gasped; she took an involuntary step, then another, into the water.

"No," she moaned, "please, no. What—Soyoung, what are you doing? What are you doing?"

"It's all right," Soyoung said, and her voice was a lullaby. "Shhh—it's all right. It's all right, darling. I'm right here."

They were both waist-deep in the water now, facing each other. Soyoung reached out and took Stella's hands in hers; Stella's face was wet, red, crumpled in tears. "It was you, wasn't it?" she whispered. "It was your voice. It was your voice in my head all along."

Soyoung smiled.

She said, "That day, when you came to the gorge and met me by the water—it was because I had been calling out to you. Even before I knew you existed, I was waiting for you."

A tear had made its way down her cheek. She cradled Stella's face with one hand.

"I tried to forgive you," she said. "I really did. After you betrayed me, I promised myself that I would turn the other cheek. I tried to dull my pain with alcohol. I tried to distract myself with my art. But she was the one who couldn't forgive you, Stella. She was always there, whispering in my head, reminding me of how unfair it all was—my whole life, filled with nothing but one injustice after another. Why couldn't I have been born in Seoul or Boston instead of being Chinese country trash? Why wasn't I the one who got private tutors and fancy toys and the biggest room in the whole apartment? And what was so utterly repulsive about me that not even one Ivy League school would deign to give me a chance?

"I did everything for you, Stella. I picked up after you. I washed your clothes. I listened to your silly daydreams and inane worries like they were the most fascinating things in the world. I *earned* my place by your side. I argued with her when she asked for you. Did you know that? I defended you to her, even after you had betrayed me, even after I had given you the greatest gift of your life for nothing. I begged her to let you go."

She was crying now. She let go of Stella's hands and raised the back of her hand to her face, wiping it noisily. It took her a moment to compose herself.

"In the end, though, I saw the truth. She was right. You had a choice to save me like I'd saved you, and you didn't. You left my call unanswered. You created an injustice in the universe, and for that . . . for that, I have no choice but to put an end to all of this.

"I'm so sorry, Stella. I can't make peace with the fact that you have chosen to exist in this hideous world without me. I won't be able to sleep at night, knowing that one day, you will meet another small, petty, worthless man who will tell you that you are too fat, that you are too stupid, that you do not deserve to be loved; and you, being you, will believe him. I can't let you do that, Stella. Not again. So I have no choice but to save you from yourself."

There was a long silence.

"Are you going to kill me?" Stella asked.

Soyoung's face was pale, mirroring Stella's. Her long, dark, waterlogged hair clung to her frame, and her tears fell steadily into the water, one after another.

"I'm so sorry," she said. "I'm so, so sorry. I wish there were another way."

Stella nodded, resigned.

"Do it, then," she said. "I don't want to be here anymore, anyway. I . . . I want to go."

She closed her eyes, and Soyoung pressed her lips to Stella's forehead.

"I'll be so gentle, I promise," she said, and her voice quavered. "It'll feel just like going home."

It was nearly twilight when Soyoung returned to the law library. There was a window she used to get into the basement, an innocuous one she'd left unlatched from the inside. She slipped through it under the cover of darkness, and at the end of the hallway, she opened the door to a small, windowless archival room and switched on the light.

Behind the cobwebbed shelves of boxes and binders, steps from the couch where she slept and the neat stack of empty beer bottles, she had set up her easel, a glass of water, and a half-dried inkstone; the painting she'd been working on sat there unfinished, a smattering of dark shapes and lines. Propped up against the wall were the canvases she had finished. Four more. Four more, and she'd have enough for a portfolio to apply to art school with. She was the closest she'd ever been.

Soyoung sat in front of the easel and picked up her brush. For a long time, she remained motionless, gazing at the swirl of black shadows on the canvas; then, slowly, the brush fell from her hand. She slipped from the stool and coiled into a ball on the floor, and there, in infinite silence, she began to weep.

ERIN

June 2017

From the fancy florist near Bryant Park, I picked up the luxurious bouquet I had preordered: roses, hydrangeas, carnations, and olive branches, wrapped in brown paper and a satin bow. I carried it with me on the train back to Hoboken, a burst of blush and white sweetness in my arms.

Sophia gasped softly when she saw it. Her eyes filled with tears; as she took the bouquet from me, she leaned in and kissed me on the cheek. "Thank you," she said. "It means everything that you came."

"Please," I said. "You know I couldn't have missed this."

Sophia nodded, hugging the flowers to her chest. She was wearing a simple linen white dress that flowed on her; she looked radiant. There was life in her again.

She said, "I still can't believe you're leaving tomorrow."

"I know," I said, "but remember what I said. A year's time."

I saw her look down and smile, sadly. But all she said was "Have you had a chance to see Brian Tsai's photographs? They're spectacular. He really has such a special connection with quails."

The Hoboken Art Collective was a converted warehouse just steps away from the Hudson. The ceiling above us was exposed, revealing long stretches of metal piping and wiring that buzzed quietly as the people below laughed and mingled. Eight Asian American photographers had been invited to show their work in the exhibition, which snaked around the space in a mazelike structure, a single photograph affixed to each white wall. There was a photo of a nude elderly man at the entrance to the maze; a placard nearby identified the artist as Abigail Tagawa.

I was looking at the photo when Paul emerged from the maze, holding Ory's hand. There was a stilted silence as we looked at each other; then Ory cried out, "Hi, Erin!" and ran up to me. I knelt and hugged him.

Ory was solemn as he said, "Are you really leaving?"

I nodded. "I'm going back to Florida tomorrow."

"I don't want you to go. You're my friend."

"You're my friend, too," I told him. "And I'm sad that I have to go, but I think it's better for everyone that way."

I got to my feet, and Paul took Ory by the hand again. "Well," he said, not meeting my eyes, "good luck with everything."

Then he tugged Ory's hand. "Come on, time for bed. Let's get you home."

I'd made it more than halfway through the exhibition when I finally saw Sophia's photographs. It was the same collection I'd seen that day on her coffee table, but with one new addition. It was a photo of a pair of scissors lying on the floor, surrounded by clumps of short black hair. I stepped closer, trying to tell if they were mine. Had she taken them that day, after she'd cut my hair? The hair in the photo looked different. It was curly.

I heard footsteps behind me and turned, ready to yield the observation space to the next visitor. That was when I saw him.

Auggie Flores.

He was wearing a flannel shirt and his trademark black-rimmed glasses, and a messenger bag swung from his shoulder. For a long time, we just stared at each other. I saw his eyes travel over me, my short hair, my eyes, my cheekbones.

Quietly, he said, "Shelley Hu?"

Hearing my name in his mouth—instinctively, I shivered. I took a step back. My arms flew up, and I crossed them in a defensive stance before I managed to say, "What are you doing here?"

"Oh, um, Sophia Moon invited me." He nodded in the direction of the mixer. I could hear glasses clinking, people laughing. "She's one of the artists. She said she could hook me up with—never mind, that's not important right now. What are . . . what are you doing here?"

"What the fuck are you talking about, she invited you? How do you even know her?"

I saw him hesitate.

"We only met, like, a month ago," he said, finally. "We're . . . we go to the same support group. For mental health and stuff."

Below me, the floor tilted. Auggie looked at me apprehensively.

"So," he said, "how are . . . how are things?"

"How are things?"

"Yeah." He scratched his head, a nervous tic. "Ever since it happened, I've been wondering . . . I've been wondering how you were. I kept thinking that I should have reached out to you."

I said nothing. Auggie scratched his head again.

"Look," he said, "I didn't mean for it to happen like that. I swear I didn't. That day, when I saw you on the subway, I only filmed it because I thought it was funny. You know how it is. You see some freaky shit in public in New York, you take a video to show your friends. And I had, like, two thousand followers on Twitter. I never thought it'd go viral and spin out into this big national story. I wouldn't have posted it if I'd known."

"You wrote an article about it for the *Gazette*, though," I said. I had to bite down on every word to keep my voice from shaking. "You wrote not just one article but three."

Auggie looked down at his shoes.

In a small voice, he said, "Not that it makes it okay, but . . . that article got a lot of clicks. It was the kind of story that just naturally sells. And at the *Gazette*, we get paid based on that. We get a bonus if a story hits a certain amount of page views."

"Right, so you sold me. You sold me for page views and a measly fucking bonus. How do you sleep at night? I'm genuinely asking. How do you sleep?"

Auggie swallowed. He looked up at me.

"That law firm you were working for," he said, "they represent white-collar criminals. Big banks that defrauded tens of thousands of ordinary people out of their homes. Did you know that?"

"I wasn't working on those cases," I said, stung. "My focus was on IP."

"Right, but who do you think paid the rent on that shiny Midtown office? How do you think they built that brand? How do you think they paid for your computer, your office supplies, maybe even parts of your salary? You worked for a firm that defended criminals. Oligarchs. Fucking oil and gas companies. Like it or not, you sold your time to them. You sold your labor. So, just . . ."

Auggie waved a hand. "It's fucked up," he said, "but it's capitalism. People like you, me, we're all rats. We're just trying to survive out here."

I was speechless.

I watched as Auggie reached into his pocket and came out with a loose cigarette. "Have you seen Sophia around?" he asked.

"Why?"

"She told me that Ira Glass was going to be here. I've been trying to get a meeting with him for ages. My background's in print, but I've been dabbling in audio for a while now. Started my own podcast to talk all things politics, pop culture, whatever's floating around in the zeitgeist. And I really think this has the potential to hit it big with a national audience, you know? I just need a . . . a fucking kingmaker. I need someone with the clout to listen to it for five minutes and tell me they can hear what I hear. That's how anyone makes it in this business. Talent's a dime a dozen. But you have to schmooze your way around town and kiss a hundred asses until you find the one person willing to sign a check."

But then his shoulders sagged. "Anyway, she swore he was coming, but it's been an hour and he hasn't shown, so I think I'm going to bounce. These photographs are basic as fuck, anyway."

It was so absurd that I started to laugh. I said, "You're a piece of shit."

"I know," Auggie said. "I work for the *New York Gazette*."

He turned to go, and that was when I saw it: a flash of white. I heard her voice.

"Shelley?"

Behind Auggie, Sophia had appeared out of nowhere. He and I both looked at her, startled, but she was smiling. She looked calm. Cheerful, even.

"Oh, good," she said. "Shelley, Auggie, I see the two of you have met each other. Or remet, I should say."

She came closer, and instinctively, I took a step back.

I said, "Sophia, what's going on? He's saying he knows you. He's saying you invited him. Did you go to the support group without telling me?"

And at the same time, Auggie said, "Hey, so is Ira here, or . . . ?"

Sophia was still smiling. Brightly, she said, "Oh, he's out back by the water, talking to my friend. I can take you to him and introduce you, but we'd have to hurry—Ira's saying he has to leave soon, but he's interested in hearing about your podcast."

Auggie's whole demeanor changed. He stuffed the cigarette back in his pocket and straightened up. "Shit. Shit, yeah, let's go. Let's go catch him before he leaves."

"Sophia—" I began, but Sophia stepped forward and took me by the wrist. "It's all right," she said, and something in her voice made me close my mouth. "Come with us, and I'll explain everything once we're outside."

At the other end of the maze, we pushed our way out of the back door. Behind the building were two gaping dumpsters and a dusty patch of grass. The Hudson was dark, silent, shrouded in a fog so thick that I could not see the glittering city beyond it. "I spent all night writing up, like, fifty story ideas to pitch him," Auggie was saying as Sophia led us to the water. "Maybe a whole spin-off investigative series, he could bring me on as a guest host—"

Abruptly, he stopped talking. The area behind the warehouse was empty.

We were alone.

Auggie turned back to us. "Where's Ira?" he asked, still hopeful. "Did he already go back in?"

Next to me, Sophia smiled.

"Extraordinary," she said. "Just absolutely extraordinary."

Auggie gaped at her, and I said, "Sophia, I still don't understand why we're out here. I don't understand why *he's* here."

Sophia squeezed my hand.

"It's all come to this, darling," she said. "It's time to lay everything out in the open. It's time we settled this matter, once and for all."

She turned to Auggie.

"The truth is," she said, "we've been plotting against you."

He blinked several times. He laughed, but the sound that came out was nervous, high-pitched. "Plotting? Plotting to . . . to do what, exactly?"

"Oh, Auggie," Sophia said, her voice gentle. "Oh, you poor, sad thing.

"There was a time when we had a special plan in store for you. For weeks, Shelley was on your tail, tracking your movements after you left work at the *Gazette*. She even followed you to one of your support group meetings. You don't even remember her being there, do you? She was there under disguise. The name she used was Erin Callaghan."

Auggie glanced at me. I thought I saw a glint of recognition through his glasses.

"At a certain point, though, Shelley decided to let you go. She was gracious. She had risen above it all. I, unfortunately, was not convinced. Why, after what you'd done to her, should we let you walk free? Why do you deserve mercy when you have never shown it to another person? It was a simple question of injustice. It was a question of what you owed the universe.

"So I began coming to your support group. I turned up every week with sob stories about my broken marriage, about my dead bedroom and my boredom and contempt towards my husband. I signed up to help you with your overwrought, vapid newsletter, and I listened patiently to your failures and your disappointments and your dying dreams. I gathered the information I needed to . . . well, to destroy you."

Behind us, I heard the sound of water slapping against concrete. The currents in the Hudson were picking up. A wind had come out of nowhere. I saw Sophia's hair float off her shoulders, drifting softly into the night air like a mass of black clouds. Her grip on my hand tightened.

I started to feel a chill in my fingers.

Sophia said, "There were three of you, you know.

"For Shelley's boss, Gene Struzik, a man who sexually harassed and silenced her, we determined that his sins should cost him his career and his marriage. We collected evidence of his disgusting nature. And when we brought this evidence to his wife, to his employers, we were met with a deafening silence. They chose to protect him instead.

"As for Amy Cloverfield, the passenger—well, we had better luck with her. She was a woman, after all, and an indisputable bitch; she was less likely to have people in her corner."

She smiled at me, and I said nothing. The skin all along my back was tingling, the hairs standing up. Auggie's mouth was lolling open. He looked small, foolish.

"Amy—Amy Cloverfield," he said, sounding out the name. "Why does that sound so familiar?"

"Didn't you hear? She jumped off the GW Bridge last month."

Auggie clapped a hand to his mouth. A moment passed before he said, "Fuck. I . . . I reported on that story for the *Gazette*. I had no idea. I—"

I saw his face change.

"Are you s-saying," he began, and there was a tremor in his voice now, a thin, metallic quality to the words, "that you had . . . that you . . ."

And for the first time, Sophia hesitated.

She wasn't looking at him anymore. She was looking at me. Her face was almost apologetic as she said, "The thing I need you to understand more than anything is that I had no other choice."

My ears were ringing.

I swayed on the spot.

I pushed her hand away and took several steps back until I hit the railing, until my back found something solid and metal to lean on. My voice came out as a croak. "Sophia, what . . . what are you talking about? What did you do?"

Sophia bit her lip. She was quiet, weighing her words; her eyes were on the water.

"I promised myself a long time ago that I wouldn't listen to her anymore," she said.

"I was eight years old when I allowed her to take my brother. That night, when I heard her voice, calling out to me—you have to understand. You have to understand, Shelley. He'd called me a thief. He'd cut up that dress, that beautiful lavender dress my umma had given to me. No one had believed me; no one had listened. And so when I heard her calling out my name that night, telling me that I was precious, that I deserved to be loved, that she would make me the most special little girl in the world, if only I would come to see her in the river—how could I have ignored her? How could I have stayed away?

"It was my stepfather's fault, too, in a way. He'd always bragged about that condo, how it was right on the waterfront, how the river was just steps away. That night, I got up from my bed. I followed the sound of her voice. I walked through the park, and it wasn't until I was deep in the river that I realized . . . that I realized it was too late.

"It took me years to come to terms with the fact that what she'd given me that night in the Han River was never a gift. It was a lie, a cursed bargain. I wasted years and years, feeding her bottomless appetite, giving her all the people she wanted, even the ones who didn't . . . who didn't deserve it, the ones I regret . . ."

She closed her eyes, and I saw it then: a glimmer on her cheek. A teardrop.

"But that night in the garden, when I saw how wounded you were by our failure, when I saw the defeat in your eyes . . . I knew then that I had to make another bargain with her. I had to give something back to the water."

The Aruba trip.

The scuba diving accident.

Gene was certified, the obituary had said. He had been diving for years.

"Did you—" I said, and my teeth began to chatter. "D-did you k-kill Amy, too? What—what did you do?"

"I hadn't intended on killing her. She had lost everything. She had paid you back for what she did to you—but then you went and told her everything. You told her about our plan. I don't blame you for what happened, of course. It was your story, your pain. You had every right to tell her. But it did mean that I couldn't afford to leave any loose ends. I had to clean it all up for you, and for that, I needed the water's help, too.

"I struggled, of course. I struggled with it for years, to the point where I broke from her and walked away. But I see it now, Shelley, why it has to happen. Why it has to be done with water. Water cleanses us; she washes away our sins. Ever since I was a child, I have known that many, if not most, people don't deserve to live to walk this earth. But no one is above judgment, my love. No one. And people like that deserve to be given back to the water.

"It will take Gene and Amy a long time to sail the river of forgetting. To cleanse themselves of their ugliness and atone for their sins. But they'll get there, in the end. They will earn the opportunity to return to this world one day, new and clean and *good*."

Sophia turned back to Auggie.

"You should take your shoes off before getting in," she said, and in her voice was a kindness. "They'll weigh you down in the water."

He didn't reply.

As Sophia bent to take off her shoes, he stood there watching her, silent, motionless. *Run*, I thought, with a sudden, desperate rush of comprehension. *Run!* But I could no longer move my tongue. It rolled up against the roof of my mouth, my saliva congealing around it, and I could only watch as Sophia walked up to him.

"Come with me," she said. She held out her hand.

Slowly, his hand came up through the air. Her fingers closed around his. In the darkness, I saw her white dress glow.

And hand in hand, they began to walk into the river.

No, no, no, I thought wildly, listlessly. My heart was racing. Every pore in my body was wide open, every hair standing up, every molecule crying out. *It's not real, it's not real, it's not happening.* But I saw them. I saw the small splashes they made as they waded in, her dress unfurling in the water like a flower, the stiffness of his legs as they carried him dutifully after her. In the water, Sophia smiled at him, and her gaze was tender, almost compassionate.

"I know what it's like," she told him. "Trust me, I know.

"I know what it's like to spend your whole life chasing the things you'll never have. To be eaten away by jealousy, worn down by disappointment after disappointment. I'm sorry for what this life has been for you, Auggie. But here's the good news: You're going to get another chance. You're going to move forward, just like this river, and you will be born again, in another place, in another time, and you will start your next life anew."

She kissed him on the forehead before she let him go.

For a moment, I saw Auggie's head bobble in the water; he was turned away from me, and in the thick of the fog I could not have seen his face, could not have heard him even if he had cried out in his last moments. Then the water lapped at him, and in the next instant, he was gone.

"Breathe, my love. *Breathe*."

Her hand was on my back, rubbing it rhythmically, and I opened my eyes and saw stars. "Easy," I heard Sophia's voice say. "Let's take a deep breath together."

She was drenched from head to toe. Her white linen dress clung to her frame, and the water in her long, dark hair was dripping onto my pants, my shoes. I closed my eyes and took a deep, shuddering breath.

Sophia was holding both of my hands in hers. She said, "I want you to listen to me very carefully."

I said nothing. My eyes were still closed.

"The first thing I want you to know is that you're safe. No one can ever hurt you, not while you're with me. Do you understand that, Shelley?"

I managed a shaky nod.

"Good." I could hear her smile. "Now, the next thing you need to know is that you don't need to worry about this. What you saw just now—it never happened. We will never speak of it again.

"And finally, you're going to give me your phone."

When I tried to speak, my voice was a rasp.

"W-why?"

"It's your alibi," Sophia said. "Proof that you will have stayed here all night."

She squeezed my hands. "This is what you're going to do. You are going to go home and take a nice bubble bath to calm your nerves. I'll stay here for the rest of the night with your phone. If the police ask, we'll say you were here all night. There's so many Asians at this event, they'll never keep all of us straight. Then, at midnight, I want you to go to our bench in the garden and wait for me. I'll answer all of your questions then, I promise. I'll explain everything."

She let go of me, and I felt her hand in my pocket, grasping for my phone. When I opened my eyes, I saw it clutched in her fingers, the case glistening in her grasp. And with that, I felt the final sliver of hope leave me.

No one else would come. No one would save me. It was just me and her, the way she'd always intended.

"Sophia," I said, "what . . . what happened to you in the Han River?"

She was quiet for a beat. Then she reached out and cradled my face in her hand, gentle.

"I died," she said, "and I came back. For that, I had to pay a price. Haven't I told you again and again? Nothing in this life is free. It's all earned, all of it. For years, I thought she had lied to me about the things she could make happen for me. I had lost faith. I vowed to stop nourishing her with the people she wanted, because nothing she had given me in return had ever been worth it in the end, not my parents, not Stella, not Paul, not Casey. But then . . . but then she gave me you.

"You were the best gift she has ever given me, Shelley. No one else comes close. No one else compares. That night in Santorini last summer, when I was standing on the patio, looking out at the sea while Paul slept in the room behind me, my phone buzzed with a Twitter notification. It was a video of you. And when I watched the video and I saw your pain and your humiliation and your vulnerability, I saw it all so clearly. How could I possibly think of ending my life when you were out there, waiting for me to save you?"

It wasn't real.

Any moment now, I'd wake up from this and find myself back in my mom's apartment, sweaty from a long nap on a cool bamboo sheet, the creaky ceiling fan spinning above me. My grandmother would be chopping fruits in the kitchen. My grandfather would be watching a soap opera about emperors and palaces on TV.

Any moment now.

Sophia took both of my hands in hers, and as she smiled at me, I saw it again. It was the same look she'd had in her eyes the night she and I had gone into the city, the night we had toasted Gene's death. It was pure, effervescent joy. It was triumph. It was euphoria.

"Do you see now?" she said. "What you mean to me? The lengths to which I'll go to keep you by my side, to make sure no one in the world can ever hurt you again? I messed up with Lizzie, I admit that. I hurt people who shouldn't have been hurt. I've hurt Ory, too, and I'll spend the rest of my life making that up to him. But I can do better, Shelley, and I will. I'll be the person you want me to be. From now on, I'll be so good. I'll be discerning. I'll only give her the people who deserve it, who mean nothing to this world, whose loss won't be mourned.

"You're not boarding that flight to Orlando tomorrow, my love. I am so sorry, but I can't let you do it. We're so close—we're so close! I've been meaning to tell you: I got the job at Ogilvy. I start there on Monday. I'm going to leave Paul, and you and I can finally walk under the sun together. No one else will ever love you the way I do: I love you wildly and boundlessly, without morality, without shame, without any of the silly confines this world puts on us. I love you in the same way I've always wanted to be loved. That's all it ever was."

Her eyes were pools. They reflected back the moon and the stars. In a previous life, they had captured me, drawn me in.

"Casey," I said, and I saw the tiniest tremor travel over her face. "What . . . what happened to her? When she left you. What really happened?"

There was a long silence.

"It doesn't matter," she said, finally. "It was a different situation. A different time."

As the water murmured behind us, Sophia pressed her forehead to mine.

"You told me yourself, remember?" she said. "You're not her. You'll never be her. I know you'll keep your word, my darling. I know you'll be good for it for the rest of our lives."

ERIN

The house was silent as I stumbled inside, not even bothering to take off my shoes. I ran straight to the guest room, flipped on the light, and began throwing my things into the open suitcase. I had put off packing until the eleventh hour, and now I was paying the price. There were shirts, underwear, art supplies, my dad's picture, sunscreen, deodorant—fuck it. I could buy everything from scratch. I could start again.

Footsteps, muffled by house slippers. Fuck. I jumped up and turned around, breathing hard, and saw Paul standing there in his pajamas. He looked at me, surprised. "Are you okay?"

My heart was pounding. As we stared at each other, I took a deep breath, willing my pulse to slow down, willing the words to come out smooth and rehearsed. "I—" I began.

I took another breath. I smiled.

"I came back early to finish packing," I said. In my voice, I could hear the panic behind the cheer, but I couldn't tell if he did. "Don't want to miss my flight back to Orlando tomorrow. It's first thing in the morning."

I saw Paul's eyes travel from my open suitcase to the unpacked items scattered on the bed.

He said, "Where's Sophia?"

"She's . . . she's still at the show. It's still going strong. Lots of people."

I held my breath. A long moment passed.

And then I saw Paul's gaze move down.

I looked down, too, against my better judgment. He was staring at my shirt, at a large spot of dampness that had formed on my chest and blossomed across the front. Sophia's hands. Sophia's hair. Sophia's tears. She had risen from the water and taken me into her arms, and in doing so she had branded me. I knew then, with a sinking finality, what would happen.

Paul stepped into the room.

He closed the door behind him.

Instinctively, I took a step back. Then another. I said, "Paul. Paul, don't do this."

"She told you, didn't she?" Paul said, and there was a strange quality to his voice, a note I couldn't place. "She told you everything."

"I don't know what you're talking about, man. I swear, I don't know anything."

He took a step towards me, and I backed up. I found the wall with my hands.

"Look—look," I said, and I could hear the desperation now, "I'm leaving right now, all right? I'm not waiting until my flight tomorrow. I'm packing my shit, and I'm calling a taxi. You'll never see me again. You'll never hear from me. I'll change my phone number, I'll—I'll move to a different state. I'll leave the country. I swear on my life, Paul. I swear on my mother's life. I'll never say a word about any of this to anyone."

I was gasping for air now. I could feel my eyes bulging as they bore into his. Paul cocked his head, like he was weighing my words.

He said, "Tell me why I should let you go."

I racked my brain, wild, desperate, searching for an answer—and miraculously, one came. I straightened up, panting.

"I get it now, Paul," I said. "I get why you are the way you are."

In his eyes, I saw a flicker. He said nothing.

I said, "When you met her, she placed you under her spell, didn't she? She enthralled you. She told you that you were the person she's waited for all her life. And then she showed you her true colors. She made you her prisoner. You've been living in her cage for thirteen years, haven't you, Paul? You've seen all the things she's done, to Casey, to others. You live every day in fear of her, terrified of what she could do to you. I get it, I do. And I—look, I can help you."

Still, Paul was quiet. I took another deep breath.

"You and I," I said, "we can go to the cops together. We'll tell them everything I know, everything you know. They'll put her away. They'll put you and Ory in witness protection. Make it so she can't find you, she can't track you down. You're, what, thirty, thirty-one? You have literally your entire life ahead of you. This is your chance to finally be free of her. Let me help you, Paul."

I waited.

Paul looked down at his hands. He smiled.

"I was right," he said. "You really don't know her at all."

That was when I dived for him.

There was one thing I'd always remembered from a childhood summer back in Florida, when a Chinese uncle, maybe the husband of one of my mom's friends, had gathered a couple of the kids to teach us the moves he'd learned from training at the Shaolin temple in Zhengzhou. *Never go for the private parts*, the uncle had said. *It's not a part of the martial code. And it hurts like hell.*

Before I'd reached Paul's balls, though, he hit me. His hand connected with the side of my head, and the first thing I felt was not pain, but lightness. A rush of stars. I fell to the floor in a lump, and it took a moment to come to, to get back on my feet. I looked around wildly for something, anything, before I remembered. I pulled open the drawer and grabbed the framed drawing Sophia had once given me, her talisman. I spun it in my hand until the sharpest angle was facing out.

I launched myself at him a second time.

This time, I hit him. I was faster, catching him in the middle, knocking the wind out of him as I rammed the portrait into the side of his neck. I heard Paul gasp. He stumbled backwards, holding his neck, and I ran for the door. My hand was on the handle. It turned. It swung open. I was halfway out—

Until something closed around my neck and hauled me back into the room by the back of my collar. My windpipe closed up. I couldn't breathe. A force I couldn't fight was dragging me across the wooden floor, across the soft area rug, until suddenly I was flying through the air, I was being propelled forward, my body was in free fall—

My head hit the wall.

My vision went pitch-black. The world around me was silent, and for a moment I wondered if I had been blinded. It took a moment for the picture to come back, one piece at a time.

I was in the guest room.

I was slumped on the floor.

And I wasn't alone.

My face was wet. A warm liquid was trickling down my cheek, and when it reached my lips, I tasted salt. I reached for my face and looked down at the substance that now coated my fingers. It was bright red. Wet. Thick.

I heard Paul say, again, "Tell me why I should let you go."

"I—" I began, and my voice was hoarse, jagged. I put down my hand.

He watched as I tried to get up for a second time. My joints were stiff, slow and dulled by the shock of the pain. But I forced myself to keep going. I peeled myself off the wall and rolled forward, planting the palms of my hands on the floor. I looked at him, on my knees.

I said, "Please."

He said nothing, but I could hear a change in his breathing. I said, "Please, Paul. Please."

And then I lowered my body and let my forehead fall to the floor. It landed with a *thud*, the sound reverberating throughout the room, the way my mom had taught me how to do it. "Please," I said, "please, Paul, I was wrong. I was wrong about everything."

Thud. My forehead made contact with the floor again. "I never should have made a move on your wife. I should have respected that she was yours. I'm so sorry, Paul. I'm so sorry."

Thud. "She never cared for me, you know. I was the one who begged her to take me home with her when we met back at that motel in Florida. I latched on to her because I was desperate, because I was fucking crazy, because I was obsessed with her. And I . . ."

I was crying now. The tears ran down my face, became one with the crimson of my blood. I felt hot, dazed, empty. But the words poured out of me. They kept coming.

"I'm no one," I said. "I'm nothing, just a fucking cockroach. Do you think I don't know that?

"Do you think, Paul, that I don't know what it's like to spend your entire life feeling like you're invisible, like you're just a—a garbage can in someone else's life? Because I do. Your whole life, just people staring through you like you're a ghost. When you talk, they act like they can't hear you. When you scream, they ask you why you're so quiet. You spend every single day of your life dressing like them, talking like them, getting the same jobs as them, going to the same bars and cracking the same jokes—until the day you finally realize it doesn't fucking matter. The moment they saw your face, they already gave you a backstory and a personality. They've already assigned you a role to play. And nobody else fucking gets it. Not your mom, not your friends, not the person who's supposed to be the love of your life. No one else gives a shit about the fact that you're all alone, that nothing you do will ever matter, that one day you will die after a long, meaningless existence and it will all have been for nothing.

"So what do you do? You live your life the way they tell you to. You become the person they already think you are. You don't fuck around, you don't make mistakes, you don't do the things you really want to do because you're *dependable*. You spend the next forty years of your life sitting in a cubicle, showing up to a job that makes you want to shoot yourself in the fucking head just so you can pay your mortgage and have ten vacation days a year. And when you're staring down the barrel at that eternity—of course you start looking for pain. You look for excitement. You fuck people you're not supposed to. You hurt other people, too, because it makes you feel something to see them bleed. It's wrong, it's ugly, it's unforgivable, but how else can you feel like you're still a person in this world? How else can you know that you haven't wasted your entire existence away? How else can you get someone to look you in the eyes and see you, really see you, even if it's for a single day of your life, even if it's for a glimmering split second?

"I don't have a life anymore, Paul. All my hopes, all my dreams—they all died last summer on the 6 Train. I thought I could reinvent myself, come back to New York and make a new life under a new name, but I was wrong. I'll never get back what I lost. I'll never amount to anything. So this is all I have now. This is all I can do. I wait for the rest of my life to be over, and I . . . I chase the glimmers."

Above me, Paul was silent.

I bent my head to him, and the blood in my mouth began to pool, warm, salty.

Thud. My head hit the floor a final time.

I waited.

SOYOUNG

January 2005

She was treading water as she walked back to the house, the unrelenting rain thick in her socks and tennis shoes. In the foyer, she took off her shoes in the dark and felt her way to the basement, leaving a trail of rainwater in her wake.

Paul was still asleep on the mattress; for a fleeting half second, Soyoung saw his motionless form illuminated by a flash of lightning, and she ran towards him and dived.

"Paul!" she whispered. "Paul, wake up!"

She heard him groan; she had fallen on one of his ribs. "Soyoung?" Paul said, and as he started to reach for the floor lamp, Soyoung pinned down his arm and pressed her lips to his ear. "No lights," she said. "The neighbors might see."

"What's going on?" she heard Paul ask, his voice muffled. "You're all wet."

He sounded groggy, but Soyoung didn't care. "I did it," she whispered, euphoric. "The thing I said I was going to do. I did it."

In the dark, she kissed him. There was a ferocity inside her, an urgency, a yearning. She kissed him again and again, hungering for his touch, triumphant, ecstatic, and she did not stop until he took both of her hands and peeled her away and held her at bay, gently but firmly. "Soyoung, what's going on? You're—you're soaked. You're shaking."

Soyoung started, and that was when she realized that her teeth were chattering. Beneath her, the sheet and mattress had become pools. "Were you out in the rain?" she heard Paul ask.

She nodded, wild with happiness, even though he couldn't see it. "I walked for almost two hours."

"Jesus," Paul said, "what for? Why were you out there?"

Then, before she could answer, he said, "Let's get you out of these clothes."

They found their way up the stairs clumsily, Paul gripping Soyoung's hand so she wouldn't slip. In the hallway bathroom, she changed into jeans and a sweatshirt, and he used a towel to wring her hair. In the dim light of the bathroom, Paul said, "So are you going to tell me now? What was the thing you did?"

"I got rid of him."

"You got rid of who?"

"Your stepdad."

Paul's hands, in the middle of drying the ends of her hair, stopped. Soyoung smiled at him; her face was beatific. She looked at him with love, with a radiant compassion. "You'll never have to worry about him again," she said. "Nor will your mom. I solved her problem, Paul. She's free."

Paul opened his mouth, but no words came out. He said, after a moment, "Soyoung, what are you talking about?"

"In the morning, you can call the police and report him as missing. They'll find his body, but by then he'll be long gone."

"Wait," Paul said. "Just—just hang on."

In the mirror, Soyoung fixed her hair as she waited. She heard Paul walk to the garage, heard him open the door and flick the light on.

When he returned, he said, "His car is gone."

"I know. We took it out after midnight."

Paul rounded on her. "What do you mean, you took it out? Did you go somewhere with him?"

The smile slid from Soyoung's face.

She looked down at the towel in his arms. Quietly, she said, "We drove out to a wooded area about four miles from here. I convinced him that it was the best place if we wanted privacy. Deep in the woods, there was a lake. Not a terribly big lake, but big enough for a car."

She looked up. "That's where they'll find him in the morning."

There was another long, ringing silence.

"Oh my God," Paul said, and he took a step back. His back hit the door. "Oh my God."

Then he said, "But how did you—how were you possibly able to—"

Soyoung shook her head. "That's the part you don't need to know."

For a few seconds, Paul just stared at her, motionless. He did not dissolve into laughter; he did not pull her into an embrace, thanking her, overcome by disbelieving joy. He simply turned and left the bathroom, and Soyoung closed her eyes. Her body had deflated, the hope that had sustained her drained in an instant. She dug her nails into her palm and willed herself not to cry.

When Paul came back, he was holding the pair of white tennis shoes she had left in the foyer. "Are these the shoes you were wearing?" he asked.

Soyoung nodded. Paul swallowed before he said, "We need to get rid of the mud."

She watched as he rinsed the shoes under running water, using his hands to scrape off the mud and leaves that had fused with the soles. He was slow and methodical, turning the shoes on every side until all the traces of mud were gone. Then he stuffed the insides with balled-up pieces of old newspaper. "In the morning," he said, "we'll toss them in the dryer."

He stowed the shoes away in his bedroom, in an inconspicuous spot under his chair. They looked at each other. "What now?" Soyoung asked.

"We act like nothing's wrong," Paul said. "We go back to bed."

He began to walk towards the basement, and Soyoung hesitated, uncertain whether to follow him or stay in his room. Paul turned to face her, and after a moment, he said, "Come on."

On the mattress, they lay side by side, their shoulders almost touching.

Paul said, "I can't believe you did that."

Soyoung turned on her side to face him. She said, "Are you angry with me?"

"I don't know how I feel right now. I'm just . . . I feel like nothing's real. I don't know what to feel."

Soyoung nodded. In a small voice, she said, "I had to do it."

"You *had* to do it?"

"I did it for you."

That was when Paul turned, too, facing her. He said, "You did it for me?"

She nodded again, fervent. "You had already done so much for me, Paul. It was the one thing I could do to repay you."

"But I didn't do those things because I wanted you to repay me," Paul said. "It wasn't a transaction. There was—there was no counter, okay? I wasn't keeping score."

Then he said, "I did those things because I love you."

Soyoung blinked. Her eyes filled with tears.

She said, "But don't you see why I had to do it? It was because I love you, too."

In the darkness, she could hear a ripple in his breathing.

She said, "When I first met you, I thought I could read you like a book. I thought you were just like the guys back in Korea, like the guys I dated in high school. I thought I had a pretty good idea of what you wanted from me. You probably wanted sex. You probably wanted a girlfriend, someone to make you feel less alone. And I thought to myself, *Sure, I could give him these things, but why should I? He's nothing special.* Because I had always thought of myself as special, Paul. My entire life, I've been clawing back against the ugly truth that I was just another ordinary pebble on the beach. I had this stupid, stupid delusion that I deserved the sun and the moon and the stars. As a kid, I'd lie in bed and dream that someone iridescent would swoop into my life and look into my eyes and tell me that yes, I am lovable, I am irreplaceable, that they would choose me a thousand times over, *me*, Kim Soyoung, not as an afterthought, not as a consolation prize, but *me* before anyone else in the world."

She was crying softly now, the tears seeping into the pillow beneath their heads.

"Of course there's a counter, Paul. There's always a counter. I keep one in my head for every person in my life, because I had always thought that love was conditional, love was something you had to earn. But the things you did for me gladly, willingly, without my ever having asked for them—I was so wrong about you, Paul! You chose me when no one else did. When I got kicked out of Cornell and everyone I knew fell off the face of the earth, you were the only one who called me. Over and over again. When my mom told me, that was when I knew. The person I've been waiting for all my life—it was you, Paul. It was you all along."

As she closed her mouth, she trembled with satisfaction, with relief. Finally—finally!—she had told him. Finally, she had laid it all out under the sun.

She waited.

"You're crazy," she heard Paul say, in a voice that was flat, quiet.

Soyoung said nothing, and he said, again, "You're crazy. You are actually fucking insane."

In the dark, she heard him sit up on the mattress. He took a deep breath.

He said, "We need to get married tomorrow."

Soyoung's mind went blank, then.

She said, after a moment, "What?"

"I've read about it in news articles before. It's called spousal privilege. They can't force you to testify against someone you're married to."

"Paul," she said, "we can't just—"

But he cut her off. "Remember that thing we talked about?" he said. "The thing about the birds?"

She was quiet, and Paul said, "You and I, we're both broken, both of us. We're two birds that can't fly. Two birds that nobody else in the world wants. But I want you, Soyoung. I can take care of you, if you'll let me.

I can be your family. I can build a cage for you to live in. Because cages don't have to be a bad thing. They can—they can keep you safe, too."

In the darkness, he reached for her hand. Their fingers laced together, and Soyoung sat up, too. She rested her head on his shoulder, and he held her, warm, steady, rocking her in his arms.

The air in the basement was different. Everything was different. In that moment, sitting together on the mattress, Soyoung and Paul saw their two distinct futures meld into one, like train tracks converging. From then on, there would be no Soyoung, and there would be no Paul. There was only their collective fortune, however it may choose to present itself.

SOPHIA

When she returned to the garden at midnight, there was a figure waiting for her on the bench, its outline illuminated by the lanterns around the pond. Her breathing grew shallow. Her footsteps quickened. She was smiling as she made her way through the cherry trees and down the stone path; it was not until she had reached the bench that she finally saw who it was.

The person waiting on the bench for her was Paul.

Her face went white. She stood rooted to the spot, silent, motionless, and a full minute passed before she said, "What did you do to her?"

Behind Paul, the lanterns flickered. He just looked at her.

"Answer me, Paul. What did you do?"

"Nothing," he said, and Sophia almost laughed.

"Don't lie to me," she said. "She's not here. You are. Something must have happened."

There was a long silence.

"I let her leave," Paul said.

"Liar," she said, breathless. "You're lying. She would never—she would never have left. She said she loved me more than anything. She *promised*."

That was when Paul began to laugh.

There was no mirth in his laughter; the sound was bitter, brittle. "God, you're crazy," he said. "You're a crazy fucking delusional bitch."

But Sophia did not flinch.

"You're wrong," she said, her voice cold. "You don't understand. You would never understand. You have no idea how special she and I are to one another, the connection we have. She wanted to hold my hand and . . . and walk under the sun . . ."

Her voice faltered. "You're jealous," she said, finally. "You're jealous because I love her. Because loving her made me realize that every day I stay in this marriage is another day of my life wasted. That every second I spend with you is a second you don't deserve."

In the distance, they heard a peal of thunder. Wet spots were forming on the ground all around them; it had begun to rain.

Paul was no longer smiling. He stood up from the bench and rounded on her, his chest rising and falling rapidly, and Sophia stared back at him, pale, defiant.

He said, "She couldn't pack her bags quick enough. Did you know that? She didn't even bother to take most of her things. *I don't give a shit*, she said. *I just want to get out of this house and never look back.*"

"Liar," she said, trembling. "Liar."

"Go check her room. Take a look for yourself if you don't believe me."

Rain was falling steadily on both of them now. Sophia's white dress clung to her, once again damp and shapeless. She opened her mouth, and Paul said, "Go. Take a look. The evidence is right there."

"You're gaslighting me. It's not true, it's . . ."

"Soyoung," Paul said, and his voice had become cold, hard. "It's time to face reality."

She said nothing. Paul said, "All these years, I've entertained your little fantasies. I've propped up your façade because I didn't want to hurt your feelings. But when are you going to face up to the truth? You're thirty, turning thirty-one this year. Think about it, Soyoung. If you were destined to become a successful artist, wouldn't it have happened by now? If you were as talented as you say you are, why is the only place that's agreed to show your art an affirmative action program in a shitty warehouse? And if you thought you deserved to be with someone so much better than me—why is it, then, that they never stay with you? Why is it that they always walk away?"

He waited. Still, Sophia said nothing.

Paul shook his head.

"I'm going back inside," he said. "Ory might wake up and start looking for us."

He had begun to walk away when she spoke again in a small voice. "Paul. Wait."

In the rain, they looked at each other. Sophia said, "It was you all those years ago, wasn't it?"

"What?"

"At Cornell. You were the one who tipped off the campus police that I was living in the library. All those years, I thought it might have been Stella Cheung or Lillian Pietrowski, trying to get back at me for what I'd done. I didn't even want to entertain the possibility that it was you. But you knew. You knew where I was better than anyone. The day after we talked on that bench, the police came for me. They knew exactly where to look."

She said, "It was you, wasn't it? Just tell me the truth."

When Paul finally spoke, he said, "They all abandoned you."

Sophia was quiet. Paul said, "When the news came out that you were an imposter, everyone dropped you. No one at fellowship would admit to having been friends with you. No one looked for you or wondered if you were okay.

"I was the only one who stayed in your corner. I called you every day even though your mom picked up and screamed at me to stay away. I did it because I wanted you to see the truth: that you had no one left in this world but me. I was the only person you could turn to.

"Thirteen years I've stood by you, Soyoung. Thirteen years I've watched them come and go, these silly little obsessions. Every time you'd delude yourself into thinking that you'd found something real. That they wouldn't run screaming when they found out who you really were. But I know you. All these years, you've tried to wash your hands of who you are and what you've done. You blame it on the water, you claim she tells you to do things, that you have no control. But you're the one in control, Soyoung. It's always been you. You're a sociopath, a lunatic, a murderer. You are someone who is fundamentally unlovable. And in spite of all of that, I'm still here. I'm the only person who will ever accept you for who you are. I'm the only person who will choose you before anyone else. And I'm the only person who will love you the way you've always wanted to be loved."

Sophia looked at him, then.

Her voice was trembling as she said, "I should have killed you when I had the chance. When the divorce lawyer told me how hard it would be to leave you, I should have done it then. Shelley would have felt obligated to stay after your tragic death. She would have stayed to take care of us."

But Paul just shook his head.

"You can't kill me," he said. "Ory needs me."

Sophia was silent. Paul said, "I've sent Ogilvy an email from your account, telling them that you're turning down the job offer. Your son is too young. You're trying for a second child. You decided it'd be better for everyone if you just stayed at home.

"Go ahead—keep underestimating me. Keep treating me like I'm a worthless thing you can just toss in the trash. But you already know the truth. No one else in this world will ever want you. I'm the only home you'll ever have. I'm the only home you'll ever deserve."

Still, she said nothing.

"I'll leave the lights on for you," she heard Paul say.

Standing there in the rain, the empty bench behind her, Sophia watched as Paul made his way towards the back door. Upstairs, their son was sound asleep, hugging his plush shark in his bed. In the kitchen, warm golden lights glowed above the counter, welcoming them home.

The door closed behind him.

EPILOGUE

I didn't go back to Florida.
 I'd have been nuts to go back to that swamp, to that dingy little apartment where she'd once eaten fish and rice with me and my mom, had laid her head on my pillow and blown my life to smithereens. At Newark, I bought a one-way plane ticket to Phoenix, Arizona. Second-driest city in the country. Not even my mom knew my exact address.

I stayed there for a few months, subletting a studio apartment from someone on Craigslist, getting a job as a marketing coordinator at a company that sold air conditioners. I even found a therapist who took my health insurance. And for a while there, I was doing okay, if your definition of *okay* was being able to shuffle out of bed to drive to work and sit in front of a computer and stare at the microwave in the break room as it rotated your lunch. For the first few months, I couldn't sleep. I kept seeing traces of her everywhere I went: A cloud of black, soft, frizzy hair. Dainty rings on a finger. Bare feet in white tennis shoes. Whenever that happened, I'd clench my hands into fists and repeat the things my therapist had said in our sessions: *Take a deep breath in. Hold it and count to seven. Release slowly. Look at the world all around you—the sights, the sounds, the people—and remember: You are alive. You are here.*

Of course, she thought she was just treating me for generalized anxiety disorder.

- EPILOGUE -

After a while, though, something else started to set in. Maybe it was the weather, the dryness. What I hadn't anticipated about the sun in Arizona was the way it bore down on you from all directions. You rushed from your air-conditioned apartment to your air-conditioned car to your air-conditioned office the way a kid plays The Floor Is Lava in their living room. I couldn't stop guzzling water. I couldn't keep myself from jumping under a cold shower two or three times a day. And yet I was still parched.

That was when I packed my bags and moved again. It's how I ended up where I am now.

I knew, I know—I know I shouldn't have moved to a place known for its water. A city with so many lakes the map looks like someone dumped a bag of sapphires on an empty page. But I felt it out there, calling to me. I couldn't stay away.

I got a job at a big food manufacturer, one that makes name-brand cereals you'll definitely have heard of, boxes of artificially colored sugar with cartoon animals on the front. I started out as a junior packaging designer. After I came up with a major brand refresh that involved giving one of the cartoon animals a pair of sunglasses, they made me senior designer. If I keep this shit up, I can probably make team lead by the end of next year. The pay is idiotically good.

Despite everything, I've kept using the name she had given me. Erin Callaghan. For once, my mom had been right: It does make everything easier.

There's a big lake not too far from where I live, so big that it's practically a small inland sea. Standing on one side, you can barely see the opposite bank, just a thin strip of trees lining the vast blue water, the outline of gray skyscrapers in the foggy distance. I've been going there a lot lately. I sit on the pebbled beach, kick off my shoes, and let the water wash over my bare feet. When the sky darkens and the beach quietens until all that's left is the soft rushing sound of water, more and more, I find myself thinking about how easy it would be to simply let the water take you into its arms. How nice it would be to go home.

- EPILOGUE -

And it is on those nights that I cannot sleep.

Because if I were to look up and see Sophia Moon standing there, her white dress swirling in the water, her hand reaching out towards me, I am afraid that there is a chance—even after all this time, even after knowing everything—that I will tell her yes.

ACKNOWLEDGMENTS

This book would not exist without Erin Niumata and Jess Macy, who found it in the slush pile and believed in its potential from day one. Thank you for your championship, guidance, and continued enthusiasm.

Thank you to Olivia Taylor Smith for the incredible work you did to transform this book. I'm still amazed by how clearly you saw Sophia through her armor and how you empowered me to uncover her truest, most vulnerable self.

Many thanks to everyone at Simon & Schuster who helped bring this book to life, particularly Brittany Adames, Hannah Bishop, Danielle Prielipp, Jackie Seow, Emma Shaw, Beth Maglione, Morgan Hart, Nicole Brugger-Dethmers, Andrea Monagle, Sam Hoback, Mollie Finnegan, Wendy Blum, Amanda Mulholland, Lauren Gomez, Olivia Perrault, and Math Monahan.

Thanks also to Sharon Bowers and Jess Siegler at Folio, and to Jason Richman and Maialie Fitzpatrick at UTA.

From the writing community, thank you to Jessi Robledo, Elisabeth Dini, Lidija Hilje, and Stephanie Kim Johnson for your friendship. Thank you to Sharon Zink and Chris Parsons for your encouragement from the UK. My most heartfelt thanks to Eunice Kim for your generous mentorship; you told me my writing had worth right as I was on the cusp of giving up, and I'll never forget it.

- ACKNOWLEDGMENTS -

My writing is inspired by the art of those who have come before me. I first read the works of Jin Yong, also known as Louis Cha, when I was a child, and the duality of light and darkness in his stories continues to challenge my worldview. The analogy about women as roses comes from Eileen Chang's 1944 novella *Red Rose, White Rose*. I have also found great comfort in the art of Anishnabe Saulteaux artist Robert Houle.

I am profoundly grateful for the support my friends have given me in Geneva, Beirut, and DC. Serge Melis and Veerle Metten: You know what you did. Xue Yan, Eva Rivera, Dominique Faure, Jan Turk, Ruth McLachlin, Andrew Tait: Thank you for listening to me whine about all the rejections, and for encouraging me to keep going. Madeleine Brandes, Kija Kummer-Brown, Guly Maimaiti, Désir Mporamazina, Matija Potocnik, Rebecca Whiting, Bernard Khalil, Kaylin Fabian, Daniel Chen, Joanne Lim, Lindsay Bigda: Thank you for being all-around good humans.

Special thanks to my therapist, Olivia, for your warmth and steadfast support. Thank you to Dr. G. T. for saving my life.

And of course, thank you to my family.

ABOUT THE AUTHOR

Lai Sanders is an American writer and nonprofit worker living between Beirut, Lebanon, and Lyon, France. Over the past decade, she has worked on issues like climate change, Indigenous land rights, and women's rights. She holds a master's degree in international affairs from the George Washington University and a bachelor's in business from Emory University. Her first name is pronounced like the English word *lie*.